THE LAST NEHISI

RED REALMS BOOK 1

WARWICK EDEN

ISBN: 9798767406722

Cover artwork by www.daniellefine.com

www.warwickeden.com

Warwick Eden is an ex-engineer with a weakness for cheese and wine, nineties music, and a slightly unhealthy obsession with trains.

Currently working in the IT industry and understandably frustrated by current AI capabilities of the *real* world, Warwick finds writing novels the only means of bringing to life these ambitions and ideas.

The author currently lives in London with partner, Jess, and daughter, Lily.

PART I

184 YEARS AGO

THE GREAT MASSACRE

DALR, ELLAGRIN

It felt like an ethereal dream, as beautiful as a snowflake and as fleeting as one. I was standing in the middle of an immense hall with Jula, dressed in my finest new gown.

"This is the Great Hall of Ellagrin," Jula had explained, bending down to my level. She held my hand rather tightly as more guests arrived, milling around us.

I ignored her. Jula was Mother's handmaid, not mine. Saima usually took care of me but she was ill that day and couldn't come. I was annoyed at that so I continued to snub Jula. There was much to look at but as more and more guests entered, my annoyance grew for their towering forms threatened to obstruct my already-limited view of the Hall. I strained to look past their infuriatingly tall frames as they ambled about, oblivious to the small child in their midst.

The Great Hall of Ellagrin extended upwards into the distance. Its endless walls of pure white gleamed with such blinding brilliance I had to squint in order to see where they ended. The height of the hall was matched only by the expansiveness of the chamber itself. Stretching as far as the eye could see, the vast hall was flanked on both sides by a series of colonnades leading the eye from the entrance on one end, down a hundred yards, all the way to the raised dais on the other. Behind the colonnades lurked more discreet seating spaces consisting of seats and daybeds, partially obscured by drapes, some diaphanous, others thick and velvety.

The ornate colonnades in particular filled me with inexplicable fascination. I traced my fingers along their carvings, completely absorbed and oblivious to the comings and goings of the people around me. The graceful indentation of leaves, exotic flowers and fruit—a nod to Ellagrin's 'agricultural heritage' according to meddling Jula—seemed almost alive and would have appeared completely real to me if not for the pale milkiness of the alabaster they were carved from. Up and up the column I traced until my fingers could no longer reach them even on tiptoe, then followed the intricate curves with my eyes instead, noting the carvings of crops gradually giving way to naked, sensuous forms, intertwined and coupling in all manner of positions.

Presently a chime sounded clearly in the distance and the bright lights dimmed, leaving only the colonnades glowing translucent in a pale luminance of their own. Jula pulled at my hand.

"Stop Jula—" I started but she quickly knelt down to my level.

"Look Lady Vittoria, *look*!" She nudged me gently and pointed.

Nothing could have prepared me for the spectacle that followed. Not even the numerous descriptions from the idle chatterings of Saima, Jula and the other maids gleaned over the past few weeks came close. To this day people still talk about it; a spectacle of wealth and unimaginable decadence, of hedonism and excess at a scale that no one in living memory has ever seen again. I simply remember it as a glorious, golden reverie.

The first to enter the Hall was our King, Salah-Eddine the Great. Lean, commanding, his hair slightly peppered with the grey of his years, he was clad in traditional Nehisi garb and a rich velvety robe of crimson so dark it was almost black. Underneath, a glimpse of his gold tunic and harem pants made from the lightest of silks rippled slightly as he strode past. The King was accompanied by his consort, Queen Noraddine, who glided gracefully by his side.

In contrast to the King's austere appearance, the Queen was a vision of ostentatious splendour. Her slender figure, barely hidden beneath a gossamer-thin hooded mantle was adorned in a delicate web of interlocking chains of gold, each barely a hair's breadth and threaded with jewels that glinted like a thousand droplets in the sun.

"She's *beautiful*!" I whispered in awe.

The Queen did indeed possess a glorious, sensuous body. Sheathed only at the most intimate parts, it had been rubbed and perfumed with oils that it gleamed with the vibrance and perfection of a pubescent female.

"The result of a sheer fortune spent on rejuvenation treatments," Jula muttered enviously. I didn't understand what she meant, only that the woman who glided past us was in my eyes, the most wondrous, golden creature I had ever seen.

Behind the Queen were the other Lords and Ladies who, like my parents, were Nehisi aristocrats. Red and gold visions of velvets, silks and gossamer though not as lavish as the Queen's, floated past in shades of reds and golds like autumn leaves, each adorned in jewellery that glinted and sparkled in the soft light of the Hall. I craned my neck trying to spot Mother.

"Where is she, Jula?" I had whispered, tugging at Jula's hand. "I can't see her. Has she walked past already?"

Jula turned towards me and put her finger on her lips sternly, meaning I was to stay quiet. I pouted. All this shushing and telling me to be quiet. I didn't like being told. I didn't like Jula. I wanted Saima. Defiantly I looked right past Jula trying to imagine she wasn't there clutching my hand, as if not trusting me to stay put, and decided to entertain myself with thoughts of what to tell Mother later in order to get her whipped for being rude to me.

A lady clad in a flowing robe of rich mahogany walked by, her face partly hidden within the cowl of her cloak but I recognised the signet ring on her finger. Its pretty little garnet stone glinted in the soft light and winked at me.

"Mother!" I called out. I felt Jula's hand stiffen in mine.

The lady paused and turned. A familiar face smiled.

Mother.

She moved gracefully away from the procession towards me, arms outstretched. I yanked my hand out of Jula's and ran to her just as she put her arms around me, shielding my impetuous movements with her cloak and guiding me gently away from the unfaltering procession. Then holding hands, we stood side by side and watched the increasingly wondrous parade pass by, like a bejewelled carnival of exotic beings.

Following the Nehisi were the Ellagrins, the hosts of the event. Unlike the provocative airiness with which the Nehisi wore their clothing, the Ellagrins were taller and stouter, and revelled in their playful costumes of rich brocades, heavy satins and intricate embroidery. They also covered their faces in fanciful masks and half-masks, some whimsical, others grotesque, but all decorated with feathers or covered in the iridescent scales of exotic reptiles. In the dimness of the hall I stood entranced, like one mesmerised by the glow of a fire, as they filed past, each more wondrous and elaborate than the one before. Finally, when the last of the guests had entered the Great Hall, its heavy doors swung shut with a clang and the festivities began.

This was the most boring and tiresome part of all celebrations. Crowds and clinking glasses, carousing and chaos, guests dancing to the robust beat of Nehisi music piping through the Hall and liveried servants, all towering above me, bumping me around like tall ships oblivious of a floating buoy. Unlike me, they glided expertly between the guests, balancing trays laden with exquisite morsels and amber liquors, serving and occasionally dodging blows from them (for it was usual for both Ellagrins and Nehisi to strike their servants). It was also usual for Ellagrins and Nehisi, as Mother explained to me before, to indulge in the rituals of court celebrations and it wasn't long before the mingling of the guests moved on to the many dark corners of the Great Hall accompanied by the sighs and sounds of a more intimate nature.

I had been instructed to stay with Jula. This I did with little fuss as I was accustomed to in parties such as this. Jula had brought me something to eat: a small plate of venison smothered in a syrup of sweet molasses, some greens and a handful of pickled nuts. Having ensconced myself in a mound of soft cushions, I was content to sit and merely observe the goings on around me.

The Hall was dim with only the pale glow emanating from the columns. Flickering candles cast dancing shadows and shapes about, lulling me to sleep. It was dark but I could see Mother lying on one of the daybeds, her eyes half closed. Beside her was Father and another man whom I could tell from his taller build and blonde hair, was an Ellagrin. Father leant over to kiss Mother as the other man joined them both in the daybed.

All around me were similar sights and sounds in the background. The sighs and hushed moans of men, women, Nehisi, Ellagrin, uninhibitedly entwined in coitus much like my parents. I snuggled further into the cushions of the low settee and continued eating. I knew from previous occasions that it would be some time before they'd come back for me. Alone in my corner, I looked round. I couldn't see Jula anywhere. She had disappeared off somewhere, probably gossiping in one of the corners with the other maids. Comfortably cocooned in the soft cushions, I soon drifted off to sleep.

Another gong chimed, this time a little louder than the first one it seemed. The guests stirred and began to assemble towards the front of the Hall where the dais stood.

"Come little one." Father's voice arose me from my dreamy state. Mother was standing beside him.

"I'm not little," I protested sleepily. "I'm nearly five."

Mother smoothed her hand over my hair.

"Are we going home now?" I asked, rubbing my eyes. It was past my bedtime, I was sure of it.

She smiled and patted my cheek. "Not yet Vittoria," she said. "Don't you want to enjoy the party some more?" Then arranging her robe and putting up her hood as before, she and Father led me towards the crowd that had assembled facing the dais at the front of the Hall. The tall Ellagrin had disappeared, presumably into the very same crowd. I craned my neck to see what the fuss was about in the front.

"Your Highnesses, King Salah-Eddine the Great and Queen Noraddine, my Lords and Ladies..." The Master of Ceremonies' voice rang out, loud and imperious. "I give you His Excellency, Emperor Mikael of Ellagrin!"

The Hall erupted in applause.

"Where, Father? Where?" All I could see were the backs of finely dressed guests in front and around me clapping.

"Look Vittoria," said Father, tapping at my shoulder and pointing to the front, "that's the Emperor of Ellagrin!"

I struggled on tiptoe to see past the crowd in front but failed to see beyond the infuriating wall of silks and satin. So Father lifted me onto his shoulders to enable me to get a clear view of the Emperor on the golden dais in front.

"Oh! The Emperor's a golden eagle!"

Father chuckled at my description of Emperor Mikael. An eagle indeed. The Emperor, commanding and clad in red and gold, donned a golden mask the shape of an eagle's head. He lifted his hand to still the applause.

"Welcome...."

His voice resonated around the Hall, deep and clear as the tolling of a bell. There was an expectant hush all round.

"For millennia, Nehisi have partnered with House Ageron, forging alliances between the two races and bringing forth the Golden Age of Prosperity," said the Emperor. "Today we, House Ellagrin, take our turn to forge our ties with the Nehisi. Today we usher in a New Age of Wealth and Harmony between our peoples." He lifted both arms. "To the Age of Wealth and Harmony!"

Emperor Mikael extended his hand towards King Salah-Eddine, bidding him join him on the dais. Our King strode forward and stood beside the Emperor, smiling beatifically at the cheering crowd.

"He hopes for too much," Father said quietly. Father held onto my ankles and glanced at Mother. "This gesture from Ellagrin will not be sufficient to lure our King away from House Ageron."

Mother nodded with an expression on her face that spoke of concern. "I fear this Ellagrin emperor," she said in hushed tones. "He is irascible and prone to impulse. Our King should never have agreed to this celebration. To accept one's hospitality without payment in return would be taken as an affront by Ellagrin."

Father nodded grimly.

"Look Father!" I called out, digging my heels into Father's sides in my excitement.

Emperor Mikael had brought forward a smallish vial and it glinted prettily in the palm of his hand.

"Is it an egg?" I wriggled atop Father's shoulders trying to get a better look.

The 'egg' was oval and transparent save for its base which was coated in enamel and encrusted with precious stones, a look echoing the ancient Faberge eggs of Old Earth of millennia past. Suspended within it was a single plant, a sapling with several white iridescent buds on the cusp of flowering.

"It's a glass vial, little one," chuckled Father.

The Emperor held it up for all to see. "I give you the Light of Nehisi," he said and presented the vial to King Salah. "For centuries, you have sought to recover the flower that symbolised your people. The plant that, like you, comes from the Ether."

King Salah nodded solemnly.

Emperor Mikael continued, "We have, with our knowledge of biotechnology, engineered this replica of the original Light of Nehisi. Grown within the Ether for the last two years, it will flower each solstice so that once again your people may worship and gift these flowers in your celebrations of the Uthsava of Emancipation."

There were gasps from several Nehisi guests and cheers erupted from all around.

"What does he mean, Father?" I asked but Father pointed towards the King.

"Shush. Listen, Vittoria..."

King Salah took the vial carefully into his hands and proceeded to speak. "My people and I thank you, Emperor Mikael," he said, smiling in fulsome appreciation. "On a glorious occasion such as this, it is easy to forget the humble beginnings of our people." He paused for a moment and then continued, his voice although thick with accent, was laced with smug assurance.

He looks very pleased with himself.

"All this," the King gestured grandly, "was made possible because one fateful night, centuries ago, an Ageronian gave sanctuary to a tribe fleeing persecution."

"That's us, Father!" I bent downwards to tell Father. "He's talking about the story of us Nehisi—"

"Shush, Vittoria." Father waved my attention back towards the front.

" ...that tribe was us. Nehisi. Who would in the course of the next few centuries, share our knowledge of the Ether to bring about Bridged travel to the galaxy." The King spread his arms out, his teeth glittered within his broad smile. "With that came the Golden Age of Prosperity. Indeed with most of our kind wedded into House Ageron, we consider ourselves to be most fortunate members of the House."

He turned to face Emperor Mikael. "Whilst we have some influence over Bridged travel, unfortunately taxation policies for goods and trades across it... these are matters between both House Ellagrin and House Ageron." King Salah held out his hands self-deprecatingly. "We are but a simple people borne of the Ether and we draw our strength from it."

The Emperor appeared to stare ahead into space, taking in King Salah's words in silence.

"What are they saying Father? Is our King saying sorry?"

"Shhh, little one... *listen...*"

"However rest assured my friends," continued the King

hastily, "that with our... *encouragement,* I am sure both Houses and ourselves the Nehisi, will continue to prosper together."

I looked down at Father to see him shaking his head gravely.

Still smiling, King Salah held up the Light of Nehisi for all to see and the hall erupted in great applause. From my perch atop Father's shoulders I saw our King hand the delicate egg-shaped vial containing its precious contents to Queen Noraddine.

She is very beautiful. Like a golden fairy...

Then a spurt of red splattered across the golden fairy's face and chest. The queen looked down at her bloodstained chest and screamed.

King Salah staggered. Behind him, the Emperor withdrew his sword from the base of the King's skull and ripped off his eagle mask.

"For the glory of Ellagrin!" he shouted and with a blood-curdling roar, brought his sword down on Queen Noraddine, splitting her lovely face in two. Then the Ellagrins amongst the crowd, expressionless behind their gaudy masks, unsheathed their daggers one after another.

Mother cowered, covering her mouth in horror. "That's not the Emperor!"

"Trap…!" choked Father.

Everything after that happened very quickly. Father pulled me down from his shoulders and grabbing me and Mother, we ran for the exit. We were running so fast my feet barely touched the ground.

Mother, looking frantically left and right as we went, spotted Jula crouching behind one of the colonnades. She grabbed Jula and together we all ran.

We were nearly at the other end of the Hall when a figure stepped out in front of one of the colonnades. I knew him to be an Ellagrin for he was tall and fair-haired. His mask, no longer concealing his face, dangled round the base of his neck. He was holding his sword, its smooth blade mottled with bits of flesh and dripping with blood. Father drew his sword and gestured Mother to take us around the other side. And as Mother pulled me and Jula away, I heard the rustle of steel blades locking together.

"Quickly Vittoria," urged Mother.

We ran towards a discreet alcove by the far side behind a colonnade, away from the crushing stampede of screaming guests running for the main entrance. I recognised Father's friend at the massive door, banging his fists against it frantically.

Not everyone can coax an opening into the Ether, Mother once said. These would be the ones that couldn't. Many more pushed up behind him, pressing him against the heavy panels, desperate to flee.

The Ellagrins closed in on them from behind, their swords raised in postures echoing the harvesting farmers on the colonnade carvings I had traced earlier. I looked away as the distinct crunch of metal on flesh filled my ears.

We were crouched down near the daybeds where Mother had lain earlier. Here, heavy velvet drapes hid us from view although they did little to dampen the screams.

"Mother, what's happening?" I had asked. "Where is Father?"

Beside me Jula whimpered, shaking like a leaf.

"Mother, I want to go home..." I didn't like it here anymore.

"Vittoria, my baby..." Mother was trembling. She could barely fix my cape with her shaking fingers. "Baby, do you remember our game of hide and seek?"

"Yes, Mother," I replied. I pouted and stamped my feet

petulantly. "But I am tired. I don't want to play that now. I want to go home, to my bed."

"You are a good girl," continued Mother looking at me. Her eyes were wide, just like Saima's when Father said he would throw her out the balcony for not attending to me first before the laundry, and her breath came short and sharp. I could hear screams and the pounding of footsteps drifting closer and closer.

"Baby," Mother said, her voice quivering a little, "we must play this one last time, okay?"

I nodded reluctantly.

"Good...good. Do you remember the special place we used to go to? The one with the bright lights and soft sweets?"

Oh! The Confiserie! I nodded eagerly at the memory as images of rainbow coloured bonbons and iced buns flooded my mind.

Mother continued. There was an urgency in her voice now. "I want you to go there, baby. Take Jula with you. It will take you a few hours but don't stop until you get there, okay?" She looked at me a little uncertainly. "You have to find it yourself this time. Can you feel the place baby? Can you *sense* it?" Mother was clutching me so tightly it hurt a little.

I nodded. "Yes Mother," I replied. I could see the shape of the place and the candy clearly in my mind and yes, I could feel it in my bones.

"Good," said Mother, satisfied. "Seek it my darling. *Go* to it." Standing up, she faced Jula and tore out her own earrings.

Why didn't she take care to unfasten them? I could see a little blood trickling down her neck as she thrusted them into Jula's hands.

"This is all I have that you can take," Mother said to Jula. "Not my ring as it will betray your identities. She will lead you to a town somewhere on the planet Ceos. Do *not* seek any

Nehisi. *Never* seek them for as long as you both live and *never* divulge who she is or where you are from to anyone. We are being... *annihilated.* Please—" her voice broke, "take care of her. Now go. *Go*!"

Jula held on to my hand. I looked up at her. *Silly Jula.* She was white-faced and shaking so I grasped her hand a little tighter hoping to give her some reassurance. Then with a fluid stroke of her wrist, Mother cleaved an opening out of thin air in front of us, no taller than I, its inside dark as onyx.

The game of hide and seek had begun.

I tugged Jula's hand bidding her to follow me. As we stepped through, I heard Mother give a little gasp. I turned round an instant before the opening closed behind us, only to see her breathe out a mist of red droplets. She mouthed the words 'I love you' then collapsed onto the floor.

Behind her stood the tall Ellagrin who had mated with her an hour before. His sword was pushed through her heart, its tip pierced her chest. Around the glint of metal, blood seeped through the front of Mother's dress and a dark bloom spread against the mahogany velvet just as the walls of the Ether closed behind us.

Somewhere in the distance behind the dais, a lady-in-waiting wounded and bloodied, hung onto a precious vial as she made her own escape into the Ether...

2 YEARS LATER

CEOS, AGERON

Vittoria stuck her hand a little further down the heap and wriggled her fingers to get a better hold.

Got it! She pulled it up quickly. It was slick with fat and a thick globule dribbled down her wrist as she brought it closer to take a sniff. *Nah, no good.* In fact it nearly made her gag. This one wasn't good for eating. She tossed it aside and went in again.

She was small for a seven-year-old. Waist-deep in a bin of scraps, the mound of discarded rubbish threatened to engulf her undersized frame as she rummaged through it. This time, she fished out a discarded rib. *Promising.* She held it close to have a good whiff, even risked a quick lick-test this time. It was slightly sweet with the hint of molasses but more importantly, there were still bits of meat attached to the bone. *But not enough for both of us.* So she took out the glass shard she always kept handy for stripping meat, scraped whatever she could get off and popped it in her mouth. It was sweet and savoury all at once.

She leant back against the side of the bin, sighed and

looked up, savouring the tiny morsel for as long as she could. Looming over her, the back of the grand old building whose kitchens probably served this to its rich clientele, stretched upwards to the night sky. There, the stars seemed to sparkle and fizz like the pops of flavour in her mouth.

I ate something like this once... An image threatened to resurface in her head but she shook it off quickly. Sometimes it felt like a distant dream. Like it never happened.

Maybe it never happened. But whatever it was, she didn't like remembering the past. *Neither does Jula,* she realised, glancing at Jula, flopped unconscious in the corner with her Stim syringe still in her arm sticking out at a funny angle.

I'll have to take that out afterwards before she falls on it. Jula's last accident with those things turned all of her lower arm up to her fingers black but much as Vittoria tried, Jula just couldn't stay away from them. *Please, just one more time Vittoria, Jula would plead. Please...* and it would start all over again. After all, Jula was the adult and what could a little girl like her do?

They had moved countless times now, from city to city, each a wonderful agglomeration of beautiful basilicas, golden monuments and triumphal arches, heaving with a rich and bustling populace. They moved sometimes to avoid the soldiers and sometimes to escape the people who sold Jula those Stims. It was easy to stay hidden in these large cities, easy to remain faceless in the throngs of people too wealthy and too self-absorbed to notice anything beyond how the War was affecting their precious availability of fresh bloodfruit and smoked scomber.

Yes, maybe it was never real.

Here, it was hard to imagine anything remotely like their old life. A stinking back alley behind the row of fancy restaurants long closed for the day and deserted save for a few rats who had probably gotten away with the better morsels by now.

* * *

SHE HAD CALLED HIM RAT-BOY, not to his face obviously but in her head, because he had a small, mousy-shaped face and a way of skulking around like a rodent. His skulking was particularly quiet that night. So quiet she had not heard him approach.

Rat-Boy was always accompanied by his mate Luca, a wiry lad with a foul mouth and an even fouler temper. The two were by no means top dog in the streets but they ran with the Caballo gang and this gave them sufficient cachet to work easier and weaker targets on the side in their free time.

They cornered her just as she was climbing out of the bin. Nearby, Jula slumped against one of the doorways, was out cold and oblivious. Vittoria cursed under her breath, kicking herself for not paying attention and listening out whilst searching the bins.

Stupid! Stupid! Stupid! This could well be the last few moments of her sorry existence, for being careless. Trembling, her left hand felt for her pocket knife whilst her right held on to her glass shard, taking care to keep it concealed behind her palm.

They were approaching her purposefully now, having worked out that Jula was in no shape to join the party or call for attention.

"Whatcha got there lil' bitch?" Rat-Boy called out. He unhooked the rope he always wore at his waist like a long keychain and began swinging it. The woop woop sound of the rope spinning round and round grew louder as he drew nearer.

"Scavenging for food again, lil' mouse?" he laughed, continuing to swing his rope.

Woop.

Woop.

Woop.

"Disgustin'," chimed in Luca. "Worse than vermin, eating out of the bins..." He spat towards her feet.

"Don't worry," said Rat-Boy, "we're not here to take your food."

Woop.

"We just want your money."

Woop.

Woop.

Then the sound stopped as he stood and faced her. Towering above her by at least a head, his breath steamed over her in the chill of the air.

"I don't have any money," Vittoria said, her hands in her pockets, and looked at him. "That's why I was searching the bins."

Rat-Boy's body bristled at the answer and he swung his rope out over her head, aiming to tighten the noose as soon as he had it circled around her neck.

Vittoria ducked to evade, then thrust her penknife towards his ribs.

But Rat-Boy had instincts and they were sharp. Also he was much thinner than his baggy clothes let on, so by the time her blade cut uselessly through his layers of shirt, it had barely nicked his flesh.

"Bitch!" cursed Luca whose only role in life as he saw it, was to be Rat-Boy's muscle-guy. He lurched forward and knocked the knife out of Vittoria's hand. Then he grabbed her from behind. With his arm locked around her neck and shoulders, he went for her left hand, now sans knife, and twisted it at an angle designed to cause the most pain.

Then, as soon as Luca held her in place, Rat-Boy landed one in her stomach. Her legs went and she doubled up in pain, coughing and unable to breathe.

Slam. Another punch below the ribcage. Pain welled up in her eyes and her peripheral vision went dark. Hell, her central vision went too.

I can't see!

She felt Luca yanking her up again. He was laughing hysterically and she sensed this was the moment Rat-Boy would finish her off. Sure enough, Luca had thought the same and even eloquently voiced it out loud too.

"Finish 'er off!" he said, holding her up.

Her head lolled to one side and in the corner of her eye, Vittoria saw Rat-Boy reach for the folds of his tunic. A glint of metal showed as he drew something out.

His makeshift machete. I'm done for.

And then just as the machete came down, Rat-Boy crumpled to the ground like a puppet whose strings had been suddenly cut.

"What the fu—?" went Luca.

Blood trickled from Rat-Boy's lips and as he fell forward, the cause of the trickle became clear. A gladius protruded from the back of his head, thrown with such force his skull was nearly split in two.

Luca gagged, releasing his hold on Vittoria in shock.

She stood frozen to the spot and closed her eyes to shut out the sight in front of her. She heard him turn to run. Then the neat little swish of a gun being fired and the thud of his body landing on the ground behind.

"You can open your eyes now," came the voice. It was low and gravelly but gentle. "They won't bother you again."

Vittoria opened her eyes and looked back at him.

He didn't wear a vizard that day but she couldn't for the life of her recall his face. The shock perhaps but his eyes, she remembered. They were black. Pitch-black, piercing and strange. And they reminded her of a lizard's.

And so that was how Lizard Man came into their lives.

"You have to be more careful next time," he chided gently. "You need to be more prepared."

"What makes you think I wasn't prepared?" she had retorted.

He looked down at her. The glass shard was still in her right fist, facing forward. She would not have missed Rat-Boy when the machete came down. They would have gone out together. She would have taken him with her at the very least.

"My apologies," Lizard Man said. "I seem to have underestimated your... *preparedness*." He lowered her makeshift weapon gently, tucked it back into her pocket and said with amusement, "I should have known. After all, the female of the species is deadlier than the male..."

Then he beckoned her to follow him. "Come," he said, "shall we have something to eat?"

* * *

AFTER THE RAT-BOY INCIDENT, Lizard Man popped in and out of her life every now and again to check on her. Vittoria guessed he was in the military, leaving every so often to fight the ongoing War or something. She didn't care much for what the War was about, except that it meant people seemed less wealthy and with less *ore* to spend in their fancy restaurants, that too meant less scraps in the bins.

Jula was also always ranting on about them having to stay out of sight and away from soldiers, so she avoided seeing

Lizard Man every time Jula was around. Or awake. Likewise, it seemed Lizard Man never turned up to see her when Jula was around either. He never really interfered with their day-to-day lives although he did teach her the art of thieving.

That was a game changer.

Despite the continuing war, there was still wealth around for the taking.

But only if you knew how to swipe and pilfer. An unseen flick of the wrist here, and a deft dip there was all it took if ever she was in desperate need of funds. And once she'd gotten the knack of it, it became a useful source of income. She and Jula never needed to raid the bins again after that.

Sometimes for kicks, he'd bet her a few *ore* to steal the town sentry's gun and outrun the other sentries on duty. Vittoria guessed Lizard Man had a thing against sentries, even though he was a military man himself. There's a difference between a Red and a dog, he would say. He was a Red, a legionnaire of the empire, a real soldier, not one of the uniformed miscreants that proclaimed themselves security enforcers of the town.

He finally gave up on giving her that particular challenge when she returned one day, arms to the brim, with *all* eight town sentries' handhelds.

GROWING UP

CEOS, AGERON

Vittoria's chores that day had confined her mostly to the kitchen. She grappled with the plate and scrubbed hard, trying not to let it slip in the soapy water. Her fingers were pink and pruned from prolonged soaking in the hot water but her attentions were far from the task at hand; Lizard Man had popped in and was talking to Karl. He had been away for the last couple of months and she strained nosily to hear what he and Karl were discussing.

Lizard Man had got her the job here at the pub run by Karl, an ex-Red and confirmed bachelor, doing the cleaning and washing up. They weren't really friends, Lizard Man said, just that he'd been drinking at Karl's long enough to be *almost* friends, that's all. Besides, he had explained to her, thieving wasn't really a proper job as such and it was getting riskier the bigger she got.

Like Lizard Man, Karl was the easy-going type and didn't seem to have any qualms with taking a youngling on. After all, Vittoria was tall enough to reach the sink and sturdy enough to not drop the glasses or plates. By contrast, Karl didn't want Jula near his drinking glasses.

Jula wouldn't bother turning up to work anyway, thought Vittoria, scouring the saucepan vigorously with the ball of steel wool. She wondered for a split second where Jula was that day. Jula hadn't come home last night and Vittoria hoped she hadn't gone anywhere near those new Stim dealers in the neighbouring Baldunia district.

They slept in the pub basement, behind the barrels and crates, she and Jula. Karl didn't mind them lodging there and Vittoria reckoned it was because she and Jula doubled as some sort of cheap security anyway.

"He came in and asked her for one of our new brews..." Karl's voice floated in from the front of the pub.

Vittoria's ears pricked up. *Is he talking about me?*

"...couldn't read the labels so I had to come out and show her," continued Karl, "otherwise she'd be charging him five *ore* for a pint costing me eight. Now I can't change where I place 'em otherwise she won't know which one's which."

Vittoria leaned back to see if she could hear better from there. Karl was talking about her, she was sure of it. The stool wobbled.

Crash! She slipped and fell backwards.

"Oi kid! Careful with my glasses!" Karl hollered from out front.

There was a pause as Vittoria listened out intently. They had stopped talking.

Then, "C'mon out 'ere," yelled Karl. "He wants to talk to ya."

Vittoria picked herself up, wiped her hands and came out.

Lizard Man looked up from his drink. If he was smiling a 'hello' at her, she wouldn't have had a clue; he always wore the vizard and he was never much of a talker.

Karl turned back to face him and continued talking, as if he had forgotten it was he that called her out in the first place. "Well, I reckon she should probably learn to read and write at her age," he said, topping Lizard Man's beer up. "At least learn to read beer labels. What do you think?"

Lizard Man swivelled the beer in his glass and pondered a moment. "You could take her to the orphanage, I suppose," he said. "They teach them to read and write there."

"*What?*" Vittoria piped up, hands on her hips. "What do you mean? Take me where?"

She must have looked a picture—hands akimbo like some indignant washerwoman, barely taller than the row of glasses on the bar—for Karl let out a snort and a chuckle.

Lizard Man directed his gaze at Karl who went back to polishing his beer glasses with renewed interest. Then he turned to face her.

"They'll teach you to read and write at the orphanage," he explained, his voice deep and rolling like far-off thunder. And you wouldn't have to work. You'd get food and lodgings for free. What do you think?" He paused and waited patiently for her answer, his own thoughts and expression closed to her as usual, unreadable by virtue of that impassive vizard of his.

"I'm not going!" Vittoria blurted out. "They have *rules* there," she said. "I've seen it! You can't go in and out as you please and they have... *curfew*!" She spat out the last word like a curse.

Karl stifled a grin and Lizard Man let out a small chuckle.

"Besides," continued Vittoria, not waiting for a reply, "they can't afford anymore orphans anyway. Donations are so slim these days they won't take me in!" She stopped to catch her breath and looked at them hotly.

"She has a point," said Karl, eyeing Lizard Man through a polished beer glass under scrutiny. "With the ongoing war, most benefactors will be sitting on their ore, not donating them to some poor orphanage—"

"Anyway, if I go, Jula will have nowhere to go," Vittoria added.

"Jula can take care of herself," said Lizard Man. He let out a disapproving grunt. "You don't even know where she is at the moment anyway, do you?"

"Probably at Decebal's," muttered Karl quietly, "...for her daily hit."

"Yeah, but she always comes back here," protested Vittoria hotly.

Karl shrugged at Lizard Man. "When she remembers..." He nodded towards Vittoria. "But her shifts pay the rent so..." Karl wasn't fussed as long as rent was paid and none of his beer glasses got broken.

Vittoria clenched her fists. "You can't dump me at the orphanage. If you make me go, I swear, I'll... I'll run away!"

Karl shot a bemused look at Lizard Man, then turned back to putting his beer glasses away.

Lizard Man seemed to back down. "As you wish," he replied.

A long pause followed where no one said a word. Lizard Man resumed his previous pose, nursing his beer and the only sounds in the pub that morning was the occasional clinking from Karl putting the glasses away. Vittoria wasn't sure if this was a stand-off or a victory on her part.

Then after a good five minutes or so, Lizard Man reached into his pocket, took out a small puck, no bigger than a two decima *ore*, and skimmed it across the countertop towards Vittoria.

She stopped it with her palm and picked it up. "What is it?" she asked, turning the pewter-coloured puck over in her hand.

Lizard Man beckoned her over. "Here, let me show you." He turned the small disc over and showed her the tiny switch at the bottom to turn the device on. "This is the *Lex Dogma,*" he explained. "The Imperial soldier's handbook."

Karl glanced up from behind the counter with interest.

"Every soldier has it," said Lizard Man. "It's a Red's code of conduct." He flicked the switch on and instantly, projected holos of swirling letters floated before her eyes.

"Look, it's mostly mnemonic holos," continued Lizard Man. He looked at Karl and kind of explained, "...and because many recruits can't read or write anyway, this is a good way to get them to learn both letters and the code itself." He scrolled through the holopuck to show her its contents. It contained a mixture of imagery, vids and various questions and acrostics to help one learn the soldier's code. "Give it a try," said Lizard Man, placing the puck in her hand and downed the last of his beer.

KARL HAD COMMENTED it wasn't exactly a school textbook, but within six months, he too had to admit the Lex Dogma did the job. Vittoria had learnt how to sound and read all the words in it and by Lizard Man's third visit, she even knew the legionnaire's entire code of conduct and rules by heart. Trouble was, she'd also broken most of them too.

But more than anything Vittoria wanted to be like Lizard Man. "Teach me how to fight," she said and he did.

He taught her some moves whenever he could. Hand to hand combat mostly and a few knife skills, but it was sporadic for he would disappear for months on end at times.

To fight the war against the Ellagrins, Karl had explained.

Vittoria understood. She could see the changes brought

upon by the war to their everyday lives. Shortages were becoming more and more apparent and for the first time in living memory, there was scarcity of food. Locally grown transgene crops now replaced Ellagrin imports and Karl had even started experimenting with brewing his own beer. There was even talk of a plague spreading on the capital planet of Amorgos, started by the Ellagrins.

"But don't worry," Karl said. "We're winning and the invading Ellagrins are being forced to flee." However the same time he said that, the news vids were blaring the announcement that the Arnemetiaen Gateway had fallen. "Never mind," said Karl. "I'm sure that will get fixed. It'll be back up once more. Things will go back to normal, you'll see."

But Vittoria wasn't so sure. A lot had changed in the past few years, too much to ever get back to what it used to be. Most citizens used to be well-off, affluent. Even the servants. But now, due to the spillover effects of the war, few could afford servants and the remaining rich holed themselves up in their villas. With burgeoning unrest from the population, the streets, now unpoliced, were awash with violence and brazen theft. It was only pockets like Karl's neighbourhood which were never respectable to start with, that remained relatively unchanged.

Lizard Man dipped in and out of their lives, turning up usually when she least expected it. There on the street he'd be standing, waiting for her, somehow knowing she'd pass that way. How he did that considering she never took the same route twice, she couldn't tell. Once she doubled back, thinking someone was trying to mug her, and managed to ambush him instead. She couldn't see his expression beneath the vizard but she could tell he was grinning.

"Thought you could jump me, huh?" she said, standing

over him as he lay prostrate, after she had whacked him to the ground.

"No," he had replied, "but it's probably your birthday..." Then he got back to his feet and gave her a shortsword. It was standard army issue but well-made, lightweight, and bore no markings.

"Next time I see you," he said, "try using that instead."

THE LAST SIGHTING

CEOS, AGERON

At fifteen, lean and slightly gangly, Vittoria leant over the bar, flashing Jula a smile as she gave it one last wipe. They were at Karl's at about nine in the morning and she was cleaning up after last night's revelry by the regulars to celebrate the end of the war with the Ellagrins.

Jula had come in to wait for her whilst she finished up. She was very good that day and hadn't even asked Karl at the bar for a drink even though it was stiflingly hot.

That seemed to be the norm of late. Days were hotter and drier than it had ever been. Even Karl's potted palm which had survived years of cigarette burns and discarded beer was beginning to shrivel and dry up in the pervading heat. Karl said it was something to do with the twin suns causing the climate to change. Well, climate change or not, it sure was hot and she was sweating moisture by the bucket.

"So what are you going to be doing after you slack off then?" asked Karl with a twinkle in his eye.

"Not much if you keep me working here past my shift, slavemaster," Vittoria retorted, "and on my birthday too."

Despite her riposte, she suspected Karl would kick her out before the morning was through. There wasn't much cleaning that he couldn't do himself and she reckoned he'd just wanted an excuse to give her a couple more ore. She grinned inwardly. *As it's my birthday...*

Karl gave an unconcerned grunt in reply.

"We're going to visit that new market near Portus," Jula spoke up.

"Maybe get some lunch there too," added Vittoria, bagging up the empty bottles behind the bar and sweeping vigorously.

Karl harrumphed. "Sounds like a *terrible* day out," he said. "All the aristocrats will be there, prancing around now that the war's officially over. It's going to be packed."

Vittoria shrugged his teasings off. Nothing was going to get her mood down. It was one of those precious, perfect days. One she and Jula hadn't had for so long even she couldn't remember ever having one. Jula was sober and there was going to be a good meal to look forward to later. Hell, Karl even said the war was over. Vittoria felt really happy.

And then things got all bad again.

A couple of men burst into the pub. They were town sentries, apart from one dressed in civilian clothes and obviously looking for someone as it was too early for drinking, even by Jula's standards. Vittoria had stopped and leant on her broom to watch.

Looking back, she could not have guessed it was Jula they were after. Jula had stayed out of trouble for months and whilst she wasn't clean of drugs, she had kept away from loan sharks and the usual trouble so it was a huge shock when the man in plains clothes turned to point accusingly at Jula saying, "That's *her*!"

One of the sentries stepped forward and yanked Jula off

her stool. Vittoria remembered dropping the broom and sliding over the counter to face him.

"What the hell do you think you're doing?" she challenged him.

"This 'ere's the one who took the money," continued the civilian, jabbing his finger at Jula. "I 'ad another customer at the stall and placed it on the counter for just a minute. Next thing I know, it's gone! She'd swiped it and run off!"

"But I don't even know you," stammered Jula. She looked at him and then at the sentries. Her eyes darted about wildly. She was scared. Authorities scared her.

"Right! You're coming with us," the sentry snapped.

"Wait a minute," interjected Karl who up until now had remained silent in the background, polishing his beer glasses. "What proof have you got that she's responsible? That she was even there?"

"Here!" said the man, opening his palm to reveal Jula's tattered old fake ID. "Proof enough for ya? I managed to grab it off her before she took off with the cash." He glanced back at the sentry holding Jula's arm and nodded diffidently, "Some of that was meant to be the payment. Y'know, for the other night's game..."

The sentry waved his remark off and still holding Jula, pulled her roughly towards the door.

"Oww, nooo," whined Jula, wincing at his hardened grip. She scrabbled in panic like a cat about to be drowned.

"Stop!" shouted Vittoria. "You're not taking her anywhere." She stood at the doorway, bravely facing them and blocking the exit. She was barely the shoulder height of the sentry that towered over her.

"Move aside, girl," he said, brusquely and pushed her aside with a laugh. His companions followed behind, shoving roughly past her on their way out and dragging Jula down the street with them.

Vittoria ran after them.

"Stop!" she yelled, her shouts echoing emptily down the street. It was still fairly early in the day and with most shops still closed, there was no one around to help her. Assuming they'd care to do so in the first place.

"You can come bail her out when you bring payment with you," replied the sentry, turning back briefly with a self-satisfied smirk on his face.

"NO!" shouted Vittoria, her tone enraged. She had had enough.

I'm done with acquiescing.

Anger swelled within her like a tsunami cresting, ready to smash and obliterate anything that stood in its path. She looked around. The street was deserted. There were five of them, all standing in a convenient huddle in front of her. Karl she sensed, was still watching at the doorway behind. She weighed her options as she stood there, looking at them. They were bunched together close enough; a running stride towards the group whilst cleaving an opening into the Ether and she could take them all with her.

Then leave them marooned in the Ether to die. Slowly.

After that, she would take Jula and they'd continue their day as planned.

But then Karl... What about Karl? Karl would have to be sacrificed too. No witnesses. There was no alternative if her secret was to be kept safe. No loose ends, Lizard Man always said. If she let Karl live, he would be a loose end. She had to decide. And quickly.

Fuck it. She was always giving in. *NO. Not anymore. They were all crooked anyway. It would be every man for himself. It always ended up that way. Even with Karl ... it would only be a matter of time when she and Jula were of no use to him any longer.* She balled up her fists, stepped back, and got ready to sprint forward.

Then a hand grasped her shoulder, stopping her, holding her tight.

"No," he said, his voice quiet, sombre.

She struggled to get free but his grip held her in place.

"No! No! No!" she screamed frustratedly, "Come back!"

The sentries had turned their backs on her and were marching Jula away.

She wrenched herself free from Lizard Man's grip but they had disappeared round the corner into the main street.

It was too late.

She swung round to face him. Behind, she saw Karl disappear back into his pub, shaking his head.

"You had no right!" she yelled at Lizard Man, shaking. Her eyes were red and wet with anger. "Why did you stop me?"

"For your safety," Lizard Man replied, his deep voice like rolling sand. "Your outbursts attract too much attention. We spoke about this before. No one must ever know of your ability." He moved closer. "You understand that, don't you?"

She snatched her dagger from her belt and slashed at him to get him to back off. "I didn't want this!" Vittoria continued raggedly. "I just want Jula and you let them take her away from me!"

Lizard Man clasped his side with one hand and grunted. She could see blood seeping out between his fingers where she had cut him.

"You are the last of your kind," he said softly. "I have to protect you, even if it is from yourself." He reached out towards her but she slapped his hand away. Lizard Man remained silent, deep in thought, like he was weighing up something. Then he appeared to have made up his mind.

"Vittoria," he started, hesitantly, "we have to leave here. I have to take you somewhere, with me." He glanced towards her and continued, "There is something you must know...."

She said nothing but continued to glare defiantly at him, tears streaming down her face.

Lizard Man turned his expressionless vizard up towards the sky. "The suns," he said quietly, almost to himself, "...it is almost time. We need you, Vittoria. You must come with me—"

"*No*!"

"We'll come back for Jula. I'll bail her out I promise, but first, you have to come with me."

"No!"

"Listen to me—"

"No! No more! I'm done with doing what everyone says. I could've taught those dogs a lesson!"

"I told you, you can't be seen doing that out in the open—"

"I was *defending myself*!"

"Vittoria—"

"I HATE you!" she screamed. "And I never want to see you again, you hear me? NEVER AGAIN!" In an instant, she opened the portal.

It took him less than a second to realise what she was about to do.

"No! NOOOOO!" He lunged forward to grab her but it was too late! She had slipped into the Ether.

And the opening closed.

* * *

HE WAITED FOR HER. Then searched for her all over the empire but to no avail. She could not be found anywhere.

Days turned into months and months into a year.

Then another.

And another.

Soon, the years coalesced into decades and in time, the twin suns of Ageron began to deteriorate and with them, the decadent beauty of its cities.

The Golden Age of Prosperity was over.

Another fifty years would pass before the rays of the decaying suns turned blood red, giving rise to Ageron's better known name of the Red Realm.

Its inner planets, those closest to the suns, were first to be affected. Scorched by the torrid heat, the trees began to die out and erratic heatstorms soon replaced seasonal monsoons. People tried to flee but where could they flee to but to the less habitable outer planets?

Another century would pass.

And another.

And as the Realm languished in the shadow of its fading suns, the sheen of its glory days forgotten, Lizard Man sank into an ever deepening despair. For only he knew the catastrophic cost of his mistake. He had lost Ageron's only hope.

He had lost the last Nehisi.

PART II

PRESENT DAY

CEOS, AGERON

VIDAR

"Hurry, hurry, hurry!" hissed Vidar urgently as the footsteps echoing down the corridor grew closer and closer. The guards were approaching fast.

His partner held up a hand to silence him and in one fluid stroke, deftly lifted the Eldur from its opened coffer. As the first guard stepped into the chamber, he grabbed Vidar with the other hand and they disappeared into the shadows.

The guard stopped in his tracks. He paled. The stone was missing; the metal cask that housed it was wide open, laid bare like the open cavity of a body, its living pulsating heart unmistakably gone.

"Sound the alarm!" he shouted. "By Dyaeus, it's *gone*! The Eldur has been stolen!"

As one of his men fled, trembling, to raise the alarm, others swarmed in, turning over every square inch of the vault to look for the intruders. But there was only one way in and out —the same way they had come in—and apart from themselves, the chamber was empty.

It was as if the Eldur and whoever who took it had simply disappeared into thin air.

* * *

IT TOOK NO MORE than a second, two at most, but Vidar didn't understand how they had managed to slip out of the vault and arrive here.

They had stumbled through a dark passageway of sorts. There, the blackness was total and viscous, enveloping him like a thick, cool blanket. He had been gasping for air, as if he were underwater although not quite because he wasn't suffocating. Strangely enough, he was convinced he hadn't been breathing either. Not air anyway but something else. Something heavier, more fluid. Something that made him nearly gag. In the darkness, he had tried to ask Tors what was going on but when he opened his mouth to speak there was no sound. Before there was time for panic to set in, they had emerged back into the light.

"OK, you need to warn me *before* you do that!" Vidar spluttered, struggling to get his breath back. This had happened once or twice in the past. He didn't like it then and he was certain he still didn't like it now. "*Before*, not after!" he said crossly. "I wasn't prepared!"

Tors shrugged nonchalantly, saying nothing as usual. He was standing motionless, facing Vidar, his face hidden behind the vizard that he never took off.

Vidar guessed he was thinking; of what, he could not be sure. Tors was a man of few words. In the ten or so years they had worked together, Vidar had never known him to say anything more than what was necessary to get a job done.

The man has no life, thought Vidar. By Dyaeus, he had tried to get Tors involved in the necessities of life—drinking, gambling, women—but even the talents of Annetta the multi-skilled pleasurologist and her Stim syringes were not enough to entice Tors out of his shell. *Although he did have a rather protracted fling with that Lady Valentina for a while,* recalled Vidar, *though I'm sure that was work-related.*

Vidar chuckled. Lady Valentina had been what Vidar termed a 'repeat client' of theirs in the old days, although it would seem with her many advances towards Tors, it was clear it wasn't just her husband's mistress' jewels that she was after.

I would have gladly retired as her kept man, thought Vidar, wistfully recalling Lady Valentina's womanly curves and her unlimited access to her husband's funds, *but sadly she only had the hots for Tors.*

The only thing Tors did for fun it seemed, was work. A wasted talent by Vidar's estimation. But Tors was very skilled and more importantly, he always paid his accomplices handsomely. That is, if they did as they were instructed and asked no questions, and Vidar was content enough not to be the first to challenge the status quo.

He looked around. They were standing in an alleyway, under a dank stonework arch flanked on both sides by rows of abandoned shanty houses pressed together like sagging wedges of damp, mouldy loaves.

A century ago, these would have been sought-after traditional cottages. Vidar could almost imagine it: cheerfully painted to appeal to those looking for quaint Old Earthian-style holiday homes with pretty planting in the front and cobbled paving that would have been clean and well-maintained. Now, all that remained was a sad remnant of the past.

Everything's dying, thought Vidar, noting the stunted shrubbery and mildewed paved front gardens, a stark difference to the beauty and opulence that used to be the norm in his childhood. He looked further up towards what looked like the main street. A faint glimmer of lights hinted at signs of life. The air was damp and smelt of piss.

This is not the same street we come from, Vidar thought to himself. He looked around and sniffed the air—it was damp with a pervading scent of moss and algae. *The air was dry when we first went into the vaults,* he thought. So dry it prickled his throat he remembered, yet now the atmosphere seemed humid, choked with moisture. *By Dyaeus, this doesn't even feel like the same area...*

Vidar felt a little bewildered but said nothing. Jobs with Tors sometimes left him a trifle perplexed but Vidar was not one to let that bother him for long.

"We're in Salopia, or somewhere near Salopia, I think..." Tors mentioned casually. It was as if he had read Vidar's mind.

Salopia's on one of the outer planets, thought Vidar perplexed. *This is not even on the same planet we came in on!*

But Vidar was a simple man and technicalities such as ending up inexplicably at a different location to where they had started rarely troubled him. As far as he was concerned, as long as they got out okay and with the loot, he was golden.

As Tors took the Eldur out from the old leathery pouch to inspect it, any doubts Vidar had, promptly evaporated along with any accompanying feelings of bewilderment. He watched as Tors balanced the stone gingerly in the palm of his hand. It was small and would have fit snugly even with if he'd clenched his hand tight.

The Eldur gave off a faint iridescent glow from within and pulsated slightly as if it were alive. As Tors lifted it up to eye level to gain a closer look, it cast soft, strange illuminations against the vague contours of the vizard that concealed his face.

Vidar wondered for the umpteenth time why he never took this off.

The vizard which was a subtle shade of granite, had a smooth texture, fine as porcelain. Moulded to the contours of the face but only enough to give hint to the humanoid features beneath, it had raised parts for a nose, two symmetrical indents for where the eye sockets would be located and a faint suggestion of chin and jaw where the chromatographic skin of the vizard tailed off, just above the collar bone.

Perhaps he's disfigured underneath, Vidar contemplated idly. *Or not Ageronian.* Or maybe and most likely, thought Vidar, it was simply because he was wanted by the authorities.

Tors was turning the Eldur over in his hand, examining it with care. It seemed to flicker ever so slightly each time he turned it. "Eldur," he murmured. "Some call it Ice Fire, the most valuable natural element in the galaxy. So precious for something so unassumingly small."

"What do you reckon it's worth?" asked Vidar in a half whisper. He blinked as the Eldur's light gleamed at him, rhythmic and alive. "Ten million *ore*? Twenty million?"

"Well, depends. How much would you price a life at?" replied Tors, his gaze still transfixed on the stone. "Or five hundred thousand lives? A single shard like this is enough to power a spacecarrier across to the far side of the galaxy."

Vidar whistled softly at the thought. "Many will pay handsomely for the chance to leave the Realms without having to wait their turn in the Exodus. But didn't you say this one's not going to be used in a ship?"

Tors nodded. "This consignment's been commissioned for a different purpose altogether." He jiggled the stone gently in the palm of his hand. "This, my friend," he said, "is destined to adorn the neck of a special lady, not dissipate away in the bowels of a ship's engines."

Vidar whistled again. "He must be unimaginably wealthy…," he said and added with a chuckle, "and stupid."

"An aristocrat," said Tors. "Perhaps a member of the House itself. They pay the best."

Vidar shook his head in disbelief. "Amazing isn't it," he said. "Fancy wearing that around your neck, knowing full well it contains enough energy to blow up a continent!"

Tors shrugged again and placed the Eldur safely back into the pouch. "It's just a rock Vidar," he replied, "just a rock."

"Well," sighed Vidar as he reached for his cryptopay device, "I'm just a man of simple tastes I guess."

Tors nodded and took out his docket to scan in Vidar's cut of precisely thirty thousand *ore*—his share of payment for the job.

Vidar grinned, his sharp, pointed teeth glinting slightly as he shoved his docket back into the folds of his tunic. "Anytime you need a hand in the next job boss, you know where to find me," he said, patting his pocket with satisfaction. Times were hard and unlike most of the population, Vidar knew they were doing much better than most.

Much, much better than most. Moreover, he liked the simplicity of their transactions; he did his part and asked no questions. It was uncomplicated and Tors always paid (and paid well) at the end of each job, regardless of when and how or even if he ever managed to shift the goods. Vidar liked that. It was almost like having a proper job. Almost.

"C'mon, let me buy you a drink before you split eh?" he said merrily, but when he looked up, Tors had already disappeared.

With a careless shrug and spring in his step, Vidar made his way out of the alley, guided mostly by the stars above and the lights in the distance.

DRAEGER

Seven thousand miles away, beneath the same stars but buried deep within the labyrinthian sanctum of the Red Palace, matters of great political consequence were slowly unravelling.

"How long do they think he has left?" Lord Draeger asked the Chancellor as the doors of the Emperor's bedchamber closed behind them.

The corridor of the Red Palace was deserted, filled with a deathly quiet that seemed to keep both servants and courtiers away. Lord Draeger, tall, dark and laconic, gestured for them to walk and converse at the same time, his air of grim countenance echoing the gravity of present circumstances.

"We don't think your father will live past the week, my Lord," replied Chancellor Rasmus. His footsteps rang off the stone paving and echoed down the cold corridor. Lord Draeger, by contrast, strode soundlessly. "It will be best if we prepared for it," the Chancellor continued. He paused, glanced at Lord Draeger and added, "If *you* prepared for it."

The Chancellor was a tall, lanky man with eyes as grey as

the evening mist but sharp as a wolf's. Over the centuries, as he watched Lord Draeger mature from boy to man, his hair had gradually progressed from graphite to pebble and now, settled at a dignified shade of flint, it matched his iron-hued tunic and cloak of dove-grey.

Draeger remained silent.

"Have *you* given it thought, my Lord?" the Chancellor pressed. "If he asks? *When* he asks?"

Draeger gave an almost imperceptible shake of his head. "I am still ... considering," he replied. The prospect of the decision that lay imminently ahead weighed heavily on his mind and he gave a deep sigh.

At the middling age of two hundred and twenty-three, Draeger felt the full weight of his responsibilities as Supreme Commander of his father's armies and as firstborn of House Ageron. Until recently, it had never been a task that bore thinking about.

Having survived growing up in the dangerously perilous confines of the royal household, he was trained by the finest in combat, strategy, politics and accorded no special treatment whatsoever that came with him being the first born of Emperor Ageron III. However at present, the extent of his involvement in matters did not concern the straightforward matters of battlefields nor combat. The Emperor was dying and the question of succession and the responsibilities that accompanied that inevitability loomed.

He shook it off for the moment. It was something he did not wish to think about just yet. "It has been two months since I've been back here," he said, changing the subject.

The Chancellor nodded understandingly. "The riots , I hear, have been sprouting up all over the Realm," he said. "It cannot be easy, putting these out."

Draeger remained in silent agreement. *Fighting the War was far simpler than containing these riots.* And it had been a war that cost all parties dearly, not least the Nehisi, now extinct.

Eradicated by the Ellagrins.

Draeger longed for something else besides the depressing multitude of problems that besieged them. Some good news perhaps. Or at the very least, a distraction. "Now what news here at the royal court, Rasmus?" he asked. "Anything worthy of note?"

"Well," continued the Chancellor with a hint of notoriety in his voice, "there has been a recent theft..."

"Hmm?"

"Apparently Lord Darius' personal vault was broken into a few nights ago."

Draeger let out a cynical snort. "I have no interest in the contents of Lord Darius' personal vault," he said.

"Ah, but an *Eldur* was stolen," came the reply.

Draeger turned to look at the Chancellor. His eyes darkened. "Does Lord Darius expect us to send troops to find it for him?" He clenched his fist. "Eldur is for the Exodus. For the people. Lord Darius should count himself lucky we've not thrown him in jail for hoarding one. Consider this never reached my ears or I shall make an example of him to the others."

The Chancellor merely nodded. It was a response he had expected.

Lord Draeger frowned. "The rich have taken to building their own ships instead of waiting their turn in the Exodus like everyone else. We have to put a stop to this."

The Chancellor agreed. "Corruption is endemic in the Exodus programme and this has no doubt stoked more riots." He paused and then continued, "We are however weeding that out before things get out of control. Our efforts have already caused quite a few outcries within the royal circles."

"Good," said Lord Draeger. *He sees everything, the Chancellor, and thank Dyaeus, he is one of the few impervious to the scourge of corruption within our ruling class.* He glanced at the Chancellor, recalling many a time where the old man's canniness and unimpeachable integrity had helped keep the Senate in check.

"On an encouraging note," piped up the Chancellor, "the *Carinthia* is nearly ready, my Lord. We are in the final phase and the last ten thousand passengers will be contacted and processed in the next few months."

Lord Draeger paused a moment. "This will be the last ship leaving for the Ellagrin system this decade," he noted.

"Indeed," confirmed the Chancellor. "And you will be pleased to know that build on the next tranche of spacecarriers has begun, my Lord."

"Excellent," said Lord Draeger approvingly. "With the departure of the Carinthia, we should see the riots lessen somewhat. At least until when the next batch of ships are ready. That always gets people's tempers flaring." He shook his head and gave a deep sigh. "Time and patience appear to be in short supply these days."

"An unfortunate but understandable reaction from the masses," said the Chancellor patiently. "Speaking of the Carinthia, my Lord, what of the settlement treaties for its passengers?"

Lord Draeger nodded.

Elena.

"I shall speak to her," he said.

"It is fortunate for us that Lady Elena has her brother's ear," the Chancellor commented. "House Ageron would be in dire circumstances if it weren't for these settlement treaties."

Lord Draeger's mouth grew hard. "It is an uneasy truce between our two Houses," he said, "and a tenuous one. Niklas could turn around anytime and renege on these treaties. Then where will we be?"

The Chancellor returned a knowing look. The problem they faced was not a new one but one that had been hanging over their heads for close to two centuries now, ever since the twin suns of Ageron had begun to fail. The war between Ageron and Ellagrin may have ended in a truce for over a century now but unfortunately for them, that very same war also saw to the destruction of the Gateways connecting the main planetary systems of the galaxy. Without the Gateways, the only means to leave the Ageron system was via spacecarriers, colossal ships to take their people away to the next planetary system closest to them; the planetary system of Ellagrin.

Ships that take decades to build.

A deep chill went through Lord Draeger. *Time is running out.*

And it had already begun. *The planets closest to the suns are already affected—heatstorms, freak weather fronts and tsunamis. It will only be a matter of time before they become uninhabitable.*

But upheaval of entire populations to the outer planets was neither straightforward nor the solution to the problem. *Much of our outer planets are barely habitable,* Draeger reminded himself, *whilst others face overcrowding.* This was the problem his father had faced and now it seemed, it would soon be his to bear.

As Lord Draeger departed the Palace and boarded his shuttle for the residence of Lady Elena, a sense of foreboding swept over him.

The beginning of the end had begun...

ELENA

The quarters of Lady Elena were modest by Ageronian standards. Although not as lavish as she was accustomed to, it provided her with sufficient comfort and more importantly the discretion that came with living in an exclusive neighbourhood.

Tucked in a quiet corner of the piazza, it stood at the end of an established row of terraced townhouses, all clad in white stucco, each exuding the dignified but unmistakable aura of Old Money.

Of course they weren't the original buildings. Nothing went back further than a few centuries at most and nothing carried real historical substance. Everything was a copy, a reproduction of a past whose memory had been handed down generation after generation for millennia. And even more ironic, this was a past from a different world altogether—Old Earth. The world of their ancestors and a world that the inhabitants of this system, having settled here millennia ago, had themselves never seen or known, other than from ancient records and accounts passed down the generations through word of mouth, stories and such.

It was evening and the twin suns had begun to set. The nearer one called Romulus, being larger and more imposing, along with its twin Remus, slightly smaller and higher above the horizon, had cast their rays on the neat residences, bathing their frontages in wine. The stonework had been absorbing the suns' unrelenting rays all day and the air shimmered from the emanating heat. It was a harsh, dry heat that withered most vegetation, save the tough sapless barbthorn hedges, dark and dense, which gave the neighbourhood its deceptively verdant and genteel look.

"You are late," chastised Elena. Her startling cobalt eyes glowed with a luminosity of their own as she lay on her gilded chaise longue.

Lord Draeger moved noiselessly across the room towards her to kiss her hand.

Lady Elena made no attempt to rise from where she was.

"My apologies," Draeger murmured, "I was... detained."

Elena waved his apology aside with a languid gesture of her hand. "I shall have to think up a form of punishment to compensate," she teased.

"Nothing too severe I hope," said Draeger, "for I have something for you..."

Elena sat up. "Something?" Her eyes lit up. "Something nice?"

"Perhaps...," came the answer. From the folds of his cloak, Draeger drew out an almost shabby-looking pouch, made from some sort of pelt. "Close your eyes," he said which Elena did without hesitation. "Now open them," said Draeger.

Elena drew a sharp breath of delight as her eyes reflected the iridescent glow in front of her.

Draeger looked on with amusement. Elena loved jewels.

Always had.

"Eldur," she whispered breathlessly, lifting the stone from Draeger's hand. "You brought me an Eldur. " She fingered it delicately. "Some call it Ice Fire and I can see why. It is beautiful...," she said, mesmerised.

Draeger looked at her. Lady Elena was an exquisite beauty. Elegant, slender and fair-haired, she looked more like a fragile porcelain sculpture than one who, through the subtle skills of persuasion wielded power and influence amongst the Doges that backed House Ellagrin. For Lady Elena was royalty itself, a pure blood Ellagrin and sister to none other than Niklas, the present Emperor of Ellagrin.Elena flung her arms round Draeger. "How wonderful!" she laughed gaily. "I shall commission a necklace to wear this around my neck at the Winter Carnivale!"

Draeger gave her a disapproving look. "Not unless you want someone slitting your throat at the ball my lady."

Elena draped her lovely arms around him. "Nonsense," she said, "they would not dare."

Draeger raised an eyebrow at her, this time almost one of reproof but Elena dismissed it with a devilish smile. "Tell me," she said, her expression suddenly serious. "I hear rumours from the Red Palace. Some say the Emperor is likely to pass soon. Is this true?"

Draeger nodded.

"Hmmm," pondered Elena. She lifted an eyebrow. "And you will ascend...?"

"That will be his decision, not mine," corrected Draeger.

"But he will choose you," she said matter-of-factly. "I know so." She looked at him intently. "But will you accept?" she asked. "Will you be Emperor?"

Draeger did not reply.

Elena dismissed his omission with a casual laugh. "Perhaps

if you become Emperor, I shall be your Empress," she said. "Or perhaps," she continued with a wicked glint in her eye, "when there is no Ageron left, you could be my consort."

Then just as quickly, her mirth dissipated only to be replaced with a darker afterthought. "I can just imagine the look on Niklas' face if that happens. Oh, the irony of it..."

"Hmmm," murmured Draeger.

"Anyway," said Elena turning back to her gift, "an Eldur that's not destined for one of your ships. How did you manage that?"

Draeger shrugged. "Let's say I commissioned the services of an underground specialist."

Elena feigned her surprise. "Are you saying you enlisted the services of a *criminal* to get me my little Eldur?" She eyed him in mock chastise. "The Supreme Commander himself?"

"Procuring something like an Eldur and gifting it to one still recognised as the enemy of House Ageron is not an undertaking that can be advertised nor commissioned legally, my lady,"replied Draeger looking down at her in mock sternness.

Elena played with a strand of her golden hair, twirling it with one finger, and looked at him, wide-eyed and playful. "I'm hardly the enemy," she laughed. "Besides, we have been in a truce for over a century and a half now. And what about this procurer you enlisted then?" she asked. "What is he like?"

Draeger shrugged carelessly. "I don't know,"he said. "No one does. He keeps his identity a secret, although his exploits border on the legendary."

"Really? *Tell* me," Elena pressed. She leant seductively on his arm.

Draeger relented. "The man that procured this stone for me," he said, "is rather well-known in certain circles for his ability to source just about anything in the Realms."

"A *thief?*" asked Elena, with feigned incredulity.

"A very good one too," answered Draeger. "So good they nickname him *Prometheus*. Rather apt in this case don't you think? Did you know, it was he who slit the throat of Cardinal Benedict?"

"Cardinal Benedict? The one who was found in the quarters of the Arnemetiae Boys Orphanage with his pants down?" Elena smiled wickedly at the recollection.

"Yes," said Draeger. "The fool decided to pay this man a thousand *ore* less than promised for the Chalice of Lucalia he procured for him."

"Ah...," murmured Lady Elena.

"They had arranged for the exchange to be held at the sacred Temple of Atheron. So when the Cardinal refused to honour the original agreement, Prometheus slit his throat there and then, in front of a most unfortunate group of young acolytes on a faith trip."

"Oh," murmured Elena with a raised eyebrow, "that *is* most unfortunate." She gave a quiet little laugh. "And how did this Prometheus escape? Didn't the priests stop him?"

"No," answered Draeger. "Apparently he threw the chalice into the temple furnace and then walked casually out the front door, but only after making sure it had melted completely first. One of the most important cultural treasures of the empire... obliterated."

"A loss of little consequence then," said Elena wryly. "I find religious relics dreadfully dull don't you? This man however," she mused, "this Prometheus..., I find *most* intriguing."

"No one has seen his face," said Draeger, "and we know very little about him."

"How *romantic*..." murmured Elena, draping her lovely arms around him. Elena felt him inhale sharply. She knew the power she possessed over men and relished it.

"So what is it that you seek in return my brave, generous lover?" As used as she was to favours from her admirers, Elena was no fool. A gift as generous as this demanded something in return.

Draeger lifted her chin to face him.

Her gaze, replete with confidence only a moment ago dissipated quickly, to be replaced by uncertainty and to her own surprise, a tinge of fear. She gazed back at him. His piercing black basilisk eyes, like infinite abysses burned into her with such intensity, reminding her that this man was after all a killer and one who had been doing so very successfully, at a colossal scale, for over a century.

"Is everything always a transaction with you?" he asked, amused.

Elena nodded. "*Always,*" she said, with a knowing smile.

It was a rather odd relationship between them—he the Commander and firstborn of House Ageron and she, sister to the Emperor of House Ellagrin. It was her father Mikael's act of genocide on the Nehisi tribe that triggered the war between their Houses. Elena looked at Draeger and wondered what he made of that tumultuous period.

Father tried to take over the Gateways. It was his jealousy and rage at Ageron's wealth and monopoly over the Gateways that drove him mad. Mad enough to massacre an entire tribe and start a war that would destroy the Gateways. But in the end, the Ageronian armies, led by Draeger, had forced Father's armies back.

Elena closed her eyes. *The war finally stopped when the Gateways were destroyed.*

She remembered hearing the news, and her consternation as one by one, the Gateways fell. *Father destroyed them.*

A pang of reprehension. *He destroyed them, rather than let House Ageron retain its monopoly on the Gateways.*

She glanced at Draeger. *With the Gateways destroyed, your people are all now effectively trapped here in Ageron, with the only way out via spacecarriers. Ships that take decades to build.* If it wasn't for her father, there would have been no war, and the Exodus would not have needed ships. She pondered further. *But if Father had not died, and the Gateways not destroyed, Ellagrin and Ageron could still be at war until this day.*

She looked away. *Would things have been different between you and I if Father hadn't died?*

Niklas, her brother and current Emperor of Ellagrin, took after Father, preferring to project the same hate and jealousy that spawned the war in the first place, but Elena had much more practical sensibilities. Ageron, she recognised, had money. Lots of it. And Ellagrin, weakened by the war they didn't win, needed money badly.

A few billion ore is far more useful than national pride.

And so, through a grudging truce of sorts between the two Houses, Ellagrin's economy gradually grew, decade by decade, slowly supplying Ageronians with biotechnology and variants of agricultural plantae hardy enough to survive their harshest climates.

But now more than ever, Elena sensed that things were beginning to tip ever more in Ellagrin's favour.

"I need a small favour," replied Draeger. "Nothing much. Just some treaty settlements for the passengers of the Carinthia."

The fate of his people. He puts that above all else, she thought to herself. *Even me... .*

Out loud she said, "And yet you give me this Eldur." Elena smiled at the irony. "Are you intending to send one less ship in future?"

"We can always mine for more Eldur,"replied Draeger casually. "However this one is particularly exquisite."

"You flatter me," said Elena and snapping back to business she asked, "So, how many?"

"A little over a million. We are sending smaller numbers at a time now to minimise impact from rebel disruptions. The Carinthia sets off for Ellagrin this winter."

"A million refugees," said Elena thoughtfully.

"Expatriates," corrected Draeger.

"*Refugees*," insisted Elena drily. "Rich ones, but refugees nonetheless."

Draeger said nothing.

She continued, a little less severe this time, "This is not sustainable you know. There is not enough land in all of Ellagrin's planets to accommodate all Ageronians, even with all their wealth. Don't forget, we are still in the midst of a standoff and you..." she said, stroking the side of his face, "are not our friends. Not even allies."

"Emissaries were sent to the Tilkoen system almost a hundred years ago," said Draeger, "but Tilkoen is distant. By the time we reach them and complete negotiations for settlements there, it may well be too late."

Draeger disentangled himself from her arms and looked out the window. The suns, now almost below the horizon, cast their dying embers of red across the square, covering everything in the ubiquitous crimson haze and living up to the empire's nickname of the Red Realm.

"The twin suns are dying faster than anticipated," he said, "and their atmospheres have expanded far more quickly than we had predicted. Their proximity has triggered heatstorms on the innermost planets and those planets themselves are becoming unstable. Natural disasters on a planetary scale seem to be occurring more and more frequently." He shook his head, his expression was grave. "It's not just heatstorms. We're getting the whole spectrum of freak weather occurrences: hailstorms, hurricanes, even tsunamis. As economic hardship from these disasters affect more people, more will support the Rebellion."

"But surely the Exodus, this expatriation programme that has been going on for over a hundred years now, this *must* show your people that House Ageron is doing all it can," said Elena. "Surely they must see the millions evacuated and resettled on Ellagrin, that efforts will continue until the evacuation is complete. What can the Rebellion possibly do for them that House Ageron cannot and has not?"

"They do not believe the empire are doing enough or have their interests at heart." Draeger shook his head. "The recent spate of scandals involving aristocrats buying their way out of the Realm has not helped. All this and the population control laws we've introduced are seen as suppressive, even tyrannical."

Elena shrugged. "Population laws are necessary to reduce the birthrate in order for population levels to be sufficiently low enough to fit the last few outbound ships. I would have decreed the same. You'll never finish evacuating the entire population if they keep on reproducing like rats. Those reasons are simple enough for the populace to understand surely?"

Draeger smiled. "It would seem no one likes to be told what they cannot do regardless the reasons behind it." He chuckled. "You wouldn't believe the extremes the *Amore Libero* cultists go to in order to make their point across. And the Exodus itself..." Draeger sighed. "People are impatient and the rebels resent the fact that expatriation is by state lottery. They believe corruption is involved."

Elena shrugged. "Yes," she agreed, "a small amount of corruption cannot be helped. Some are, after all, more equal than others, and with all resources spent on building ships, I would imagine there is little leftover to pay for natural disasters and the population's current social needs."

Draeger sighed. "Regardless, with the recent surge of natural disasters affecting entire cities, people are getting nervous. Everyone wants to leave and no one wants to wait decades to do so. But that cannot be helped. For now, I need to make sure those selected for the Carinthia have a destination to go to."

Elena nodded. "Very well," she said, "I shall talk to my brother. The settlement treaties shall be agreed upon in order for the passengers of Carinthia to put down roots on Ellagrin soil. At the usual price but..." She turned to face him, her delicate brows furrowed, "I fear Niklas will not indulge me so easily in future. My frequent requests annoy him and he tires of me. Ellagrin cannot take in the inhabitants of all twelve of your planets, even at the price offered. You will have to find another way to save your people."

As she rose to leave, she turned back to gaze levelly at him. "Or just let them die," she said. "The end will not come in its totality for another few centuries yet. Ageronians may be able to comprehend a timescale that far but the other shorter-lived species—the humans, the Ashgarians and and the handful of marooned Tilkoens that have ended up here—what do they care? Most of them are destitute and with no access to rejuvenation, they won't live beyond the end anyway. Humans even less so. These will not weep nor care for the generations to come."

She paused at the door, turning back to face him one last time. "So you see, my love," she said with a faint smile, "there is after all, nothing to worry about."

With that she blew him a kiss and withdrew from the room, signalling the end of their meeting.

AGERON III DIES

The royal bedchamber was hazy with incense and oppressively heavy and full despite its size and the relatively small number of people in it. In the corner, Queen Alin stood impassively amidst the other weeping consorts, Emperor Ageron III having expressed his wish to keep them and their constant fretting, genuine or otherwise, away from his bedside. A few senior members of the Senate, Praetors Lord Patrin and Lord Albertus, hovered nearby in sombre silence, and in the far end of the chamber, other lesser members of the royal household stood by murmuring amongst themselves in hushed voices.

The room was dim and heavily muffled by the sumptuous drapes that hung on the walls and around the bed. It was richly decorated; its ceilings and cornices covered in intricate carvings echoing the patterns of the antique tapestries that adorned the walls. Sculptures, some a millennia old, lay dotted around like the toys of a child left carelessly mid-play, whimsical fancies in a scene of understated opulence and beauty. Subtle reminders that despite everything, House Ageron was still the richest and most powerful empire in the galaxy. The floor was the only surface left bare. Bereft of rugs or carpet, it was made of wood, so lovingly polished and preserved it gleamed like dark treacle, smooth and warm to the touch.

Wood, thought Draeger as he looked at the courtiers standing silently in the corners of the room. *How many of you even know what wood is, or have seen where wood comes from?* For a second, his thoughts left the room and a fleeting memory of golden sunlight filtering through a canopy of leaves filled them.

Autumn. The woods. They had milder seasons then, not the harsh arid heatstorms of today. And forests. Days that were filled with golden sunlight, not the dying crimson haze that gave rise to the Ageron's better known nickname of the Red Realm today, but bright, glorious, golden sunlight that warmed your face like the touch of an angel.

"Lord Draeger," said Chancellor Rasmus, his quiet voice bringing Draeger back to the present. "His Excellency wishes to speak to you." The old man drew back and gently extended his hand towards the Emperor's frail figure.

Draeger followed in the direction of the Chancellor's hand, approached his father and sat softly on the bed beside him. "Father," he said, bowing his head in greeting.

Ageron III lifted his head and looked at his son. His eyes although dimming, still displayed great lucidity behind them. "The Oracle has not yet awoken," he rasped. There was difficulty in his breathing and his speech was faint and slurred.

"It has not awakened for nearly two hundred years, Father," replied Draeger quietly, "It may never awaken before we leave the solar system."

"We are running out of time," the dying Emperor continued. "You know it too. The ships take too long to build and..." Ageron gulped a few shallow breaths in succession, "before long, we will have spent all our resources for materials and supplies. Treaties with the enemy cannot be depended upon, the hatred between the two Houses runs too deep."

Draeger nodded, "We are still searching, Father."

"You must find the Key," Ageron pressed. "The last Nehisi, the Key to reopen the Gates. The Oracle had warned us about this... Without the Gateways, billions will die."

Draeger bowed his head. *That's not all the Oracle told me,* he thought to himself, remembering.

"My son, I have left you much to do. To find an Eldur in a sea of stars..." Ageron gave a little sigh.

Draeger lifted his bowed head and looked at his father. The sigh was not one given out of weakness. Indeed, apart from his current condition, the old man had few. His withered body had become almost unrecognisable, but the eyes—they were still those of the father Draeger grew up with. The man who had spent more time involved in the affairs of the state than with his own sons (of which there remained only two). The man who expected his sons to function without fear or emotion, to do what was necessary to rule a hundred billion peoples comprising a multitude of races, species and a plethora of cultures, morals and beliefs. And what was necessary in maintaining the Realms in the course of the last two centuries included the war, retaliation for the massacre of the Nehisi, and countless skirmishes from factions wrestling for power. In every single one of them, Lord Draeger, Supreme Commander of the armies, had carried out his father's orders with lethal efficiency and without emotion.

Now the hour to proclaim the next ruler of the Realms had arrived. Emperor Ageron III lifted his head weakly and looked at his sons. Draeger—tall, hunched over the bed like a dark hawk, his aquiline nose and basilisk eyes inherited from his mother the great Sorceress Yinha—was dimly visible in the flickering candlelight, and standing a little further behind, his brother Akseli The Younger—resolute, rugged and yet regal in certain aspects, a trait unmistakably passed down from his mother, Queen Alin who was, without doubt, in the corner of the room somewhere, waiting for him to expire.

"The Kingdom is yours...," said Ageron. His dulling eyes lingered over Draeger. "If you so want it. I would also wish it so. My first born...."

Draeger looked at his father for a moment. *If I accept, my imperium will extend from commander of the armies to control over the Senate and the Praetors of all twelve planets. All will answer to me and me alone. The empire will be mine....* In short, the offer was not only one of succession, it would be one that would give him total and utter control over House Ageron.

Draeger looked up into the darkness and pondered a moment. In his peripheral vision, he observed his younger brother Akseli standing at the side, his head bowed in sombre respect. Despite that, he sensed a palpable sense of disquietude from Akseli, an undercurrent of desire, accompanied by a helplessness from knowing that both their fates would be determined by Draeger's decision in the next few moments.

He hungers for it, Draeger realised. *He wants to be Emperor....*

He let his thoughts run with the idea. Akseli was always the more loquacious one, better at talking to people, the one whose words could convince them even if the actions that followed didn't necessarily match up. But he was also the more ambitious of the two and Draeger knew well of his brother's ambitions.

However Akseli will never be a threat. As Supreme Commander, there was never any question where the power lay. *He who controls the armies, controls the Realms.* Ambition was after all, part of their lives as sons of the Emperor and a proponent of survival too. One only had to look—in the course of the last three and a half centuries, out of Ageron's litter of over three hundred male heirs, Draeger and Akseli were the only two that survived.

Is there any harm in all this though? pondered Draeger, toying with the idea. *After all, I will still control the armies, and the day-to-day governing of the people by the Senate, Akseli can deal with.* The thought of the incessant politicking and negotiating, the endless discussions with the Praetors, slick and slippery with their demands, the backstabbing petty royals in their attempts to advance their statuses within the Senate—it was the last thing he wanted. As Supreme Commander, his chain of command was far more straightforward. Apart from a few exceptions, the Legati answered to him and him alone, and his orders were followed without question for the military operated separately to the Senate, leaving its Praetors to manage the tedium of the day-to-day administration of the empire.

It is much simpler this way. After all Draeger did not negotiate. The only negotiating he ever did was with the end of his sword. He thought about the interminable hours his father spent negotiating and discussing matters of the state, a stark contrast to his role as Supreme Commander.

What have I to lose by letting Akseli play King?

There was an imperceptible exchange of looks between father and son, then Ageron III smiled. It was a smile of how glorious things *could* be, except they both knew it was not to be.

Draeger spoke. "I am honoured, Father," he said, "but I believe Akseli will be better suited to affairs of the state whilst I carry on in my capacity as Supreme Commander of the armies and continue with the search for the Key." He looked into his father's eyes. "I will watch over him, Father, and I will serve him as I have served you."

Ageron nodded. It was as he had expected. His eyes shifted to the figure standing behind Draeger.

Akseli stepped forward and knelt before the bed.

"Then so be it," said Ageron lifting his voice as loud as he could muster. "Akseli The Younger, second son of Ageron… is *Emperor* of House Ageron."

And then, with a final exhalation, he closed his eyes for the last time.

ELENA

Elena stood by the balcony window, her glass of *amarinthe* in hand, and gazed disinterestedly as the mob surged past below.

Another mindless herd of disillusioned fools, she thought as she watched them shout and wave their banners about. The constant rioting of late was getting tiresome. *Perhaps it's time to leave the Realm.* With all this heat and havoc, the cool, lush greenery of home in Ellagrin was looking more and more the attractive alternative. *An option these people do not have,* she noted, well aware of her vastly different circumstance.

"These riots appear to be worsening," she murmured, still looking out of the window.

"The people are restless," replied Draeger. He was sitting in her apartment, glass in hand, contemplating. "The recent spate of natural disasters we have had on the inner planets hasn't helped." He looked up from where he was seated and went on. "The heatstorms at Anavio in particular have put a strain on resources. The people are worried and anxious to leave."

Elena nodded. "And how is your brother Akseli handling all this? Has it been a month yet since the coronation?"

"A little over a month," answered Draeger, "and we have been evacuating people from cities hit by heatstorms everyday since. I have had Akseli broadcast his speeches to the people to reassure them," he continued. "To remind them that the Exodus Programme is progressing as expeditiously as possible and whilst selection of evacuees is conducted by state lottery, no one will be left out."

"And is that working?" asked Elena wryly.

"The Emperor possesses great statesmanship," replied Draeger. "He placates the people..." and then added rather drily, "and my armies ensure they remain placated."

Elena suppressed a chuckle. *So nothing has changed then. He who controls the army holds real power.* Her lips curled in amusement. *Akseli can't be happy about this.*

"I hear Ageron himself offered you the throne. Why did you not take it?"

She turned away from the window. "That would have given you complete control over the Realms, " she said. "You don't need Akseli." She looked at him and wondered. *What I would give to have that kind of power in Ellagrin...*

Draeger stood up, picked up the decanter from the sideboard and walked slowly across the room towards her. "I believe this arrangement works better," he said. He looked across her shoulder and out the window. The mob had disappeared around the corner and the street below was quiet once again.

"These riots are organised by the Rebellion," he said, mulling. "And they've not stopped there. Their attempts to steal the empire's resources are hampering our shipbuilders' progress."

"So I hear," said Elena. "They seem rather brazen about it too, from what I've seen in the news."

Draeger nodded. "They blasted a hole into one of the central vaults last week, trying to steal an Eldur. And the week before, raided one of the shipbuilding plants at Segontia for propulsion drive parts." He shook his head. "The antics of the Rebellion are becoming a hindrance."

"But why are they doing this?" asked Elena. "To sell to the black market? To fund their cause?"

"They're after the same resources for themselves," said Draeger. "The Rebellion have been building a spacecarrier of their own, did you know?"

"Really?"

Draeger nodded, filling her glass. "The *Tethys*. They have somehow cobbled enough resources to build their own ship." He gave a heavy sigh. "Their continuing actions not only sabotage our efforts on the Carinthia, they impact the build of our next tranche of carrier ships. These rebels will stop at nothing. Anything to get their message across—they want control of the Exodus."

"Interesting," murmured Elena. "Do they think they can run the Exodus better themselves?"

"They don't think we're conducting the Exodus quickly enough," Draeger replied, and after a brief pause, "or equitably enough...."

"Ah." Elena understood. Most of these she knew of already, curtesy of the gossip within the social circles she moved in.

"The past few incidents of rigged lottery results, in particular the latest one, has not helped in matters," said Draeger grimly.

Elena nodded. *The recent scandal involving Lord Aridius.*

"Aridius' involvement in passenger tickets for the Carinthia," continued Draeger, affirming her thoughts. His mouth twisted in bitter grimace. "That incident has brought much damage to the egalitarianism of the Programme."

"I can imagine,"murmured Elena empathetically. *Yes, that one. Akseli was not too happy about it, but **not** because of Aridius' misconduct...*

"A dozen of the Aridius family's closest friends could not *all* have possibly won the state lottery for passage on the Carinthia," continued Draeger.

Elena remained silent, recalling her source's account of Akseli's outburst: *'That fool Aridius would have got away with it had he not insisted on including the mistress, her parents and all three of their bastard offspring as well!'*

"Akseli has demanded an inquiry into this,"continued Draeger, "and short of public flogging, Lord Aridius has been stripped of his title."

Elena glanced quickly at Draeger. *So, he doesn't know about his brother's involvement...*

"Corruption aside, the weather patterns are becoming too irregular for our prediction models to work properly," said Draeger. He frowned. "And we cannot divert too much manpower or resource from the Exodus to rebuild the cities destroyed by these epic natural disasters."

He placed the decanter back on the sideboard with a thunk. "People can understand why their cities are left to go to ruin but at the same time, to have to wait years for the ships to be ready, to see the fruits of their sacrifice, *if* at all they get the chance to... that is a tall ask."

"Indeed,"agreed Elena. She recalled what it was like here, almost a century ago before the suns grew hotter and the trees began to die out. *In the days before the War, before the Gateways fell, Ageron oozed with wealth and her cities were lustrous and golden. Her people, even the poorest, were in want of nothing. Oh how the mighty have fallen...*

"Which brings us back to this business of your people wanting to leave on their own, without having to resort to putting their entire faith in the Exodus," said Elena. "Ah! That reminds me..."

She smiled impishly and went towards the tapestry that hung on the wall just before the bedroom area. She lifted it to access the safe hidden underneath. "What do you think of this?" she asked brightly, bringing out a necklace—the Eldur in its new setting. Elena put it on and walked up to Draeger, twirling this way and that to make it glisten and pulse in the light. "Do you like it?" she asked.

Draeger smiled. "It is very fetching," he answered.

"Well," said Elena seating herself on the chaise next to him, "I happened to wear this to a private soiree the other night..."

Draeger shot her a sharp glance.

"A small and very private affair, don't worry," added Elena, eyeing his concerned look with wicked relish. "At Lady Ceciro's." She paused to look at him and then continued. "Lord Darius wasn't there but his mistress was...."

Elena leant forward, fingering her necklace lightly. "And according to her...," Elena lowered her voice conspiratorially, "Lord Darius' vault was broken into last month. A vault which rather coincidentally held an Eldur promised to her for her new tiara." Elena's lips curled. "An Eldur remarkably similar to mine, it seems," she said, searching his face closely, "although I suspect, contrary to her deluded hopes, I doubt very much jewellery was in the forefront of Lord Darius' mind." She gave Draeger a knowing look but Draeger remained impassive, refusing to rise to the bait.

Elena gave a little laugh. "Perhaps I should wear this to Lord Darius' dinner next week," she said aloud, "and see what he thinks of this."

"Don't," Draeger said, finally rising to the bait and giving her a stern look.

Elena's lips curled with mischief. "Oh, but think of the fall-out, "she said wickedly. "The social circles here are dreadfully dull. How amusing it would be, don't you think, if it transpired that Lord Darius' painstaking plans to secretly evacuate were lost to the frivolous form of a lady's ornament instead."

Draeger shook his head.

Elena laughed inwardly. She enjoyed getting him riled up.

"Please don't tempt fate," Draeger urged. "My gifts to you may be for your entertainment but they do not involve scandal, least of all those that will add to my current list of problems."

Elena dismissed his concerns with a pat on his arm. "Don't worry my love," she said, "I was merely jesting." She gazed at him. "But, I *was* thinking—" she said.

Draeger groaned.

Elena ignored his grumbling. "I was just thinking," she said again, "this thief you enlisted to procure my Eldur, this *Prometheus,* he could have been at Lady Cicero's gathering." She sat up, her eyes bright. "You know how it is in these aristocratic circles... we talk and well, we *talk*." She looked at him intently. "Who's to say, perhaps this Prometheus is one of your royals?"

Draeger shrugged. "That is a possibility, yes," he said, "but what of it?"

"You know how I like mysteries," said Elena. The prospect of uncovering this mysterious criminal excited her. "Surely it can't be difficult working out who this Prometheus really is. Do you think he also works for the Rebellion?"

Draeger shook his head. "I doubt it. If he were, he wouldn't be stealing for private buyers."

"Hmmm," murmured Elena, thinking.

Draeger looked her. "Don't get involved," he warned. "Men like Prometheus are dangerous, especially when Eldur is involved. They are mercenaries and this isn't some trivial pursuit for amusement. I have enough on my plate as it is to deal with at present."

Elena gave a sigh. "Very well," she said. "I shall have to find other ways to amuse myself whilst I'm here then."

She settled herself comfortably on the chaise in resignation but deep down, Lady Elena wondered…

VIDAR SPLURGES

SCANDAL! PROMETHEUS STRIKES AGAIN!

Vidar chuckled as he passed by the holo headlines projected at the news stand. He didn't stop but as he sauntered past, he chanced to glimpse the accompanying clip of some Lord denying it was an Eldur that was stolen by the legendary jewel thief.

Vidar reflected on the irony of it all. *So, they're hiring us to steal from each other—from one Lord to another.* He gave an amused snort. These Eldur heists were indeed lucrative!

Vidar continued his way through the genteel neighbourhood, commonly known to locals as the Italian Quarter. He liked walking down its elegant avenues. Here, the pretty cobbled streets were open and empty, and the air clean. A far cry from the less salubrious downtown where one had to not just hotfoot through its filthy, smelly tenements but endure its far less attractive populace at the same time.

Even the twin suns seemed to beam down more benevolently here, tinting the entire street in an attractive glaze of reds and pinks. Vidar could feel a dry heat prickling slightly at his throat but it was a good, dry heat and the air was still with none of the fine sand and dust that usually came whenever the wind blew.

He sauntered down the street, whistling as he went, every so often turning his head to admire the attractive, well-heeled female residents strolling past. Life was good and Vidar walked with the assurance of a man relaxed in the knowledge that he had money in his pocket. Lots of it, thanks to the recent job for Tors and enough to start a new life, if he could be bothered to be careful enough with it.

It was late morning and the threadbare lining of his tunic scratched hotly at his neck as the suns approached their zenith. *I probably should have ordered those new shirts earlier,* he thought to himself, feeling a little self-conscious of his slightly scruffy state amidst the well-kept surroundings. Who knew these things needed a day to be 'tailored'?

Well, it can't be helped now. I'm late as it is...

He reached the end of the avenue and turned left towards a rather handsome apartment block. Its entire ground floor, once a hotel foyer and a well-known restaurant, had been tastefully converted into the plush offices of Caelum and Co. Realtors. Entering through its sleek, dark doors, he was met by the receptionist and shown to the rather swanky waiting area in front. As he sat, Vidar looked out through the one-way glass windows at the apartments opposite.

These must be about the same size as the one I'm getting....

His eyes followed their attractive frontages up to the stylish wrought-iron balconies overhead; a few of these had their doors open to let the air in and he tried to see past the diaphanous curtains that rippled as the occasional breeze snatched at them.

He wondered who lived in these. What was it the rental lady said before? Second homes to wealthy businessmen, a few pied-a-terre's for kept mistresses and the rest, family homes of aristocrats inherited over the generations.

I could get used to this kind of lifestyle, he thought, fanciful images of an idyllic lifestyle forming in his mind. Purchasing one of these outright was most certainly out of his league but a few months rental here, his wallet could afford.

Maybe I'll get some girls in to liven things up a bit, he mused. But they'd have to be the classier ones of course. Better dressed and definitely less uncouth; not the ones from the tenements like Lucia and her companions, not that there was anything wrong with Lucia and her 'sisters'.

The women Vidar knew were mostly prostitutes, paid escorts at best. Fine company who'd happily share his *amarinthe* and comfortable bed, preferably when he paid them for the privilege, though on occasion, in particular when he was short, they often obliged him on account of his charms and easy-going manner.

Hell, I might even get friendly with the neighbours, he thought gleefully to himself. *A posh totty perhaps....* All women, no matter what background, were always his type. And with regards to those women, Vidar fancied the same applied to him too. His lips curled at the recollection of the ladies he passed by earlier.

"Mr...Valerius?"

A smooth voice arrested Vidar from his daydreams. A slim-looking lady stood in front of him, hands clasped together in a polite waiting gesture.

"Valerius?" Vidar repeated rather hazily, then hastily added, "Valerius! That's me! Er yes?"

"My name is Camilla,"the lady said. "We spoke over the comms earlier."

Vidar nodded.

"This way, sir," she said leading him into the inner office.

It was a simple room, functional but tastefully furnished with a desk, two chairs facing each other and a large abstract painting on the wall. Camilla motioned for Vidar to sit down and brought some details up on the holo projector in front of them.

"Let's see," she said primly as the image of the apartment flashed in front of them. "Number 2, Portuno Gardens?"

"That's the one," said Vidar flashing her a smile. *Definitely a tad too conservative, but it never hurt to be charming with the ladies...*

Camilla stood up and walked to the large painting on the wall. It was made up of various swirls and colours which seemed to unfurl and churn almost imperceptibly on its own.

But Vidar was too busy regarding her instead. *Too aloof,* he thought, *and too bony besides ...* as his eyes swept over her stiff svelte frame. Vidar liked his women curvy, womanly at the very least and this one looked far too frigid for his tastes.

Camilla reached out and pressed her index finger lightly on a teal splodge on the right-hand side of the artwork. There was a soft whisper as the panel of the painting split in half, sliding open to reveal rows and rows of clear transparent cubicles behind containing a variety of keys.

Vidar noted that whilst most of these were the standard biometric cardkeys, there were quite a few ancient metal ones as well. It was one of these traditional keys that she removed from its compartment.

An abloy. Beautiful, he thought, admiring its multifaceted design. Vidar had a thing about locks and keys, and abloy keys, whose ancient design rendered them virtually impossible to pick, held a special place in his heart.

Camilla returned to her desk, proffered a professional-looking smile back at him and brought the display up to show him the dates. "So it's for six months?" she read out, looking at him for confirmation.

"That is correct," Vidar replied, smiling.

"Will you be looking to extend it further past the six months sir?" Camilla asked. She gave him an appraising look.

"Er, no," said Vidar. Then feeling compelled to provide something by way of explanation, added, "I travel a lot you see. Business...."

Camilla nodded perfunctorily. "That's not a problem," she said primly. "You can always let us know should you wish to extend or find something new," she continued, her long fingers tapping fluidly on the projected keyboard, entering the necessary details into the system.

"Sure," replied Vidar and scanned in payment through the holographic docket.

The instant it gave a discreet beep, Camilla's face sprang to life with a wide smile."Thank you Mr Valerius, the payment has gone through," she said, beaming.

Vidar noted wryly that her voice had a tinge more enthusiasm in it this time.

"And here are the keys," she said placing them in his hand. "I trust you know how to work these sorts of old keys?"

"Yes I do, thank you," Vidar said and stood up to go. He tossed the keys lightly up and down in his hand as he reached for the door.

"Oh," he added, smiling casually and pausing as he opened it, "I meant to ask... do you know where we could get a *kofi?*"

Camilla looked up from her desk, the cheerful look she wore a minute ago totally wiped out. Vidar found himself looking at a completely passive face, almost blasé. "Hmm?"

Not interested then, thought Vidar. "I meant," he said slightly louder this time, "is there any place nearby, a cafe perhaps where I could get a *kofi* and a bite to eat?"

Camilla's face finally registered a flicker of a reaction. "There is the Bluebird cafe," she answered. "Round the corner, five minutes' walk, on the right. Look for the blue and white awnings."

"Thanks," said Vidar, tilting his hat and left.

A FEW HOURS LATER, Vidar sauntered past the blue and white striped awnings of the Bluebird cafe and entered the tiny establishment. The cafe was bright, cheerful and from the looks of its clientele, a little more upmarket than the ones he was accustomed to.

Definitely should have ordered my new shirts earlier, he thought, acutely aware of the discreet glances cast towards his direction as he walked up to the serving counter.

The girl behind it, slim, pretty, gave him a quick once over before asking rather haughtily, "Having here or taking away?"

Vidar gave her an easy smile and replied, "Having here. One *kofi* please."

"Sugar? Molasses? Syrup?" she asked. Her tone, abrupt, sounded almost like Camilla's.

Vidar leant on the counter and gave her a wink. "No thank you," he replied unruffled, "it's sweet enough I reckon."

The girl ignored his remark, poured the thick, dark steaming *kofi* into a dainty cup and handed it to him briskly. "You can pay here," she said curtly, pointing at the slim reader perched at the side of the counter and turned to wipe down the counter.

Vidar scanned his payment in, collected his *kofi* and looked around to find a seat, aware of the eyes of other customers following his every movement. *They can smell it when you're not one of them.*

He stopped midway, as he pondered where to sit. The cafe

was rather full, something he hadn't factored in a minute ago. *Now how to not embarrass yourself eh?* he wondered, looking around.

His eyes rested on the pretty burnished head by the window. Slender and attractive, she played with a strand of her blonde hair as she sipped her drink, but unlike the others, he noticed she hadn't bothered to hide the fact she was observing him, and with interest. He took his hat off towards her, half expecting her to look away, as most ladies of her kind tended to do, but to his surprise, she didn't. Instead she smiled confidently back at him.

"May I?" he asked, approaching her table.

She eyed him casually and nodded.

Vidar smiled and sat across her, sharing her table. It was smaller than he'd anticipated and he found himself facing her in a rather intimate setting.

Up close, she was elegant and even more beautiful than he had originally envisioned. Her blonde tresses, loose and tumbling, gleamed like cornsilk and her eyes of startling bright cobalt seemed to pierce right through him. But it was her demeanour that struck him — slightly aloof and rather prim on the outside but underneath... underneath that lurked something else. Something more basic, dangerous perhaps.

She's not afraid, he observed, gamely returning her gaze.

"So," he said, leaning forward, "do you come here often?" *Of all stupid, banal chat up lines!* Vidar kicked himself instantly. "I meant," he added hastily, "is this your local *kofi* place?"

The woman looked at him. The sides of her mouth curled slightly in amusement. "This is my favourite haunt, yes," she replied eyeing him with a glint in her eye. "I like to come here to observe the local... wildlife."

Vidar took a sip of his *kofi* and leant back. "This might

become my favourite too," he said. "I'm Valerius," he said, holding out his hand.

"Nice to meet you,Mr Valerius," the woman replied, resting her palm delicately on his outstretched hand.

Vidar noted she did not volunteer her name. *No matter, I like a challenge.* He drew closer and bent to kiss her hand. It was soft and had a faint floral scent that lingered.

"Are you from around here?" she asked politely.

"No. I've just moved to this neighbourhood."

"Oh…?" Her eyebrow rose.

He liked the way only one of them did that.

"So where are you from?" she asked casually leaning on her elbow.

Vidar felt a little warm under the collar. He replied easily enough though. "Oh, all over. I travel a lot."

"And now you've come here," she said, her eyes still fixed on his. She took a little sip of her kofi. "So what do you do for a living, Mr Valerius?" she asked lazily.

"Oh, Business," replied Vidar, "you know, procurement of *things…*"

"How interesting. What sort of *things*?"

Vidar cleared his throat. "Oh… a bit of this and that," he said. "I source things for er… private clients. Valuable art, jewellery," he waggled his eyebrows at her a little, "…the occasional Eldur. You know, Ice Fire. A bit of everything really."

"How intriguing…."

He could've sworn her eyes gleamed at the mention of the Ice Fire. *That hook always works with women.* Vidar shrugged nonchalantly. "It pays the bills," he said, smiling cocksurely.

She leant forward suddenly. "You're not the legendary *Prometheus* are you?" she whispered, holding him captive in her intense gaze.

It took all of Vidar's will to stay calm. He decided to stay silent, choosing neither to deny nor divulge.

She's definitely interested...

"Anyway, I must go," the lady said, rising from her seat.

Perhaps not.

Vidar rose hastily from his seat, trying not to look crestfallen.

The lady nodded towards him and smiled. "Well, it was good to meet you, Mr Valerius," she said graciously.

Vidar gave a wistful sigh in silence as the sight of her lovely derrière glided gracefully towards the exit. Then he gave a start—she had paused at the doorway.

Their eyes met.

There was a coolness in the blue of hers, a shrewdness and something that hinted at business and only business as they inspected him.

For a brief moment, Vidar stood frozen, uncertain but transfixed.

Then the spell was broken as she released him from her gaze, turned and left the Bluebird cafe.

VIDAR'S NEXT JOB

Vidar sat on one of the beams of the warehouse, waiting. He was smoking his cigarette and thinking, his legs dangling a good twenty feet above a few hundred crates of synth aphrodisiacs and libido enhancers. Above him, the rafters trembled slightly from the heatstorm raging outside and he could hear the incessant swish of fine sand hurtling against the cladding outside.

Good job I arrived early, he thought, realising he had forgotten to put his anti-thermals on. *Outside in this storm, I'd be roasted without them.* He could tell this one was particularly harsh. With the unpredictable climate nowadays, it was not unusual for citizens caught unawares in such storms to suffer second or even third degree burns when exposed to the burning hot winds ripping through the city.

Not everyone can afford good anti-thermals. He remembered what it was like before he worked for Tors, before he had any *ore* to spend on basic protective clothing.

Vidar whistled cheerfully. Well, it was certainly nice and cool here inside the warehouse with its heatproof sidings and triple insulated cavity walls but from the sound of the storm raging outside, he reckoned it could be hot enough for third degree burns today.

I wonder if the storms here on Amorgos would ever get as frequent as those on Anavio and Bellun, he wondered. Amorgos was certainly not as close to the suns but nevertheless, at a middling distance from them, the last few years had seen a surge in temperatures and heatstorms. He gave a cynical snort. *Probably in a few years time and then it'll be skin grafts all round for anyone caught without protection!*

Vidar drew in his cigarette, leant back and exhaled languidly. To him, a few years in the future was ages away. His thoughts turned to the job in hand. It had been only two months since the last heist and already Tors had summoned him again. There was going to be another. Business was obviously booming. At this rate, without time to properly fritter away previous earnings, he could stop working for some years after this.

By Dyaeus, I might even extend the lease on my plush apartment! He smiled. *Maybe I'll bump into her again.*

Vidar noticed he was still thinking about that woman he met at the cafe. He wondered if she lived nearby. She had said the cafe was her favourite haunt, which seemed to imply she did.

Who knows, we might be neighbours. He imagined having her over to the apartment and grinned inwardly.

Neighbours with benefits...

The sound of the door broke his reverie. He looked down. A hooded figure had entered and without looking up, stopped just below where he perched.

"You're late," Vidar called from above.

Tors nodded. A man of few words as ever.

Vidar leapt down and landed next to him, light-footed and

silent as a cat. Stubbing his cigarette out on the crate next to him, he asked, "So my friend, what fun excursion are we embarking on next?"

Tors turned to face him, his vizard static and expressionless as always, despite its fairly flexible exoskeletal material. Then, an almost imperceptible twitch round the nose area and a sniff.

A sniff!

Vidar chuckled. "I don't believe it," he laughed. "Is it possible that you have a ... cold?"

Tors gave him the finger and produced some plans. "These are the blueprints of the base we're hitting tomorrow night," he said. Even his digitally altered voice sounded fluey.

Vidar looked at the plans: engineering facility, top-tier lock-down security. This was no walk in the park. Difficult, but not impossible. "But these facilities are massive, like entire neighbourhoods. Do you know the exact location of the target?" he asked.

Tors nodded. "I'll get us to the unit itself. You'll have to handle the security system."

"Sure, no problem," replied Vidar confidently. *Standard alarm systems. I could do them blindfolded.*

Tors nodded. "This time next week, same day. At midnight we hit it. On the dot."

"Next week? So soon?"

Tors turned towards him sharply. "You're not ready?"

"Of course I'm ready," Vidar replied indignantly. "I'm always ready."

"Good. We have to move fast. This one's hot."

"Ok boss." Vidar gave a mock salute.

"I'll get us in as usual," continued Tors, "but you'll have to deactivate the sensors in order for us to grab the Eldur."

"Oooh!" remarked Vidar. "Another Eldur. Are we specialising in this stuff now?"

"We have to be a bit more careful in this one," Tors said. "It's a grade one Vim, earmarked for large carrier ships. And there are rumours the Rebellion are eyeing it too."

"Ah," said Vidar, "if the rebels are after it and we're stealing it from the empire, then who are we stealing this for? Not another rich bastard?"

"Kind of," replied Tors. "A private buyer. The less you know, the better."

Vidar shrugged. "It's all the same to me, my friend," he said easily. "It's all the same to me." He looked at Tors. "Y'know," he said, "after a few more of these, we could retire you and I...."

Tors looked at him dead straight.

Vidar could almost picture his facial expression. *I bet he's looking at me blankly underneath that.*

The words relaxation and fun didn't exist in Tors' vocabulary. Retire was probably a word he'd never heard of. *You're not the legendary Prometheus are you?* she had asked him at the cafe, her interest roused. Vidar snickered to himself. What was it with the idea of Prometheus that drove these women crazy?

They probably imagine him to be some tall, mysterious, smooth talking persona, thought Vidar. *That's what they all think, these crazy women.* Vidar sighed inwardly. *If only they knew.* Emotionally retarded, grumpy, a workaholic, and not to mention without a drop of fun, the real Prometheus standing before him was anything but.

"You know," he continued, pressing Tors further, "... retire?"

No answer.

"I meant as mates," Vidar clarified quickly, just in case. "You know, me and my harem, you with maybe a new hobby?

And both of us somewhere less scorched. Maybe Vasa? They have good beaches there—"

A loud thunk interrupted him, its echo reverberated throughout the warehouse. Probably a large chunk of debris hitting the wall outside. Vidar considered the ever-frequent heatstorms and added, "Or maybe ask one of your rich clients to give us a ride out of the Realms?" *Maybe it's time to think about leaving ourselves, just like all these rich lords...*

Tors sniffed for a whole minute and then cracked the joints at the back of his neck. "Get your gear tested and ready," he said finally and handed him the plans.

Vidar hunched over, slouched like a teenager on strike. "You suck the fun out of life, you know?" he grumbled.

Tors shrugged. "We'll go through the plan in three days' time. Usual place, same time as the last," he said. "Be ready."

Vidar threw his hands up in the air. "You need to get laid," he muttered, "You *so* need to get laid...."

Tors sniffed and turned to leave. "Don't be late," was his only parting comment.

Vidar sighed."Sure thing, boss," he replied and sat back against one of the crates to wait out the storm. "Sure thing."

THE EYES HAVE IT

He couldn't stop thinking of her. Every time a pretty blonde passed by or a flick of golden hair caught his eye, Vidar would stop to see if it was her again.

I didn't even get her name.

He could've kicked himself for that. He hadn't seen her for weeks now. *Perhaps she's gone on holiday. Or moved away. Or maybe she lied and this isn't even her local neighbourhood.*

Vidar gave a resigned sigh. There was no help for it. He donned his hat and walked out of his plush apartment to go for a walk. Like the day before, and every other day before that, he found himself heading once again, as if on autopilot, towards the familiar blue and white striped awnings of the Bluebird cafe.

You need to stop doing this, he told himself. *The food there isn't even that great.* Despite the stern reminder, he found himself walking up to the counter just as he did the day before.

"Back again?" came the disdainful greeting from the girl at the counter.

"The usual please and a cannoli," replied Vidar, leaning forward and giving her the full benefit of his beaming smile.

The girl's eyes glazed over with the same derisive look reserved for those deemed inferior to the establishment. She deposited Vidar's cup of *kofi* and his cannoli on the counter with a clatter.

Vidar ignored her cheerfully and pondered which seat to take today. The usual one at the back perhaps as it generally gave him a discreet view of anyone entering the cafe. All in hope of catching a glimpse of Her.

I need to get a hobby, he thought to himself. *This is technically stalking. Besides, I'm going to be fat with all this kofi and cake.* Balancing the cup and plate carefully in his hands, he turned round to look for a seat.

His heart skipped a beat.

There in the corner! The recognisable tilt of the head, its burnished sheen of honey and gold. *Could it be...?*

She was reading a book. He approached tentatively. As he neared, the head looked up and the unmistakable pair of cobalt eyes regarded him.

It's Her!

"May I?" he ventured.

"Mr Valerius," she said, her lips curling into a smile.

She remembers my name!

She gestured to the empty seat across her. "Please..."

Vidar didn't need to be told twice. He slid into it without delay and sat facing her. "What a coincidence seeing you here," he said, trying to sound casual despite his pounding heart.

She nodded. "Are you not working today, Mr Valerius?" she enquired, smiling almost coyly.

Vidar cleared his throat. "I ah... am taking some time off at the moment," he said, "to research my next project."

"Ah," she said nodding, "so you work for yourself. How agreeable for you."

"It has its benefits," admitted Vidar. *Best get some information about her this time, Vidar* he reminded himself before enquiring. "And how about you?"

"Oh, I don't work," she said with a laugh. It was however, without arrogance and she continued as one would when stating a fact, "I am fortunate enough not to have to work."

"Ah," commented Vidar, smiling knowingly, "it's great to be able to enjoy the finer things in life." *You blathering fool, Vidar!* his inner voice rebuked. *What would you know about that?*

She looked at him amusedly. "I was born during the Age of Prosperity," she explained, "and my family's businesses provide for my lifestyle."

Hmmm, an older chick, figured Vidar. That could be anything from approximately two to three hundred years ago. Vidar put her at a middling two centuries old. *Still, she's hot as Hebe though....*

"I was born towards the end of the Age of Prosperity, before the War," he said. *Best stick with the facts as much as possible. Less likely to trip yourself up that way...*"But even so, things seemed better then than now."

She nodded in agreement. Her hair gleamed in the sunlight forming a soft nimbus around her head.

Vidar looked on mesmerised.

"Indeed," she said, stirring her *kofi* languidly. "Six centuries is long enough for the decline of an empire, even one as wealthy as Ageron." She smiled at him. "It was a different world then, you know," she said, "...before the Gates fell." Her lips curled at the memory. "Ah, the celebrations, the extravagance, the *decadence*...."

She chuckled amusedly. "In those days everyone had servants. Even our servants had servants. And the best parties to be had were in Amorgos, with the best from all over the Realms—musicians from Vasa, flowers from Olicana, roast hams from Ilia..."

Vidar only nodded. *I only remember the chaos,* he answered in his heart, recalling what the reality was for him in those days. *I remember the fighting that continued outside the walls of the wealthy and the privileged, long after the war ended. There was no music, no flower decoration, no Ilian delicacies, only the clamour of riots, tear gas decorating the streets, and me punching the lights out of a man in the dregs of Cosicana for a piece of rotted ham hock.*

She fanned herself with the napkin and Vidar found himself silently holding his breath as his gaze discreetly followed the line of her slender neck and hovered at the cleavage of her pale breasts.

"And the heat, " she added with a distracting heave of the chest. "For a while, I lived at another residence as far out as Olicana." She twirled a strand of hair, not taking her gaze off him. "Olicana is much cooler but too far from the amenities of Amorgos, don't you agree?"

"Indeed," Vidar nodded, his smile polite but his voice tight. *The last heatstorm I got caught in nearly killed me. In fact, it nearly killed all of the inhabitants of the city I was in. That day, two thousand died as an unexpected heatstorm swept through the city, scorching everything in its path. Those people never had the option of living anywhere else ...*

Vidar watched as she nibbled at a slice of fruit from her crostata.

"We used to grow these," she murmured looking at its ruby-red segments. "Bloodfruit. We grew these outdoors, in our orchards. This was a long, long time ago." Her eyes took on a far-off look, "Before the suns grew hotter and the trees began to die." She licked the sticky sap off her fingers daintily. "Those varieties were sweet and deep-flavoured," she said, "not like these insipid indoor transgene crops nowadays."

Vidar nodded and sipped his *kofi* politely. He remembered his first bloodfruit. *It was an indoor aerofarm I broke into; with a homemade jammer device to stop the alarms from going off.*

Vidar smiled inwardly at the recollection. It was his first foray into electronics, and the start of what would become his profession. *That transgene, indoor-grown bloodfruit was the sweetest thing I'd ever tasted in my entire life.* He looked at her. *Second sweetest thing perhaps...*

"Well at least there is still *amarinthe*," she sighed, picking up her glass.

"I'll drink to that, my lady," Vidar smiled, genuinely this time, then raised his to clink hers.

At length, they rose to leave the cafe and Vidar tried once again to ask her name but she merely smiled. He walked with her towards the exit. *Perhaps if I accompany her to her place...*

Outside, he stopped short as a massive shadow loomed over him, obstructing the rays of the late afternoon sun. Vidar backed off a step and looked up.

The man was big, wide and very tall.

Ten feet perhaps, or eleven, thought Vidar. He wasn't even sure the man had a neck—he could barely see all the way up past his chest.

The giant looked down at him. He was as ugly as he was tall, his face was dark and pitted, with small eyes that resembled raisins embedded within folds of his forehead. Instinctively Vidar moved between that thing and her and hesitantly reached for his gun.

"Why I do believe you are trying to be gallant," she laughed, putting her hand on his hand to stop him. She gave his arm a gentle squeeze. "You may stand down Mr Valerius. This is Varg," she said. "He's my bodyguard."

Vidar gave an uneasy chuckle, but suitably relieved, relaxed his hold on the gun. She smiled at him and moved away.

"Good day Mr Valerius," she said, dismissing him as her giant followed.

Shame about the oversized pet, Vidar thought. He looked on after them for a while, then decided to take the scenic route back to his apartment.

The evening was still warm and he liked walking past the row of artisan bakeries before cutting across the patch of green towards Portuno Gardens. As he came up to the entrance of his building, he paused and did a double take.

She was standing diagonally across the road, at the entrance of one of the larger, grander townhouses, fishing her keys out of her purse whilst her giant waited awkwardly beside her.

Vidar gave a little wave. As they exchanged amused looks, she laughed and called out across the street. "Do you mean to say you live round here, Mr Valerius?"

"I do, indeed," replied Vidar, grinning and pointing upwards. "Second floor."

"And I live here," she said, pointing at her front door with a smile.

Neighbours! Vidar looked to the heavens and made his first ever prayer of thanks to Dyaeus. Then he glanced across the street again.

She had dropped her keys back into her purse and was crossing the street towards him. Varg lumbered slowly after her and mercifully stopped a polite two feet away from the them.

"I guess this makes us practically neighbours," said Vidar, trying not to grin too widely.

"So it would seem." She lifted an eyebrow at him.

Vidar felt his knees weaken a tad. "Well, I think it's fate," he said leaning closer, forgetting Varg for a split second.

Then he remembered and pulled back quickly with a nervous glance at the giant's direction. But Varg looked on impassively, still as a rock.

Doesn't look like there's much between this big oaf's ears. Perhaps he's just all muscle and nothing else. Vidar plucked up a little courage. "Would you like to come up to mine… for a drink?"

She paused to consider for a moment. "Why not," she said. "Although I hope you don't mind," she continued looking at him wryly, "if Varg comes along."

Vidar looked up at Varg, impassive and solid, and smiled. "Sure," he said, giving her his arm, and led the way.

* * *

VIDAR OPENED the door to his apartment, feeling rather self-conscious. The apartment had come furnished and he hoped the style of furnishing met with her approval.

"It's very nice," she murmured, looking around and then headed towards the balcony.

Vidar gave her a modest smile. "Thank you," he said. "Although I think it needs a woman's touch, personally."

She walked around the balcony, her fingers trailing the wrought iron railings lightly and then came back inside. "Do you have anything to drink?" she asked.

"Drink?" Vidar stuttered. *By Dyaeus, I don't even have food in here, never mind drink!*

"Sure…" he said and headed casually for the sideboard where a crystal decanter stood. Vidar lifted it and sniffed it cautiously. *Amarinthe? I hope this is drinkable—this has been here since I moved in. Who knows when this was last used....*

Confidently, he took two fluted glasses from the tray and poured the drink into them. Vidar didn't bother offering Varg one although the thought did cross him mind to let Varg try the drink first. He handed the glass over to her tentatively.

She sat down at the sofa, curled her legs up and sipped it. "Brandy?" she said, surprised. "I didn't think you were a brandy drinker..."

Not amarinthe then. Vidar shrugged casually and smiled. The drink tasted pleasant enough but strong, like liquid fire, and much more potent than *amarinthe*. He put his glass down and sat beside her, still eyeing Varg standing impassively by the wall.

"Don't mind Varg," she said. "He's just the help." She leant closer to face him.

Vidar found himself holding his breath. *By Dyaeus, she is stunning.*

She touched her collarbone absently, and ran her fingers downwards towards the top buttons of her bodice, her shapely breasts rising and falling seductively with each breath.

Unwittingly, Vidar's eyes trailed downwards towards them.

"May I see your bedroom?" she asked suddenly.

Vidar nearly spluttered his drink. "Sure," he replied, too surprised to move from his seat.

Her smile widened, as did her legs as she climbed on top of him, straddling him as she went. "Take me there," she ordered, undoing the first few buttons of her bodice in front of his very eyes.

Vidar stood up as he was told. He lifted her, his arms holding her at the buttocks, and staggered towards the closed double doors. He freed a hand to fumble at the doorknob and turning it, they tumbled into the bed beyond. Behind, Varg followed his mistress dutifully into the room without a word.

She lay on the bed, arms flung wide open, and smiled suggestively at Vidar.

"Come...," she instructed, and lifted her skirt.

Vidar stopped breathing for a moment. She was completely naked underneath. He obeyed keeping his eye on Varg even as he climbed on top of her. Varg, standing against the wall, towered over them.

"Must he?" Vidar protested half-heartedly.

"Varg *always* follows me," she said wryly, pulling Vidar towards her and undoing his trousers.

"Everywhere?" asked Vidar, eyeing the great, hulking figure.

"*Everywhere,*" she replied. There was a gleam of amusement in her eyes. "But don't worry. You won't notice him. He's here to watch over me, not watch you."

But Vidar wasn't so sure. And he had a feeling she liked being watched, not watched over. "Shouldn't I at least know your name first?" he asked hesitantly as he crouched over her.

She threw her head back and laughed, offering up her delicate neck to him.

"Elena," she said as she wrapped her legs around him and breathed into his ear, "my name is Elena...."

PART III

THE REBELLION

MARCUS

When Marcus first moved his division into their latest hideout, he never imagined he'd have to walk nearly a kilometre of abandoned subway tunnels in order to reach the engineering team. He was beginning to get breathless by the time he strode into the part of their base which they had claimed for themselves and nicknamed the Smithies. Scanning quickly as he strode past each workroom, he finally stopped at the third one where a woman, tawny and rather muscular sat hunched, her back facing him and the open door.

Pihla was bent over her cluttered workbench, deep in concentration, straining to get the ejection port to click into place atop the customised slide of the gun. Beside her, a soldering iron sat patiently amidst tiny mounds of metal parts and electronic components, leaking thin tendrils of smoke.

Marcus stood deferentially at the doorway, letting the distinctive smell of vaporised solder waft up his nose as he waited for her to finish her task.

"What do you want boss?" she half-grunted without looking up.

Marcus grinned. *She has eyes on top of her head, at the side and on the back too.* "Just wanted to check something with you," he said, stepping in and walking up to her side where she could see him.

"What about?" asked Pihla, not taking her eyes off her task at hand. Customising a Empire-standard B12 plasma was not a straightforward task.

"Team Helots are in their final phase of build. We've been asked to procure the power source."

Pihla stood up and shoved the entire weight of her body onto the stubborn device. There was a sharp rasp of metal against metal until finally, the ejection port slotted into place with a grudging screak. Satisfied, she sat back down with a sigh. "Yeah, so?" she asked, wiping the sweat off her brow with a greasy rag.

"So I'm going to need to know what size Eldur you think the Tethys is going to need," he answered. "Y'know, what size and grade of Eldur would a ship this size utilise?"

Pihla glanced at him sharply. "You don't mean to say the engineers haven't specified that up front?" She gave an incredulous snort. "You can't be serious!"

Marcus shook his head. "No…," he said patiently, drawing out his words slowly as if good-humouredly explaining to a child, "that's not what I said. They *have* specified it but I thought I'd get a second opinion from you before I spend the next few months planning to break one out of a maximum security vault, that's all."

He looked at her, his eyes twinkling in amusement. "Sourcing Eldur takes a lot of time and effort you know, and I don't want to go through all that only to discover it's not fit for purpose."

Pihla offered a placated grunt. "Well, a ship of Tethys' size will need a grade Two sized Eldur at least," she said. She squinted up the barrel of her gun, examining her workmanship. "With grade one Vim for the necessary propulsion properties. Won't be easy sourcing one of those..."

Marcus nodded, satisfied that her answer matched the specifications he'd been previously given. "Oh, they're not that rare," he added casually.

"And you know that for a fact, do you?" asked Pihla, looking up and glancing at him.

"I do indeed," replied Marcus knowingly. "This here's not just a pretty face you know," he continued wryly.

Pihla put the gun down to give him her undivided attention. She regarded him briefly.

Marcus, fair-haired and open-faced. The first time she met him, she had dismissed him as a lightweight. However his boyish charm and easy going manner belied a crafty resourcefulness underneath. More than that, he did really have his ear to the ground. In fact, Marcus had eyes and ears everywhere, from all kinds of sources, even ones they were theoretically at war with.

"I believe you," she said, nodding as she gave the gun a vigorous rub to clean it.

"The Empire has at least a handful of these larger ones," Marcus went on. "It's just a case of picking the one that's easiest to get at—"

"—without getting caught," finished Pihla.

"Without getting caught," agreed Marcus with a steely smile.

Pihla snorted. "Well, let's hope it's still where it is by the time we get around to stealing it," she said.

"What do you mean?"

"I mean, like last time, when he got the Eldur before we even finished our recce—"

Marcus let out an annoyed huff. "We have enough on our hands without having to contend with maverick small-time thieves in our way."

"I'd hardly call him small-time," retorted Pihla, "looking at some of the jobs he's pulled. Who does he work for?"

Marcus' eyes took on a faraway look. He shrugged. "No one as far as I know," he said, "Hell, no one even knows his name, hence that ridiculous nickname the public's given him. Prometheus!" Marcus let out a scornful snort. "He appears to be a lone operator. Mercenary. But he's good, I'll admit that. By Dyaeus, I'd enlist his services if we could afford it."

Pihla gave a chuckle.

"Well, we won't be slow this time," Marcus continued grimly. "The stakes are too high in this one. Brasidas said the Tethys will carry at least half a million."

Pihla whistled softly. "I'm just glad we're not the team in charge of logistics," she said. "The sheer organisation of passengers must be unthinkably complex."

Marcus nodded. "And long," he said. "Two years in fact, and each team operating completely independently, without knowledge of each other in case of leaks to the authorities. Even then, we've lost two groups—had to cut them out of the passenger list."

"Perhaps we are no better than the Exodus and its lottery method," Pihla remarked carelessly and then straightaway regretted it.

Marcus gave her a cutting look. "No," he said.

Pihla saw that his fists were clenched into a ball.

"We are *not* the same," continued Marcus. "That state-run lottery, if you can call it that, is a joke. The rich pay their way and buy their places from the poor and desperate."

Pihla bit her lip. She had forgotten about Lora.

"We have a choice," said Marcus, pressing his point further. "We can take control of our own future, and not leave it to fate, and certainly not to the empire. He turned to stand at the doorway and looked out into the passageway.

Lora, thought Marcus. *Lora. Never again.*

It was Lora who'd saved him from living like a roughneck after he'd escaped from his previous life as an Ashgarian slave. Lora who saw something past his felonious exterior and begged her father to give him a job in his merchant business. Lora who decided to put their newly married names down in the state lottery and against all odds won them each places on the *Almirante,* the Exodus ship before the Carinthia, the ship halfway across the galaxy to Ellagrin by now.

Marcus' face twisted at the memory of it all. It was Lora who did everything, who took charge.

I didn't know the ways of the world then. I couldn't even read. But how could he have been so ineffectual, so naive, so weak? He should have spoken up, intervened, done something. Anything. Instead he held back, the stupid boy from the backwaters of Vasa who did nothing whilst Lora fell ill. The fool who discovered too late that Lora had sold her place to an aristocrat who paid her doctor to tell her she could not be cured. The fool who didn't dare expose the doctor for they were having a baby.

She was carrying our son...

It was illegal of course. Population control laws dictated only those who'd won the lottery for birth licenses were permitted to have a child. She had begged him not to retaliate against the aristocrat but as her illness progressed, it became clear she wasn't getting any better and neither was the baby.

She made me swear I would go regardless of what would happen to them.

He didn't of course. He even promised the doctor his ticket in exchange for her treatment. But Lora died anyway.

Never again.

That's why he was here. To put right what had become endemic in the Realm. To atone for the past. To make amends. His heart didn't yearn for her anymore. The years had dulled that to a faint memory, distilled it down to an idea of a person that once was. An idea that that had come to represent the state of the Realms today and everything that was wrong with it.

An idea that spawned the Rebellion.

Marcus glanced at Pihla who was fiddling with the gun in silence. He gave a sigh. It would not do to dwell in the past. There was much to do and the mutterings he had been hearing on the ground worried him. The state-owned Carinthia was due to launch soon and as such, security, already high in the first place, was even higher now.

"We have to be even more careful now," he said to Pihla. "The authorities will be sniffing around even more than usual with the Carinthia's imminent launch. Anything we do will require extra care or we risk exposing the Tethys."

He had a bad feeling about the next job. But this time, feeling or no feeling, they didn't have much of a choice. The Tethys was almost ready and like the Carinthia, it needed an Eldur to fly.

VIDAR

The engineering facility was a sprawling grid of hundreds and hundreds of miles of gleaming, white-walled corridors, all identical and completely indistinguishable from one another. It housed sections—whole areas each the size of neighbourhoods—where repair and maintenance of machines were carried out by other machines.

The empire's legal chop-shop, thought Vidar looking at row after row of identical doors, *except at a colossal scale*. There was nothing to see for the doors were all closed but behind them and all around, he could hear the thrum of machinery whirring away.

Engineering facilities like this were commonplace all over the Realm. This was where everyone: manufacturers, farmers and small businesses sent their broken down equipment, harvesters, machines and service bots to be repaired, updated or recycled. Vidar felt giddy just staring at the kilometres of white stretching ahead of them. There were no identifying markings or signs inside the complex. There was no need—the entire facility was run by machines.

No wonder they moved the Eldur here, he thought. *It'd take forever to find it even if every room here had its doors open.* He picked up his pace, careful not to lose sight of Tors who was walking in front. Vidar shuddered at the thought of getting lost here.

Tors turned left at the next corner and stopped in front of the second door, one of fifty identical doors in that row. According to him, they were now standing just outside the door that led precisely to the unit that contained their Eldur.

The one door out of a hundred and thirty-three thousand identical doors in this facility, noted Vidar. After their fiftieth job two years ago, Vidar had stopped wondering how Tors always managed to hone in on their target just like that. He merely concentrated on his part of the job, which chiefly dealt with disarming systems, both manual and electronic. With a deft flick, he removed the cover panel and proceeded to scan the controls.

Tors was leaning against the wall.

Vidar thought he looked a little weary and wondered if he was ill, although he'd never known Tors to succumb to anything as mundane as flu.

"Can you work any slower," muttered Tors, grumpily. He produced an irritable snuffle.

Vidar stopped in his tracks and gave him a look of rebuke. "I am an *artiste,*" he huffed. "These things cannot be rushed, unless you want security crawling here in an instant."

Tors responded with another sniff followed by a grunt. Moments later, the doors slid open noiselessly.

"Your Excellency…," bowed Vidar sarcastically and let Tors enter first.

The unit was vast. And quiet too, save for the soft whirring from the rows and rows of processors and diagnostic terminals that filled the space.

No broken hovertugs being repaired here, thought Vidar. *This one looks more like a control room of sorts rather than one of the other repair assemblies.*

They walked down the main aisle silently, glancing around as they went. Every now and again, an automaton would whizz past, a sterile white vision with mechanical appendages that hung far below its blocky torso, whirring its way to an errand or to plug into a terminal to perform whatever task it had to carry out, oblivious of their presence.

The two walked on, passing row after row of processors until at length, they reached what Vidar guessed was the halfway point of the vast chamber. A square-shaped opening stood before them and in the middle, suspended in an anti-gravitational lightshaft, was the shard of Eldur.

"Showtime," whispered Vidar, taking out his toolkit.

The lightshaft pulsated slightly as his jammer began interfering with the main signal until at long last, it matched it in cadence allowing Vidar to intercept and close off the master. There was low hum as the mechanism wound down, enabling Tors to reach out and grab the Eldur.

"LOOK OUT!" yelled Vidar suddenly.

A beam streaked across the room. Tors leapt back, just in time to see part of the metal casing of the lightshaft warp on impact from the shot. Behind him, someone jumped forward, leant over and swiped the Eldur.

With a shout of wrath at the audacity of it all, Tors swivelled round, raised his fist and aimed it at the encroacher's temple. He punched down hard. The man arched back but did not manage to clear the blow in time. The Eldur flew out of his hand and skittered across the smooth floor away from them both.

Oh no, no no... Vidar cursed as his eye followed the Eldur coasting all the way into obscurity beneath a bank of processor units.

The man staggered backwards, slightly dazed and reached for his gun.

Vidar glanced at Tors. "Uh-oh," he muttered. *That's going to really piss him off now...* He knew what would happen next; he'd seen it before.

Tors reached into his tunic and pulled out a thin, slither of a dagger. His opponent lifted his gun confidently and aimed to fire.

Vidar sighed. What these fools never realised was that when it came to Tors and his knives, the knife always won. Even against a gun. That was how ruddy quick Tors was.

"Oh no you don't!" came a voice from behind and a blurry swirl dived at Tors, propelling him off his feet. Tors crashed down as the force of the tackle sent both men skidding across the floor.

By Dyaeus there's two of 'em!

Tors stumbled, recovering quickly in order to intercept the next blow. A jab and a punch as the vicious struggle ensued with Tors striking swiftly and tactically in order to eke an advantage against his taller and more heavily built opponent.

Vidar noted that Tors was visibly slower in his reflexes today. *What is wrong with him today?* Worryingly Tors' attacker was getting quite a few blows in.

"Uh-oh," said Vidar again, agitatedly this time as he could hear sentries approaching. The shot and ensuing commotion had alerted security. The autobot sentries were already making their way down the main aisle, the unvarying clamour of their strides echoing down in the vast chamber. "We have to *GO*!" he yelled, waving madly at Tors. "*Sentries*!"

The sentries, now no more than a few yards away opened fire. Tors and the big guy split apart and ran for cover. Vidar cowered, crouching behind a row of terminals, unable to move. Opposite him, the smaller man had recovered sufficiently from his dazed state and was running towards the side exit. Vidar looked longingly as he disappeared through it.

The sentries let loose yet another barrage of shots.

"Shit! Shit! Shit!" Vidar swore, hands over his head and flinched in fright when molten metal from the panel beside him trickled down, nearly burning his sleeve. Frantically he looked around for Tors. He was a couple of rows back, squatting behind a row of machines and leaning against them, head back and chest heaving. The other guy, the large one, was several rows behind, also shielding from the heavy firing. Vidar tried frustratedly to get Tors' attention.

What is wrong with this guy? Why isn't he moving away?

Then the firing stopped for a brief moment. Vidar heard voices, shouting , then footsteps pounding down towards them. *Those don't sound like sentries.*

Vidar had a bad feeling about this. Sentries didn't march out of step. *Guards* marched like that…

"Hell! Guards!" yelled Vidar to Tors. "It's not just the sentries! I can hear guards! *Live guards*! You said this was an *autobot* facility!"

The guards had now arrived and the sentries paused from their firing as their non-machine counterparts issued them new orders.

Vidar peered over to take another look. Not just their bog-standard commercial guards but *Imperial guards!* "They're Reds!" he yelled. "What in Dyaeus' name are Reds doing here?" Vidar thumped the back of his head against the panels behind in exasperation. *Now this would be the moment to get us out of here!* He gestured wildly at Tors but the guy wasn't even looking his way. *What the hell's wrong with him today?*

Tors was trying to get up. His legs wobbled and Vidar could see him heaving with the effort. And then, "Atchooo!"

I don't believe it! He's down with flu? Man flu too, from the looks of it! Well, flu or no flu, this was not the time to wallow in it.

What the hell, thought Vidar, *I'm gonna go for it. He'll follow me from behind.* With a yell of bravado, he lunged for the side door, waving Tors to follow suit.

Tors' attacker sprinted forward too, throwing a couple of shots towards the Reds to cover himself. Vidar glanced back. Tors had stopped mid-way and was taking refuge behind the next row of terminals.

Shit! Shit! Why isn't he coming? thought Vidar frantically. He could see Tors sitting down weakly, leaning on his side. Across the aisle, the other man had almost reached the side exit by now. The Reds had joined the sentries and had begun firing again. Through the aisle, Vidar could see that Tors had still not moved. He was still sitting on the floor and his arm was limp around his waist. A dark patch seeped out on his tunic, just below the ribcage.

He's been shot!

Vidar cursed. The side door was now so near he could almost reach out and touch it. Tors on the other hand was at least four, maybe five metres away.

Now this would be the perfect time to cut business ties, thought Vidar. He glanced at the exit, then at Tors and then back at the exit again. *Besides,* he told himself sternly, *how well do you know the guy anyway?*

He shook himself and got ready to go, but his conscience jabbered on: *The guy never talks to me. Ten years of working together. Ten years! I know nothing about him and he doesn't want to know anything about me. Or my girlfriends. ESPECIALLY my girlfriends.*

He glanced back at Tors again. The poor sod was trying to

get on his feet . He wobbled and clutched at the terminals for balance. *You don't owe him anything, Vidar,* he told himself. *Although he* **is** *a good employer. And the best jobs* **do** *come from him. Plus, I won't get paid for this if he dies.* Vidar looked longingly at the door and then at Tors.

The air grew thick with smoke and the unmistakeable smell of stun-gas wafted over. It burned to breathe as more canisters were released in their direction.

Vidar covered his lower face in the crook of his elbow and breathed in through his mouth to lessen the sting. *Time to get out of here.* He looked at Tors one last time.

Ten years. Ten ruddy years...

Then Vidar stood up, swore and bolted back towards him.

"COME ON!!" he yelled as he reached Tors. Arm around his waist, he hoisted Tors up and together they sprinted back towards the side door.

Tors managed the first few strides but crumpled down again.

"By Dyaeus, we've got to move or we're sitting targets!" urged Vidar, coughing and panting heavily. He looked towards the door: two, three metres at most. They would make it if only Tors could run. But he couldn't and with Vidar merely dragging him along, they'd almost certainly be within firing range in seconds.

Then a movement to his side.

Vidar whirled round. Tors' attacker, the larger one, had turned back and was sprinting towards them. Before Vidar could react, the man single-handedly yanked Tors up and hauled him towards the door.

Vidar sprinted after them. They made it through and Vidar slammed the door shut behind them.

"Way out!" the man panted, still holding Tors over his

shoulder and pointing up the stairs. He was tall, muscular and obviously very strong.

Vidar looked at him, unsure. Wasn't he and Tors at each other's throats wrestling for the Eldur only moments ago? And now he was helping them? Was this a trap?

Doesn't seem likely, Vidar told himself and there was no time to ponder as the sentries would be here soon. They were now in some sort of stairwell and the man was heaving Tors up the stairs.

"Why are we heading upstairs?" panted Vidar.

"The roof...," came the reply.

"The roof?" Vidar repeated incredulously. Granted they were near the top level of the facility but the roof itself, Vidar knew, happened to be approximately a thousand feet above ground. There was no exit from the roof, no way to get to the ground unless you threw yourself off the building. Why was this fool heading towards the roof?

They had reached the top of the stairs. The man's accomplice was already there waiting for them. If he was surprised to see Vidar and Tors, he certainly didn't have time to show it. At the big guy's signal he wrenched open the hatch door and they all clambered out onto the exposed roof.

Vidar struggled to stay upright. There, the roof being a singularly smooth and flat surface, strong winds tugged viciously at them, threatening to blow them off their feet.

The accomplice nudged Vidar, pointing vigorously. Vidar glanced up from his crouched position, squinting in the face of the whipping gusts. Atop the gleaming metal surface of the roof was a hyperglider, shimmering like an apparition, in partial stealth mode.

Dragging Tors, they hurried towards their only means of escape, staying low and almost crawling at times to avoid being blown off in the process.

Several metres ahead, the door of the hyperglider lifted open. A tanned, brawny woman stood at the opening.

"MOVE YOUR ASSES!" she yelled, so loudly Vidar could hear her words over the howling of the wind.

Behind them, the hatch door blew open with a reverberating clang, the solid slab of steel peeled back like ripped cardboard. The sentries burst through like a throng of metal insects and were piling onto the roof. In their wake clambered the Reds but they forgot the strong winds and whilst the sentries' magnetised clamps allowed them to stay on the roof, the ripping gusts hit the Reds, taking with them those who had emerged standing upright. Screaming, they slid along the roof, flailing and grappling uselessly at the smooth surface but finding no purchase on the polished exterior of the building.

The winds took them straight over the edge and down a sheer drop of a thousand feet. Behind, other Reds rapidly adopted the crouched position in order to advance towards the fleeing threesome.

"RUN!!!" yelled the big guy, sprinting for the aircraft.

Vidar swore as they all ran for the hyperglider, dodging the rain of shots that fell upon them.

The woman at the aircraft was firing their way, furiously trying to pick off the sentries behind them. She stopped firing when they reached the aircraft and glared firstly at the big guy, still carrying Tors, and then at his accomplice.

"Extra bods?" she snapped. "We don't have space!"

The smaller man started to give an apologetic shrug whilst the big guy charged straight in.

"Pihla, we have to GO!" he growled, eyeing the woman.

Scowling, she slammed the door release and darted into the cockpit. The aircraft began to lift off.

"GO! GO! GO!" the big guy yelled, dropping Tors onto the floor of the aircraft as Vidar dived into his seat.

Outside, hanging onto their advancing machine counterparts, the Reds closed in.

With seconds to spare, the hyperglider pulled away from the roof and sped away just as the next barrage of fire power was discharged at them.

DISCOVERY

"Is he dead?" asked Vidar peering closely at Tors' body.

They were in some form of makeshift residence housed underground, somewhere within a section of disused train tunnels. Where the planks extending the platform area ended prematurely, ancient tracks peeked out from below. Layers of centurial dust lay atop these old repulsion tracks, once used by glidetrains that ran beneath the city in the old days.

Fleeing the engineering facility, they had flown for a few hours, then landed somewhere on the outskirts of Alandia. Vidar reckoned they were somewhere in the northern sector of the sprawling megalopolis but he could not be sure. The additional time it took to get here, firstly through the back-streets of the city before slipping into the abandoned underground system, had certainly not helped increase Tors' chances of survival. And he still didn't know who these people were, though they appeared to be living under the radar of the authorities.

He had introduced himself as Marcus, the big guy who had

carried Tors. Now that he wasn't being shot at or running for his life, Vidar took the opportunity to have a proper look at him.

The man was tall for an Ageronian, at least a head taller than himself, and flaxen-haired, almost blonde enough to be mistaken for Ellagrin descent if it weren't for his brown eyes. He had the build and bulk of an Asgharian cage fighter and Vidar was sure the man's tackle on Tors earlier contributed to his partner's critical state.

"Well...?" asked Vidar.

Marcus bent over to inspect the limp body. "Not sure," he replied. He prodded the body lightly with the butt of his dagger.

No reaction.

Tors was as still as a cadaver and with his padded suit, even Vidar couldn't be sure if he was breathing or not.

"He your friend?" asked Marcus, looking for a good spot to slit open the vest in order to examine the wound.

Vidar nodded and lit a cigarette. The sight of blood always made him slightly queasy. "Yeah," he said. "Friend, partner... More partner I guess." He thought about it more and then shrugged. "Work mates really..."

"Huh," answered Marcus, selecting a spot and sliding his dagger neatly between flesh and material. He felt for movement around the ribcage. "I think he's still breathing," he said.

"Not dead then?" said Vidar hopefully. Breathing was generally a good sign of life.

"Mmm, on second thought," said Marcus, "I'm not sure. I *thought* I felt the ribcage expand but I could be wrong. Doesn't look like there's any movement, is there?"

Vidar didn't look. "He's a good employer though," he offered, casually looking up at the cavernous arches overhead.

Vidar didn't like looking at dead bodies and whilst hoping Tors wasn't dead, didn't want to risk it anyway.

"He...," murmured Marcus a little doubtfully. "Hmm..." He had slit the heavily padded vest open and two shapely breasts had tumbled into view.

Marcus covered them up again quickly. Thankfully, Vidar was still admiring the architecture overhead.

"You say he's your friend, eh?" Marcus asked again.

"Yeah," said Vidar, slightly irritated at Marcus' insistence. *What was this? An interrogation?* "We've been working together for more than ten years. He's not the sociable type and I'm the closest thing to a friend to him. So yeah, you could say that..."

"Hmm..." Another pause from Marcus.

"Hmm what?" asked Vidar impatiently this time. "So is he dead or what?"

Marcus didn't answer. Instead he continued, "You know what your friend looks like?"

Vidar stopped short. "What he looks like?" he asked, still pondering the architectural merits of the ceilings above. "Er, no."

Marcus put down his dagger with a deliberate clunk. "You don't know what he looks like?" he said rather incredulously. "Your friend. Of over *ten years*?"

"Well, he never shows his face," Vidar replied defensively. "He doesn't like it!"

"You've been working with him for ten years and you're telling me you've never seen his face? Not even once?"

"Yeah!" replied Vidar, spitting out his cigarette butt. "That's right!" He was annoyed now. All these questions. Fumbling at his pocket, he took out a new stick and proceeded to light it, eyes still firmly away from the body.

"What is your problem?" Vidar went on. "He doesn't like people seeing his face. I tried once, many years ago, and he damn well nearly killed me for that!" Vidar puffed agitatedly at the memory, breathing life into the new cigarette's glow. "I've never asked since."

"Well, the breathing's extremely shallow so I'll need to remove the vizard to fit an oxygenator on," said Marcus. He lifted Tors' limp hand, held the thumb and positioned it lightly at the side of the vizard, just behind the jawline where he guessed the release clasp lay.

"No *wait*!" protested Vidar, realising what he was about to do next.

Perhaps it was the years of conditioning, but Vidar suddenly felt very uncomfortable at the thought of unmasking his friend. Like performing some sacrilegious act.

"*What?*" snapped Marcus holding Tors' hand mid-air, annoyed.

"But *no one* sees Tors' face," said Vidar. " *I've* never seen his face."

"You will now…"

"Well maybe I *don't* want to see his face,"continued Vidar worriedly. He thought about it some more and said, "Maybe it's so disfigured and so horrific I won't be able to un-see it. Maybe he's not even humanoid…." His voice trailed off.

"Oh, he's humanoid alright," said Marcus bending over to take a closer look at the release mechanism. As he pressed Tors' thumb against it, it gave off a faint beep, followed by a very tiny hiss, like a leaky balloon. The deactivated vizard became flaccid, resembling a rubbery mass of skin and sagged back onto Tors' face, scintillating slightly as its electrically enhanced illusory properties ceased to work. Marcus peeled the vizard aside.

"WHAT THE FU…?!!" Vidar jumped out of his chair and swore, then leapt on his feet again as the burning cigarette landed on his lap.

"You didn't know your friend's female?" asked Marcus, clearly amused.

Vidar ran his hands through his hair repeatedly. He was beginning to become what Tors often referred to as 'agitated'. None of this made sense. It was like discovering your brother was actually your father. Or mother. Something like that. He was finally about to say something when Niko entered the room, medical kit in hand.

Niko was the smaller guy who first tackled and tried to grab the Eldur from Tors. Behind him walked in Pihla, the tawny woman who piloted their hyperglider, holding an oxygenator set.

"Oh," said Niko, eyeing Tors with arched eyebrows. Then looking at Vidar's face, said it again with wry emphasis, "*Oh...*"

"Hand me the suture Niko," Marcus cut him short, looking at the gaping wound. It was pretty bad and she'd lost a lot of blood which probably contributed to the weak pulse.

Niko opened the kit and passed him the suture.

Marcus took it and grabbed the oxygenator mask from Pihla which he administered with the speed and familiarity of one who had done this more than once before. There was a slight shudder from Tors as the oxygenator started pumping its concoction of chemicals into her lungs and by the time Marcus had sutured her wound, she had begun to breathe more deeply and on her own.

"Blimey," said Vidar, sitting back down pale-faced and bewildered. "I don't understand it...."

Niko looked at him and grinned, "Looks like your friend's turned out to be the girlfriend you never knew you had!"

Vidar spluttered. "He's not my girlfriend," he said glaring indignantly. "He... *she* I mean."

Niko's face creased with laughter. This was too much for

Vidar and he leapt to his feet, fists clenched and advanced at Niko.

"Whoaa— " Pihla stepped in between the two of them. "Stop it you two," she said, looking sharply first at Niko, then at Vidar.

"No thanks to *you*," Niko said, looking hotly across at Vidar, "we lost the Eldur."

"*We* lost the Eldur?" replied Vidar indignantly. "We lost the Eldur? We lost the fuckin' Eldur because of *you*, you interfering small-timers!"

"How dare you!" yelled Niko. "We saved your sorry asses!" He raised his fist and started towards Vidar once more.

Marcus stepped between them this time. "We need an Eldur," he said grimly, then looked at Vidar, "and you are going to help us."

"Well, we can't go back there to the engineering base," said Pihla. "It'll be crawling with security by now."

"Well, we'll have to find another source then," said Marcus, "and quickly—the order needs to be fulfilled by next week."

"Order?" asked Vidar. "You guys stealing to order?"

"Sort of," Marcus said vaguely. "It's for a spacecarrier."

Vidar whistled. "A carriership," he said, "that's not the Carinthia?"

Marcus looked up noncommittally.

Vidar exhaled through his teeth. "How do you even keep something that colossal from the authorities? And who's going on it?"

"The ones who need to leave the most, not the rich who have bought their passageway on the Carinthia," said Marcus simply.

"Problem is where to find another piece of Eldur at such short notice," said Pihla. For all her brawn, she seemed the most analytical of the three.

"The base will be locked down after our recent bust-in," said Marcus. "We'll have to look in nearby Ilia but that's at least a few days journey which cuts it too thin for my liking."

"What's the rush?" asked Vidar.

"The ship is ready," explained Pihla. "It just needs the Eldur to power it. The longer we delay, the bigger the risk of the authorities discovering it and disrupting evacuation plans. And we can't risk that."

"Well thanks for the offer," Vidar said, exhaling his cigarette smoke into the air, "but Tors and I are freelance operators." He flicked his cigarette and looked at Marcus coolly. "We don't concern ourselves with the treasonous activity, being law-abiding citizens and all that. So if you don't mind, we'll be on our way soon."

There was a harsh clatter as Niko kicked his metal chair aside and drew up menacingly against Vidar. "You were right Pihla. We shouldn't have helped them both back there," he growled not taking his eyes off Vidar. "Well, *you're* going nowhere. You're both staying here until we decide what it is we need you to do for us."

"The hell I am," replied Vidar. His eyes flashed angrily. "There is no other source of Eldur on this planet that you can get at. That's a fact, believe you me, otherwise me and Tors would've gone for it instead of that fortress of a facility. You haven't a solution; there is no viable option that will give you an Eldur by next week."

"We *have* to find one," said Marcus.

"*There... is... none,*" replied Vidar. "I tell you, Tors' intel is as good as it gets."

"Then we should just snuff you two out," threatened Niko, "seeing as you're of no use to us." He drew his gun and pointed it at Vidar.

A tense silence followed.

Then from behind, a voice, clear, undigitised and distinctly not-male rang out. "There is another option."

They whirled round.

Tors was sitting up, partially covered in a blanket.

Vidar blinked. He had often imagined him, no *her*, under various guises but he could never have in a million years, imagined this.

She had long hair. No longer compressed and hidden within the vizard, it tumbled over the tops of her bare shoulders, black as a raven's. Vidar had always thought of Tors as an athletic type of man, a sword fighter. Instead, in front of him was someone with a slightly delicate air about her although, and he checked himself again, there was an unmistakably wild, feline menace beneath those piercing green eyes.

"Ah," said Marcus cheerfully, "you're awake. *Alive* even! This... your friend?" He eyed her with a gleam of mischief and pointed at Vidar who was funnily enough, looking upwards again.

"You say there is another option," Marcus continued, clearly interested. "What is it? Could there be another Eldur somewhere on this planet?"

"Could be," answered Tors. "It mayn't have left the planet yet."

Vidar glanced at her as she continued.

"We did a job recently," she said. "There's a chance you could still get it before the owner leaves Amorgos."

"Good," said Marcus, nodding. "I did think you two would come in useful."

Tors leant back. She was visibly tired, but managed a scornful snigger. "But what makes you think we'll help you?"

"Because," said Marcus, "I can give you what you want."

Tors smiled thinly. Her green eyes seemed to cut right through him. "And what would that be?"

"A place on the Tethys," said Marcus. "It'll be the last ship besides the state-owned Carinthia, that will leave for the Ellagrin system within this decade. The next generation of space-carriers won't be ready for another twenty years at least, assuming the total destruction of our Realm hasn't happen by then, or this empire of ours hasn't descended into chaos."

Tors laughed again, this time disdainfully. "No thanks," she told him point blank. "We're not interested."

Vidar looked at her, surprised. "We're not?"

"I don't care much for where they're heading," she explained dismissively. "Besides," she said, giving Marcus a critical look at his fair hair, "I hate the Ellagrins. Far too blonde."

Marcus shifted uncomfortably under her penetrating gaze.

"Er, are you sure we don't want the seats, Tors?" asked Vidar again. He was fairly sure he might want one. Or two if they could spare it. *I could bring Elena with me...*

Only last week heatstorms decimated the twin cities of Cauda and Ebusus before authorities had time to save anyone. Natural disasters on an epic scale seemed to occur more frequently these days and without warning. A one-way ticket out of the Realm was the thing everyone wanted these days.

"There is only one seat," Marcus said. "Only one," he reiterated. Then pausing, he leant forward to look at Tors in the eye. "*You* may not want a seat on the Tethys," he said quietly, "but perhaps your mother might."

Vidar sat forward with a jerk. "Mother?" he repeated.

Marcus nodded. "Foster mother perhaps?" Friend?" He regarded Tors with unsmiling eyes. "Now, I have to admit I'm guessing here, but I see no common features between the two of you..."

"I don't have any kin," replied Tors airily. "You are mistaken."

"Oh no I'm not," replied Marcus drily. His voice changed. It became sharper, harder and deadly serious. "I am never mistaken," he said. He approached her, his tall form towering over her and said, "The great Prometheus, procurer of the unobtainable. We have been following you closely for some time now. You appear to have no past, no permanent abode, no family but strangely enough, through the years, you seem to always cross paths with a particular woman. A homeless Stim addict of no consequence, with no apparent connection to yourself, a person with no history. A shadow. Yet each time you intervene to keep her out of trouble." He paused and smiled, half to himself. "Yes," he continued self-assuredly, "it would seem this woman, this woman called *Jula*, could mean something to the famous Prometheus..."

"Come off it!" snorted Vidar. "I've known Tors for years and I'm the closest to family he... I mean she's ever known. She has no one. No roots, right Tors? Right??"

Tors remained silent for a while. Her eyes had turned a hard, steely emerald. At length she spoke, "Where is she?"

"In one of our safehouses," Marcus answered. "You know, she's wanted in relation to a missing loanshark case downtown. " He looked at Tors and continued. "Also, that mysterious gang attack eight months ago and more recently, a double murder in the Baldunia district. Two small-time Stim dealers..."

Tors shut her eyes at the mention.

"We have her detained," said Marcus, "but we won't turn her in if you help us. And in return, we'll give her a seat on the Tethys to take her away from here and from the authorities. She can start her life afresh."

Tors remained silent for what seemed like a long while. "Very well," she said in the end, closing her eyes, "I'll show you where it is."

"We will?" asked Vidar incredulously. "What? Are we a charity now…?"

Tors looked at him. Her eyes were cold with no light left in them. "Let's just get this done and be on our way. Take it as your next job from me," she said quietly. "After that, we will have no dealings with these people."

Vidar returned a reluctant look but said nothing further.

"Good," replied Marcus, seemingly oblivious to the soured mood. "Rest up as best you can. I'm afraid there will be little time to heal as we need to prepare. Who and what will you need? We have the expertise, kit and weapons. Whatever you want."

Vidar snorted. "Pfffft! No thanks to you, my gear's back at the facility. We'll need a bit more than the few noddy spanners you have back here."

"I'm sure we'll find you what you need," said Marcus and gave Niko and Pihla a nod.

They stood up and went to pull open the sliding doors on each side. The opening doors revealed a huge hall beyond, bustling with activity. Hundreds of people working away in a cavernous old station concourse: some hunched over rows and rows of tables assembling weapons, teams fixing and maintaining military vehicles, and others packing ammunition.

Vidar's eyes widened. "What the…? What by Dyaeus…? Who *are* you??"

Niko grinned and slapped him in the back. "We're the thorn in Akseli's side," he said, "the gnat in his face, the splinter in his arse—"

"Welcome," interposed Marcus, stepping back to allow them full view of the hall and its people, "…to the Rebellion."

This time Vidar's mouth stayed agape and his cigarette dropped.

INTERLUDE

Meanwhile, deep in the Red Palace, inside the private office of Lord Draeger, the mood was far more sombre.

"The Rebellion are getting bolder by the day," commented Chancellor Rasmus after they had viewed the footage of the failed heist at the engineering facility.

Draeger stood facing the window, his dark frame a grim outline against the ancient casements as rays from the setting suns cast thin fingers of eerie light around his hawkish silhouette."Play that first part again," he said, turning around.

The Chancellor replayed the footage and the scene between the two figures tussling for the Eldur in the warehouse projected in mid-air again.

"*There*!" Draeger pointed out, "… and these other two..." He rubbed his fingers together, thinking, and commented, "They are obviously two different parties."

"Different parties after the same Eldur?" asked the Chancellor.

Draeger nodded. "Even though in the end, one assisted the

other with escape." Clearly the altercation was unplanned, but there was something else that he couldn't put a finger on.

Akseli shifted restlessly in his chair and stifled a yawn. The three of them had been discussing matters of the empire for several hours now.

"Well, I say we should get the Praetors themselves to do some work," he said. "Amorgos is Praetor Albertus' responsibility. I say make him earn his keep. Get him to do something to stop the Rebellion. The Praetors are supposed to govern their planets but Albertus does nothing but sit idle, growing fat on his salary. Why not assign him some of your soldiers to catch these rebels? It is time he did some work for a change."

Draeger shook his head. "No," he said firmly. "I will not have my Generals take orders from any Praetor."

And I would sooner trust a rebel than trust a politician. He glanced at Akseli and continued, "At any rate, I have General Titus using the legions from Amorgos to evacuate Dumnorium and Artalia at the moment, before the next wave of heatstorms destroy those cities. We won't be done with this any time soon and I will not waste these men on idle jaunts chasing a few rebels."

Akseli raised his voice. "But if as you say, the rebels are impacting us, then we should put an end to their activities. We could hunt them, flush them out. *Hang* them."

Draeger noticed his brother brighten at the thought. *I wager he's thinking that stringing up a few rebels might make for a good show at the Esplanade.* He noted that there hadn't been a public execution for centuries. *And all my brother can think of in this time of difficulty, is a show of barbarity....*

"Not now Akseli," he cut his brother off firmly. "We have more urgent matters at hand. Our legions have been posted all over the Realm to quell these riots. Let us leave it at that for now and monitor the situation. It is not the Rebellion that affects us most at the moment."

"But—"

"*Leave* it Akseli."

Akseli retreated into sullen silence.

"My lord," the Chancellor spoke up as he switched the holo projection from the security footage to the 3D map of the planets in their system. He pointed at one of them. "About the recent devastation at Anavio... will you be making an appearance sometime soon?"

The survivors. Draeger groaned vexedly. "Are the survivors taken care of now?" he asked.

"Yes,"answered the Chancellor. "They have been moved to rescue shelters ready to be rehoused in the next few weeks. We could do with some presence from the empire though."

Draeger nodded. "Akseli," he said, "will you see to that please. The people will be grateful to see their Emperor."

Akseli looked as if he was about to say something but Draeger cut him short. "And bring supplies with you," he said. "An Emperor bearing gifts will fare even better with the populace."

Akseli's expression soured but Draeger ignored it, dismissing his brother's reaction as petulance. *There is too much to do without my having to check if he is reconciled with his duties as Emperor.* "I have to fly out to Segontia to discuss the next batch of ships," he said turning to the Chancellor.

"Can some of the Praetors not assist with that, my lord? " asked Chancellor Rasmus. "You are stretched as it is."

Draeger shook his head. "I have some of my Generals doing the rounds but this time, not the Praetors."

Akseli shot him a surprised glance but remained silent.

"They cannot be wholly trusted Rasmus," Draeger continued, explaining his decision. "Their offices leaked the locations of suppliers the last time and it will only be a matter of time before the locations of the assembly facilities are leaked. If that happens, we will have bigger problems to contend with."

The Chancellor nodded in agreement. "I understand," he said. He hesitated a moment and then ventured, "There is one other matter my lord. A small one..."

"What is it?"

"The..., " Chancellor Rasmus cleared his throat delicately, "the Lady, my lord. She shouldn't be on Ageronian soil. Should the public get wind of this..."

Elena. Yes, she is still here. Draeger nodded.

"I understand," he said. "I shall have a word with her and I will escort her back as soon as possible."

"Very good, my lord."

"She has been good to us Rasmus," Draeger added. "We shall have resettlement treaties for the Carinthia soon."

"Very good, my lord," said Rasmus. "To have successfully persuaded the Emperor to acquiesce to these settlement treaties is no small feat. The lady has a subtle touch."

"It will not be enough though," said Draeger.

The Key, the last Nehisi...

His heart sank at the lack of progress they'd made on this front. He moved towards the table and sat down with a heavy sigh. "We have yet to find the Key and we are running out of time."

"The Oracle foretold of the emergence of the Key around this century," said the Chancellor, "the same way it foretold of all the other things that have come to pass: the genocide of the Nehisi, the deterioration of our binary suns, the dying of the Realm. The Key will surface eventually, I'm sure. At any rate, everything that can be done is being done—the Exodus and our search for Key which we will continue to do so for as long as it takes."

The old man moved his fingers mid-air to hone in on a particular spot on the planet Amorgos—the city of Lagentia. "My lord, what about access to the Lagentian Gate?" he asked. "The city remains sealed for now but if we find the Key," he cleared his throat, "*when* we find the Key, what then? Will the city be safe enough for the people to enter?"

Draeger's brows furrowed. *He speaks of Lagentia, the City of the Dead.*

Akseli let out a dismissive snort. "The city's been sealed for centuries now, and nuked. Twice. The only thing that could possibly survive after all this time is superstition, Rasmus."

Draeger turned to his brother and corrected him. "That ... *thing* still lives and whilst it remains in Lagentia, we cannot get our people safely through to the Gate inside it."

"Indeed," agreed Chancellor Rasmus.

Draeger looked across the table at the Chancellor and leant back as the old man continued explaining the logistics of transporting the citizens to the old city and through the Gate to Akseli.

Lagentia... the old capital. The sights and the sounds replayed in Draeger's mind as vividly as if it were yesterday...

THEY WERE RUNNING towards Lagentia Central Station. It was sweltering and the heat, magnified by rays of the sun trapped within the hastily erected domed forcefield around the city, had raised the temperature to almost unbearable levels. As he ran, the soles of his boots seemed to soften with each stride, melted by the hot tarmac underneath.

Ahead, the city had been overrun by a sea of black. And it did indeed look as if the sea had engulfed the streets and much of its buildings, for it undulated and moved and writhed. A billion tendrils, moving as one monstrous, quivering mass, making its way gradually but unmistakably towards the Gate.

"The Gate must NOT be opened at any cost!" he had shouted to his men.

They were approaching the main concourse and the Lagentian Gate was in full view. Except it was completely covered by the LON.

*The **L**ight **O**f **N**ehisi...*

He winced at the irony of the name itself, for what was once a plant symbolic of the Nehisi tribe, was this dark, heaving mass enveloping the Lagentian Gate before his very eyes.

The Gate! Its elegant arc, silver in colour and untarnished underneath, was clad in black and dripping with dark vines that wriggled and moved purposefully. Beside it, the Gate control room was completely filled by the hideous creeper, moving and pulsating within. Somewhere inside, in the midst of the congestion, a scream erupted, raw and primal.

"Someone's trapped in the control room, my Lord!" yelled one of his men. The soldier had crept as near as he could to the room without touching the LON. "I can see him! It's the *Customs Vilicus,* m' Lord!"

Head of Customs himself. And Nehisi. Draeger recalled noting the last fact with great unease.

The roar of blowtorches filled the air as the men began to incinerate their way towards the trapped man. The LON writhed and Draeger noticed its tendrils lashing with increasing menace.

WATCH OUT!" he had shouted to warn the men. From his slightly raised vantage point, he could see the creature lunge towards them.

Too late!

Tendrils descended from every part of the building, coalescing into a huge grotesque tangle, and reached for them. Screams erupted as the quivering mass engulfed the soldiers one by one, their blowtorches dropping to the ground as the creature gorged itself on them. Then it turned back to the Customs Vilicus himself.

Through the windows of the control room, Draeger could just about make out the man, strung and pinned to the power receptacle by the LON. The Eldur inside it had long been removed, in order to prevent the Gate from powering up. Likewise its beacon which would have also been present in the slot on the control panel was also missing, long gone and destroyed in the war. But despite all this, the LON was undoubtedly stringing the Customs Vilicus up in attempt to reactivate the Gate.

"It's using him to open the Gate!" Draeger had yelled, reaching for his gun.

There was a whirr as the arc of the Gate began to emit a soft, white glow. As it flickered to life, the Customs Vilicus began to scream in pain.

That thing knew the Gate could not be activated, not without a beacon and a power source, recalled Draeger. *Yet it knew, somehow, that a Nehisi could force open the Gateway again...*

But the Gate was draining the man. The more it sucked from him, the brighter it grew. It was an excruciating way to die.

It's trying to escape somehow.

A tunnel had begun to form—a bright, white spiral, gradually enlarging and extending impossibly inwards. Draeger cursed and pulled his gun out. Reluctantly he aimed it at the dying man through the thick tangle of the LON, and shot him clean in the forehead.

The LON gave a bone-chilling shriek as the Gateway tunnel shuddered and shut down again. Then like a hideous giant viper, it swung round to face him.

Hostus, the young centurion, pulled out his sword and lashed at the LON before it came into contact with Draeger. Draeger joined in with further strokes cutting through the LON, leaving decapitated bits of its form lying limp and shredded on the ground.

"This way!" Draeger had yelled, leading his men towards the city's exit. Despite their best efforts, the LON was advancing towards them, threatening to engulf them. "Use your swords," he said, "they are more effective!"

They hacked their way through the pulsating thicket. The LON stayed mostly out of their way.

It knew to avoid our swords. It was very much sentient.

Every now and again, shifting parts of it moved revealing the tangled mesh of flesh and bones of soldiers some not yet dead, struggling futilely.

They were being eaten alive.

Draeger remembered the retching from some of his men who witnessed this as they made their way to the exit. The LON kept a distance away from them but nevertheless, it closed up behind them as they went, sealing any hope of turning back.

As they neared the exit, Draeger had turned around to look back at the city. Lagentia looked as if a shadow had fallen across it. Its tall spires darkened as the LON swallowed it up like a dark, dense fog. Screams and cries for help in the distance gradually diminished as the LON continued to engulf each dwelling.

"How many in the City still?" he had asked.

"Ten thousand, my Lord," his man Hostus had stammered. "Ten thousand *at least.*"

With no way to get to them.

"My Lord, …. it's… it's trying to breach the exit. If it succeeds..." The centurion turned and pointed at his men hacking desperately at the sallying, slithering mass, trying to keep it back.

It had taken me no more than a minute to decide.

Draeger recalled his words to Hostus. Words that resounded with all the weight of the death sentence they carried: "Seal the exit. Seal it *now*. Let nothing and no one through."

Young Hostus had looked at him for a brief moment and nodded.

He knew...

Then the centurion ran back towards his men to give them orders to close the city doors.

And so ten thousand voices were sealed in to their doom.

After that came the Hex, overlaying the city walls and forcefield dome: a solid structure, fashioned out of a complex layering of hexagonal grids, impermeable and impenetrable to air and light. But when the absence of light or air was found to have had no effect on the LON, plasma bombs were then dropped in the Hex.

Many times and repeatedly.

Then nukes. Twice.

Yet still it lingers on in its stony crypt, resisting our every attempt to wipe it out.

Draeger's heart grew heavy. *And now, if we are to access the Lagentian Gate once more, how by Dyaeus will we get our people into the City of the Dead safely?*

BACK IN THE ROOM, CHANCELLOR RASMUS' voice gradually came into focus, bringing Draeger back to the present. The old man and Akseli were still discussing the possibility of evacuating the citizens via the Gateways once the Key was found.

Draeger followed their debate silently. The Chancellor was reminding Akseli that Lagentia was not the only option where Gateways were concerned. Unspeaking, Draeger agreed with him. *We have after all, more than one Gateway linking us to the other planetary systems of the galaxy. But it has to be Lagentia as out of all the Gateways, it is the only one that connects us to Ellagrin, with whom we have settlement rights agreed.*

"What about the other Gateways, my Lord?" asked the Chancellor as if he had read Draeger's mind. "What if the Key could reopen those too?"

Draeger sat back and ruminated.

The three Gateways linking House Ageron to the other Great Houses in the galaxy: House Ellagrin, House Tilkoen and House Yoon.

Gateways were always named after their Ageronian endpoints, a fact alone that demonstrated House Ageron's dominance over all the other Houses in the galaxy during the Age of Prosperity. The Lagentian Gateway was therefore named after the Lagentian Gate in the city bearing its namesake here on Ageron, despite its other endpoint being the Namsos Gate on the planetary system of Ellagrin.

Similarly, in the old days, the Arnemetiaen Gate connected the city of Arnemetiae in the Ageron system with the Sansari Gate in the Tilkoen system.

And finally, the gateway that once connected the Leodis Gate in Ageron's oldest academic city of Leodis to the Huangshan Gate in the far-off planetary system of Yoon was known by all, simply as the Leodis Gateway.

Draeger sighed.

Ah, the days when travel to the next planetary system was but a short walk across a Gateway tunnel. How simple it was then to travel to Ellagrin, to Tilkoen and to Yoon, planetary systems light years apart from each other!

By Dyaeus, how we took that for granted!

"The Leodis Gateway is as good as gone," he said, replying to the Chancellor's question. He closed his eyes for a second, recalling Yoon and its stratospheric mountains of ice and snow.

"The Yoons destroyed their own gate long before the War escalated," he continued. "They took it down completely." He wondered if their gate had been irretrievably destroyed or merely deactivated on their end.

I wouldn't put it past them to destroy it completely. During the War, the Yoons had made a conscious decision to withdraw from the rest of the galaxy. Destroying their last link to the rest of civilisation seemed a logical step in their plan.

Draeger leant back wearily. "I don't know, Rasmus," he went on. "Even if we find the Key, I don't see how this will reopen the Gateways." He looked at the old Chancellor. "If you remember the incident with the Customs Vilicus all those years ago—I cannot see how a similar approach would be viable. The gateway would have to be kept open indefinitely if we are to evacuate *all* our people and this is not something even the most powerful Nehisi can do." He shook his head. "And I don't see how this Key can reopen any of the Gateways when one or both gates on either endpoint are now without their beacons."

The destruction of the Gateways had been the most disastrous consequence of the war.

The beacon at the Lagentian Gate was wiped out in the skirmish against the Ellagrins and in the case of the Arnemetiaen Gateway ...

Draeger paused to remember... *We had moved to expunge the Ellagrins from Arnemetiae, so they fled through the Gateway into*

Sansari. They destroyed the beacon at the Sansari Gate to prevent us from catching them. He sighed. *They would have been ordered to do so regardless.*

Draeger remembered their mad Emperor. *If the Gateway could not belong to him, then it would belong to no one.*

"And yet the Oracle told us to find the Key and our people would be saved," said Akseli with a sneer.

"There are simply too many if's and how's," said Draeger, for once agreeing with his brother's skepticism.

The Gateways were artificial constructs, built using Tilkoen technology and formed by the interaction of the Gates on each end. He simply could not imagine how the Key would be able to re-enable these.

The Gates themselves were powered by Eldur and together with the aid of beacons on each end (holding the location of the opposite endpoint), formed a Gateway, a persisted state through the Ether. It was a physical tunnel which allowed people to travel across vast distances, from one place to another, instead of having to traverse the Ether, the transdimensional subspace that existed between worlds which only the Nehisi could access.

"If, and it is a big if," Draeger continued, "the Key could somehow find a way to reopen the Gateways, then the Tilkoen system may be our next best option. But until we hear back from our Emissaries, we cannot be sure they will take us in. For now, the Lagentian Gate which links us to the Ellagrin system remains our first point of investigation once the Key is found."

"Indeed, my lord," agreed Chancellor Rasmus.

Draeger stood up and signalled the end of the meeting. "But one hurdle at a time," he said. "Leave Lagentia to me. We will cross that bridge when the time comes."

He nodded at the old man, then turned to Akseli. "I understand your reasons for going after the rebels Akseli, but let us not forget, the Exodus is our main priority and this is where our efforts should be concentrated. The Rebellion are mere flies. Swat them if they come too near but do not let them distract us from our task. Our troops are dispersed everywhere at present, containing these riots. We cannot afford to spare precious men in order to chase a few rebel ghosts."

"Of course," agreed Akseli.

Draeger nodded and rose to leave. All that had been discussed today troubled him but no more than expected.

However something else niggled. Perhaps it was Akseli's mood, but it seemed to him there was something in his brother's demeanour that appeared to suggest his sentiments did not quite reflect his words.

PART IV

ECHOES OF THE PAST

PIHLA REMEMBERS

Pihla gave a little whimper in her sleep. This was the part of her dream she didn't like.

"Pihla, *hurry*!" There was worry in Pappi's voice as he urged young Pihla, then barely six years of age, along the bright tunnel of the Arnemetiaen Gateway. "Mamma is waiting for us at the end. We have to get to Mamma, Pihla..."

"Yes Pappi," answered Pihla breathlessly as Pappi pulled her along with one hand and with the other guided the rented hovertug with their things. They were on their way towards the city of Sansari by foot.

Pihla knew they had to walk. Pappi said that it was because the Ellagrins had taken over the city of Arnemetiae and vehicles were not allowed inside the Gateway tunnel under emergency law. Walking beside them were others also trying to get back to Sansari before the next skirmish between Ellagrins and Ageronians suspended use of the Gateway again.

Across on the other side of the walkway were those heading the opposite direction—from Sansari towards Arnemetiae. The hushed throngs of people walking briskly, hurrying with the sole purpose of reaching the other end as soon as they possibly could, added to the tension in the air.

A loud whoosh broke the quietness in the tunnel. Pihla looked up to see a fighter zoom past overhead.

Pappi hurried her on. "Mamma is already on the other side waiting for us Pihla," he said worriedly. "We have to hurry…"

Another one roared past overhead.

"What's happening Pappi?"

"Fighterships Pihla," answered Pappi and then half-whispered to himself, "Ellagrin *Hauks*…"

Behind the Hauks resounded the deep drone of a larger ship, a Destroyer. A few more Hauks shrieked past overhead and many on foot cast worried glances upwards at the increasing numbers of fighterships hurtling past. People started to move faster and faster.

"C'mon Pihla," said Pappi, holding her hand tight now. Last to fly past, a Destroyer, roared overhead.

Pihla dropped her toy mouse in fright. "Mausa…!"

"No Pihla, we don't have time!" Pappi snapped but Pihla stood transfixed.

Her eyes were trained not at him, but *behind* him.

"Pappi…" she pointed.

Her father turned back to look. His face drained instantly.

The massive corridor of white at the Sansari end of the tunnel was darkening rapidly, as if the lights were being switched off section by section. Each successive length of tunnel switching off with an echoey *clunk … clunk… clunk…*

Pappi was a Gateway engineer and though he knew what he was seeing, still he could not believe it. Other travellers had stopped to gape at the strange sight as if in a trance; sections of tunnel blinking out into darkness and getting closer and closer.

"Pappi…" whimpered Pihla, reaching out for his hand.

Then Pappi seemed to snap out of his dazed state and into action. Dropping the handle of their hovertug, he picked Pihla up in his arms and began to run—back towards where they had come from.

"What's happening Pappiiiiii...?"yelled Pihla as they bounded for the Arnemetiaen Gate. By now, others too were running away from the encroaching darkness as well.

"The Gateway...," panted her father as they neared the turnstiles at the Arnemetiaen exit. She could sense the fear and disbelief in his voice. "It's shutting down!"

"But Mamma!" yelled Pihla as panicked travellers ran alongside them. She had one arm around her father's neck but the other reached out helplessly back towards Sansari, towards the rapidly encroaching darkness. "What about Mamma? Mamma! Mamma! Mausa!"

Her father didn't answer back. He was huffing heavily by the time they reached the turnstiles.

The customs guards there must have seen it too for they had opened the barriers to let everyone through. The big round indicator lights above each entry ramp shone brightly, green and continuous, as throngs of people rushed through.

Pappi took one last look behind him, his eyes wide with fear. With one last heave of exertion, he leapt through the opened barriers just as the bright, white tunnel behind them blinked into oblivion.

* * *

"YO, WAKE UP!"

"Nooo!" Pihla woke with a start, remnants of her dreams fading quickly. She wasn't in a Gateway tunnel, she was here, in her quarters, underground, and thankfully within the safe confines of the rebel base.

Niko was standing in front of her. "You have to take these to that Prometheus woman," he said bluntly, holding out a packet of bandages and a *Medisyringe* in front of her. He had the expectant look of a ten-year-old who didn't know what to do with the casserole on a night in without the parents.

Pihla sat up and rubbed her eyes. "*You* do it," she said. "Why are you asking me to do it?"

"'Cos you're a woman,"Niko replied flatly, "and well, this is womanly stuff. You know…" He shrugged pathetically.

Pihla glared at him, now truly awake. "No, I don't know," she replied flatly.

"Well, you're a woman…" Niko began slowly, trying to explain, "and she's a woman. And I'm not dressing up her wound and shit." He looked at Pihla and held out his hands in a gesture of helplessness. "Besides," he said a little plaintively, "she scares the hell out of me…"

"Chicken shit," said Pihla, grabbing the dressing off him. "As if I have nothing else better to do today."

Niko grinned at her. "Imagine that," he said, "the infamous Prometheus himself…I mean herself. Who'd have thought eh? It's like meeting a legend or something."

Pihla shrugged. "Trust Marcus to find out something like that. Makes you wonder what else he has his eyes and ears tapped into."

Niko handed her a loaded syringe. "Here, take this too. She'll need antibiotics as well. Do you think they're going help us? Her and the other guy?"

Pihla snorted. "They're not helping us out of the goodness of their hearts," she scoffed. "They're just doing it because Marcus' got one up on her."

"What about that side-kick of hers, Vidar? He seems open to our cause—"

"Ppppft! Are you trying to convert him to the Rebellion?"

Pihla shook her head. "You're wasting your time Niko. That one only listens to the jingle of *ore,* not to Marcus' orations of political ideals. And I doubt he'd take orders from anyone but her anyway." She grinned at him. "Just like you only take orders from me," she added.

Niko shot her a withering look. "Just because you recruited me doesn't mean you're my superior. Besides," he added sneeringly, "I'm not in Engineering..."

Pihla patted him condescendingly. "It's alright," she said. "Nobody's perfect."

Niko pulled a face.

Then Pihla hesitated a moment. *Should I ask him? What if he doesn't want to tell me?* She plucked up the courage to ask anyway. "So, you're going on the Tethys then?"

Niko shot her a searching look. "You heard?"

Pihla nodded.

"Well, actually,"—he was hesitant—"I turned it down..."

Pihla's heart skipped a beat. "Why? Why did you turn it down?" *Was it because I wasn't going?*

Niko shrugged. "I can't," he replied. "I'm needed here."

She perked up. *'We'll go together,' he had said to her before. 'You're like a choleric older sister to me, one I can't shake off. We're family—'*

"Besides, I found out they only assigned me one seat. I need one for Mariana as well."

Mariana. His sister. Of course.

"So anyway, I spoke with Marcus and he's promised us two seats on the next ship after the Tethys. A couple more years here, a few hundred years from now at Ellagrin. Who cares? It's not gonna make a difference to us as new settlers anyway."

I'm an idiot. He doesn't think of me as family. Why would he? He already has a sister, a real one. "That's great news," Pihla said. She swallowed hard.

"Yeah," he nodded, smiling. "What about you?"

Pihla froze momentarily. *Who am I kidding. I have no family here. That's why I need to get out of here. Then from Ellagrin, a couple of years' journey to Tilkoen. To the only family I have left there...*

"Yeah. I might talk to Marcus about the next one too." She tried to sound casual. "Don't wanna leave it too long. Engineering will be trained up by then. I've got Lukas shadowing me now and he's already overseeing most of our day-to-day operations." She fingered the bandages and syringe restlessly. "Anyway, I'll get these over to that Tors woman."

"Sure thing,"nodded Niko. "Thanks again, mate."

Pihla nodded and ducked out out as quickly as she could.

THE CORRIDOR OUTSIDE was getting busy with people coming back from the night shift. Pihla walked briskly, jostling against the flow, at times shoulder brushing against shoulder when oncoming traffic was heavy, and made for the stairs.

Despite the extensiveness of the old underground network, at least half of its passageways remained unexplored and unused. What was used a lot though, were the smaller dead-end tunnels—ones that had been closed off at one end. These served as storage rooms, sleeping quarters and even the occasional canteen for those on their way to and from their shifts.

From there, it was a quick sprint down the dark tunnel along Sector 3 which housed another row of sleeping quarters. They had put Tors and Vidar in two of the spare rooms there.

Right next to the rest of us, noted Pihla disapprovingly. She still didn't understand why Marcus trusted these two enough to have helped them escape the engineering facility in the first place. But Marcus often operated based on reasons only known to himself and whilst she didn't fully trust these two, she trusted Marcus.

She stopped outside Tors' room and rapped on the door. "It's Pihla," she announced loudly, "I've got your bandages—"

The door opened and Tors stood before her, dressed in the faded clothes loaned to her a few days ago. Standing behind her was Vidar. They looked as though they'd been interrupted and weren't too happy with that.

Pihla looked at them both. "Am I interrupting something?" she asked innocently.

Tors ignored her question and then turned back to face Vidar. She left the door ajar for Pihla. "You can leave the bandages on the table," she said and gestured impatiently for Vidar to continue.

Pihla saw a safe in the room, mounted on a makeshift wall constructed out of pallets and discarded wooden frames. "What's that?" she asked.

Vidar gave a snort. "What do you think?" he retorted sarcastically.

Tors arched an agreeing eyebrow but said nothing.

Then Vidar turned his attention back to the safe and slid the jammer against its front panel. He took out a slim wrench-like implement from his front pocket and with a deft flick, clicked the door of the safe open. "Voila!" he exclaimed, putting down his tools triumphantly.

Tors looked at her stopwatch. "Three minutes,"she said eyeing it critically. "At this rate, our mark could've had a *kofi*, made the bed and had a chat with the guards by the time you finished. "

Vidar threw her a pitying look. "You try breaking a level six, reactive-scrambler cryptolock with a nosy interrogator in the background..."

Tors stared at him apathetically.

Vidar gave a sigh of resignation and asked, "Again?"

She nodded and he began setting the safe back again to repeat the procedure.

They're rehearsing the whole damn thing, thought Pihla. She studied the room a little closer; the bed had been moved up against the wall to make space in the middle and the mattress, table and chair she noted, had been placed at a specific points on their side to demarcate the boundary of something. *No wonder they asked for the layout.* She marvelled at the sleekness of their operation. *By Dyaeus, they leave nothing to chance—from floor plans, to timings, to kit. The entire sequence.*

As Tors and Vidar repeated their practice run, Pihla could see why Marcus wanted to recruit them. Then she looked at Tors—tough yet fragile, a little like Lora—and wondered. *Perhaps her skills are not the only reason he wants to recruit her. But it's not going to work. She cares for nothing and as for Vidar joining the Rebellion, he only takes orders from her.* Pihla nodded to herself. *They are mercenaries and that one*—she looked at Tors warily—*that one's a lone operator.*

"You need anything else or are you just here for the conversation?" asked Tors, sarcasm oozing out of her. She looked at her stopwatch for the results of Vidar's second attempt and gave him a nod of approval. "Under two minutes," she said. "Good. I'll let you go rest up. We'll catch up later to go through the rest of the details."

"Sure thing, boss," Vidar replied, packing up and ostentatiously walking past Pihla as if she wasn't there.

Tors turned her gaze to Pihla and nodded at Vidar's direction. "If you've got nothing else, the door's that way," she said curtly.

Pihla gave her a measured look. "You don't like taking orders, do you?" she said.

"Not under duress," said Tors, "especially from a craven like your leader."

"I don't think Marcus liked forcing your hand this way. He didn't have a choice that's all," said Pihla. She went on, "Marcus always keeps his word. Once the job's done, he'll release your foster mum. She'll get her ticket out of here and you won't see us again."

Tors let out a cynical grunt in response and as Pihla walked out the door, she asked her, "And why are *you* doing this?"

"Doing what?" asked Pihla.

"Helping Marcus," replied Tors. "Helping the Rebellion."

Pihla paused a moment. "For the right to decide my own future," she said. And then she thought of the day at the Arnemetiaen Gateway all those years ago. Of Pappi who was no longer here, and of her Mamma, stuck at the other end, light years away in the Tilkoen city of Sansari, and she shrugged.

"And for the same reason *you* are I guess," she said. "For our mothers..."

A TEST IN TRUST

The meagre shafts of crimson daylight through the sunpipes were already fading by the time Marcus and Tors reached what appeared to be the edge of the underground network. Ahead, the tunnel forked in two, both in such state of disrepair that part of their walls had crumbled away over the centuries. Exposed brickwork showed up, their rectangular shapes yellowed and cracked like rows of rotting teeth, and a little distance down along both tunnels, the old repulsion tracks stopped. It looked as if they were probably never laid down in the first place.

"Where are we going?" asked Tors.

To her annoyance, Marcus didn't answer. "It's much easier if I just showed you," he said. "It's just a few minutes' walk from here and it'll definitely be worth your while."

She pursed her lips in annoyance but grudgingly followed his lead. They had walked through much of the length of the rebel base to get here: from the Spence, which she learnt was short for dispensary, past the Arsenal where weapons were kept, through the living quarters and mess hall and then the

Smithies where metalwork and repairs took place. Tors didn't balk at the trek as it enabled her to nosy around and gauge the scale of their operations.

Always useful to know about the competition, she told herself. If the Rebellion were likely to go after the same sources of Eldur as she was in the future, then she wanted to know as much about them as she possibly could. She filed each bit of information carefully away in her head as they went along, and added to her mental map of where things were in this sprawling underground maze.

Behind them, the overhead lamps were just starting to light up. One by one, they replaced the dimming red sections of tunnel with their artificial yellow glow. However, in front where the tunnel began to fork, the line of lamps stopped.

These sections are probably unused, she guessed, *as it doesn't look as if the wiring has ever been extended through these in the first place.*

Marcus took out his torch and turned it on to light their way. The air was much staler than where they'd come from and Tors marvelled at how vast the network of tunnels were. It was strange to think that only a few miles directly above them on the surface was the Ageron's capital city, Alandia, bustling with people going about their daily business.

"The actual glidetrain network more or less ends there," said Marcus, pointing at where they'd come from. "Our base sits within much of that network, which maps to roughly the footprint of old Alandia before the Age of Prosperity."

He took the left tunnel and led the way, his torch illuminating slices of the way little by little as he pushed ahead. "We've just come from roughly where the northwest sector of the city is today, so now, where we're heading is actually directly below the city centre."

They pushed on, walking along the tunnel in semi-darkness, the rhythmic crunch of gravel underfoot echoing down the tunnel.

"So did you grow up here on Amorgos or on one the other planets?"asked Marcus casually.

Tors rolled her eyes. With Marcus it was always questions. She could feel her heckles rise already. "Well you seem to know an awful lot about me already," she replied, refusing him the satisfaction of an answer.

Marcus was silent for a moment. "It's only since we started taking interest in getting the Eldur for ourselves that I began to take an interest," he said. He chuckled. "And that was when we realised we were obviously not the best in the business of er… procurement."

The explanation seemed to placate her. Tors shrugged. "All over," she answered. "Jula and I lived all over. We moved a lot."

"Yeah, me too," said Marcus easily. "Mostly when I was growing up. I only ever settled here on Amorgos when I got involved in the Rebellion." He glanced at her. "It has become quite a close-knit community over the years."

Community. Tors recoiled at the word. *Scary.* Just her and Vidar would have been too much of a 'community' in her opinion.

She wondered if any of the rebels would actually give their lives up for something as abstract as a cause? *Whatever fight these people think they're fighting, I wager they'll be off like a shot the moment the Reds come knocking.* Inwards, she scoffed cynically. *Rat-Boy would've sold me out for a mere pack of cigarettes.* Then again, she recalled the greetings and salutes Marcus received from the rebels they'd passed by on their way here. They seemed to genuinely like and respect this oaf.

"So why the Rebellion?" she asked, changing the focus of the subject back at him.

He lifted an eyebrow and gave her a where-do-i-even-start look.

"Corruption," he said. "We've had decades of corruption and nothing has changed. The elite get preferential treatment. We're all desperate to leave this place before it goes up in flames and yet our fates are decided by others. The Exodus selection is in the hands of the few rich and powerful. You've seen it for yourself. By Dyaeus, you may have even assisted some of them for all I know."

Tors shrugged. "Not all of the elite get to buy their way into the Exodus. A few get in. So? It still serves its purpose for most of the population."

Marcus stopped and turned to face her. "If you believe that, you'll believe anything ," he said angrily. "Especially now with the violent climate changes, real lives are at stake. Everyone wants to leave the sinking ship and the elite are muscling in, stealing the places of common citizens. And they do this with *impunity*—I mean, look at Lord Aridius, and before him, Numerius. And what about the scandal with Lord Tiberius? The list goes on."

Tors gazed levelly at him. *Yeah and your blackmailing me puts you right up there, along with them, on the principle stakes.*

Marcus continued his tirade. "Anavio alone experiences a few hundred heatstorms every week. No corner of that planet is spared. The poor don't have a choice. They have no place to go. They can't install protection against heatstorms in their homes and they can't afford heat protective clothing. Children suffer third degree burns each time they get caught in a heat-storm." He kicked a piece of rock angrily. "The richest empire in the galaxy and House Ageron lets the entire city of Cauda burn in a heatstorm. The Emperor says we cannot afford to provide anti-thermals for every citizen, yet every royal household in Alandia has a heat protective dome over their villa."

Marcus went on. "Don't you see? We have to take back control over our destiny somehow. Many will not survive long enough to get onboard the next ship out of here."

Tors shrugged, remaining unconvinced. Greed, self-interest, injustice. The strong preying on the weak. These were laws of nature as universal as the predator-prey cycles of the natural world. None of it rankled her nor did it ever occur to her that they were things that could be put right. She looked at Marcus cynically. *Well, whatever gets you up in the morning mate, just don't be standing in my way...*

The tunnel ended in a closed-off heap of rubble. To the right, just off the platform, was a flight of concrete stairs leading upwards. Tors followed Marcus up the stairs, wincing a little; her wound was healing but it still caused her some discomfort when she moved too much. Soon, they emerged at the top of the stairs onto the concourse of an old station.

Only the skeleton of the building remained and it looked more like a cavernous indoor farm rather than a former train station. Endless rows of raised troughs made from old sleepers and other salvaged parts of the building stretched before them, filled with rows of vegetables, their dark shapes visible under the red and blue indoor lights. A gentle murmur of conversation from the men and women working between the rows of planting echoed around the vast space and Tors detected the faint sound of water trickling gently through pipes in the background.

She almost didn't recognise her.

Standing beside another woman, a cabbage in her hand, she didn't look as gaunt as Tors remembered. She had put on a little weight and with her cheeks filled out for a change, she looked almost healthy. They were laughing and she was pointing animatedly at the cabbage before she looked up and across towards Tors.

"Vi…?" She looked unsure, dazed almost, as if not quite believing her eyes. Then all of a sudden, Jula dropped the harvested cabbage and ran across towards Tors, jumping over the rows of vegetables like a hurdles as she went.

"Oh by Dyaeus, Vittoria!" She hugged Tors tightly, surprising her with her action.

The Jula I remembered was never lucid enough to recognise me, never mind hug me. Tors hugged her back, a little uncertainly. "Ouch," she said, wincing a little.

Jula pulled back worriedly. "You okay?" she asked, looking intently at Tors.

Tors nodded. "It's fine,"she replied. "Just an old wound."

"Are you hurt?" Jula sounded genuinely concerned.

Tors looked at her. *It would never have crossed the old Jula to ask.*

"Is that… really you?" she questioned out loud.

Jula laughed. "I could ask the same," she said, looking at Tors closely. Her eyes for once, were clear and focussed, not glazed over in stupor.

Tors breathed in sharply. Somewhere from the recesses of her mind, from old buried memories, she remembered and recognised this Jula. The Jula who laughed with Saima and who played with her when she was but a child.

"I thought you were dead," continued Jula, wiping her tears roughly with the back of her hand. "Look at you—you're a woman!" She grasped Tors on her arms, her eyes still glistening.

"After the incident at Karl's, they finally let me out. I came back to look for you but you were gone." She sniffed. "Karl said you hadn't been back since. Not once. Anyway, I stayed around for a while hoping you'd come back but you didn't."

Tors remained silent. *I was around, watching. You just didn't know it.*

Jula swallowed thickly. "After that I moved on to the next district. I had to. I couldn't stay..." She hung her head in shame. "Decebal was getting unreasonable and I couldn't repay him for the Stims after all that interest I'd racked up." She looked at Tors, the fear from that time still etched in her eyes. "He came after me..."

I know... But Tors merely nodded. The words would not come out.

"But I got lucky," continued Jula, her eyes widened. "Some other loanshark took him out before he could get to me!"

Tors nodded but said nothing. *I know,* she answered Jula in her heart. *And it wasn't some loanshark. But that was the only way to resolve the problem. Decebal would never have let the mounting credit go.*

She couldn't take her eyes off Jula. How surreal it was to be having a proper conversation with Jula and here she was, tongue-tied.

"They cleaned me up real good here," said Jula, as if she sensed Tors' wonderment. "And you know what?" She looked at Tors unflinchingly. "I think I can do this," she said. She grinned at Tors and nodded. "I really think I can stay clean and well, be this way from now on."

Tors continued to listen, dumbfounded.

Then Jula beckoned her friend over, the woman she had been talking with earlier. "This is my friend Marie," she said, introducing her to Tors.

Marie gave Tors a smile and turned to give Marcus a nod of acknowledgement.

"Marie's entire family's going on the Tethys," said Jula.

Marcus nodded. "All the people you see here are," he explained to Tors, pointing at the others working around them. He grinned. "I thought I'd show you *who* we were doing all this for, seeing as I had explained to you the why."

"We're going to live off the land in Ellagrin," continued Jula happily, "just like this." She looped her arm round Marie's. "Turns out I'm pretty handy with growing things," she said, giving Marie's arm a squeeze.

"The community will support her," said Marcus . He looked at Tors thoughtfully with his brown eyes.

There it is again, she thought to herself, *that 'community' word...*

As Marcus turned to ask Marie and Jula some questions, Tors pondered. This time, she understood what Marcus actually meant and saw what this actually did and could do for Jula. *She has friends to support her now. More importantly people who will form part of her life and her support system. People who will help keep her on the straight. Something I could never do for her...*

This time, it felt like Jula actually had a shot at this.

She glanced at Marcus who was joking with Jula and Marie, tugging at some carrot tops in the far end. There was something goofy about him despite the fact they all looked up to him as their leader, and something inside her softened. He had taken a risk in bringing her to see Jula, essentially revealing to her where Jula was, and perhaps risking his only leverage at getting the Eldur.

You fool, she scoffed at him inwardly. *You trusting fool. Even I wouldn't trust someone like me.* With Jula's position now known to her, she could now whisk her away at any time.

However, as she looked on at the two women teasing and laughing with Marcus, she found to her surprise, that her resolve to play him out diminished.

Perhaps this is not such a bad deal after all, she reflected. *And perhaps he's not such a fool after all, although I bet Vidar won't be happy about this. Still, it will give Jula a new life and a chance to start anew.* That alone was worth everything.

She looked on as Jula waved a bunch of leafy greens at her from afar. Tors found herself smiling back and for the first time in a long while, the weight of responsibility upon her shoulders felt just a little bit lighter.

NIKO

The instant Niko walked into her apartment, he felt something was wrong. It didn't look ransacked, but felt *thinned out,* as if some of its contents had been removed. It had been a year since he'd last seen her. That couldn't be helped—as sister to a known member of the Rebellion, she would have been watched in case he attempted to make contact. It had taken much care and planning on his part before he could even risk coming here today.

"Mariana?" he called out cautiously as he picked his way through each room, eventually ending in the bedroom.

The curtains were drawn but the material was so worn and thin, it let enough light through to enable him to see without turning the lamp on. A single bed, its thin mattress and an even thinner blanket took up most of the small room. An old mirror and grandma's old wooden dresser, so old Niko often wondered how it wasn't crumbling to dust, filled the wall on the other end.

Mariana was very proud of her dresser, often showing it off to friends. 'It's an antique' she would say, 'and probably worth a few thousand ore 'cos it's made from trees', although neither she nor Niko had ever touched or known a tree their whole life. Trees had not existed in the Realms for over a century now. The closest thing to a tree were the the shorter, hardier barbthorns and other similar, smaller shrubs. But then the world of yesteryear was so different it would have been unrecognisable to those of his generation.

Before the Exodus, as Nana used to say, long before the twin suns started failing, the Red Realm was more commonly known as Ageron. It was the Golden Empire, the Age of Prosperity, Nana called it, and so prosperous its cities oozed wealth and its citizens lived in unimaginable decadence.

Niko remembered sitting on the floor, elbows resting on his hunched up knees, Mariana on Nana's lap, listening to her stories of her own childhood days, enraptured by every detail.

'Every household had servants, even mine', Nana said, 'and there was so much food. Fresh food: juicy oranges from Lassos, sticky red bloodfruit from Vasa, crunchy pomum, picked from the orchards outside Alandia and sweet, fresh greens, grown from the earth and outdoors under the golden twin suns'. A far cry indeed from today where those lucky enough to avoid the earthquakes or heatstorms, barely eked a living to survive.

Well, we shan't have to live here for too long, thought Niko. *Wait until I tell her Marcus has promised us tickets on the next ship out of here.* He tapped the top of the dresser absently, trying to decide what to do next.

The taps sounded hollow.

Niko stopped abruptly, then slid the top drawer open. It was empty of clothes. Heart thumping, he pulled each one, one after another.

They were all empty.

Shit! he thought to himself. Something was very wrong here.

Panicking, he accessed the comms panel and searched for the most recent entry: *Official announcement*, it flashed, received only moments before he had entered the building.

"Shit! Shit! Shit!" he cursed and hastened out of the apartment and into the street outside, looking around desperately. Had the Reds taken her? Did they know he was coming? Was it the last heist? Did they figure out it was him?

The evening crowd was a sea of grey-looking faces, people on their way home from work, as weary as their grim surroundings.

"Fratello!"

A familiar voice. Mariana!

Thank Dyaeus.

She ran to him. "I can't stay long," she said breathlessly. "Oh by Dyaeus, fratello.." She hugged him hard and whispered in his ear, "I *won*! I won the lottery..."

"What?" Niko looked at her disbelievingly.

She nodded, tears in her eyes. Looking around to ensure they weren't overheard, she continued in a low voice, "Yes, the message just came in a few minutes ago. I have a place on the Carinthia! But I have to leave immediately for the pickup point. You know the drill."

Niko nodded. He was speechless. The Exodus—Mariana had actually won a place!

Winners were informed at a moment's notice and mandated to proceed to a secret location disclosed by the State in order that details of the evacuations remained secret. There were no goodbyes, nothing. If you didn't proceed immediately, you'd lose your place. And from the secret collection point, the evacuees would settle on the ship itself with no further contact with the outside world. And when the time came, they would make their journey in longsleep, to designated settlements somewhere in the Ellagrin system.

When Niko got his voice back, he said, "That's good. *Good!*"

She HAS to take this. There may not be a ship after the Tethys, no matter how confident Marcus is.

"But I can't go… not without you!" Tears streamed down Mariana's face. "I can't fratello, I *can't*…" Her small body convulsed in sobs.

He grasped her shoulders with both hands and looked at her streaked face. "This is *great* news, Mariana." He said that slowly, trying to impress upon her how happy he was for her and how important this was. "Mama would be so happy."

Mariana tried to hold back her tears. This would be the last time she would set eyes on her brother. Ellagrin was light years away and she knew that by the time she reached it, he would be long gone. This was why the empire evacuated families together but Niko was part of the Rebellion, a wanted man, and therefore in the eyes of the empire no longer a legitimate part of it.

"Now *go*," he said gruffly, almost pushing her away.

She hurried off, looking back one last time before disappearing into the crowds.

MARCUS' PAST

"Right, I'm off for my shift at the Smithies now,"said Pihla, stopping outside Marcus' quarters. " Marcus told me to fetch you and so I have." She gestured at the door in front of them. "And here we are."

"What does he want?"asked Tors.

"Our esteemed leader has decided that you and Vidar should probably have something to defend yourself with in tomorrow's job," Pihla said. "I'd do that for you but I don't know what grade weapons you and Vidar are allowed, so best you square that with the boss yourself."

Tors remained silent.

Pihla shot her a look. "He's not the enemy you know," she said.

"I find that hard to believe," Tors replied.

"Marcus is...," said Pihla, looking up as she searched for the right word, "a revolutionist." She nodded. "In every sense of the word." She looked at Tors with her intense amber eyes. "The way I see it, the Exodus is one thing but it may be too late for many of us. The likes of Lord Aridius are buying their way out by commissioning their own spaceships at the expense of the empire's expatriation programme and there is no way to stop them from doing this. Marcus merely wants the right to take matters into our own hands. To build *our* ships *ourselves* if we have the means to. Not wait around for the possibility of being selected for the next expatriation flight."

Pihla stopped outside the door. "Anyway, I'm not one for preaching," she said, rapping it loudly. "I shall leave you to it." She waved and sauntered off in the opposite direction, whistling.

With an impatient sigh, Tors pulled the door open. *Let's see what your Righteous Deliverer wants to talk about,* she said to herself as she walked in without waiting for an answer.

MARCUS' quarters were larger than the ones she and Vidar had been given, but unlike theirs, this one had its own ensuite shower. Marcus was standing just outside it. He grabbed a clean shirt from the chair nearby and walked towards her. He moved like a panther and his sleek muscles rippled as he advanced. Without her vizard, Tors felt strangely exposed and a little self-conscious.

"Good, I see you're here," Marcus said with a smile. His tousled hair was wet and tumbled over his left brow, dripping slightly onto his bare chest.

"Pihla said you wanted to see me,"replied Tors, curt.

"Yes," said Marcus, towering over her small frame.

Tors looked at him coldly. *Just because I'd agreed to help you obtain the Eldur doesn't mean we have to be on conversational terms. Stop wasting my time, you oversized twit.*

"So," he continued, pulling his shirt on, "I thought we

should have a look in the Arsenal and pick out what you and Vidar will need for tomorrow."

Tors raised an eyebrow. "It's a heist," she remarked drily, "not a military offensive or a tea party. How much kit does one need?"

Marcus cleared his throat. "Well, er, we shall see then. Let me show you the Arsenal and you can tell me what you require. I understand you've not been inside."

Of course not. You and your goons wouldn't let me so much as look at a gun. Tors let the silence roll on and after an awkward moment, Marcus opened the door and led the way.

Their footsteps echoed hollowly down the tunnel as they made their way to the Arsenal. Marcus unlocked the door and stepped aside to let her go first.

A low hanging lamp flickered to life as they entered, its swinging circle of light illuminating racks and racks of guns lining the brick walls. A few rusty swords hung from the corner, corroded by green trails of moisture leaking through the ceiling. The room, like others in the base, had a flagstone floor, smooth and worn from years and years of feet. The air here smelt of damp, metal and gasoline. Although the piddly little lightbulb was not bright enough to illuminate the entire space, Tors could guess from the way their footsteps echoed in it that this was a cavernous chamber.

An arsenal all right. Tors gaped internally.

"You have quite a selection here," she said, "and some fine-looking antiques too." She examined an ancient semi-automatic from one of the racks with interest.

"Yes," said Marcus, "but mostly we have standard stuff and a few modified inventions of our own too." He tossed her what looked like a burst gun which she turned over to examine. It had the sleek look of a plasma-28 but with a slightly different barrel. *Good weight though.*

"Plasma burst gun?"

"Neutrino."

Tors arched an eyebrow, impressed. *Some modification. I'd happily pay a thousand ore for something like this.*

"Pihla's idea," said Marcus, "Canny one that. Her Tilkoen pedigree shows through. You know, Pihla heads up the Engineering team and all these modification ideas come from them."

Tors turned the gun over to look for the release clasp.

"Here," said Marcus reaching out, "it's not obvious where it is." He laid his hand on top of hers and placed it on the slidestop which, as he had pointed out, was not in an obvious position. "And you activate it like this," he continued, guiding her into position, his arms above hers. Leaning over, his face almost touched hers and she could feel his breath on her cheek ever so slightly. He smelt of fresh soap and old leather.

Unwittingly, she breathed in deeply and found herself liking it. And liking it far too much. "This one's fine," she said, abruptly pulling back and conscious of the discomforting rise in heat on her cheeks, "and maybe a compact plasma-32 for Vidar."

Marcus nodded with equally uncharacteristic awkwardness. "Sure," he mumbled hastily and strode towards the other end of the chamber where the handguns were stored.

Tors looked around her. *Perhaps I need a replacement vizard,* she thought, trying to shed the vulnerability she had been feeling as a result of being without one. She guessed this end of the room was probably used as a war room of sorts in the past, before it held racks for the guns.

Maps lined one corner and on the row of cabinets pushed up against the wall, tall stacks of papers stood tentatively under the intimidating racks of guns—old papers, maps, news cuttings and gun schematics.

Sigh... but no vizards. Tors flicked the papers over idly as she waited for Marcus to retrieve Vidar's piece, looking at the clippings, some so old and yellowed, their ink barely visible.

ALANDIA NEWS, dated 3502. Lord Caius onboarded the Almirante at last minute.

Questions raised on state lottery corruption.

SCANDAL! Doctor found guilty of attempting to steal Exodus ticket from patient.

THERE WERE other news cuttings too:

NATIONAL REALMS BULLETIN: Lord Mircea and family flee the Realms aboard private space carrier. Latest protests linked to burgeoning problems with unauthorised emigrations. Public disgust at court sessions set after family left the Realms.

AND SOME MORE RECENT ONES:

ALANDIA NEWS. Scandal! Lord Aridius stripped of title for rigging Exodus state lottery.

TORS FLICKED THROUGH THE PAPERS, scanning their content. *Strange. They all have a similar theme running through...*

Then she felt her fingers touch something cold and metallic. Her interest piqued, she pushed the few sheafs of cuttings aside. Nestled in between them was a metal tag, strung on a thin chain, like a dog tag. She examined it.

An old ticket! The ones the Exodus programme used to issue in the early days before the electronic versions. It had the passenger name inscribed on it, on top of the crypto key mount and stamped across it, the word VOIDED.

ADMIT : One (Adult)
Ship: Almirante
Name: Marcus Thaddeus

"HEY, GIVE ME THAT!"

Tors dropped the tag, startled.

Marcus snatched it before it even reached the table and slid it over his neck, his demeanour no longer cheerful nor obliging.

"Here's Vidar's gun," he said, tossing the piece to her. He seemed closed off. A different person.

Next he handed her an elegant, thin dagger. "To replace the one you lost in the engineering facility," he said gruffly. Then, dismissing her, he said, "Briefing's tomorrow at o-seven-hundred. I'll see you and Vidar then."

Tors nodded, clutched the two guns and turned to leave. She didn't look at his face. She didn't have to for she recognised the signs. Pihla was wrong. This was not a man driven by idealistic dreams of a better future.

This was a man haunted by his past.

PREPARATIONS

They were in the mess room, packing in any last minute items for the job. Tors reached to close her rucksack, tugging at the thin strap stuck in its zipper. It wouldn't budge, staying steadfastly lodged between the teeth of the zipper.

Marcus reached over to take the bag from her, to help. "So how'd you do it?" he asked casually as he examined the strap.

Questions... again. However, try as she might, Tors couldn't seem to stay angry at him. "Do what?" she asked. She was annoyed, but at herself. It annoyed her that she couldn't even stay cross at him for long.

"You know," Marcus said easily, "move in and out of a situation so quickly."

"What do you mean?"asked Tors, directing her gaze at him. It was sometimes hard to gauge if Marcus was serious or just making idle conversation.

Marcus brought himself closer and Tors' skin began to prickle with anxiety. *What is wrong me me?* she thought, slightly flustered.

"Here," he said, dropping her bag into her hands, its strap now free from the confines of the zipper. "So, the last time we tracked you and Jula," he said, eyeing her interestedly, "it was in a blind alley but by the time we looked for you, there was no one there. It was like you both disappeared into thin air." He leant closer and looked at her intently. She felt the heat rise in her cheeks again.

"So how'd you do it?" he asked. "How'd you get out so fast?"

Tors stared back at him, waited sufficiently long enough to make for an uncomfortable pause, then replied coolly, "If I tell you, I'll have to kill you. Trade secrets of a thief and all that."

"Huh," replied Marcus casually, although his eyes never left hers. "A magician never reveals his tricks I guess..."

Tors moved away to examine some visors on the table. Her heart was still pounding. *What's come over me? Maybe I should ask to borrow one of these.* She hastily picked up one, pretending to look at it. *Is it the lack of a vizard that's unsettling me or is it all these questions?* she wondered. She eyed him surreptitiously and wondered in mild horror. *Or by Dyaeus, am I actually finding him distracting and* ***not*** *in a disagreeable way??*

"Where's Vidar?" Pihla voiced, looking up.

"Scouting the target area," replied Tors, switching back to matters at hand with relieved rapidity. "He's been keeping a close eye on the apartment all week, making sure the Eldur and its occupant hasn't moved. He should be back soon."

"Hmmm," said Pihla, then asked Marcus. "You sure you don't want me and Niko coming with you on this one, boss?" She looked across to Tors and added, "No offence. It's not that I don't trust you..."

"None taken," quipped Tors with a careless shrug.

Marcus shook his head. "No," he replied, "you and Niko

stay on behind. We can't have too many people in the area. It's too risky."

Niko grunted and turned back to Tors. "Well, your friend's been out for some time now," she said. "You sure he's scouting and not getting wasted at the nearest watering hole?"

Right on cue Vidar sauntered in, whistling.

"You're in a good mood," commented Niko, eyeing him as he walked past. Niko had his passive-aggressive voice on. "What have you been up to?"

"Oh, nothing much,"replied Vidar airily. "Went out for some air after my reccie, sampled the pleasures of Alandia…"

Tors glanced at him. *He's practically on cloud nine,* she observed. *Tomcat.* She rolled her eyes at him.

Pihla gave a husky snicker. "Careful Vidar," she teased, "if she's one of those downtown pleasurologists, you might catch something that'll shorten your days. By Dyaeus, it might even shorten something else too hah!"

Vidar shrugged the taunts off carelessly. "Love…," he said half-dreamily, "love will make everything right."

"Well now's not the time for that," said Marcus cutting him short. "And as the job is tomorrow, no more going out of the base from now until it's over," he said eyeing him keenly. "We can't afford to attract any attention."

Vidar shot him a wary look and then smiled. "Sure," he answered easily, "I was just making the most of my time outside that's all."

"Everything's just one pleasure ride for you, isn't it?" Niko grumbled, chucking his rag into the bin with an annoyed flick.

"What is wrong with him?" asked Vidar.

Pihla laughed. "He's just grumpy," she said and threw some spare clips at Niko. "Oi!" Pihla pulled a face, trying to get his attention. "It is *you* who should be the one making the most of your time. Not wasting it moping around. Oi….*hamster*!"

Niko ignored her completely.

"I don't understand—hamster?" Tors looked at Pihla quizzically.

"Niko's human," Marcus interjected to explain, "which means his life span is less than a third of the average Ageronian's. And probably half of Pihla's."

"I'm half Tilkoen, half Ageronian," said Pihla proudly, "but I'm banking on inheriting my Ageronian father's longevity, rather than my mother's." Her muscular arms gleamed like bronze as they moved up and down polishing the mechanical BZ-1 in her hands.

"Pihla was one of those marooned here years ago when the Gates got destroyed," explained Marcus. "As you can tell from the Tilkoens here, they can live for over two hundred years," he added, "but humans last no more than a century at most."

"Without rejuvenation that is," chipped in Pihla, "which we all know he can't afford."

Marcus nodded. "Hence the hamster reference," he said. "Short-lived as a hamster. Although," he added kindly, looking at Niko, "at your tender age, there's plenty of time yet to be thinking of these things eh, Niko?"

"Ah," said Tors diplomatically and resumed her task. It was sometimes difficult to tell humans and Ageronians apart. Niko was, after all, pretty tall for a human.

Niko ignored Marcus' remark, picked up his bag and walked off in a huff.

Pihla raised a questioning eyebrow at Marcus. "Something must've put him off," she said. "He usually takes my jokes well."

"Mmmm…" answered Marcus noncommittally. He waited a moment after Niko left, then lowered his voice. "He went to see his sister the other day. Nearly missed her too."

"Yeah, so?" Pihla questioned.

Marcus gave the door a quick glance to make sure Niko

was out of earshot. “She won the state lottery,” he said. “She’s going on the Carinthia.”

“Oh,” replied Pihla as the brevity of that statement dawned on her. “I see,” she finally said and without a further word, carried the guns out of the room.

AN UNEXPECTED ENCOUNTER

Elena tapped her fingers lightly on the leaden marble desk and pondered her next move. Cadmus, his manservant had just informed her that Lord Draeger had been away from the palace for a week now and was not due back for some days yet.

Probably somewhere still quelling the riots, she thought. *If that's the case, he's probably not even on Amorgos at the moment.*

Her delicate eyebrows knitted into a slight frown. She was here to give him the snippet of information she had chanced upon. *A little gift. After all, these were the same people causing him no end of trouble from the sounds of things but where by Ysgarh was he?*

She let out a little sigh of frustration. *I can solve it myself easily enough,* she thought. But then, did she have sufficient men for the job? And what if they outnumbered Varg and his team of two? She shook her head. *I can't tell Niklas or ask to borrow some soldiers as I can't have him know about my whereabouts.*

Niklas and his irascible nature. *I shouldn't even be here in*

Ageron in the first place. If he knew of even half of what I've been up to here, he'd kill me. She shuddered. Her brother's jealousy held no bounds. *He cannot be controlled. He wishes to have me and to keep me only for himself.* Her hand subconsciously felt for the hidden snuff box she kept in her skirt, containing her contraceptives. If Niklas knew about her lovers...

She shifted uncomfortably in the seat. She was playing with fire, she knew. Handling Niklas was like roulette, even with the distractions she ensured were placed between him and her. Annette, Inger, Lise—she knew his type based on his inexplicable fixation on her. They were chosen because they were all variations of the same theme.

One day these women will no longer be enough to distract him.

The image of Lise flashed unbidden to the forefront of her mind. The foolish girl must have did or said something wrong.

She dressed almost exactly like me for one.

And that night, Niklas was in no mood for a poor copy, an insult to his tastes. Lise's body bruised and bloodied was found in his chambers the next day, her face beaten into a pulp.

But Niklas would never kill me, she told herself. *It was not like this when we were young. He didn't have Father's temper then.* In fact, he protected her.

Growing up, Father was violent to them both and it was often Niklas, being the older one, who stood between her and Father, often standing up to him. Sometimes to his own cost. Some nights when she was too afraid to sleep, she would crawl into his bed instead and both of them would fall asleep in a huddle.

But as he grew older, Niklas had become more and more like Father, and by the time he finally ascended the throne, the transformation was complete. He was irascible, secretive, suspicious, even more so than Father, and convinced that House Ageron was out to destroy Ellagrin.

Elena shook her head. No, Niklas was definitely not an option, but her source had warned her and she was fairly confident he was not lying.

Perhaps I should just return to Ellagrin, she thought conceding that perhaps this was not to be. But information, especially good information should be acted on and used, not wasted and Elena was not one to waste an opportunity if one presented itself. She fidgeted, thinking of how she could make use of it without Draeger.

She stood up, walked to the door and peered out again. The corridor was empty. She let out a resigned sigh. It was not to be. *No matter,* she thought, *your loss.* She put her cloak on and rose to leave. Closing the door behind her, she turned—

Only to bump into Akseli.

The Emperor himself.

"My, my… what have we here," Akseli said with a drawl.

Elena looked at him, his flaxen hair gleaming under the light from the wall sconces in the corridor. *We are cousins after all,* she contemplated, noting certain similarities in their features. Their hair colour for one. "Your Excellency," murmured Elena.

Akseli gave her an appraising look. "What are you doing here?" he asked. "Looking for Lord Draeger?"

Elena nodded.

Akseli flashed a smile. "My brother's in Othon I think. One of the outer planets anyway, quelling some riots. Didn't he tell you? Or is he too busy for you nowadays?"

Elena's cheeks grew a little hot but she replied coolly, "I wouldn't know what Lord Draeger gets up to, your Excellency. My social calendar is far too busy to accommodate him and he, well, has no social calendar, as you know."

Akseli gave another smile in reply.

"And how is your mother, Queen Alin?"

"She is well, thank you," replied Akseli. "Busy I gather, although what it is exactly she is busy with, I have no idea nor any inclination to find out."

Elena smiled and nodded politely. She knew Queen Alin well. A difficult relationship with her own mother Elisabet, it was in Alin, her father's sister, that Elena found someone she could talk to. And throughout her formative years until the War severed relations between the two Houses, Queen Alin had remained her constant companion and confidante. *Only she could temper Father's mood swings, but when she left to marry your father, Ageron III, he became worse. And Niklas and I bore the brunt of that...*

"And how are things here in the empire?" she inquired politely. "I hear your visit to Anavio recently was much lauded and your speech to the victims of the devastating storms most reassuring. You have a flair for engaging with the populace, Your Excellency."

Akseli gave her a bitter look. "Don't mock me Elena," he said. "I tire of the position I find myself in, playing second fiddle to my brother."

Elena lifted an eyebrow, feigning surprise. "But you are the Emperor of the Red Realm," she replied. "That's hardly playing second fiddle. I on the other hand..."

She thought about her role in the courts of Ellagrin with Niklas. As accomplished as she was in matters of governing Ellagrin, she knew that at the end of it, she was a woman after all. *In all the history of Ellagrin, never has there been a woman in power.* The Doges—governors appointed solely by the Emperor—would never allow it.

"Emperor!" Akseli laughed scornfully. "But whom does the real power lie with in the background?" His eyes blazed. "My brother has the support of the armies and because of that, he has the Senate's ear, not I."

Elena remained silent. Power, she knew, did not always sit with the ones in prominence. She had learnt from a young age how this game was played and by the time Niklas ascended, the Doges too learnt that Elena was the only one who had his ear. *And if they were ever to go against me, they had better have Niklas' support behind them...*

"Emperor!" Akseli spat the word with contempt. "That title will be worth nothing once the Exodus is complete." His eyes bore into hers. "Do you know what you are doing?" he asked, clutching her arm suddenly. "When you persuade your Niklas to authorise all these settlement treaties of my brother's?"

Elena gazed at him levelly. If his sudden outburst startled her, she did not show it.

Akseli did not wait for her reply. Instead he continued. "You are merely expediting my continual descent to oblivion as Emperor."

Elena eyed him steadily as he went on.

"Once all Ageronians leave the Realm, there will be no one left to rule," said Akseli. He dropped her arm and his mouth hardened to a thin, bitter line. "Do you think my people will still swear allegiance to me when they are comfortably established in Ellagrin?"

Elena shrugged. "It will not be an easy life for them though. There is not enough space for all Ageronians in Ellagrin. Don't forget, we are five planets where you are twelve. At the moment, there is no satisfactory solution in sight as yet."

Elena patted Akseli's arm to calm him down. "I am in two minds about the Exodus too," she said, looking at him, "despite what I do for your brother. Think about it. There will come a point where it will put a strain on both land and resources in Ellagrin. Even Niklas can see that. He is already saying you should look to House Tilkoen to take some of your people in."

Akseli shook his head. "Tilkoen is too far from us," he said. "It is far enough as it is for us to get to Ellagrin."

"But not too far once you're in Ellagrin," Elena pointed out. "The Tilkoen system is no more than seven or eight years' journey from us. There will be land enough to spread out. The Tilkoens are like ants, preferring to congregate densely in their cities, leaving much of their planets untouched. It is most likely that when the time comes, Niklas will insist that some of your people be relocated from Ellagrin to Tilkoen."

"Perhaps," admitted Akseli grudgingly. He gave an exasperated grunt. "There's no end to our compounding troubles at the moment with the riots, the natural disasters besieging us, the damn Rebellion." He leant against the wall and looked at her intently.

Elena didn't like that. *He looks like Niklas when he's toying with something twisted in his mind.*

Then the pieces clicked into place. An idea formed in her head. *A solution to my little problem!*

She leant forward and met his gaze. "Well," she said, "as luck will have it, I may have a little something to cheer you up. Tomorrow night. If you so care to drop by my apartment then..."

Akseli eyed her warily and Elena gave an entertained chuckle.

"It's not *that* I have in mind, your Excellency," she continued, laughing out loud. "Even *I* am discerning enough to know that I'm not your type." She smiled. "I may have a little present for you if you and your guards drop in then," she said. "It will be worth your while, I guarantee it."

Then she patted his arm and made her way down the corridor to leave the palace.

PART V

CONVERGENCE

MARCUS

It was nearly time. Marcus knew it was about one in the morning and therefore time to set off as he could hear the stir of the first shift coming back from work and the second shift heading over through the tunnels to sub them. He and Tors were waiting for Vidar in one of the smaller mess rooms. He looked on as she took out the dagger he'd given her to polish it.

She handles it like an Ashgarian, as if it were an extension of her. "You know any Ashgarians?" he enquired casually.

Tors looked up and stared straight through him. "No," came the reply.

"Oh," replied Marcus. "Only because you handle your blades like one. That's why I asked." He tried not to sound intimidated.

He looked at her again, surreptitiously this time. Her attentions had returned to her dagger and she was rubbing its blade vigorously with an oiled cloth. It glinted under the incandescent light above the table where she perched, its gleam reflecting off her eyes, making them glow green like copper on fire.

Marcus felt an emotion stir within him. That surprised him. It had come from a part of his heart that had been sealed off since Lora, an emotion he had not felt in a long time.

She is like an Ashgarian, he observed. *Wild, amoral and with total disregard for authority*. Strange to think she'd be the one to bring back memories of his unusual upbringing with the strange tribe.

Before Lora, Marcus had spent much of his life amongst them. Ashgarians were slave traders. Fierce and nomadic, they moved around from one place to another, frequently pillaging rural and unprotected outposts in the less developed parts of the galaxy.

He was seven when a clan of Ashgarians plundered his village. Too small to be sold, they kept him and he was raised in the master slaver's household to serve as sparring practice for the master's children. Fortunately Marcus was a fast learner and though not as big as the average seven foot Ashgarian youngster, he was light on his feet and somehow survived to become a worthy sparring partner for his master's eldest son.

Marcus sighed inwardly. It was pointless hoping Tors would join him and the Rebellion. *The Ashgarians wouldn't understand our reasons for the Rebellion either. They don't believe in causes nor, Dyaeus forbid, in doing something that didn't directly benefit them or their pockets.*

Now more than ever, Tors reminded him of the them. *She cares for nothing. Not the Rebellion, not the Empire and perhaps not even herself. So maybe she has Ashgarian blood in her—she's certainly as cut-throat and lawless as one*. But then Asgharians were dark-skinned and heavily built. Like tanks. And she wasn't. Come to think of it, he was getting rather distracted by the way she was built: her unruly hair, black as the dead of night, her startling eyes, the way her head tilted whenever she pondered.

He thought about her some more, all the time trying not to stare at her too conspicuously. *Will she rip me apart if I say something else to her? I should say something. Make conversation....* It was a daunting prospect talking to Tors, and Marcus felt his resolve begin to ebb away.

Say something! Marcus dug his fingernails into his palm and launched straight into conversation.

"So..." he asked, as casually as he could muster, "You up for tonight?" *By Dyaeus, that sounded like a chat up line!* He could've kicked himself.

Her raven locks were pulled back in a high chignon, exposing most of her neck. Marcus couldn't help admiring the slenderness of it. And she had a habit of twirling the stray strands of hair before tucking them behind her ear. It reminded him of the time he first met Lora—the slightly queasy fluttery feeling in the stomach, like a cross between diarrhoea and heartburn.

"Yes."

Oh good—she answered! "How's the wound?" he asked.

"Healing."

"Shall I take a look?"

"No," came the reply, terse and a trifle too quick. "That won't be necessary." She glanced at him when she said that, and that caused him to stop breathing for a minute.

*Those eyes...**breathe** Marcus!* He averted his eyes from her gaze and swallowed. "Okay," he said, "but make sure you stay close. I'll get the stone. We go in and out. Quick. No drama."

"No," Tors corrected him, her voice contemptuous. "*I'll* get the stone. *You* keep an eye out for security."

Marcus chuckled. He didn't think she'd let him take over. "Not much of a team player, are we?" he teased.

"Look," he continued as casually as possible, leaning close. He wasn't sure how she would react to his audacious move but what the hell. "We're on the same side here," he said, trying to catch her eye. But she was faced downwards, tightening the calico brace around her midriff and wincing slightly as she did so. At that moment, she looked tired, almost vulnerable and he had the sudden urge to reach out and take her in his arms to protect and reassure her.

"You don't have to play this solo act all the time you know," he said gently, "and *sometimes,* just sometimes, you need to know there are others who will be here to help you." Marcus' voice broke a little towards the end. "You aren't alone anymore…," he said softly.

And then she looked up, and her eyes met his.

By Dyaeus, she's beautiful, he thought, aware of this strange emotion stirring in him as he looked at her, making him feel inexplicably warm. He hoped he'd maintained a straight face.

Tors held his gaze, then drew herself up to him. Her lips were almost touching his. Her breath soft and quivering seemed to mirror the flutterings in his stomach.

He found himself holding his breath. *This is IT! She's finally going to relent.*

"I think…," began Tors, a curl half-drawn on her sensual lips.

By Dyaeus, he could get lost in those fiery, green eyes. *Take me,* Marcus said in his mind, *take me now!* "Yes..?" he gulped innocently.

"I think," Tors continued, tracing her finger over his lips, "what would really help me is knowing that *sometimes,* just sometimes… you and your merry men will stay out of my way and let me finish my job!" Her eyes flashed fiercely like daggers as she drew back and glowered menacingly at him.

Marcus wilted slightly in her piercing glare.

She spoke now, quietly and dangerously. "And when tonight's job is done and Jula is safely on the Tethys," she said, "you and I are done, you hear me? We are *done*."

THE JOB

Over at one of the houses overlooking the piazza, three figures slipped in noiselessly through the servants' entrance at the side. It was the early hours of the morning and the air was dry and chilly.

But not as chilly as the exchange we just had, winced Marcus recalling his failed move on Tors to win her over. He rubbed his gloved hands to keep them warm. *No matter, I shall have to work on her,* he thought, ever the optimist.

Like shadows they slid past the servants' quarters at the back and into the main living area of the house. There, in the hall with its sumptuous decor of marble and glass, stood the main staircase leading upstairs. As was previously observed, there were no guards, this being a private residence.

The staircase was curved and elegant, made of pale marble and crowned by a black wrought iron bannister. Long and continuous, it led gracefully upwards onto the landing where a row of doors stood in silent attendance.

Cautiously, Marcus walked up the stairs behind Tors and Vidar.

They had just passed the second door when Tors stopped and gave the signal. Then silently she turned towards the third door and pushed the handle gently downwards to open it.

They found themselves in a small lavishly furnished parlour, an anteroom which led to a slightly larger one behind. The curtains were open and the sky outside glowed faintly with the orange hue of the city's light pollution, illuminating the room sufficiently for them to view its contents. A gilded chaise longue stood in the middle of an otherwise empty area and diaphanous drapes hung along the far end, partitioning and partially obscuring the bedroom beyond.

Tors gestured to Vidar, pointing at the wall tapestry beside the drapes.

Gingerly, Vidar lifted it to reveal the panel of the safe underneath. He grinned, laid his toolkit noiselessly on the floor and set to work.

Like a well-oiled machine, thought Marcus. Their manner suggested a familiarity that could only have come from having worked together countless of times. As Vidar laboured on, Marcus looked round the room nervously.

This is why they're the pros and I'm not. Unlike Tors and Vidar who looked as if they could be unlocking a flycycle in the park, Marcus felt distinctly ill at ease, edgy, his nerves directed particularly towards the bedroom beyond the drapes where a sleeping form nestled in the canopied bed.

A gentle rustle of the satin sheets made him stiffen. Marcus held his breath as a bare and shapely arm lifted and then settled again on top of the sheets. He breathed a sigh of relief. *The sooner this is over, the better...*

Moments later, the safe gave off a soft click. Vidar gestured at its opened door with a silent but triumphant flourish and moved aside so they could see.

Swiftly, Marcus reached for the Eldur, glowing faintly in

its dark recess, ignoring Tors' indignant glare. He was a little surprised to see the stone embedded within the form of a necklace when he pulled it out. Nevertheless, he took it and tucked it safely in his pocket. Then he motioned Vidar to close the safe and they started making their way out of the room.

"You know," Vidar said out loud suddenly, making Marcus and Tors jump. He had a strange expression on his face.

Marcus' heart sank into the pit of his stomach.

"You know," Vidar said again, looking at Tors, "you never once asked me if I wanted to go."

Marcus glanced nervously beyond the drapes.

Tors had moved towards Vidar but he raised his hand to stop her.

"You never, *ever* asked me if I wanted that ticket on the *Tethys*... a ticket out of this hell hole," he said, looking at her. "That junkie mother of yours, she'd be too stoned to even know if she's out of the Realm." His voice grew hard and bitter. "All these years of being your partner. Has that never counted for anything?"

Marcus could feel his heart pounding in his chest.

This is bad...

He looked at Vidar, trying to work out how to take him down without too much noise. They needed to do something now and quickly. Tors too, had remained silent. Marcus knew she was thinking, trying to figure out the next move too but before any of them could do anything, a cool voice arrested them.

"Now what would three strangers be doing in my quarters at such an hour?"

Marcus turned towards the smooth, provocative voice. It had come from the bedroom and he could just about discern the outline of a naked woman through the drapes, coming closer towards them. The same shapely arm he had seen moments before, parted those drapes and a tall blonde woman, breathtakingly beautiful and in complete state of undress stepped through. She did not appear the least concerned with her appearance.

Marcus looked away quickly but Vidar stood still, unabashed and transfixed. *Why doesn't he look surprised?* thought Marcus.

"Please do not try to run," the woman said composedly. "My guards will shoot if you do." As if on cue, several guards appeared noiselessly and stood behind all three of them, guns trained and at the ready.

"What the *hell* is the meaning of this?" Marcus demanded, looking at Vidar.

Vidar gave a harsh, derisive laugh. "This? *This?*" he sneered. "*This* is me looking out for myself, this is."

He let out another bitter laugh. "This is me having had enough. Enough of this stinking, dying, shit hole we live in." He looked at Tors with increasing rancour. "I tried to tell you many, many times," he said, "but you wouldn't listen. You may not want to leave the Realm, but I do. *I* do! I want to get out of here, before the whole place goes tits up and *he* ..."—he pointed at Marcus, wagging his finger energetically, his lips pursed and bitter—"he offered you a ticket! A ticket you were going to waste on that junkie! And she's not even your real mother! Well, I've managed to find my own way out of the Realm. Not only that but I shall leave in style!" Vidar looked at the naked woman, angry and panting.

She smiled at him and to Marcus' surprise, Vidar smiled back smugly.

"Tell me," the woman said to Vidar teasingly, "why should I afford you such special privileges?"

Marcus looked on with great unease. *This woman and Vidar...*

Vidar laughed with a forced easiness. "Look, I brought you the leader of the Rebellion, like I said I would. I don't think any of your boys here could have done that." He said that defiantly at first, and then with a look of entitlement in his eyes added, "Besides, we have an understanding..." He trailed off, looking at her with the expectant eyes of a pup.

The woman's eyes flicked over Vidar's face. Marcus thought they were the coldest, bluest eyes he had ever seen in his life and they glittered dangerously, sending the hairs on the back of his neck standing.

"You know," she said silkily, "where I come from, it is forbidden for commoners to consort with royals." She walked up to Vidar, extended her arms and lifted his chin so that he faced her. "But you're no ordinary commoner, are you?" she purred. "My Valerius..."

This time Vidar said nothing.

"Then again," she continued, letting her arms fall to her side and then walking languidly behind one of her guards whose gun and indeed line of sight were still trained resolutely at Vidar, "I am not one to break with tradition either..."

There was the brief look of confusion on Vidar's face as he struggled to comprehend what she meant. Then a gasp as his face contorted. He looked down and for a split second watched with surprise at the rivulet of blood running down from the neat, smoking hole in his chest. He collapsed on the floor in a heap.

NOW! Marcus' reflexes kicked in. He yanked backwards, surprising the guard behind. A second forceful stroke followed, this time his forearm, smashing down on the man's neck, snapping it like a tree branch.

At the same instant, Marcus glimpsed Tors shift position to face her captor. There was a brief glint of metal as she whipped out her dagger and drove it into his groin. But as her arm retracted, another jumped her from behind. With his right forearm clamped around her chest, his left moved to break her hold on the dagger, causing it to fall to the floor with a clang.

Tors struggled to break free.

Marcus leapt forward to help her but he wasn't quick enough. One of the guards, a freakish giant of a man, stepped in between them and knocked him back. Marcus scrabbled back on his feet as the brute advanced. He could see Tors struggling to dislodge her attackers, her hand clawed at the iron grip around her neck and her feet teetering, trying to find enough solidity to lever them off her.

She reached out towards him with her other hand. *Help me!* He could see it in her eyes.

"Get *him*!" The woman pointed at Marcus, her eyes shining with a terrible intensity. Her words seemed to propel the other guards into action.

There were too many of them. It was a lost cause.

Either I get out now or I won't. Marcus cast an anguished look at Tors, then turned, sprinted across the room and hurled himself out through the balcony window.

* * *

IT TOOK the guards barely a minute to secure the apartment along with Tors in it.

"Are you sure you don't want to go after him?" Lady Elena asked, looking up from Vidar's corpse on the carpet and then at the Emperor Akseli. There was a touch of disappointment in her voice. The evening it seemed, had not quite turned out the way she had envisaged.

Akseli stepped over the body casually. "My lady," he greeted.

Elena nodded irefully towards the smashed window. "He's one of the rebel leaders you know, "she said, picking up a robe from the chaise and slipping it on. "My little present from me to you that I hinted at yesterday. That as well as the prevention of the theft of my necklace...." The frustration and dissatisfaction in her voice was now obvious. Her plan for Akseli to foil the theft of her jewel and bag himself the leader of the Rebellion in one go had failed on both counts.

Draeger would not have failed.

However, she kept her vexations to herself as her diplomatic instincts dictated. There was no gain to be had from irking the Emperor of Ageron.

"No matter," Akseli replied, seemingly unperturbed at the loss. "The rebels are predictable as rats. I will get him and your necklace back soon enough."

"Hmm," murmured Elena, glancing at Tors, "but for now, all you have is this..."

Akseli yanked Tors towards him to examine her. "Perhaps this one has information, or would you rather I disposed of it?" He took her by the hair and pulled her close, so close his face was virtually upon hers. Then he raised his gladius and pressed its blade at her throat.

Akseli looked at the girl. She had the most startling green eyes, atypical for an Ageronian and even more surprising, she had returned his gaze without flinching. He was not used to that. Usually they crumbled and begged but this one was different. Then he felt the cold of a blade against his midsection and looked down at the sliver of a blade discreetly poised to slide between his armour plates and into his lower stomach at a moment's notice.

Akseli stiffened. *Now* that unflinching gaze made sense. Those green eyes shone with lethal potency as Akseli lowered his gladius and slowly released his hold on her.

Perhaps I won't kill her just yet, he thought, not taking his eyes off her. *Besides, she's not unattractive.*

There could be some use for her before he disposed of her. Pushing her towards his guards, he instructed to them to remove the dagger, tie her and take her away.

Lady Elena lifted an eyebrow but said nothing. "The other one," she said, indicating at the broken window, "unfortunately escaped with my necklace."

"We will retrieve it," replied Akseli. He eyed the girl again. " This one will help with the investigations," he said. "I apologise for my men's incompetence at letting that happen in the first place."

Lady Elena dismissed his apology graciously. "Your presence alone is enough, your Excellency," she said. "And thank you for your kind offer."

"Not at all," replied Akseli. He looked at her and continued, "However I will say this. Your being on Ageron soil puts you at unnecessary risk. I fear neither my brother nor I will be able to guarantee your safety should this become public knowledge."

Lady Elena assented. Even with the settlement treaties between the Houses, there were few Ellagrins in Ageron these days. "I understand, Your Excellency," she replied. "you will be pleased to know that your brother will be escorting me back tomorrow."

"My lady," nodded Akseli, satisfied, and took his leave.

THE PRIVATE PORTAL

Elena pulled at his hand as they stepped through the portal into her palace.

Draeger could tell she was glad to be back at Ellagrin, its oxygen-rich blue skies and verdant vegetation not only a calming contrast to the red, arid harshness of Ageron, but physically a welcome relief to her.

They had come through the private portal, known only to a few, including himself and Akseli. A gateway through the Ether, similar to the commercial Gateways of ages past, it was the last of its kind in the entire galaxy. It was built by his father Ageron III for Akseli's mother Queen Alin, in order that she might travel between the Red Palace on Ageron to her Summer Palace on Ellagrin with ease and in secret. Small and but a fraction of the commercial gateways, it was a extravagant endeavour which functioned only to transport no more than one or two individuals at a time.

Sadly too small to be a lifeline for the billions of our people...

"Come," beckoned Elena seductively, "stay a little while with me..."

He pulled back. "I cannot," he said firmly. "I have to return to the Palace. Akseli informs me he may have information on the whereabouts of the rebellion by tonight."

Elena laughed. "It may well take him some time to extract that information," she said a little cruelly. "Your brother likes to take his time with interrogations and I think this one, he intends to have fun with..."

Draeger looked at her. In some ways, Elena resembled his brother; they both possessed the same callous streak within them. He wondered what she knew of his brother's prisoner, and how.

Elena touched his face lightly. As if reading his thoughts she explained, "Some rebels broke into my apartment last night. I'm afraid they managed to steal my Eldur."

"I see," replied Draeger and asked, "I trust you weren't hurt?"

"No," answered Elena. "Fortunately, his Excellency was passing by and managed to capture one of them. Another was killed on the scene but the third escaped."

Draeger nodded and wondered how it was that Akseli could have chanced to pass by Elena's place at that hour. It was all too convenient.

"Yes, Akseli mentioned they were part of the Rebellion," he said. "People are getting desperate to leave Ageron and the Rebellion meddling in all this is not helping matters." He looked at her and ruminated. They had been doing this for some time now: political partners from opposing sides, negotiating behind the scenes. Dancing a delicate dance with the political fates of their two Houses hanging in the balance.

He studied her briefly and wondered what it was exactly that they had between them. Why had she helped him all these years? *If it wasn't for our joint efforts, a truce would not have been reached and the war would have continued until this day.* Her brother, Niklas, was impetuous, his temper too bilious for matters of the state.

He has his father Mikael's madness in him. Without Elena's subtle hand in tempering her brother's impulsiveness, Ellagrin would have continued down the path of war started by Mikael and into financial ruin. So was it for love or for self-preservation and personal gain? In the end, he decided it was a mutually beneficial arrangement; Elena was far too calculating for anything else.

Elena played with a strand of her golden hair, twisting it thoughtfully round one finger. "So what if the people want to leave on their own ships?" she raised. "Does it matter if some wish to take their fate in their own hands?"

Draeger's face became serious. "Because without law and order, there will be anarchy. Chaos. The strong will survive at the expense of the weak and the wealthy will monopolise our resources to build their own ships. There is already corruption across the Realm which we are trying to stamp out. The Exodus at least ensures resources are managed and the evacuation done fairly." He shook his head in frustration. "The Rebellion's activities slow our progress in building the next tranche of ships. We are having to divert our efforts in order to protect the resources used to build and furnish these ships."

"The people are worried of course," said Elena. "A perfectly normal reaction. It is natural after all for rats to leave a sinking ship."

"Yes it is," admitted Draeger, "but even if they manage to build a ship that will endure the voyage, where would they go? Without agreed settlements, they will be refugees. Or worse, if intercepted by the Ashgarians, they will be enslaved and sold like cattle."

Elena shrugged. "There is no solution without its flaws,"

she said. Her eyes flickered momentarily, "unless you find the Key of course..."

Draeger glanced sharply at her. *How much do you know about the Key?* Nothing had been uttered outside the walls of the Red Palace and with the age-old grudging truce between the two Houses, there had been no talk of the Gateways for centuries.

He thought of the work that lay ahead. *No doubt old tensions will resurface if we manage to reinstate the Lagentian Gateway.* And then there was the small matter of getting into the sealed city of Lagentia in the first place. Even this solution was fraught with danger. *How will we get in without the LON getting out? It's still alive and will kill all in its path.*

"That route may take some time,"said Draeger finally. "We have not been able to locate the Key yet," he said, his lips pursed in a grim line, "and in the meantime, I have an uprising to quell."

Turning back, he disappeared into the portal again.

TORS

The guard had shoved her into the room and locked the door with a resounding click. Tors looked around to survey the chamber.

A majestic four poster bed presided over the large room, set on a raised platform and draped in heavy velvet. Gilt-framed mirrors adorned the panelled walls and in the middle, hanging pendulously from the ceiling, was a massive red glass chandelier.

Hardly an interrogation chamber, she thought cynically to herself, looking at its lavish furnishings. The far end of the Emperor's bedchamber was far more to her liking. Dominated by a majestic-looking bank of floor-to-ceiling windows, it offered her a magnificent view of the twin suns sitting low on the horizon. Together, they cast long shafts of light into the chamber bathing everything in crimson and danced off the chandelier in a million glinting shards of blood-red brilliance.

Tors clucked with contempt as she walked round the room, examining it. Its contents were hardly inspiring, with nothing of value or interest.

'I can be cruel or conciliatory,' the Emperor had said when he instructed the guard to lock her in his bedchamber, *'but it will depend entirely on you. In fact my interrogations have been known to be quite a pleasurable experience...'*

Tors gave a scornful snort at the recollection. She was in no doubt as to what plans the Emperor had for interrogating her.

Well, I shall leave you to do all that pleasuring by yourself, she thought sardonically as she examined the windows. They were sealed shut of course and did not open, although there was no use for that anyway for beyond them stood a sheer drop of a few thousand feet into the crevasse below.

Unperturbed, Tors shifted her gaze from the chasm below to the landscape beyond. Into the horizon extended the razor-sharp peaks of mountains, their distinct outline and sheer magnitude unmistakable even to a child of the Realm. From the dizzying heights of their craggy peaks, they plunged downwards into the blackened abysses below where valleys, bone-dry and uninhabited lay in the shadows. There was only one place in all of planet Amorgos this could be. The only place with a fortress perched high in the Red Mountains.

The Red Palace.

She was a prisoner here, in a place where famously the only known way in and out was by air. However that did not worry her in the slightest.

She cast her mind back to the last few hours. *I should have seen it coming,* she thought with regret.

He was executed.

She sighed. Vidar and his women. Women were always his weakness, and he talked too much. She shuddered. *Except this time, the woman in question happened to listen...*

She trailed her fingers along the beautiful mother-of-pearl inlay of the table. On top lay a small tray littered with a few rubies glinting in the last rays of evening light. Absently, Tors picked them up and dropped them into her tunic pocket. *At least Marcus got away with the Eldur,* she told herself. That was perhaps a conciliatory outcome of the whole debacle.

She wanted to leave now, to get back to Jula, and she hoped Marcus had started getting Jula and her friends to the Tethys, to leave before things got worse. *Who knows what else Vidar divulged...*

The sound of footsteps outside wrested her back to matters at hand.

"Time to go," she said to herself and with a deep breath and a seasoned movement of her wrist, she cleaved an opening and stepped into the Ether.

* * *

LIKE A WELCOMING OLD FRIEND, the familiar cool darkness enveloped her as she walked in, and its fluid essence filled her lungs as she breathed. She felt at ease, cocooned. This was her safe place where no one else could get to her.

The transversal winds of the Ether whirled around her, pushing her this way and that. As Tors walked on, straining slightly against them, she could sense a natural endpoint somewhere ahead. Like all endpoints, it exerted a subtle tug on her subconscious. She kept an eye out for it. These naturally occurring openings out of the Ether always reminded her of holes in a rock, like small windows into other worlds.

'Vittoria, can you tell me why a natural endpoint is useful?' Mother would ask.

'Because you can exit the Ether into a world through a natural endpoint.'

'That is correct," Mother would say with a smile. 'But why is an endpoint like a one-way mirror?'

'Because, you can leave the Ether through it but you can't enter into the Ether through one.'

'That's right, good girl.'

The mechanics of the Ether was something Mother said every child should know. One could exit from the Ether into a world via a natural endpoint but there was no way you could enter the Ether through one.

'That is why we Nehisi are so important, Vitorria. We were needed to make openings ***into*** *the Ether. Did you know long, long ago, our ancestors made those openings? And then clever people like the Tilkoens built Gates to keep them open for everyone.'*

'Like the Lagentian Gate, Mother?'

'That's right, Vittoria.'

'But those Gates look different, Mother. They're bright and white! The Ether is thick and dark... like molasses.'

Mother had laughed, although in any memory of her, Tors could never quite recall Mother's actual voice or face.

'You are very clever, Vittoria,' Mother had said. *'The bright tunnel is what we call a Gateway. It joins the two Gates on each end. The Lagentian Gateway joins the Lagentia Gate here in Ageron to the Namsos Gate in Ellagrin. You see, not everyone can go in and out of the Ether like us. They need help—they need a tunnel to get from one endpoint to another. A Gateway. So the Tilkoens built one for them.'*

Like others with the 'gift', Tors had been taught how to 'coax' the Ether—to make an opening into it—in order to enter and exit the Ether without artificial Gates.

'But back to the natural endpoints, Vittoria. Like ancient travellers, Vittoria, we must learn to recognise certain endpoints from inside the Ether. Endpoints which will lead us to the places and planets we like, yes? Like the Confiserie on Ceos or the sand caves of Litore. Would you like that?'

'Yes, Mother.'

By now she could make out the dim shimmer of the endpoint she was after in the distance. It was fortunate that this one happened to be nearby.

Sometimes it took months and in many cases, years before the next endpoint was found. Even then, it could lead to a planet too far from where you wanted to be in the first place. In these cases, it was sometimes quicker to just conjure up a temporary opening at a suitable location in order to exit the Ether, although that option was not without risk, especially if one was unfamiliar with where that temporary endpoint led to.

But in this case, there was a natural endpoint close by and even more fortuitous, it was the one she was after. She could sense it. It was one she had used before and would take her to Olicana, a nearby planet, but one at least a few days' flight from the Red Palace. Far enough she decided, for by the time the Emperor sent out search teams for her, she would have disappeared into its population.

However, something seemed to be tugging at her subconscious. Something she couldn't shake off; a strange exertion which she had never felt before.

A call. Something was calling her back, *compelling* her to do so.

What by Dyaeus is this?

Tors tried to shake it off and continued on her way. But still it tugged. Like an insistent urging to go back to where she had left the Palace.

This is ridiculous. Tors tried with all her will and headed purposefully towards her endpoint but the pull could not be ignored. Reluctantly she turned back, walking until she was almost where she had started out.

There. That felt like the correct spot. The closest she would get to that tug from here.

This is madness!

She closed her eyes to check. Yes, this would take her back to the Red Palace. Back into the clutches of the Emperor.

But the pull was too insistent, so Tors took a deep breath, made an opening and stepped through it before she had time to contemplate her foolishness.

THE ORACLE

The claustrophobic feeling of the cramped corridor surprised her. She sensed she was back in the Red Palace but this time, in a different part of the place. An older section of it. It was deathly quiet and as far as she could tell, deserted as well.

Tors examined her immediate surroundings. The passageway, narrow and windowless, had very low ceilings. Flickering wall sconces cast a soft golden light against the dark panelled walls and the floor was covered with a sumptuous carpet, deep green and luxurious, muting any possibility of sound in the place.

Enveloped by thick silence, Tors started walking, guided by this strange feeling within. She had no idea where she was heading, only that she had to heed this irresistible pull she felt, and it was somehow telling her to go this way and that. The corridor led to another, and another. Every so often it would diverge into other corridors, all virtually indistinguishable from each other. She walked on, following only the strange pull she felt, her hand lightly sweeping the panelled walls as she tread noiselessly through the warren of passageways. They twisted and turned this way and that; some with steps leading to the next corridor, others simply sloping upwards or downwards. She sensed with each turn, that she was getting deeper and deeper into the bowels of the mountain.

An hour must have passed and she guessed her absence would have been discovered by now. This was madness. She should be in the Ether, away from here but try as she might to free herself from the mental pull she felt, it pressed at her even more until it became impossible to do anything but follow it. On and on she went, its intensity increasing with every step. Her head had started buzzing now, like it was filled with static. Then just before the next corner, that sensation peaked with an overwhelming hum. She staggered at the forcefulness of it and leant on the wall to steady herself.

Here. It was here, behind this wall. *But why the overwhelming urge to go towards such deafening static?* She looked for a way in.

There! A door!

With the static now screaming in her head, she fumbled blindly for the handle, turned it and stumbled in.

The moment she stepped over the threshold, it stopped.

Tors staggered in with great relief. She was in a room, lit only in the middle by a single spotlight from above. Darkness swallowed up the rest of the room, its walls and ceiling all invisible in the gloom, giving her no indication of its size. A lone stone pedestal stood in the middle, illuminated by the stark circle of light. There appeared to something on top of it. She moved closer to have a look.

And there it was.

Tors shuddered slightly. It lay suspended in mid-air, inside what looked like an oversized glass cloche. Curled up, it resembled a human foetus, wrinkled and hairless. Its eyes, thick and heavy-lidded, were closed and it looked very, very old. Ancient beyond belief and yet, resembled something born prematurely. She felt the hairs on the back of her neck stand, and she wanted to run away but again the same tug took hold of her. The same urge beckoned her to come closer. As powerless as a marionette in a dream, she lifted the cloche and reached for the creature. The instant she touched it, a jolt, intense as a thousand volts, coursed through her body. Her muscles spasmed involuntarily and for an instant, her mind, overloaded with a dazzling white brilliance, saw nothing but whiteness.

Then it stopped.

As her vision gradually came back she looked down. Its eyes, pink and liquid, had opened and it was staring at her. It spoke.

"I see you," it said, acknowledging her presence. It had a strange sing-song voice and each word it uttered seemed to rumble with great effort and weight.

Their eyes locked. Then it spoke again. "You are the last. Pity."

"What do you mean?" Tors asked.

"Nehisi. The first sentient species born of the Ether and perhaps the last." As the creature paused, she felt its strange gaze pierce through her. It was as if her entire soul were laid bare with nowhere to hide.

"*You* are the last Nehisi," it said. "You are the Key."

"The Key?"

The creature nodded almost imperceptibly. "The Key to the Gateways," it rumbled softly. "You must open them once more. To save the people of Ageron."

"I don't understand," replied Tors. "The Gateways no longer exist. They were destroyed centuries ago."

"You must open the Gateways once more," it pressed, its voice like far-off thunder, "or billions will die." The creature blinked for a second, its rheumy eyes still heavy with lassitude. "But before that, an obstacle," it said. "An unfortunate one. A pity I did not foresee it becoming sentient." Its eyes blinked independently of each other, pale and wet.

"A creature, also of the Ether," it continued. "You will have to destroy it before the Gateways can be opened. A battle..."—it looked at Tors again, its eyes strange and pressing—"Deliverance and decimation, the Ether provides the agents of both. But only one can win and the fate of all hangs in the outcome."

"What do you mean? What battle? I'm no soldier and this is not my fight," protested Tors.

The creature looked at her. Its pink unseeing eyes sought deep into her memories, probing and searching. It searched far back and deep. Images of memories buried away flicked through her mind. An image, a familiar sound, a scent. More memories: the Great Hall of Ellagrin, Jula shushing, venison, sweet molasses. Mother, her naked breasts, the tall Ellagrin and his sword.

The blood. Dripping blood.

Tors fought back at it and tried to bury it again but it was insistent. It would not have her refuse, so it continued to rifle through them. It wanted to show her something. It *needed* to show her something. And then it found it—the fleeting image of a lady-in-waiting fleeing with a vial in her arms. An egg-shaped vial containing a dark green sapling with iridescent white flowers.

"Why? Why her?" asked Tors.

"Not the female," the creature corrected, "the *seedling*."

"The *plant*?" asked Tors.

"Yes. The Light of Nehisi."

Another memory. This time not hers but the creature's. A city—deserted, crumbling and ancient. It was overgrown with creepers. Except they moved far too actively for a plant, their black tendrils twisting and writhing, engulfing everything in its path.

"What is this place?"

"Lagentia."

Tors recognised the name: Lagentia, the former capital of Ageron which had laid abandoned for centuries. So this was what the city now looked like inside. "It was sealed because of a toxic leak," she said, remembering the news in the past.

"Not a toxic leak."

A further image. A massive structure with its distinctive tessellation of hexagonal grid-like patterns.

The Hex.

The Hex was an impenetrable structure erected to seal the entire city. Inside, the creeper covered much of its surface. It was climbing it, probing, seeking.

So the Hex was built not to seal chemicals in, but to prevent this from getting out. Tors grew cold at the realisation. But the Hex was old and disintegrating, and the creeper moved and probed incessantly. A crevice, a weakness. In time, it would find a way. Tors shuddered. She felt its presence and it filled her with a sickening dread. Its leaves were dark, almost black but the flowers — the flowers were unmistakably white and iridescent.

The Light of Nehisi.

"Yes," the creature confirmed as Tors' childhood memories found their way back to the forefront of her consciousness.

The night of the Great Celebration. The Great Hall... the Great Massacre. The plant in the vial...

"The Light of Nehisi," confirmed the creature, detecting her thoughts, "but it is no longer a plant. It has evolved. It desires to return to the Ether. To spread. If it manages to do so, it will. Until everything it touches is consumed."

"How did this happen?"

"The Ellagrins engineered it as a bio weapon. A Trojan horse." It chuckled at the archaic reference. "Foolish, vain Nehisi," it continued. "Even after the massacre, they kept it, cultivated it and gifted it to each other. They did not know it contained their genetic markers. That was how they could be targeted, infected without detection."

Infected, thought Tors. So that was how within less than a decade of the Great Massacre, all surviving Nehisi died out. She hadn't known this then; she was too young to be aware of events, and besides she and Jula were in hiding on the other side of the Ageron system, on Ceos. She had looked up the old news records years later when she was older.

After the Massacre, the Nehisi had fled back to the capital, seeking the protection of Emperor Ageron III. Fearful of further attacks from the Ellagrins, he placed them under protection in Lagentia. Those who lived elsewhere relocated to the capital where they could live, guarded by its resident army.

They called it the City of Light.

Gradually, reports of infertility amongst the Nehisi began to surface. After that, the unexplained deaths. Soon, they were dying by the thousands with no apparent cause except for the fact that no other species appeared to be affected. And then the toxic leak...

"Today, that city is no longer. It bears a different name today—" said the creature.

"The City of the Dead," finished Tors. Eventually they all died. Every single one of them in that city. Even the non-Nehisi perished for the city had to be sealed along with all of its inhabitants due to the alleged toxic leak. Any Nehisi fortunate enough to have escaped died anyway, eventually. They all did. Except the only one who didn't come in contact with them or the Light of Nehisi: her.

"You must kill it," said the creature. "It is no longer a pathogen. No longer an agent that disrupts its hosts. It has become sentient and now seeks ways to procreate. If it cannot combine with a species, it will consume it. It must be stopped before it destroys all life."

An uneasy feeling of dread filled Tors. "Can't the army destroy it? Burn it? Nuke it?"

"They have tried over the years. And failed."

"But this is not my fight." Tors recoiled from the image. "I want no part of this. Besides, it is contained. It cannot escape the Hex."

The creature closed its eyes. There was weariness in its nuance. "Some battles you do not get to choose," it said. "You must kill it. No one else can because it is a creature of the Ether, as are you."

"I am nobody. I'm not a soldier and I'm not even Ageronian. And I can't fight something like that..." The image haunted her. It was alien, monstrous. Her stomach churned.

"You are Nehisi. He will teach you."

"Who's he?"

"He who found you, Vittoria."

Tors froze at the mention of her old name. "What do you mean?" she pressed. "Who? Who has found me?"

The creature ignored her questions. "You must not fail," it said. "Destroy it, then open the Gates. Save them, before it is too late."

Visions of continents burning filled her mind. The twin suns collapsing. The planets spiralling out of control. Billions and billions of Ageronians perishing.

"Save them…," it whispered. The creature withdrew, its thick eyelids flickering blindly for a second before closing in slumber once more. Gradually it began to curl back into a ball, retracting tighter and tighter until only the tips of its hairless toes showed.

In her mind too, she could feel its presence receding, like a fading mist, until it was no more.

"Wait!" Tors exclaimed, dropping the cloche she had been holding all this time. It hit the floor with a resounding crash and smashed into a thousand pieces, but the creature remained inert, suspended in mid-air.

Then sounds of scuffling outside the door brought her back to the present.

Guards! They were trying to break the door down.

"Now would be a good time to leave,"muttered Tors to herself and made ready to cleave an opening for herself. She felt the air in front of her quiver. And then nothing. She tried again and once more, nothing.

This has never happened before, she thought to herself panicking. And then the mental static returned. She pressed her hands to her ears in futile attempt to block it out. The static had picked up again as soon as the creature fell back into unconsciousness and like a crescendo rippling through her mind, this mental interference clouded her mind, preventing her from opening the portal.

She let out a low curse as the sound of guards trying to break the door down punctured through the static. Tors hastened to the opposite end of the room. In the dim light she could just about make out its circular shape and its walls comprising a series of arched alcoves.

There has got to be an exit somewhere. There just has to be! Fumbling hurriedly, she pressed her palms against the wall, following it and feeling her way as she checked quickly from left to right. She continued her examination, fingers hastily tapping away at the smooth recesses of each alcove until suddenly her fingers pushed into thin air.

Her hunch had paid off! A passageway cleverly hidden in plain sight behind a dark illusory trompe l'oeil of an alcove!

Behind, the door flew open with a resounding crash. Tors whirled round. A flurry of red cloaks filled the doorway. And just as the guards entered, an arm reached out from behind Tors and pulled her into the shadows.

LIZARD MAN

"This way!" hissed the figure urgently as Tors' eyes darted about trying to see who it was. It was too dark to make out anything except what resembled a brief gesture beckoning her to follow.

Who by Dyaeus is this? The one who finds me? The one that creature mentioned? Do I follow? Should I?

But there was no time, no alternative, and besides her head was spinning with the static, so Tors followed and they slipped silently through the hidden passageway whilst the guards searched the room.

They ran down the low corridor and after a while, Tors noticed its panelled walls cease and join to rock in the form of an underground tunnel. Behind, she could make out the shouts and sounds of the guards hot on their heels. *They must have found the hidden passageway!*

Onwards they continued, quickly and noiselessly, ever descending, until at last the tunnel opened up into a cavernous gallery bathed in sunlight. It was a natural cave, eroded over millennia, and in its middle sat a hyperglider.

"Quickly," the figure urged as they hastened into it.

"Who are you?" Tors demanded.

"There isn't time. Strap yourself in," he ordered, rapidly initiating take off. Tors felt the ship hum and vibrate as it started up.

Moments later it lifted off.

Tors looked out of the window towards the platform they'd just left, fast diminishing in the distance. Several figures were running onto it now, and she could just about make out their red cloaks. A minute slower and they would not have made it.

SHE TURNED her attention to the man next to her manoeuvring the ship. There was not much that she could determine; the vizard that obscured his face would almost certainly have altered his voice digitally as well.

He wore a typical Ageronian soldier's outfit: long sleeved tunic and fitted bottoms in standard black which clothed a lean, muscular physique. The long red cloak of the guards' uniform covered the rest of him. He was tall and as she soon found out, rather terse.

They had now left the exosphere and were making their way through space. Tors glanced curiously at him. "Where are we going?" she asked.

"Casar," came the reply.

"Casar?" she asked. "Why?"

Casar was the backwater of the Red Realm, known rather less salubriously as the Hovel of Ageron for it was as backward and as it was impoverished. There had always been nothing of note on Casar, apart from their desalination plants and a handful of outposts, even in the Age of Prosperity.

"You will be safe there," he replied.

Safe? What does he mean by that? Besides, I don't need your help to be 'safe'. Tors waited to hear more but he said no more to elucidate. She surveyed her companion critically. Obviously a man of few words and ordinarily a trait she welcomed except this time she had questions. Lots of them.

"Why are you masked?"she asked, breaking the silence.

"I work for the Emperor," came the reply. "It would not do for anyone to know my identity."

"Who *are* you?"

"An ally," the stranger replied turning to face her. His featureless vizard gave nothing away.

It struck Tors how Vidar must have felt over the years. "What do you mean?" she asked. "And what do you want from me?"

"I have been looking for you for some time," he said. "You awoke the Oracle."

"The Oracle?" Tors blinked. "You mean that... *thing* back there?"

He nodded. "That 'thing'," he said, "has been asleep for over two centuries. No one has ever been able to awaken it, and the few who tried have paid the price."

"What do you mean?"

"Those who have touched the being have either died or become mad. The Oracle possesses knowledge so infinite that all who come into contact with it will succumb one way or another."

He shook his head in disbelief. "That is what I had been led to believe. Until now." He continued to face her, saying nothing further for the moment.

In the absence of any visible facial expressions, Tors guessed that he was staring intently at her.

Then he sat forward suddenly, and asked interestedly, "It talked to you. What did it say?"

Tors looked at him and wondered. He seemed to know a lot about the creature. Was he a member of the royal household? Was he with the Emperor? Her conversation with the Oracle remained fresh in her mind but she wasn't sure if she wanted to share it with this stranger. Who was he and could he be trusted?

But he didn't wait for her answer. Instead he continued, muttering to himself, "The Oracle waking up can only mean that the time is near. We must prepare."

"Prepare what?"

"Prepare you," he said as he turned back to steer the ship. "To fight."

"Fight? Why would I be needed to fight? I'm not a soldier," said Tors. The Oracle mentioned a teacher. Was this him? This made no sense. She contemplated making her escape. Yet something niggled; there was something familiar about him.

"Well, they say the female of the species is deadlier than the male," he said, "so perhaps you'll be up for the task."

The phrase shot through her system like a bolt of lightning. Tors froze. It was a phrase she had not heard since she was a child.

It's him.

As if he too sensed it, he turned to face her again.

"Hello Vittoria, we meet again," he said stretching out his gloved hand. "I don't believe we were ever properly introduced, even before. My name is Hostus, at your service."

"It's you!" breathed Tors. "*Lizard Man.*"

Hostus nodded a little doubtfully. "If that helps with the association, ye-es. Although I hope, the name… that was merely a childish impression at the time?"

Tors nodded, flushing slightly. Lizard Man was her nickname for him when she was a child growing up on the streets of Ceos and he certainly didn't look very lizard-like to her now. She wondered why she'd nicknamed him thus in the first place.

"I don't understand," she said. "How were you in the Red Palace? How did you know?"

"Some of us have been waiting for your arrival," he said. His voice sounded a little different. Probably the vizard's vocalisers, but the tilt of his head as he talked and the way his expressionless vizard pointed at her direction when he spoke was unmistakable.

Lizard Man.

So Lizard Man's name, all this time, was Hostus.

"The Oracle has never been wrong but it has been difficult to locate you, especially with the Emperor looking for you at the same time." He sighed. "After you took off, I looked for you. For years. For a while, I thought all was lost." He shook his head in disbelief. "All these years I looked and all this time... I never realised you and the mighty Prometheus were one and the same."

"I don't understand..."

"You will, soon," replied Hostus. "There is much you have to know and learn. You have been off the radar for so long."

Tors regarded him thoughtfully. "Hostus," she repeated the name he mentioned to her slowly, trying to remember the past. *I don't think we parted on good terms.* She tried to recall what'd happened except it was so very long ago; almost two centuries ago to be precise and much of that had been a blur.

"I prefer to be called Tors if you don't mind," she added. *The Vittoria I used to be died a long time ago.*

Hostus nodded. "As you wish," he replied.

VILLA CASTRA

They flew on for the next two weeks, crossing much of the entire length of the Ageron system and taking care not to stop at the bigger planets of Ilia, Olicana and Othon in order to avoid detection.

Once or twice Tors thought to bail out on him. *I have after all, fared just fine without him all these years,* she thought to herself. *And what about Jula? I need to get back to her to make sure Marcus keeps his end of the bargain.* But somehow, something kept her there. Curiosity perhaps. It certainly wasn't sentimentality and besides, she finally remembered the last time they parted and why she was still angry with him.

Towards the final leg of their journey, after having made a brief stop at Deva to appear as if they were trading supplies, Casar, the farthest planet in the Realms blinked into existence upon the ship's display. Security clearance on entering Casar's airspace was minimal as could be expected of the backwater planet.

The ship skimmed the surface of Casar's vast ocean and headed west until it reached Salinae, one of the few outposts along the western coast of the continent. Tors had a look at the brief description of Casar from the ship's data. It was a peculiar planet, consisting of only one continent covering about two percent of its total surface area and a few million small islands scattered about its vast ocean.

The only planet in all of Ageron with an abundance of water, noted Tors but not without irony, for its water was too chemically concentrated to be detoxified and desalinated easily. *Water, even if purified, would sadly be too far to be shipped to the planets that needed it most.*

"Salinae," said Tors as the name flashed up on screen. "Can't say I've ever been to that town before."

"We're not going there," said Hostus. As he said that, the ship banked right and sped on over the town.

From the cockpit, Tors could see the terracotta rooftops of the township's residences, sitting short and squat below them. There were no skyscrapers in Salinae or anywhere else on the planet for that matter. A small, lacklustre outpost, all Salinae had were some facilities for storing grain and goods and a few plants for processing the ocean water for local consumption.

Eventually even these squat dun-coloured buildings diminished into the distance behind them. The dusty roads that carved each neighbourhood into neat little squares gradually lost their grid-like rigidity towards the outskirts of the town, engulfed by sand dunes which heaped around its edges, towering over the town like waves suspended in motion, waiting for the day when Nature would reclaim the town.

It's no wonder no one wants to move here. Casar may be the farthest planet from the suns but it's still a dump. With no natural water, no cultivatable land and no resources, Casar's climate was one of extremes. Its vast continent, hot and arid, seemed as torrid and unforgiving as the Emperor himself.

On and on they flew across the breadth of the continent

until at length, the darkening expanse of the ocean reappeared below. Here, small islands dotted the sea, sparkling like shiny hard sequins scattered carelessly by a child. And there were many; Casar had millions and millions of little islands, spread over its vast ocean, virtually uncharted and all too small and craggy for habitation.

How ironic, mused Tors. Unlike its large, flat continent, these tiny, jagged islands were covered with rich vegetation. It was as if Dyaeus himself had decided, in a wicked stroke of irony, to bless these small snatches of land, too small to be of any use, with fertile soil instead of its single largest landmass —the continent.

Tors stared out the window. They were heading towards the island ahead. This looked no different to the thousands they had passed before but as their ship approached, Tors could see that despite its jagged peaks the island was fairly large.

Probably wide enough to fit a town comfortably within it, if only it were flatter. They were headed towards a particularly treacherous looking mountain face with no hint of slowing down or changing course.

We're going to crash headlong into it!

However, before she had the chance to say anything, the ship banked sharply and she found herself staring at a long, thin crevasse, cleverly camouflaged by the ridges of the mountain.

"Hold on," said Hostus and with barely a second's warning, the ship teetered on its side and slipped through the crack.

Moments later, a tiny landing platform, hewn out of rock appeared and the ship touched down lightly inside the mountain.

"Welcome," said Hostus jumping out to stretch his legs. "Welcome to the island Caecus."

* * *

THEY WALKED out of the ship into a vast cavern. The landing had been carved out from the mountain itself and light streamed down in long, thin shafts from skylights formed out of natural fissures and cracks in the rocks above. From these apertures, light from the red suns poured in, forming pools of crimson on the concourse below.

Like a cathedral drenched in blood, thought Tors a little dramatically to herself.

"Come," said Hostus, leading the way from the landing and into the mountain itself.

They walked through a series of interconnecting tunnels, vestiges of erosion by waterways now long gone. These wound their way inwards, ever deeper, sometimes with a gentle incline, other times sloping so steeply that Tors nearly lost her footing. Every now and again the faint sound of trickling water could be heard—an underground spring perhaps—but otherwise, the tunnels seemed to go on forever, frequently branching into other tunnels as was the natural state of the terrain.

Another Red Palace, thought Tors to herself. Perhaps one of a smaller scale but a hidey-hole in the mountains no less. She had quite enough of hidey-holes inside mountains. It seemed to her that anyone who lived inside of a mountain was bad news but as she had no plans to go anywhere just yet and orders for her arrest would have no doubt been issued far and wide across the Realm by now, it was probably just as well she stayed here for the time being. At any rate, she was curious to see what would happen next.

As they turned the corner, the tunnel opened out onto a glade. Tors gave a little gasp as her eyes widened to drink in the unexpected vista of green.

I have not seen such greenery since I was a child!

Few planets in the Red Realm bore any luxuriant vegetation and in such abundance. Tors had never seen anything as lush and as verdant as this in her entire adult life. Perhaps Casar being furthest from the suns was a contributing factor. They were in a large clearing, a good three acres at least, flanked on all sides by the near vertical walls of mountain rock that towered high above them. Like a fortress wall, these had no doubt helped sustain the glade by sheltering it from the dry winds and harsh rays of the suns.

Nestled in the middle amongst several wizened olive trees was a Roman villa surrounded by well tended gardens, complete with fountain and decorative waterways.

Just like the stories of our ancestors from Rome in Old Earth. It was the most beautiful, surreal thing she had ever seen.

Hostus led her, still speechless, up to the house and into the main atrium.

Elegant columns lined its periphery, with living quarters leading off from its four sides. Tors stood in its centre, where a fountain of white marble tinkled, and leapt at the open sky above.

"There will be time enough to explore further," Hostus interrupted, "but for now, this is Villa Castra, where you will eat, sleep and train."

Tors gave Hostus a look. "Train?" she said warily. She vaguely remembered him teaching her a few combat skills all those years ago.

"*Now*," exclaimed Hostus suddenly and reached for his sword, "let us see what you're made of!" He drew it so swiftly that she did not see it, but heard the blade hiss as it left its scabbard.

Reflexes kicked in and Tors arched backwards just in time to avoid the steel from slicing her head off. *Just like old times.*

Except she wasn't a child anymore and he wasn't play fighting with her either.

I'm going to have to defend myself if I am to live to see what the toilet here in Villa Castra looks like...

Hostus swung round and from behind the pillar knocked her bodily to the floor.

She rolled to the side as his blade came crashing down, chipping the mosaic floor and missing her by millimetres. Tors moved next. From her supine position, she kicked outwards, striking at the heel of his boot and knocked him off his feet.

He landed on the floor with a thump. It was a good move, but served only to buy her a second or two's respite at most. Hostus was quick and his swordsmanship sharper and deadlier than she remembered. She needed a weapon and fast.

She ran down the corridor, flinging whatever at hand behind her in order to bar his way as much as possible. A tall standing vase came crashing down as she tipped it over, as did a carved planter. Ahead she espied an array of spears mounted on a stand and skidded to a halt in front of them, nearly slipping on the smooth floor tiles.

How apt for a Roman villa.

She fervently hoped they were the real thing. *If these turn out to be home accessories, I'm as good as dead.*

Ripping the first spear from its mount, she hurled it at Hostus, aiming squarely at his torso so that he had to slide sideways to avoid it. The spear narrowly missed its mark and hit the floor with a heavy clang.

Not an accessory then—excellent!

Grabbing the next spear, she whirled round to face him again. Now came the second assault, this time in full force. Tors met his sword head on with her spear, grunting as the momentum amplified the sheer power of his strike. An instant later, came an unexpected spring backwards by Hostus, completely throwing her off balance. She fell forward, arms flailing clumsily in front, in attempt to reign in her balance quickly but she was fractionally too late.

Crouched forward and on her knees, the tip of his blade rested on her back, pointed elegantly downwards, straight as an arrow and poised between her shoulder blades.

Tors remained motionless in her position, still bent forward, trying to catch her breath.

Hostus retracted his sword with a derisive snort and slipped it back in its scabbard with hardly a trace of exertion.

"Amateurish," he announced, as if to no one in particular. "Although," he went on, "it could have been worse. *That* could have ended up the shortest tutelage in the history of Ageron."

Tors could have sworn he was smirking underneath that expressionless vizard of his.

PART VI

METAMORPHOSES

TRAINING

And so began her training with the veritable master Hostus. The weeks that followed were regimented, relentless. A gong would chime at the crack of dawn, signalling the beginning of the day and the commencement of her fitness training.

Hostus had fashioned her a running route.

The grounds of the villa, Tors discovered, extended to well beyond the glade it resided in. Beyond, concealed by a swathe of forest were several orchards, some fields and a lake.

Starting with the path that wound round the orchards, she would sprint past the millet fields, through the forest, free-climb up the crag, then race along the jagged mountain ridge that surrounded the estate before doubling back to complete the circuit via the path by the lake.

Her 'morning run' would end just before breakfast which was served in the dining room at precisely the same time each day. This meant Tors had to complete her circuit in time or miss it completely, as exactly half an hour later without fail, breakfast would be cleared, regardless of whether it had been touched or not.

Like all other meals in the villa, breakfast was delivered by the villa's servitors—a set of hoverbots which acted as a physical extension of *Servis*, the villa's central AI. These were smallish airborne mechanical assistants which essentially looked and performed as hovering gloved hands. Initially, Tors found them disconcerting to look at—bodiless gloves fetching things and bringing them meals—but she soon got used to them.

Breakfast itself was simple but good, consisting of bread, millet porridge and thick, black *kofi*. A brief rest was allowed post breakfast, after which came sword practice, followed by unarmed combat in the form of hybrid martial arts.

Finally, the morning session would end with shooting practice before breaking for lunch. An hour's meditation provided a paltry period of rest, and training would resume in the form of street fighting, weapons practice and agility training.

All without break until nightfall.

It was a gruelling schedule and a brutal one. And for the first two weeks, Tors crawled exhausted into bed at the end of each day and slept as if she were dead to the world.

* * *

"UP!" COMMANDED Hostus as his longspear lashed down towards her crouched figure. They had been training for some weeks now and Tors was beginning to get accustomed to Hostus' harsh methods.

There was no time to get back up to her feet so she rolled to the side just as it came whistling down, barely missing her head.

"Up!" he ordered again, this time retracting the spear and then thrusting it directly at her so she had no choice but to counter or be stabbed.

Tors let out a frustrated yell and yanked her sword across to block. It took all of her strength to get it between the oncoming spear and her torso in time.

"*Get up,*" growled Hostus as the spear flew to the side after meeting her blade. In an instant, his sword was out, barely before she had time to clock the fact that he'd already moved on from spear practice. The blade came swinging round in an elegant arc, aimed perfectly to take her head off.

Tors let out another scream, scrambled to her feet and met the blow head-on with her sword, this time held tightly with both hands in order to withstand the force of his strike. The clang of metal echoed into the distance, bouncing off the surrounding mountain of rock.

"*Wait!*" she called out in protest. Sweat dripped down her nose as she rested half-bent, her hands on her knees. "Time out..." she gasped, trying to catch her breath.

Hostus stood up straight and paused whilst Tors glanced up at him, arms aching and panting like a dog.

He's going to carry on, she thought with dread but surprisingly he didn't. He merely stood there, expressionless behind his vizard and stared at her.

He thinks I'm a pitiful excuse for a fighter, thought Tors, still half crouched and wheezing in exhaustion.

Hostus reached for his water bottle and stood by the side, drinking in silence.

Tors noted with resentment that he didn't look or sound out of breath at all. Not for the first time did she wonder why she didn't just leave. Unlike Marcus, there was no collateral involved, no Jula held as a pawn. Besides, the memory of the Oracle was fading like a dream.

I could just as easily pretend all this never happened at all. Slip out through the Ether, start a new life elsewhere. She closed her eyes. She could leave if she wanted. Anytime. And no one could stop her.

Hostus cleared his throat to get her attention. "We start again," he said, curt and business-like.

Tors opened a tired eye to look at him. "It may be *your* mission to save the people of this Realm but it's not necessarily mine," she said.

She recalled the people she and Jula encountered over the years. Landlords, shopkeepers, law enforcers. None of them cared. *They all left the likes of Rat-Boy, the gangs and dealers to prey on us whilst every other passer-by looked the other way.* Her mouth hardened into a thin line. "Why should I save them?" she asked Hostus. "Some people don't deserve to be saved."

"Perhaps so," agreed Hostus, "but they all don't deserve to die. Now straighten up!" He swung his sword impatiently, decided she hadn't snapped into attention sufficiently, and proceeded to lunge forward in attack.

"Is this really necessary?" protested Tors, leaping to her feet and deflecting with her sword. "If I'm to fight this LON creature, shouldn't I be training with something a little more powerful like array blasters or pulse launchers? Anything more than just my two bare hands?"

Hostus' only reply was a sharp strike at her with his sword.

Tors moved to block but his unexpected blow loosened her grip and her sword fell to the ground with a clumsy clatter.

"Electrical devices don't work in the Ether," Hostus said. He kicked her sword back to her with a scornful snort. "This is *basic* training," he said. "Training you were meant to have done if you hadn't walked away from me all those years ago in a childish tantrum. Because of that, we have years of training to make up for. Now pick your sword up and *continue*!"

Tors' only reply was a frustrated yell before kicking her sword up into her hand again to resume their parry. "You know, you're still the same old asshole I remember," she said, lashing at him angrily.

His blade darted to meet hers. Their swords clashed as she parried and swore at him. "*Canem testiculis*!"

Damn you Hostus and your standards. When it came to the art of fighting, he seemed as obsessed as ever in his pursuit for perfection. *It was as if I'd never left.*

Hostus moved backwards, letting her advance in her anger. Then he spun around, aimed his sword at her side, and brought it down hard. It slashed at her shoulder.

"Where were you all those years?" he demanded to know. The blade caught the side of her arm, sharp and painful. A line of blood trickled down. Whilst his blows were not at full force, Hostus always made contact with his blade. He liked to make sure she remembered the cost of each slip up.

"Couldn't find me, could you?" she mocked as she flipped her sword from her injured hand to the other and hit back, this time from the opposite side, disorientating him just a little and forcing him to adjust his stance. Her lips pursed with satisfaction with the remark.

"Karl said he never saw you again. Even when Jula came back to look for you."

Their blades clashed.

Clang! Clang! Clang!

The sound of each blow echoed into the surrounding wall of rock in the distance.

Tors gave a derisive snort. "I never went back to Karl's," she said.

"Not even to his funeral?"

Tors stopped short.

Hostus struck her with the back of the hilt .

She didn't block this time and it landed smack on her face, high on her cheek. She didn't retaliate. *Karl's dead??*

Tors stood in stunned silence. "I didn't know he died,"she said after a pause. She looked at Hostus. It wasn't just her cheek that hurt. "When and how?"

"About ten years after you left," replied Hostus, throwing in one last swing at her which she blocked this time. "They said he tried to stop a brawl in his pub."

He lowered his sword and gave a grunt of regret. "Word was he got in the way of a shortsword."

Hostus stopped to signal the end of their session and tossed her her water bottle. "After I gave up waiting around Karl's, I looked everywhere," he said. "Old neighbourhoods, new neighbourhoods, neighbouring districts, workhouses, every planet, everywhere. But you had vanished into thin air."

Tors put her head back and glugged half the bottle in one swig.

"So where did you disappear to?" asked Hostus. He said that casually but she could tell he was curious. Besides, he'd spoken more to her in the last few minutes than he ever did in all of the past put together. Proof enough that this was something the normally taciturn Lizard Man *really* wanted to know.

Tors sat down on the bench and reached for her satchel. From its side pocket, she fished out a small battered old disc, turned it over and switched it on. The holo projection of letters swirled upwards into the air above her outstretched hand.

"The Lex Dogma," sighed Hostus, recognising the words and sat down heavily beside her.

"...the Imperial soldier's handbook!" They said it in unison.

Tors gave a soft hmmmph as the holo switched from

words to an image of army barracks. "I wanted to be a Red, you know" she said, "just like you. So I joined the army for a bit."

Hostus turned to look at her. Despite the blankness of his vizard, she could sense his disbelief.

"Yes," she replied, nodding her head. "I joined the Reds."

"How?" he asked. "The physicals, the checks—they would've known you were female."

"I didn't sign up," Tors said. "I just took someone's place."

"You *what*?!"

Tors nodded. "His name was Balbus and he liked to drink."

She looked at the trees in the distance and continued: "He liked to drink a *lot*." She shrugged. "And he was a loner. No women, no family, no friends. There was the added plus in that he wore his vizard all the time. Not standard army dust-storms but one like yours. To hide his burn scars, you see."

She leant back and continued. "We played cards sometimes. Then one night, he fell dead."

Hostus gave a surprised snort. "Fell. Dead?"

"Yup. Fell dead," she said matter-of-factly. "Just like that. Face down. Dead. Right into his cards too." She glanced at Hostus and continued. "He probably had too much to drink. Balbus wasn't exactly fit and healthy so I guess that finally did him in. It was the perfect cover for me to step into, so I took his place. I became Balbus."

There was a brief pause as Hostus took it all in. "Which legion were you in?" he then asked.

Tors stared at him. *By Dyaeus, we're practically having a conversation,* she thought mildly astounded. This was the most she had ever known Hostus to say in one go.

"Legio IX Valeria at Ilia," she answered. "Then about six months later, we were transferred to Othon under Lord Reku, one of the few Praetors who, as you know, is also Legati. But I didn't like his Lordship's attitude so after a year, I decided I had had enough and walked off."

"So you deserted the army," stated Hostus. He sounded terribly unimpressed.

Tors cocked an eye at him. "*Balbus* deserted the army," she corrected.

Hostus responded with a displeased grunt.

Tors shifted uncomfortably. *Does he find it contemptible that I left the army? Surely he can't possibly be angry with that. Technically speaking, I hadn't really signed up—I was pretending to be Balbus!*

"I guess I decided that the Reds weren't as honourable as I originally thought," she replied bluntly. It was true. In the days after the war when when everything was scarce, it was every man for himself, Imperial soldier or not. "When it came to times of hardship, they were the same as other people really," she said simply, recalling the chaos that ensued after the war and what people did just to survive.

"So you went back to stealing?"

Tors nodded. "I fell into it by accident really. Some Lady needed help to steal her lordship's jewels back from his mistress, and I guess it went from there." She chuckled. "Ah, the allure of a mysterious *casanove*. Women go mad for that kind of shit." She waggled her eyebrows and grinned, "I believe Lady Valentina still has the hots for *Prometheus* after all these years..."

She glanced at Hostus, expecting more questions but he said nothing more. Instead he packed up and headed for the villa.

Tors picked herself up and trudged on after him. They made their way to the dojo for the next session. There, Tors began to prepare when Hostus stopped her.

"We'll try something different now," he said.

Tors arched an eyebrow.

He looked at her and nodded, expressionless as ever. "This time," he said, "we train in the Ether."

THE ETHER

"The Ether?" repeated Tors blankly. She could sense him smile beneath his impassive vizard.

"Yes, we're going to train in the Ether," he said. "Of course, I cannot enter it without your assistance." He gestured for her to go before him, "Please..."

Tors gave him a wary look. *What, enter the Ether?*

In the past, despite his knowledge of her and the Ether, Hostus had never ever asked to enter it. She gave him a are-you-sure look and when it looked like he wasn't going to back down anytime soon, she heaved a resigned sigh, cleaved an opening into the Ether and in they both stepped.

Like a familiar blanket, the cool darkness enveloped her. She breathed in deeply, letting the viscous Ether permeate her lungs. To many, the sensation would have been fairly unpleasant, akin to drowning, but for Tors it felt as comfortable and safe as a foetus cocooned in a mother's womb. She turned to check on Hostus. He stood behind her, his cloak rippling in the usual crosswinds of the Ether. If he was uncomfortable in this environment, it certainly didn't show.

Hostus let a few minutes pass in order for them to adjust to the dimness of their surroundings before producing from the folds of his cloak, a small round object.

A *pomum,* an apple-like fruit, from the villa's orchard.

Next, he took out a small flamethrower.

An ancient relic. Why? It took Tors a second or two before she remembered. *Mechanical gadgets. Of course!* Because nothing electrical worked in the Ether. *Plus these devices come with their own cache of oxygen and fuel mix.*

Throwing the pomum in the air ahead of him, Hostus fired at it, incinerating it instantly. This occurred in total silence for the Ether carried no sound. Reaching into his cloak again, he produced a second pomum and then, making a crushing gesture, signalled for Tors to do the same and destroy the fruit.

Tors looked at him frustratedly. *And how by Dyaeus do I do that? Without a bloody flamethrower!* Then she realised what she had to do. Somewhere in the depths of her memory, something stirred. Vague remnants of an old memory.

Remember Vittoria, the Ether is but an extension of us. We can shape it, coax it, control it. Mother's words…

It took a great deal of concentration. At first, she managed to hold the fruit in mid-air but not destroy it, although she meant to. Trying to effect some tangible 'hold' on the Ether was much trickier than just the quick cut to cleave an opening into it. She had to concentrate on 'locating' the Ether in order to mold it. It was like having to think of it as something with body, with substance.

Like feeling for the solid presence of air.

The second try was only marginally better. She managed to coax a small ball of flame but it petered out before she could direct it towards anything useful.

Again, signalled Hostus, throwing her another pomum.

Again Tors tried. Firstly, to hold the small object, then to channel the incandescent force of the Ether at it. This time, she failed at both and the pomum fell to the ground.

Hostus picked it up and threw it at her. *Again,* he urged.

Again, she failed but Hostus would not stop, repeating the action again and again until Tors no longer had the energy to stand upright. By the time he finally called it a day and they returned to the villa, it was already dark and the stars had come out. Tors fell into bed, exhausted and drained.

The very next day Hostus made her repeat the same thing again. Then the next. And the next.

Over and over again.

Day followed night, and sometimes day followed day, for when they exited the Ether, the skies were lit in a soft blush, harking the arrival of dawn of the next day.

Why by Dyaeus am I doing this? Tors asked herself for the umpteenth time. *Is this really my fight? And did anything good ever come of putting oneself out there to help others?*

The days crept on and whilst countless attempts yielded no success, yet Hostus would not relent. If anything things were turning hellish with him taking her already punishing training sessions to almost sadistic levels. It began to dawn on Tors the difficulty of her task ahead. It seemed impossible. To be able to destroy an object, even one as small as a pomum would mean she would have to somehow tap into the Ether's energy and manifest it in its raw form.

But how by Dyaeus am I supposed to do this? There were no instructions and no historical accounts of this feat. Indeed with nothing to go on, how could she hope to accomplish such a task?

But Hostus would not hear of her excuses. Instead, he pushed on mindlessly, making her repeat her efforts and ignoring her pleas for rest until she felt she could not endure it any longer.

* * *

"I NEED to take a short leave of absence," Tors said as they sat down to dinner after yet another long day's training. "To see Jula—"

"No," Hostus cut her short.

Tors let her fork fall back into the plate with a clatter. "But I haven't seen her for months now. I don't know if she's dead or alive. Or if they've turned her over to the authorities." She wondered if Marcus would actually do that. *He'd better honour his part of the bargain,* she thought. *After all, he did get away with the Eldur.*

Hostus shook his head. "No. You're halfway through your training. We cannot afford distractions."

"But my training has improved—"

"No it hasn't," snapped Hostus, "and as for the Ether..." He jabbed his food critically with his fork.

"But it's only for a day," protested Tors. "I know I still have much to learn but a few hours won't change anything. I can get to Amorgos via the Ether. It will be faster and I shall be back within the day. I *promise* I will be careful."

"*No,*" Hostus said, adamant. "It's too risky. You'll be spotted the moment you set foot on any of the planets, especially Amorgos. *No,* finish your training, then we shall see. Jula will be all right."

"But—"

Hostus held his hand up to silence her.

Tors flung her napkin onto her uneaten plate and left the table.

* * *

THE FOLLOWING days were spent training mostly in the Ether. To make matters worse, Hostus had taken to conducting all their hand to hand combat sessions within the Ether as well, firstly because the Ether's viscosity demanded much more effort in movement and secondly, its disconcerting darkness tested her instinct.

To Tors' annoyance, neither posed any visible disadvantage to Hostus' reflexes nor manoeuvrability during combat. In fact, he seemed to thrive fighting in the gloom of the Ether. Depressingly, she also realised Hostus was right, for neither her mastery of the Ether nor her combat skills were at the level they needed to be.

But I still need to see Jula.

It had been months now and it worried her, not knowing if Jula was still safe with Marcus or if indeed she was still with his people. *Besides, I'm getting nowhere with mastering the Ether,* she thought to herself despondently, *so what's a couple of hours lost anyway?*

That afternoon, they faced each other in the gloom of the Ether, circling: Hostus with dagger in hand and Tors unarmed. The objective of the exercise was a simple one. It was for her to disarm him.

He moved first, thrusting the dagger at her chest.

She side stepped, avoiding the blade. It had swung so close she felt the ripple of its passing in the Ether. She brought her body back up and aimed for a punch into his side but as always, Hostus seemed to anticipate her every move.

He deflected the blow easily with a casual downward jab and because she had left herself open, landed a punch squarely at her temple.

She crumpled at the blow.

Hostus waved her up impatiently. *Again,* he gestured and lunged at her once more.

This time she ducked and tried to grab the dagger off him but her feet gave way from under her – he had booted her in the knee pit. An instant later, the dark of the Ether loomed, slamming her in the face. Tors let out a scream in silent frustration which was duly swallowed up by the Ether. Before she could get up, Hostus had leapt onto her.

Straddling her, he forced her head back with his hands. Back and back until she thought her neck would snap. He stopped just before that point and held her there. His masked face stared impassively at her.

Despite that she felt his derision burning into her.

Then, *Up,* he signalled, releasing his hold on her.

This session was getting from bad to worse. Not only was she unable to snatch the weapon off him, she wasn't even countering his strikes, neither blocking nor avoiding them. She looked with increasing despair at Hostus. She knew what he was thinking. *How am I supposed to defeat the LON if I can't even defeat a single soldier in close combat?*

Scrambling back to her feet, she spun right, made a grab for Hostus' dagger, missed, then whirled to the side. Her mind whirled too. *How can I stay here training when I don't even know what's happened to Jula? Marcus may have thrown her out for all I know. I should never have left her there.*

Hostus stabbed at her direction but missed.

Tors resumed her stance and faced him once more, well aware that she was tiring faster than he was. She eyed the dagger in his hand, so tantalisingly close.

I have to snatch it now, she thought, conscious the session was coming to an end soon, affirming her dismal fail if she didn't succeed in its one simple objective.

Hostus held the dagger loosely in his hand waiting for her

next move, transferring it impatiently from one hand to the other whilst tilting his head ever so patronisingly at her.

Now! She leapt forward, hand outstretched, eagerly reaching for the dagger.

Too eagerly.

He floored her almost immediately.

Stupid! she cursed herself. *That move was too open to ever work!* Swiftly, she picked herself up and went in for it again.

SLAM! The length of his arm pounded her to the ground.

Tors fell, stunned, the wind knocked out of her.

No! She got up again, livid at how easy he had her, and charged at him.

SLAM! Again Hostus evaded her grab for his blade, then swung out, pulled her outstretched arm towards him.

Her balance out of kilter, Tors fell face-down once more.

No! No! No! She punched at the ground, enraged and humiliated. This wasn't how it was supposed to be. She nearly had it!

Hostus straightened up and with a derogatory sweep of his hand, signalled the end of their session.

However, Tors wasn't having it.

No! she signalled. *Rematch*! she gestured vehemently. She wasn't finished; she had to have another go. She *needed* another go.

But Hostus shook his head, refusing. The session was over.

Tors snatched at his dagger one final time but Hostus slapped her off so hard it flew from her grasp. She rushed at him, glowering, fist raised, but before she could strike he had grabbed her by the neck and slammed her down on her back again.

O-VER! he signed as he pinned her down on both arms, crouching over her, so near she could see the minute chromatophores of his vizard scintillating before her very eyes. He paused, pulled back and dropped her as if he were discarding something loathsome.

She had failed. Yet again. And rules were rules.

Your rules, not mine, she thought angrily. *You won't let me try again and you won't let me see Jula! It's always your rules, not mine!* And she would not abide by that. Her eyes flashed with anger when Hostus once again gestured reaffirming that they were categorically *Done.*

So, furious, she gave him the finger, opened the portal and stormed out of the Ether, leaving him in it.

SAYING GOODBYE

Soft chatter floated up to the rafters of the converted station and from her hidden perch high above, Tors looked down. Like tiny runway illuminations, the rows and rows of red and blue grow-lights provided scant brightness with which Tors scanned each crouching figure working amongst troughs of vegetables. Entire sections of tall, short, rotund and cactoid shapes gleamed purple beneath the lights, interspersed with the venation pattern of fronds from leafier varieties glowing faintly in the dark. At last, she spotted the familiar outline of Jula.

There you are.

She sprinted lightly across the beams to the other side, just above where Jula was working, careful not to make any sound which would be amplified in the cavernous space.

It hadn't taken her very long to make her way from the rebel base to the community farm once she reached Amorgos. Jula was with her friend Marie from last time, carefully transferring seedlings from trays into the gel troughs. With no autobot assistance, this was back breaking work, bending over to insert each seedling into the nutrient-rich gel. Once or twice, the women straightened their backs to counter the punishing exertion of their labours. Tors marvelled at their care and persistence, especially Jula's.

The old Jula would never have been able to stick with something like this. Then fleetingly, it occurred to her with some guilt, that she was no better than the old Jula. Worse perhaps. *Here I am, having walked out on my training.*

She winced at the thought of having left Hostus in the Ether. *Well, he had it coming. Always telling me I can't do this, I can't do that.* She felt like a teenager again. *Just like the last time we saw each other outside Karl's, when I wanted to leave those sentries in the Ether to die.*

Another thought occurred to her, accompanied by a stab of guilt: what if he wandered off in the Ether? She shrugged it off. *He should know better.* She wouldn't be able to locate him if he did. Anyone stupid enough to do that thoroughly deserved to spend the last of his days wandering in the Ether.

A voice from below arrested her attention. A third person had approached Jula and Marie. Tors recognised his tall build and gait.

Marcus.

She strained to hear his words.

"...they'll tell us...," he said, his voice fluctuated in and out of hearing. "...rendezvous ...sometime... next few weeks. Be ready to leave at moment's notice."

The two women nodded their heads and looked at each other excitedly. Jula was clasping Marie's hands. Tors leant over as much as she dared, trying to pick out more of the conversation below.

"I won't be able to say goodbye, will I?" Jula asked.

Marcus shook his head in reply. "We tried to extricate her," he said, "but by the time we had worked out a way to get into the Palace, our sources there'd informed us she was gone."

"Do you think she escaped?" Jula asked, worried.

"Don't you worry," said Marie, patting her arm. "She's a tough one. She'll be alright."

At that point, Tors contemplated showing herself to Jula, to let her know she was okay and to say goodbye, but she hesitated. Then two young boys bounded up the aisle towards Marie. The younger one, no more than five or six, ran up and wrapped his arms around Marie's thighs, giggling.

"Mama," he said, wriggling and trying to dodge his elder brother who looked about twice his age.

Above, Tors leant back into the shadows in case they looked up.

Marie looked down fondly at her two boys. "I'm sure Tors knows you're thinking of her," she said to Jula as she mussed the younger one's hair affectionately. "After all, you brought her up through those first difficult years."

"I think it was more the other way around," said Jula a little ashamedly. "You see, mostly it was her that took care of me."

Marie squeezed her arm. "That may be, but you did your best and no matter what, you stuck with her, didn't you?"

"I nearly lost her when we first reached Ceos," said Jula, "but we did stay together. I did my best, as I promised."

Tors closed her eyes and smiled. Jula did do her best, even though her best was at times pretty suspect. From the time she got stoned and tried to get Tors to try her first puff at the age of eight, to the time when she walked off so drunk she forgot she'd left Tors, then barely seven, in the back alley by the rubbish bins. *But she came back for me the next day,* recalled Tors, *after having searched all the back alleys in the neighbourhood because she couldn't remember which one it was.*

Tors chuckled inwardly. Memories of those days flooded

back, each a struggle for survival but really quite funny when you thought about it. She stole one last look at Jula, her face etched with lines from years of hard living.

Perhaps now is as good a time as any to say our goodbyes.

It was long overdue. *I'm no good for you either Jula. Not as good as these folks are—Marie and her boys. They'll take care of you and keep you on the straight and narrow, the way I never could.*

Marcus put his hand on Jula's shoulder. "I'm sorry you can't say goodbye to her," he said, "but we cannot jeopardise the operation and besides, I made her a promise." He looked at Jula with seriousness. "A promise I intend to keep," he said.

Tors sat back down on the beam with a silent sigh of relief. *He means to honour his promise.* Jula's future was secure.

"She was always good to me..." Jula's voice floated up to the beams. "and it breaks my heart not saying goodbye."

Tors detected the grief in her voice. It nearly broke her heart too. Then, mouthing a silent goodbye, she left as quietly as she came.

SHACKLES OF THE PAST

W*ell, I suppose I should retrieve him,* Tors thought as she made her way back to Villa Castra. Hostus wouldn't have wandered off in the Ether. He knew better than to do that but there would be hell to pay for her actions.

With a deep breath, she went back to collect him. She was right. He was sitting where she had left him and when they got back, there was certainly hell to pay.

And pay she did.

He never asked where she went or what made her come back, but he did make her training twice as hard and three times longer. Endurance training now included a two mile lap around the lake on top of the usual route around the mountain ridge.

To make things worse, the seasons were getting colder and the first snows were setting in. Weapons and resistance training were conducted outdoors followed by combat training in the Ether. The latter remained frustratingly fruitless as far as progress was concerned and as for the rest of her training, Hostus had decided to conduct all sessions outside without returning to the villa for lunch or the much needed warmth.

They camped outdoors, sometimes by the lake where he would make her catch their lunch, other times high on the mountain ridge by the running route where they would subsist on a tea brewed from collected pine needles, heated on a small makeshift stove, and whatever else she could find in the traps that day. Tors was on the verge of hypothermia and vomiting with exhaustion by the time each day ended.

But still the training continued.

* * *

"*Move*!" Hostus warned as he slashed at her.

Tors reacted hurriedly, deflecting his blade with hers. The fiery rays of the evening suns glinted off their blades and the clashing and clanging of their swords echoed from the grounds of the villa into the distance.

Blow after blow, he continued to hammer her whilst she retreated, losing ground with each step.

It had been like this for weeks now—her performance declining at times, her progress stagnant at best.

"The mind must be clear in battle," Hostus remonstrated. "Yours is *not*!" His blade came whistling down at her.

She lifted hers to meet it but not without difficulty. This time, she had to use both hands to keep her sword steady.

"*There*!" Hostus pointed out again. "See? You are not focussed!" He lunged forward and attacked again.

Clang!

"Your mind is cluttered with *rubbish*!"

Clang! *Clang*!

"Are you *daydreaming*? What are you thinking of?"

CLANNGGG!

"NNYARRGHH!!" was Tors' only answer as she staggered at the force of the final blow. Hostus could be relentless when rankled.

Hostus swung round and caught the back of her legs, dislodging her off her feet.

"Ooooof!" Tors fell face-down onto the gravel.

"*This* is what I mean," berated Hostus. "You are carrying baggage within you. Your mind is full of… full of…" He lifted up his left arm in despair and with his right, rammed his sword into the ground with a sharp, frustrated thrust. "By Dyaeus, if you continue like this, we are as good as dead! *Finished*!"

Tors sat back up and leant against the base of a large terracotta pot, looking at him in weary silence.

For a moment, Hostus gazed at her without saying a word. When he finally spoke, his tone was harsh, demanding. "Did you go and see her?"

"See who?" asked Tors, too exhausted to move an inch. She spat out a few bits of shingle and rubbed her face.

"Jula," came the impatient answer. "When you left me in the Ether, did you go see her?"

"Yes, I did."

"And?"

"And what?"

"And is she alright?"

"Yes she's fine, she fine…" Tors tried to wave his nagging away. She could tell from his voice that he wasn't going to let this go.

"So you've seen her and she's all right," he said. He rasped his fingers testily. "Therefore there's nothing more for you to be concerned about, yes?"

Tors shrugged. "Sure."

Hostus shook his head, frustrated. "Your mind is clearly elsewhere and it is affecting your performance. We don't have time for this. I need you to *focus*!"

"I *am* focussed!"

"No you're not!" Hostus snapped. "You're still thinking of Jula. Your mind is not here, I *know* it. This is foolishness! By Dyaeus, *why*? *Why* do you still concern yourself with her when she'll be leaving the Realm soo—"

"BECAUSE SHE'S ALL I HAVE LEFT!" burst out Tors.

She grabbed a fistful of gravel and flung it at him. Then she turned to punch the side of the huge terracotta pot. Again and again and again until at length, her knuckles were bloodied and lacerated. She sat back down in a heap, tears streaming down her face.

"She's all I have left," she said again in a half-whisper this time, the anguish apparent in her words.

Hostus advanced towards her.

Tors cowered, her hands raised to protect herself.

"Hey," he said softly, "it's okay..." Then he knelt beside her.

"She's all I have left..." cried Tors. She retreated back into her seated position and hugged her knees tightly.

"I know we're running out of time," she said, her voice muffled inside her folded arms. "I know it even though you don't say it." She looked up, tears clouding her eyes. "I'm trying, Hostus, I really am. I'm giving it all I've got but at the same time, I don't think there's much of me left in the first place to give..."

He said nothing.

"I don't remember them," she continued, "...my mother, my father. I can't remember them at all." Tears streamed down her face. Her voice seemed small and lost.

And that was it. Somewhere beneath her once-closed centre, the gates to her heart had broken open and now, there was no way to stop the flood of emotions that surged through. The loss she felt and the unbearable emptiness that she would face once Jula was gone.

She looked at Hostus through her tears. *How could you ever understand?*

"Jula is the closest thing I have left to remind me of them. The only evidence of who I am. Who I was." She looked up at him. "She is the only proof I ever existed. And when she goes, then what? Who will I be?"

She buried her face in her hands and whispered, "I have been a shadow for so long I don't even know who I am anymore."

Hostus moved closer and gently pried her hands from her face. He tore a part of his tunic and began wrapping her bloodied knuckles. When he had done that, he spoke again. This time his voice was gentle. "Just because you can't remember their faces doesn't mean you've forgotten them," he said, slowly wiping her tears away.

"I have no memory of them," she half-whispered. "The other day, when I remembered Mother's words… I couldn't remember what she looked like." She looked at him sadly. "I couldn't even remember her voice."

Hostus touched her cheek softly. "Sometimes when we can't replay the memories in our minds, it is because they reside too deeply in our hearts," he said. Beneath the synthesised undertones of his vizard, his voice, low and gravelly came over to her with aching familiarity. It made her feel safe and it comforted her just as it did the day he first chanced upon her and Rat-Boy. The day she had thought all was lost.

He held out his hand and pulled her to her feet, his callused hand enveloping her smaller bloodied one.

"Now," he said just as he did all those years ago, "shall we have something to eat?"

THE REASON WHY

W*hy am I doing this?* Tors asked herself once again. *Is all this worth the fight?*

They had been training in the Ether for hours and hours. As she had done so more times than she'd cared to count, try as she might, there was no way she could manipulate the energy from the Ether to do what she needed it to do.

She was exhausted. Exhausted by the hours spent in there and exhausted by the days and nights spent trying to figure out why she couldn't do it in the first place. The punishing routine wore them both down, master and protege.

I CAN'T DO IT!! she screamed at him noiselessly in the Ether. *What you expect is IMPOSSIBLE!* She flung the pomum back at Hostus and whirled round in anger. *Why do you persist with this pointless task?*

Did he not get it? They'd been trying thousands of times, for weeks and weeks. If it were possible, she would have done it by now. Tears streamed freely down her face. She was glad she had her back towards him.

A purposeful pelt on her back indicated he had thrown a pomum at her.

Will you STOP it already! She clenched her fists in anger, refusing to turn around to face him.

A second impact on her back and she could see the small fruit plop down and roll under her legs. Then another.

Will you—.

Tors whirled round, her arm lashed outwards… and the pomum in mid-air, burst into incandescent fragments before her very eyes!

For a moment she stood gaping at what she had done. *By Dyaeus...*

Then Hostus threw her another pomum. And another.

With similar alacrity, she pulverised each one the same way.

When they had destroyed every last pomum they had with them, Tors threw her hands in the air and Hostus did a funny little jig in the Ether, before lifting her and twirling her round in glee.

By Dyaeus, I've DONE IT! she yelled soundlessly into the Ether, throwing her head back with joy.

THAT EVENING, when they returned to the villa, it was already dark and the stars had come out. They were both tired, Hostus even more so than Tors it would seem.

"I never thought I would be able to do that," said Tors as they sat over dinner that night. "I had never thought of the Ether that way."

Hostus nodded. "The Ether is a substance and like any substance, it can be manipulated. The trick is to be able to physically control it ."

"I think I was once told this was possible, but I don't

remember actually doing it or being shown how to," she said. Apart from the flashbacks triggered by the Oracle, she still couldn't conjure up any other memories of her childhood.

I had buried them too deep to even recall them now...

"Can *you* do it?" she asked Hostus. "Can you control the Ether?"

He shook his head. "No. Only those born of the Ether can. Even then as you probably know, not all Nehisi can manipulate the Ether. Only a small percentage of the population are born with the ability. In the past, these tended to be elevated to nobility because of their precious gift. You've obviously inherited this from your parents."

"Did you know them... my parents?" asked Tors. A spring of hope bubbled up inside her.

Hostus shook his head. "No, not personally but they would have been involved in the empire's expeditions into the Ether. It was the Age of Prosperity, at the height of Bridged Travel where our Emperor would have sent Nehisi to look for new routes to open. Ageron II would have sent many out to explore and to map these routes... that is until they all realised that it was impossible to map the Ether due to its constant state of flux."

Tors nodded, agreeing. *The currents of the Ether...*

"Which is why your people were so important," Hostus continued, "for their innate instinct of the Ether. One cannot map endpoints if they constantly move like ocean currents and without landmarks or any other guiding entity within the Ether itself, it is impossible to map the Ether."

"And the Light of Nehisi?" Tors asked, the image of the insidious, writhing tendrils resurfaced in her mind. "Does it sense the Ether?"

"The LON," murmured Hostus. He paused and then

nodded. "It is attracted to the Ether, yes. It senses it and you will need to use the Ether to destroy it."

"Destroy it…" repeated Tors. Her knees weakened a little at the thought.

"The Ether is a double edge sword," said Hostus. "It is the only thing that will destroy the LON but at the same time it is also the creature's escape route. A means by which it can spread across the universe."

"But at the moment, it is imprisoned within Lagentia. Hasn't anyone tried to destroy it where it is?"

"Yes. And failed. It cannot be destroyed outside the Ether. We tried. Many times. It proliferates too fast and regenerates before it can be completely destroyed. But we do know that it does not like heat so flames keep it at bay. Fire similar to the flames you produced back there in the Ether although not quite identical. The Ether is only way to destroy it."

"You sound as if you know a lot about this creature." Tors looked expectantly at Hostus.

He took a slow sip of his *amarinthe,* the chromatographic skin of his vizard that blended into the skin near his mouth fluctuated slightly as he did so, and sat back. "I was there you know," he said quietly, "when it happened. Horrendous oversight. The Ellagrins had outplayed us and we didn't even know it. Several months passed before the first Nehisi started dying. They fell ill at first: fever, dehydration, then organ failure, shutdown of the body and eventually death. Quarantining the sick did nothing to stop the spread. Scientists were completely baffled. The sickness also caused infertility but all these only affected the Nehisi. Every other inhabitant of the city was unaffected by the disease."

"The Oracle mentioned some genetic markers," said Tors.

Hostus nodded. "You have to hand it to the Ellagrins. They are truly the masters of agriculture. They had bio-engineered the LON to target specific marker genes, specifically that of the Nehisi. Contact of the plant to skin or inhalation of its spores would pass a specific pathogen into the host and disrupt their physiology, causing infertility and eventual death. A simple but clever device as it was tradition for the Nehisi to gift each other the LON in celebrations and social events. That, coupled with the Nehisi all living together in Lagentia under Ageron III's protection meant that within a few years, they had all been infected."

Hostus sighed. "By the time the scientists had worked this out, it was too late. The entire Nehisi population had been infected. As a last ditch attempt to prevent the extinction of the race, they tried to reverse the infertility, first by trying to reverse engineer the plant itself and then when that too failed, they cross-bred the LON with other naturally abundant species in the hope that their reproductive alleles would prevail as the dominant instruction."

Hostus shook his head gravely. "But we Ageronians were always better industrialists than agriculturists. In hindsight, we should not have tampered with something that we were not experts at in the first place. It was at that point that we triggered a jump in the LON's evolution. In one of our cross-breeding efforts, the LON as a specie crossed over from plant to animal."

He shifted uncomfortably. "The speed at which it spread was unprecedented. We had to seal the entire capital. Those who escaped the city were no luckier—they were dying anyway. In less than a decade from first exposure to the LON, the Nehisi had all but died out."

Tors sat listening. All this had been happening when she was growing up on the far-flung planet of Ceos, in hiding, with Jula.

Hostus drank from his glass and continued, "So you see,

the final joke was on us Ageronians, for the creature you see today was a result of our own doing."

Tors took a long sip of her drink. "So that's the LON," she murmured thoughtfully. "What I'll be up against…"

"Well, the good news is you probably won't be infected like your predecessors because it has made the jump to *animalis,*" said Hostus brightly. "The bad news is, how we think it can be killed…." He gave a slight shrug, "Well, that has never been tried before."

"Great," replied Tors and downed the rest of her *amarinthe* in one gulp.

THAT NIGHT she finally remembered and the lost memory came back to her in her dreams.

Mother...

She was sitting in Mother's lap and Tors could almost smell the sandalwood and orange blossom in her hair. *I'd forgotten how much I loved that smell...*

Mother moved her hair back in one languid movement, so it hung behind the shoulder.

Oh how black her hair was! Tors' gaze followed the tresses along the shoulder, up the neck and the jaw before settling on Mother's face. *She had green eyes too, like mine!*

I remember!

Tors was so happy her heart could burst.

'Why Mother? Why do we have to do this?' Tors had asked her. They had been training in the Ether and she remembered being tired and overwhelmed by the tasks Mother had set her.

Yes, why Mother? Why am I doing this? her heart asked, echoing her younger self.

'Because only Nehisi can,' Mother said. *'We are the only ones who can find these endpoints.'*

'But why Mother? Why should we risk our lives in the Ether to find endpoints for the Gates?'

And it was then that Mother had looked at her and smiled.

'Because we can, Vittoria,' she said as Tors drank in her face and everything she could in attempt to hold onto that memory forever. *'Because we* ***can****.'*

METAMORPHOSIS

As was the way with Hostus, despite her breakthrough, there was no respite and training resumed the next day. Days blended into each other, coalescing into one continuous blur as time seemed to extend and meld into the harsh winter of Casar. The days were bitterly cold and the nights raw and biting, but still Hostus pressed on with her training, always pushing hard but not beyond what he felt she could physically take.

Probably just hard enough not to kill me, thought Tors grudgingly one day when he picked her up after flooring her with a left hook she should have anticipated. *Bastardi.*

Despite that, she felt herself improving. Eventually the pain and agony receded and each day she found herself welcoming the challenges it brought her. She knew she'd always been a good fighter but now her senses, her reactive speed and strength felt considerably enhanced. The training had stirred something within her. Something she couldn't put her finger on. Something between an awakened instinct and a flashback, a sort of muscle memory from within the very core of her being that she could not ignore or shed. She felt herself changing, and it felt good.

Am I in danger of becoming another Marcus? she asked herself.

However, deep down, she realised it wasn't just the training that was keeping her there. Something else was compelling her to stay her course.

For the very first time in her life, she had a purpose. But more than that, she realised what she actually loved from each punishing day of hard graft and toil.

She loved being with him.

* * *

"HOW CAN you be so sure we're doing the right thing?" she asked Hostus one evening.

They had just finished dinner and were watching the news streams whilst 'the hands', as Tors called the servitors, hovered about clearing the plates.

She rubbed her aching arms and looked across the table at Hostus who was fixing her sword. He was replacing the binding around its hilt.

"What do you mean?" asked Hostus.

"All this training," replied Tors, "how do we know all this is going to work?" A pang of uncertainty hit her. "What if the LON cannot be destroyed? What if there is no way to reopen the Gates? What if the Oracle's *wrong*?" She turned to him, looking for some hint of reassurance.

Hostus looked up from his task. "The Oracle has never been wrong," he said. "Granted, it has been a little light with details on the Gates but amongst many things, it foretold of the dying suns, your existence and of your re-emergence. The solution will become clear when the time comes."

"Hmmm," murmured Tors, "let's hope so." She twirled her glass absently.

The news stream switched to recent protests against the imminent launch of the Carinthia. "They're certainly not happy," she remarked.

"No," agreed Hostus, "but you wouldn't be either if you weren't on the passenger list." He glanced at her and asked, "And Jula? She's bound for the Tethys is she not?"

"Yes," nodded Tors. "Marcus will hold up his end of the bargain and I believe the Tethys will be departing soon too."

"If the Imperial army doesn't get to it first—"

Tors set her glass down and glared at him. "These people deserve their chance too!"

"I'm just stating the facts," said Hostus, "but doing this on their own, without the empire's backing so to speak and with nowhere to resettle, they are refugees relying on sheer luck."

He continued. "What if Ellagrin doesn't take them in? What if the Asghar slave traders intercept them? The Tethys is defenceless."

"So what's the alternative?" asked Tors. "Stay here and be bypassed by a system that's corrupt to the core?"

She stopped herself after the last sentence. *By Dyaeus, I sound like Marcus. What is happening to me?*

"Look," said Hostus, "I don't have anything against the Rebellion other than these riots they start which I have to help put out."

He gave a small grunt as he tightened the binding around the hilt some more. "...and the disruption to the Exodus," he added.

There was a brief pause before he continued. "...not to mention the bombings and thefts."

He hefted the sword to check its balance. "...*and* the threats to my fellow Reds protecting the empire's resources for the

Exodus," he concluded, inspecting his handiwork one last time.

Tors let out a chuckle. *You have a point.*

"But..." finished Hostus, finally looking up, "it is what it is."

He held up her sword with both hands, its hilt now bound tightly and neatly with the twine-like material.

"It is what it is," she repeated with a grin, coming round the table to take it from him. Their hands touched for a moment and her breath caught as the warmth of his palms passed to her. She didn't withdraw immediately, instead stood motionless in front of him. From his seated position and hers standing up, she felt his gaze upon her.

Tors set the sword aside and leant forward, all the time conscious of his unwavering gaze. Slowly, she took his hands and placed them on her hips.

He pulled her towards him and she found herself holding her breath until at length, her arms rested softly on his shoulders and his head was buried so close to her heart she thought he would hear it thrumming.

"Tors..." he whispered thickly. The warmth of his brow resting on her chest seeped into her and as his hands gripped the contours of her hips tightly, she gazed down on him and wondered.

I know you so well, yet...

Not thinking, she reached for the back of his vizard but Hostus stopped her before her hand even grazed it.

Without uttering a word, he withdrew slowly but firmly, and she in turn, moved back, leaning against the table.

She closed her eyes for a moment and breathed out at the reprieve. *Madness. What was I thinking anyway?*

Then she glanced at Hostus. It would seem that he too, had regained hold of his senses.

He reached out for his glass of *amarinthe* and sipped it calmly, as if nothing had happened.

Then with a nonchalant wave of thanks, Tors picked up her sword and headed out of the room to retire for the evening.

COMPLICATIONS

Ka-kawooo! Ka-kawoo! The harsh sounds of the *kakawu* in the skies as they made off for their evening hunt echoed and bounced off the mountainous rock that surrounded the villa.

It was night and the sky, though clear with stars, did little to illuminate the courtyard. The entire villa was in pitch darkness, with *Servis* instructed to deactivate all occupier interactions for their training. They were still in the midst of their combat session.

It will be a long night before either of us gets any rest, thought Tors as sweat trickled down the side of her face.

Sensing a subtle stir on her left, the merest flicker like a moth's, she raised her sword in a swift confident stroke. A split second later, metal on metal clashed. Hers met with Hostus' blade with a faint chirr like a metallic cricket as the two swords glided over each other before meeting again in jarring impact.

In the dark, they danced around each other, striking and retreating, clashing, sensing and anticipating each other's moves. Like performers in a lethal caper, they had begun to think as one and so to gain an advantage, they began to make faster, riskier moves.

On and on they went with increasing intensity, exchanging blows, grappling, parrying, pushing to tease out the slightest weakness or edge against the other. They battled from the courtyard into the villa itself, inflicting damage on the exquisite frescos along the way, through the corridor and finally crashing through the glass wall into the dojo. Here, there was no corner or corridor to hide behind, just an empty arena, the perfect setting for confrontational combat.

Tors could hear Hostus breathe. It was even and controlled but audible for they had been at this for hours already and their strength was being pushed to the limit. She surmised he could probably hear her breathing as well which meant they could pinpoint each other's location fairly accurately even in the darkness.

A faint swish of the blade and by instinct, Tors crouched down, sending a few shards of glass tinkling across the floor in her haste. Her fingers touched on a longish sliver of glass. As she took it, she felt his sword slice past the top of her head like a breath of wind. Still down, she extended her leg outwards in a sweeping half arc, knocking him off balance. A thud told her that he was down and a clang indicated that he must have dropped his sword. Seizing her chance, she lunged in his direction, her sword pointed forward.

He must have sensed her coming for he rolled aside, dislodged the weapon from her hand, and then wrenching her forward, lifted her up by the neck. Pushing her backwards in a flash, she felt her head against the cold smack of stucco and plaster, and his weight against her pinning her to the wall. The cold of his steel pressed against her neck.

"Yield," he rasped hoarsely. She felt the heat coming off his body in wafts of steam, his breath short and sharp on her face.

"Only if you do," she replied, barely able to raise her voice with the weight of him pressed into her diaphragm, squeezing the breath out of her. In her hand the sliver of glass which she had sense to grab just moments before was now pressed against his groin to emphasise her point. She felt him stiffen as a result.

Conceding, he lowered his dagger slowly, letting it drop to the floor.

Then his hand reached upwards, his fingers gently grazing the slender line of her neck all the way up to her chin. As he moved closer, she heard the imperceptible hiss of his vizard retracting. His breath, now slow and predacious, fanned over her ear, sending chills down her spine and she felt his full body pressing druggedly into her.

Then the hungry urgency of his lips on hers.

The glass shard dropped from her hand and landed on the floor with a tinkle. But it was hardly noticed. A wave of heat and excitement swept over her as his hands moved downwards, one cupping her breast, the other reaching between her thighs.

"Yield," he growled in a guttural tone.

She relayed no such submission and so with both hands he tore open her shirt, letting it slide off her shoulders and onto the floor. With his body pressed against hers, pinning her hard against the wall, he stripped the pants off her and lifted her up.

She tore at him, undoing his clothes and holding onto him for she had nothing else to cling to.

With one hand palmed against the wall beside her head, he held her up with the other and pulled her closer to him. Hunger and aggression coursed through his veins but his touch remained gentle.

She wrapped her legs round his waist and pressed against him, feeling every hard inch of him between them, desperate for him to enter her.

A primitive sound escaped his chest. "Yield," he said huskily.

She closed her eyes even though there was no way she could see anything in the pitch darkness and finally relented.

Sex was urgent, savage, she as voracious as he was. In the end, they lay entwined on floor of the dojo, looking through its pane-less wall at the night sky, satiated and spent.

"I should not have done that," he said softly, caressing her back, "you are my charge and but a child."

Tors made a small noise like a half-chuckle. "The last time I saw you was centuries ago," she replied. "I am a child no longer." She touched his arm, running her fingers up and down over the sinewy ridges of his muscles and wondered once more what he looked like. He was almost certainly Ageronian, humanoid at the very least where the important bits were concerned, as she had discovered to her great satisfaction. However, as to what he looked like, she still hadn't the faintest idea.

He stirred a little and she moved her head from his shoulders as he sat up. He smelt of the forest, of earth and musk.

"I have to leave for the capital. It will be for a few days," he said.

"Alandia? Why?"

"The troops have been summoned, " he said. "More riots all over the Realms, no doubt stoked by news of the Carinthia leaving. The legions have been sent all over the Realms to quell the civil unrest."

He got up and kissed her forehead. "I shall be back in a few days," he said. "Keep training. In the meantime, *Servis* will take care of anything else you need."

PART VII

SECRETS AND SUBTERFUGE

ELENA

SUMMER PALACE, ELLAGRIN

"And the settlement treaties?" Elena asked, gazing disinterestedly at the amber contents of the goblet in her hand.

Her voice echoed hollowly down the Grand Hall, reflecting her sentiment for the place. Indeed, she would have preferred any of the smaller cabinet rooms but Niklas always insisted on working in the Grand Hall of the Royal Palace.

This place is as cheerful as a tomb.

She rubbed her arms involuntarily, thinking of the much more amenable settings of her Summer Palace. She hated it here but the Royal Palace on Namsos was Niklas' preferred base.

As was Father's, she noted. It seemed all of Ellagrin's Emperors, past and present, and their court preferred to rule from the Royal Palace. *Perhaps it is because it is called the 'Royal' Palace,* she thought sarcastically, *lest people needed reminding of how 'royal' they were here.*

The Royal Palace was where the Doges congregated to

seek audience with the Emperor, to discuss and debate matters of the state, to make deals.

The little royals, she thought contemptuously. The petty, self-important leeches of House Ellagrin who had the audacity to think they somehow shared the Ellagrin lineage. *They prefer this place because it is a warren of nooks and crannies with hidden corners to hide and whisper. To plot and conspire.*

Compared with the Summer Palace and its genteel gardens, the Royal Palace was a formidable fortress of steel and stone. *They see this as the seat of power,* thought Elena sardonically, *marinated in so many centuries of tradition it now seeps of rot.*

Ornate mirrors and gilded portraits of emperors past hung on the Grand Hall's panelled walls, looming over the two long tables on each side, cold and sombre, and doing nothing to lift her spirits.

Elena was disconsolate and her mood had turned increasingly troubled ever since she left Ageron to come back to Ellagrin.

She glanced at Niklas sitting at the table opposite, looking through the day's arbitrations, still not heeding her. The portrait of Emperor Filip II gazed solemnly down upon her. Elena looked back at it stiltedly. Something about that portrait unsettled her.

Filip II, or Filip the Technologist as the historians nicknamed him, was a proponent of biotechnology in large-scale farming, the first to push the use of technology in agriculture, little knowing how significant the consequences of his forward-thinking actions would have almost a millennia later.

Well, Father certainly made full use of your legacy with the Nehisi...

Elena studied his face. Her ancestor's achievements great as they were, were sadly eclipsed by the well-known fact that his eyes were not Ellagrin-blue but Ageronian-brown, leading to malicious gossip that his conception wasn't perhaps as conventional as he would have liked people to believe. Nevertheless, the purity of the Ellagrin lineage ended up being preserved after all for Filip II died heirless, leaving his brother (Elena's grandfather) free to claim the throne.

Here in the portrait however, Elena noted that the artist had painted Filip's eyes a compromising shade of nondescript grey. The face lean, the line of the jaw pleasantly angular and the slightly gangling neck struck a certain familiarity with her.

He looks like Valerius...

That realisation rankled her.

A maidservant attempted to fill her goblet with more *amarinthe* and Elena sent her off with a snappish command. Her eyes grew hard as her thoughts returned to Valerius.

No, he had another name—his real name. What was it? Vidar. They called him Vidar...

She swirled her drink agitatedly. What was this? Guilt? Regret? Did she miss him? She recalled the bewildered look on his face before her guard shot him.

A meaningless dalliance. Nothing more, she told herself. *I thought he would lead me to the famous Prometheus who procured my Eldur.* No, she did not regret his death, she was sure of that. Nevertheless she felt a certain self-loathing. She felt wretched.

Does it matter who I bed? Or rather, did anyone I bed matter?

She looked at her brother who had made no attempt to answer her earlier question and her thoughts now drifted towards that of Draeger and the beginnings of a plan that had begun to form in her head.

Does it matter who I sell out?

She thought about it, then shook it off and tapped her fingers impatiently.

Niklas looked up. "What?" he snapped.

"The settlement treaties, brother. I need you to authorise them."

"Treaties, treaties, treaties. Can we talk about more interesting things please. They are all you go on about these days. I have given you all the treaties you have asked for, sister. Do not vex me further with these inane repetitions."

Elena stood up and walked over. Her eyes glittering and tumultuous held Niklas'. A dull resentment began to burn in her. *YOU vexed? Whilst you dither and dally over documents you barely understand? I'm the one that's vexed brother, trying to run Father's empire despite* ***you****.*

"There is one last thing for which I need your confirmation, brother," she replied darkly, still holding his gaze. She felt him draw his breath. *So be it if I have to whore myself to have my way. Does it even matter anymore?*

She gave a careless laugh—there was no light left in it. Then she leant over, showing just a little more of her cleavage in the process and said, "The Carinthian treaty, that is all."

Niklas grunted. His eyes did not stray from her pale, milky breasts. "Is that all that will please you, sister?" he asked, standing up. He gripped her wrist tight, causing her to let go of her drink.

The goblet fell to the ground with a clang. Now fear gripped her, shaking her from her earlier haze of moroseness. She had gone too far.

Show no fear.

Elena continued to look at her brother, her face belying neither fear nor discomfort and nodded.

Niklas's face was flushed, the *amarinthe* he had been downing all night evident in his sullen, inebriated state. His eyes narrowed as he examined her face and then with an impatient flick, he said, "Very well," and let go.

Elena relaxed a little, giving a secret sigh of relief inside.

Niklas could be violent when drunk. And cruel. She rose to leave the room.

BAAMM!!

The sound of his goblet slamming the table stopped her dead in her tracks. Her heart sank to the pit of her stomach.

Stay calm. It will be worse if you run. She turned around to face a flushed and angry Niklas.

"You think this is all?" he snarled, advancing towards her. "I give you what you want and you just walk away?"

His mood has turned. Carefully, carefully...

"Of course not," she replied easily and smiled at him soothingly.

Niklas towered over her, at least a head taller, muscular and menacing.

She moved to touch his arm but before she could do that, he grabbed her by the neck and with one hand, shoved her like a rag doll against the table.

"Niklas..."she gasped. The room spun around her.

By Ysgarh, he means to kill me...

He pinned her against the table, hand clasped tightly around her neck and she found herself teetering on her toes suffocating.

"I can't breathe..."

"Do not think me a fool, sister," he hissed, his breath hot against her cheek before releasing her.

She crumpled backwards onto the table, gulping for air. *He has Father's madness. Staying with him will have me killed one of these days.* She glanced at him. *Do I run or do I stay and fight? Is all this worth me fighting for?*

But Niklas had other things on his mind. He reached for the hidden pocket in her skirt and ripped it open. Her small snuffbox fell out with a clatter.

The contraceptives!

Niklas eyed her closely. "Don't think I don't know what you've been up to," he said. He leant close, his breath hot against her ear, made her feel suddenly sick. "But fear not, my sweet sister. You won't be needing these from now on."

He does not mean to kill me, she realised. *But this is worse than death.*

He stood up straight, towering above her as she cowered with fear. "We will make new babies, you and I," he said, reaching for her face and holding it up forcefully in his powerful hand so he could look upon it uninterrupted. "Beautiful Ellagrin babies, Elena."

He released his grip and turned away. "I am tired of the repulsive half-breeds my concubines produce," he said. "Instead *you* shall give me beautiful, blonde babies. Perfect images of you and I."

He turned to face her, his eyes ablaze with insane fervour. "Together, we shall bring back the glory days of our empire!"

Elena shuddered at his words, and found herself asking once more: *Do I run or do I stay and fight? Is all this worth it?*

But as she wiped her tears away, she realised deep down that she could not run. She *would not* run.

No, she would stay and fight. And she would defend herself and claim what was rightfully hers.

QUEEN ALIN

RED PALACE, AGERON

The young steward backed away cowering as Queen Alin strode purposefully past him into the solar to see her son.

"Out of my way boy, or I shall have you skinned and hung outside these doors as a reminder to all other stewards!" she warned frostily as she entered.

Through the tall narrow windows of the Red Palace, crimson light streamed into Emperor Akseli's solar, spilling across its dark polished wooden floor in blood-red shards. On one end stood a desk and the only other source of illumination in the room: a lamp perched atop its elegant leather-clad surface.

At the desk sat the Emperor, his fair hair dishevelled and unkempt, and his hands on a girl, barely in the cusp of womanhood, sitting on his lap. Visibly tipsy, he was trying to lick the *amarinthe* from the concave of her very ample cleavage. Her pale bosoms bobbed up and down as she giggled coquettishly, clearly enjoying the attention as much as the *amarinthe*.

"Mother!" greeted Akseli as Queen Alin approached. He stood up abruptly and the girl tumbled to the floor with an ungainly thump. "To what do I owe this pleasure?" Akseli said, stepping over her and pulling out a chair.

Queen Alin sat down, folded her hands over her lap and cast an icy look at him. At the grand old age of three hundred and sixty-six, her wrinkled face was still beautiful. Nevertheless, it possessed a smile that never quite tallied with her glacial blue eyes.

Today there was no smile and her eyes looked icier than ever. "My son," she said levelly without glancing at the girl behind him, "we need to talk."

Akseli smiled. "Of course," he replied and as he turned back towards the girl, his face changed and darkened like a storm cloud. Unfortunately, she was slow to notice.

"And WHY are you still HERE??" he screamed at her.

There was a clatter as the girl kicked her goblet in fright and scrambled off as fast as she could.

Then Akseli turned back to face his mother, his manner civil once more. His eyes however, were anything but. The Queen Mother visited at times, but never for a social visit. "Now what troubles you, Mother?" he asked.

"I hear you lost the Key," she said. Her eyes glittered as she continued, "A mere girl at that…"

Once a vibrant blue, those eyes had cooled over the centuries into an even icier blue although the steely, hardened quality behind them remained unchanged.

"I didn't lose her," Akseli retorted. "She escaped. Besides, even *you* didn't know she was the Key until you saw the recordings—"

Queen Alin arose and slapped her son in the face.

His eyes blazed as the red of the welt showed on his cheek.

"Useless bastard!" she said. "You useless *bastard*! Ageron

himself would not have let things come to the mess we find ourselves today. She was already in your custody, and yet you let her walk right out of the Palace! You utter, incompetent bastard!"

Akseli bared his teeth. "Call me bastard again," he answered, seething, "and I shall cut you from your navel to your mouth."

Queen Alin regarded him unsmilingly. "Better," she said, eyeing him critically. "Much better. For a moment I thought you'd lost your backbone as well. Perhaps you have what it takes to be Emperor after all."

Bastard or no bastard, I am still Emperor of Ageron. Akseli glowered darkly.

His mother eyed him steadily. "Don't worry," she said, "I've cut quite a few heads already in the past to protect *that* secret. Do you really think I'd let that all go to waste?"

She smiled and reached out to smooth a hand over his hair. "Now tell me, how did she escape the Red Palace?" she asked, "and from the bowels of the ancient quarters no less."

"The Rebellion is my guess," Akseli replied. "After all, whoever who holds the Key holds power over the Realms."

"Mmm," murmured the Queen.

"But they would have had to have help," continued Akseli. "Not even our servants here dare go down the ancient maze of passageways for fear of getting lost, so how they found their way to the Oracle confounds me."

"Someone had to have helped them locate her in order to help her escape," agreed the Queen.

" Could it be that cretin Chancellor of ours? He has spies in every crevice of the Palace."

"As have I," retorted Queen Alin. "Perhaps it could have been the Rasmus but let me worry about him. He may well have Draeger's ear but like Draeger, he is a man of principle."

She smiled. "And men who have moral principles are often crippled by those very principles they hold dear."

She looked at him, her thoughts moving onto other matters, although clearly still troubled with the missing Key. "Now what news of the Realms then? I hear of more and more riots each day."

"Yes," replied Akseli, "riots are happening everywhere, especially around the innermost planets hit by recent natural disasters, namely Anavio, Bellun, even Trimon. The people are naturally skittish and wanting to leave."

The Queen nodded, agreeing.

"We are also seeing more and more skirmishes on Amorgos, in particular around the capital city. Intelligence suggests a large one coming up on the outskirts of Alandia itself."

"No doubt the Rebellion has heard news of the Carinthia leaving soon."

"Yes. We've also got them on the offensive too as we're tracking down the whereabouts of their own spacecarrier in order to stop it."

"Hmm," pondered the Queen, "and your brother?"

"He has been sending our troops to quell the riots and overseeing these matters."

"I see." Queen Alin contemplated a moment.

And there will be even more to quell soon, thought Akseli, studying his mother quietly, *to keep Draeger's armies spread out and away from Amorgos, away from the City of the Dead. And when I find the Key, you won't dare call me an incompetent bastard again.*

"You know," said the Queen suddenly and looked at him. "I think I know how we can flush out the Key from hiding."

"How?"

"You mentioned before the Rebellion had offered a seat on

the Tethys for one of her kin?" asked Queen Alin, referring to the Key.

"Yes, her foster mother," affirmed Akseli.

"Well," the Queen continued, "I have an idea how to get her attention."

"How?"

"The Rebellion of course," said the Queen. Her eyes gleamed. "The Rebellion will help us do just that."

A DEAL

After the Queen Mother left, Akseli remained in his solar for a while. A plan was beginning to form in his mind. But it would require the Key, the Key whom he had in his possession earlier but did not realise it at the time.

How by Dyaeus was I to know the Key was a woman, not a man! He kicked himself for letting her slip through his fingers. But no matter, plans were afoot to retrieve her and when found…

'We must be careful not to let your brother get wind of this though,' his mother had warned. She was right of course and he wondered if Draeger knew the rebel woman he'd captured was the Key.

Unlikely, as I hadn't told him anything other than she escaped, he told himself. *Besides, he doesn't know about the hidden surveillance in the Oracle's chamber.* After all who would bother to put a spy cam on something that hadn't woken up for centuries.

Akseli re-examined his options. Now that the Key had been identified, it was only a matter of time before his men located her. He frowned. *The Key… our alleged saviour and deliv-*

erer. The Key may be enough to win the Senate over to my side but its influence alone will not be enough to win over the army. No, Mother, you've not quite thought this through. The Key alone is not the answer...

Irate, he stood up and made for the door. There had to be another way to capitalise on his current advantage.

The corridor of the palace looked empty and Akseli marched down it in large, strides. He found himself making his way to the west wing, towards the boudoirs where the ladies of the court resided. Perhaps the afternoon with Flavia, Livia and whoever else he fancied would help bring some clarity.

With a plan in mind, he turned the corner at speed—and careered into her.

"Oh!" Her blonde tresses came into full view as the cowl of her cloak fell to her shoulders.

"Why, who have we here?" said Akseli, surprised. He reached out a hand to steady her.

Elena took it and paused to regain her composure.

Akseli could have sworn she looked a little on edge and it was not because of his running headlong into her. "We seem to be bumping into each other in corridors all the time," he said, looking appraisingly at her. *She looks almost frightened.* That alone was inherently out of character, particularly for someone like Lady Elena.

Lady Elena nodded without saying anything.

"You look a little out of breath my lady," said Akseli. "Perhaps you should sit down." He led her along the corridor and ushered her into his solar.

Lady Elena did not appear to resist .

Yet another thing out of character, thought Akseli, intrigued. *My, my, what is going on here?*

Inside, he handed her a glass of *amarinthe.*

Elena accepted it gratefully.

"So, what brings you back in the Realms, my Lady?" Akseli asked.

"I'm... I'm looking for Lord Draeger," Elena answered.

She seeks my brother's help or counsel? Akseli wondered.

Elena paused. Then seemingly collected her composure, she continued, explaining, "I've come to inform him... and you, that the treaties for the Carinthia have been approved. News I'm sure you both will be pleased to hear."

"How marvellous," murmured Akseli. "But I'm afraid I have no idea as to where my brother is. In fact, I've not seen him for some months now." He gave her a goading look. "Do you mean to say even *you* don't know where he is or what he's been up to?"

Elena smiled easily. "What Lord Draeger does in his own time is not my concern. These treaties... these little commercial exchanges between your brother and I are economically beneficial to both Houses. A mutually advantageous arrangement. However, there are things of his I have no wish to interrogate and likewise there are things of my own that he has no part in...," she glanced at him smiling sweetly, "nor knowledge of..."

Akseli smiled but said nothing.

"Anyway," continued Elena, seemingly back to her confident self, "I'm sure he is busy as always. Perhaps looking for the Key?"

Akseli glanced at her sharply. *What do you know of the Key?*

Then he said slowly, "Well, you'll be interested to know that we may well be close to locating the Key."

"Is that so?" Elena murmured. Her tone was indifferent but her irises Akseli observed, had widened ever so slightly. "The Key..." she said. Her eyes took on a far-off look. "Perhaps the Gateways will be opened once more?"

"Perhaps," answered Akseli. "Although how exactly is the Key to do that, we are unclear."

"I'm sure the answer will reveal itself when the time comes," said Elena comfortingly. "Perhaps the Oracle will tell you."

Akseli regarded her keenly. *For an enemy of the House, you certainly knows more than you should. Even most of the court here know nothing about the Oracle.*

He looked at Elena. *It is a dangerous game my brother plays. What if you turn on House Ageron and side your mad brother instead?* But Elena was calm and calculated, a far cry from her truculent brother. Besides, he suspected she did not always agree with Niklas.

Unlikely, Aseli decided, *but perhaps the old adage of keeping one's friends close and enemies closer could be turned to one's advantage...*

"Well," he grumbled, "you'd think so, except that bloody thing hasn't woken up to tell us that vital bit of information."

"I'm sure the answer will reveal itself in due course," Elena said, looking at him innocently. "And when the Gate is reopened, what will you do?"

Akseli gave her a long, measured look. "Well..." he replied slowly. His eyes glittered.

He had come to a decision with his plans.

He looked at Elena and said, "I was thinking of what *you* could do when the Gate is reopened..."

"Oh..?" Elena regarded him with interest.

Akseli leant forward conspiratorially. "I have a proposition ," he said, lowering his voice to almost a whisper, "for *you...*"

Elena lifted an eyebrow. "Go on..." she said.

HOSTUS

VILLA CASTRA, AGERON

It was five days before he returned to Villa Castra. In the dead of night, tired and bruised, and with the taint of death hanging around him like an unshakeable cloak of foul vapour, Hostus found himself entering her bedchamber like a moth drawn to flame.

In the darkness he could hear her breathing, even and relaxed. An almost imperceptible whisper of a dagger unsheathing indicated that she too, had heard him. Hostus dropped his cloak gently onto the floor and exhaled wearily, aware for the first time since leaving the villa of the fatigue that pervaded his body.

I have to end this.

A hundred different emotions stirred within him. *She is your ward, your responsibility,* he reminded himself bitterly. *All this...*—his thoughts churned like a torrid storm inside—*this juvenile infatuation ... it will only serve to ruin us both, and worse. There is too much hanging in the balance, too much at stake...*

It had been a hard few days and some of the riots he had to quell, in particular the ones against the common people had cast a shadow over him that he found hard to shake. War was different. The sea of faces of those perished in the War and the numerous other battles he served in did not weigh on him the same way these small skirmishes did. For these people were not fighting against an adversary, they were fighting for what they believed was the only way for them to live.

They were fighting to survive.

Unfortunately, our Emperor does not share the people's sense of urgency, he thought grimly to himself, *nor their fear for the future of them and their loved ones.*

He climbed into Tors' bed, reaching for her in the total darkness.

Lying on her side, she was naked save for the dagger which she had tucked discreetly back under the pillow.

His hand slid up the side of her body, caressing her smooth skin, skimming along the curve of her hips, down the dip at her waist and then trailing lightly across her midriff to cup her breast as he leant in to kiss her from behind.

She reached for him and as she did so, he sensed her hunger for him in her returned kisses and in the urgency of her body pressed against his.

But Hostus was overwhelmed with conflict and guilt. He had tried his best to fulfil the Oracle's instructions. As foretold, he had become her teacher and protector. But a lover—that was an irreconcilable thought. And yet he desired her with such intensity that he would have at that moment gladly sacrificed a billion lives to have her.

Perhaps I have already done so with my recklessness...

He wrestled with the enormity of the task that lay before him. Did she truly understand what was being asked of her, he wondered? Had he done enough to prepare her? Despite all the training, would she know what to do when the time came? And if they failed...

A life for the life of billions. Hers, for the life of every other living being in the Realm.

Could he bring himself to pay the final price if it came to that? *Would* he?

She turned towards him and slid closer, slowly taking his clothes off and wrapping her body around his. She sensed his conflict but said nothing as he buried his face between her breasts in the sanctuary of her embrace.

Does she know? She breathes as I breathe and she feels what I feel. And yet we only meet as ourselves in the dark. I cannot... I must not... but so overcome by his need for her, he turned to her, losing himself in her and into oblivion.

* * *

THE NEXT DAY saw training resume as normal. Hostus had suggested unarmed combat by the lake that morning. It was so early the heavens were still dark as they worked their way through each practice round, their breaths expelling thick, rapid puffs of steam in the sub-zero temperature as they sparred. Hostus had managed to outmanoeuvre Tors and twice he even dunked her in the lake's icy waters.

She was not happy.

"Even an Ellagrin farmer can fight better than this," he remarked scornfully. Swinging round and catching the heel of her boot, he threw her down with a resounding whack. Overhead a startled flock of kakawu burst from the trees, their gilded forms dispersed into the lightening sky like exploding fireworks.

From where she lay, Tors grabbed his ankle and dislodged him from his stance. His recovery was not quick enough and in an instant, she was on top, straddling him on the shores of the lake, palm on the side of his face, pushing him down, crunching through the thin layer of ice and into the icy water beneath.

As he choked and as water rapidly filled his lungs, Hostus looked at her through the shimmer of the lake's surface.

My magnificent, wild one...

She was still holding him down, looking at him eyes ablaze, as he realised with some degree of humour, that he was beginning to drown. But she did not relent and neither did he struggle.

I have been around death long enough to embrace it, he thought as it occurred to him that she might not even realise he was drowning on account of his vizard masking his face.

Perhaps I deserve death... The faces of those who died that fateful day in Lagentia reared in his mind's eye in answer to the thought. *My men died for me but many, many more died* ***because*** *of me.*

He remembered some of their faces. The citizens of Lagentia. His brave legionnaires. The young centurion...

He knew what it meant when I gave him the order to seal the city: the death of all those people still trapped in Lagentia. And then when the LON made a final attempt to breach the city doors, he and his men fought it back, kept it at bay. It was a desperate fight but in the end, they had to seal the city with themselves ***inside*** *in order to protect the rest of the Realm.*

Hostus closed his eyes as he remembered the centurion who faced death so bravely. He remembered his face, his voice, his name.

His name was Hostus...

After what felt like an eternity, and as if a trance had been broken, she released him and pulled him out of the water.

There he sat, bent over, retching and regurgitating the water he had swallowed. When he finally looked up, she was standing in front of him, tall and commanding, her green copper-flame eyes flashing with confidence.

He nodded, satisfied. "You're ready," he said.

That night he left again to fight.

BAIT

"Servis, stream news," instructed Tors. She nibbled thoughtfully at a fig as Servis projected the news in front of her. It had been several weeks since Hostus had left to join his legion and the bulletins provided Tors with little detail, other than reports of skirmishes still breaking out on most of the twelve planets. The hardest they said, were being fought on the planet Amorgos itself and in particular around the capital city of Alandia where it was reported that the authorities were closing in on the Rebellion's own shuttles to their space carrier, the Tethys.

It had been months since seeing Jula and with the increasing clashes between Rebellion and Reds, Tors had a feeling the rebels were having difficulty shaking off the empire in order to enable the Tethys to leave the Realms unhindered.

They'll be looking to launch imminently, she thought to herself. *They risk being discovered the longer they delay the launch.* She had no doubt Marcus would see Jula on the Tethys as he had promised, but how and if they had already managed to do this or not in the midst of the unrest in Alandia, she wasn't sure. She wondered too, where Hostus was at that moment. If he was in Amorgos, it was likely he'd be one of those fighting against Marcus and his supporters. Added to that, Hostus had to follow the orders of the Emperor and yet keep her whereabouts concealed from him.

The folly of men and their wars.

War only taught her one thing: that there were no winners. There were no heroes or villains. No honour or treachery. That only depended on which side you sat on.

Outside, the blizzard had calmed down and a muted silence enveloped the villa. The snow storms, a stark contrast to the milder, pleasanter weather only a few months ago, had lashed continuously for the past few days and if it were not for Servis diligently clearing the snow, the villa would have been completely buried under by now. Not that that would have prevented Tors from her outdoor training for the snow provided her with variation to her endurance runs. In fact, yesterday's run on the mountain proved an exhilarating test in reactiveness and improvisation when she inadvertently triggered a mini avalanche and ended up having to glissade her way down the mountain ridge to outrun it. Most of all, the challenges the weather presented were a welcome distraction from Hostus.

Tors wrapped the blanket around her shoulders and turned to stare out the window at the powdered ridges of the mountains surrounding the villa. Her eye traced its outline right up to the snow-capped peak where she rode out yesterday's little avalanche. She missed him terribly, his presence and his banter or lack of rather. Yet their relationship was an unspoken conundrum. He was terse with her, at times almost repellent but his touch—here, there, correcting a grip, adjusting a stance—spoke volumes. And at night, after a hard day's training, despite her advances, he would turn her away firmly towards her bedroom and head resolutely for his in the opposite direction. It was as if he himself was in turmoil but each time he returned, it would be as if he needed her more than ever.

She glanced away from the window and back to the streamed images of the armies curtailing the progression of the uprising. *Propaganda news no doubt,* she thought cynically. Official news streamed from the empire rarely contained anything else other than what the Emperor wanted you to hear.

A heading flashed on screen with some breaking news: some pods bound for the rogue carrier Tethys had been detected on the outskirts of Alandia. The image showed a close up of the mountains just outside Alandia.

Tors sat up. She recognised their distinctive shape at once. Like the jagged comb of a cockerel, those craggy structures sat over a vast network of natural tunnels, with entrance openings on one end and on the other, a vertical rock face pockmarked with holes formed from some of those tunnels. *The Peaks of Minos!*

Then it dawned on her. *This must be where they hid the shuttles for the Tethys...*

The next image showed a pod shooting out of one of the fissures of the mountain face and into space. As Marcus told her once, the shuttle pods were located all over the Realm, some at secret locations, others hidden openly at transport stations, but all poised to automatically take-off and make for the Tethys' secret location once its passengers were inside. The bulletin flicked to images of Avems hovering mid-air, their guns trained at the openings on the face of the mountain, in position, presumably to shoot down any shuttle pods that emerged. On the other side of the mountain, where the entrance to the tunnels stood, rebel troops were holding the Reds back from advancing into the tunnels, throwing every last ounce of firepower at them.

They're surrounded on both ends: the entrance to the tunnels and on the opposite side! The Reds are waiting to shoot down the pods on the opposite side of the mountain!

LIVE! REBELS TRAPPED! Screamed the headline against another image. Tors rushed forward to take a closer look. It was the image behind the headline that caught her attention. A particular face in the panicked crowd.

Jula!

The image was grainy but it was Jula alright, with Niko behind her. The footage continued, showing them cowering under the barrage of shots, then quickly disappearing into the mountain.

"Jula!" blurted Tors. "Servis, pause!"

Tors stared at the frozen footage. The image showed the army getting ready to enter the tunnels.

Jula's a sitting duck. They all are. The Reds will find her before the day is over! I have to get her out before it's too late! Hurriedly she cleaved open the portal and stepped through.

TORS

PEAKS OF MINOS, AGERON

The muffled sound of gunfire outside the caves reverberated through the tunnel, creating disconcerting echoes all around and down the rest of the subterranean network. Tors stepped out of the portal and peered cautiously. Yes, this felt about right. She was fairly certain she was in the right place.

Moving in and out of the Ether was not an exact science and whilst she knew where to exit in order to get to the Peaks of Minos, this was as near as she ever was going to get to where Jula was. She would have to trek the rest of the way through the mountain passageways in order to find Jula.

She looked around, her eyes adjusting quickly to the dimness of her surroundings. She knew this section of the tunnel well. *Vidar used to hide out here in the old days.* It was a fairly wide passageway with further tunnels branching off it, formed by the rock's natural erosion over millennia.

Now which way to find Jula? The news footage had shown Jula and Niko running into the mountain and then images of shuttle pods escaping from the other side of it, narrowly avoiding the barrage of plasma bombs from hovering Avems trying to hit them.

Now Tors knew that this complex maze of natural subterranean passages twisted and burrowed all the way from one side of the mountain to the other, where they ended in a sheer wall of rock, pock-marked with openings from those passages, overlooking a ravine a thousand feet deep. *So all I have to do is make my way towards these openings.*

She walked along the tunnel listening intently and followed the persistent pounding of plasma bombs.

A great spot for hiding and launching the shuttle pods, she noted as she walked on. *These passages are too complex to map and too deep for detection scanning.* Coupled to that, the numerous openings on the other end served as ideal exit points for launching the shuttle pods. Tors hoped she could remember the route Vidar had shown her before.

And then the tunnel led to a fork.

Ah. Which one? She looked carefully at both exits. The one to the right sported a tiny hint of a mark a few inches just above floor level; the symbol for *ecfugium.*

Meaning escape route.

So a mapped tunnel. Years ago, Vidar had shown her what the different symbols meant. Shorthand markings, he said, so that people knew which route to take and by people he meant brigands, outlaws, convicts and whoever else desperate enough to flee the authorities at the risk of getting lost in these tunnels.

So Tors chose the other exit—the unmarked one—recalling also Vidar's advice that ecfugium markings were often swapped to trick the authorities down the wrong tunnel instead. She slowed as she entered this new section of tunnel. Here, light filtered in from holes and openings overhead, illuminating the rocky contours of the tunnel's walls and sections of its floor like spotlights amidst the gloom.

A figure flit past a dim pool of light ahead.

Reds!

Another imperial soldier followed suit. Then another and another, all in perfect silence.

No doubt looking for the rebels. And Jula.

Tors stopped mid-step and backed into the side of the wall, careful to stay within the cover of darkness and away from the light that percolated through the natural fissures above. The soldiers moved on. Then something stirred behind her.

An arm reached out.

Her reactive instincts kicked in first. A short inverted punch delivered swiftly yielded results almost instantaneously. The attacker fell to the ground, landing heavily on his back, face visible under a small pool of light. To his credit, he barely made a noise.

Marcus??

The surprise was mutual and that look was evident on his face, even as he raised his finger to his lips as a warning to keep silent. Tors leant over to help him up but Marcus waved her offer down, rolled to the side away from the light and staggered silently back on his feet. It was a good minute or two before having made certain the Reds had moved on, before he finally signalled the all-clear to her.

"Well, if it isn't you, back from the dead," he said, his voice low. "How did you know to get all the way in here?"

"It's all over the news," whispered Tors, "and I know this place. Vidar used to hide here." She swallowed hard. Seeing Marcus again brought back images of that night and Vidar. *Vidar sold us out but no one deserved to die like that.*

"I saw Jula and Niko in the news feeds," she said quietly. "Where is Jula? Has she made it out in one of the pods?"

"Not yet," said Marcus, "but any minute now. Niko's taking her there as we speak, as is Pihla with Marie and her two boys." Marcus gave a weary nod. "We did well—this will be literally the last pod bound for the Tethys."

"If the Reds don't get to them first," said Tors. "This place is crawling with them."

Marcus agreed. "I'm on my way to tunnel five where the pod is parked. If we see any Reds heading that way, we're going to have to draw them away from there, you understand?"

Tors nodded.

Marcus led them down the passageway, avoiding the occasionally pools of light, their feet padding noiselessly on the dry sandy floor.

Tors wondered how anyone could remain hidden from the Reds for long when these tunnels offered nowhere to hide, and light filtering in from cracks and openings overhead obliterated any residual chances of staying hidden. She didn't have to wonder long for Marcus signalled for them to halt.

They stopped, listening intently. There was a faint echo of movement ahead. Someone or some persons were coming!

Taking several steps back, Marcus ran towards the tunnel wall, scrambled up and with a practiced motion of the arm, hoisted himself up through one of the openings overhead.

Quickly, he signalled Tors and reached out to towards her.

She followed him, leaping upwards off the wall and grasping his outstretched arm to pull herself up. Scarcely had they hoisted themselves up into the opening above, a flurry of red cloaks flashed past below. Tors held her breath as another team of Reds hurried past.

Marcus tapped her lightly on the shoulder and motioned for her to follow him.

Tors looked around. They were in another tunnel, just on a level above the one they had just been in.

Of course! These passageways don't just branch left or right, they branch in literally all directions, including up and down! So this is how they'd evaded the Reds so far; the routes to the pods cut across levels in all directions.

Deeper and deeper through the warren of tunnels she followed Marcus, avoiding the occasional sinkholes in the floor of the passageway, then going down a level again until at length, the passageway widened into a gallery. This time, it felt solid underfoot.

Almost circular in shape, the gallery, carved out naturally through erosion over the centuries, stood silent and empty, dimly lit by shards of light filtering through a handful of overhead fissures. Crowning its sides were five other entrances to further tunnels. It looked like an ancient theatre awaiting the entrance of its actors.

We must be near, figured Tors, for the air here carried the distinct smokiness of discharged weaponry.

They stopped at the mouth of their tunnel, careful not to enter the gallery, and stayed hidden in the shadows.

Marcus peered out cautiously. He gave Tors a little nudge and pointed at the tunnel diagonally across them. There in the shadows, Tors could see Marie and her two boys at the mouth of their tunnel with Pihla next to them, waiting.

Tunnel five, Marcus indicated to Tors. Then he pointed to the tunnel on the far right. There, waiting in the shadows with Niko was Jula.

The gallery was clear. Tors could see Marie and her boys gesturing at Jula to run across to join them. She held her breath. *Go, Jula,* she urged silently. *You can do it. Just a quick run across.*

But Jula hesitated.

And then footsteps! Then several forms making their way through one of the other tunnels.

Reds!

Jula retreated into the shadows as the soldiers poured into the gallery and gathered there to decide which tunnel to investigate next.

Marcus put his hand on Tors' shoulder. In his other hand, he held a pebble. Aiming it carefully at the opposite tunnel, he signalled for her to get ready to run.

He's going to create a diversion, realised Tors, *but what if that doesn't work?* Her eyes searched for Jula in the shadows of the tunnel. *If I can just get to her, if I can grab her, then I can get us into the Ether. I can get her out of here safe and sound.*

But before any of them could do anything, a faint rattle from loose gravel from tunnel five punctured the still silence in the air.

Marie's tunnel!

It was enough to attract the Reds, then—

"By Dyaeus I'LL TAKE YOU WITH ME!" Grabbing Niko's gun, Jula stepped out into the gallery and shot wildly at the soldiers.

They responded instantly with a barrage of shots.

"NOOO!" Tors reached out as Jula's body fell to the floor, but she was held back by Marcus.

Marie and her boys fled into their tunnel.

Some of the Reds moved to give chase but were stopped by their leader. "Forget them!" he yelled, calling them away from tunnel five. His eyes were trained at Tors who had given her position away.

"Get HER!" he shouted, pointing a rather impressive looking weapon at her.

Tors and Marcus turned to flee.

BOOM! Stun discharge. It hit her like a shockwave, knocking her off her feet.

Marcus pulled her back up on her feet but she could hardly feel her legs, the stun discharge having rendered them temporarily debilitated. Marcus yanked her arm over his shoulder and ran on, part carrying her, part dragging her, the Reds hot on their heels.

Tors shook her head in effort to clear it. *If I could just cleave an exit into the Ether...* but she was too disorientated to focus.

They ran on, Marcus seemingly knowing where to go. At last, they stumbled into the light of an opening ahead and onto the welcome sight of the gleaming wings of a sleek hyperglider.

Sensing her legs regaining their sturdiness, Marcus let go of her and left her to lean against the body of the aircraft for support and turned his attention to the service door release mechanism. As the door of the aircraft opened, he reached back for her. "Coming?"

She hesitated. "I don't ..." she started. She saw his eyes flick to the left of her.

Marcus instantly drew his gun.

Tors swivelled to look at whom it was pointed at. The unmistakable vizard, the insignia on the right sleeve.

Hostus!

"No wait!" She stepped in between them, blocking Marcus from having a clear shot at Hostus. "He's not with the Reds," she said.

"What do you mean he's not with them?" replied Marcus incredulously, looking at Hostus, unmistakably Imperial in his centurion uniform.

Tors sighed. "It's a long story,"she said and then turned to address Hostus. "What are you doing here?"

"My men are heading this way," he said to her quietly, not taking his gaze off Marcus.

"*Your* men?" repeated Tors.

Hostus nodded gravely.

His men, noted Tors. *The ones who were searching in the tunnels. The ones who killed Jula. So he knew. About the pods.*

"You need to leave now," Hostus continued.

"So you're with the empire now?" Marcus asked, glaring at Tors accusatively.

"No,"she replied, "It's not what you think." She shot a glance at Hostus. "*He's* not what you think..."

"Then prove it," said Marcus hotly, "Prove you're not a traitor and come with me."

"And what?" asked Tors bitterly. "Join your fight? Your war against what? For what? So that you can overthrow the empire and win your freedom? The freedom to do what?"

"Yes," replied Marcus, "The freedom to decide our own lives. To do what we want and not what the empire tells us. To be free from oppression and corruption."

"Is *this* what you want?" shouted Tors, pointing towards the tunnels. "Is this your meaning of freedom? More lives sacrificed? At what price, your kind of freedom?"

Hostus placed his hand on her shoulder. "We have to go," he said gently, "and so should he."

"No," said Marcus looking at Hostus squarely. "She's coming with *me*." He looked at Tors, willing her to come with him but she stood back.

Marcus banged the hyperglider in anger.

"Marcus..." Tors tried to explain but he had stomped inside the aircraft.

As the ship lifted off, Hostus said, "You cannot stay in Alandia or anywhere in Ageron for that matter. It's too dangerous."

"Well I can't go back to Villa Castra," Tors replied. "I don't want to anyway."

Go where indeed? she asked herself uncertainly. *Away from the Rebellion—yes, and all this—without a doubt. But where in all of the Realms can I go to avoid both rebels and the empire?*

Hostus spoke gravely, echoing her sentiments. "The uprising is fast turning into a war and what's more," he continued, concerned, "it was not by chance you came here. The Emperor made sure Jula was shown in the newsfeeds, knowing that that would draw you out of hiding."

Tors shuddered at the revelation. At the time she had suspicions that the bulletins were a ruse from Marcus to try and lure her back to him but if this was orchestrated by the Emperor then ...*what does the Emperor know?*

She looked at Hostus. "But where will I go?" She gave a bitter laugh. "Back to Ceos? I know some great slums there..."

Hostus shook his head. "We have to assume the Emperor knows you are the Key and Dyaeus knows, who else? And if the rebels find out as well, you'll have the entire Realm hunting you down. We have to hide you somewhere safe and out of the Realm," he replied. "Somewhere no one can reach you."

Tors stared at him.

Hostus nodded. "I have an idea..." he said as they turned to exit the tunnels.

THE PERFECT HIDEOUT

The familiar wood panelled corridors of the Red Palace drew an uncomfortable breath from Tors.

"Why are we back here?" she asked as they walked, their brisk footsteps muted by the corridor's deep carpet of green. They had flown here via Hostus' own ship, landed a few miles away amidst the hidden ridges of the Red Mountains, and made their way into the Palace's underground labyrinth via a secret access way.

Instinctively she pulled her cloak closer to shield her lower face but she needn't have bothered. As before, the hushed, confined passageways were eerily empty. Indeed the labyrinthine sprawl of the Red Palace was rumoured to be so large and convoluted that even the residents themselves had never set foot on more than a tenth of it.

They walked on for nearly an hour, passing door after door, until at long last Hostus stopped outside a small wooden door. It was rather unremarkable looking, with its plain dark panels and unadorned panels, but for its old, ornate door handle. Hostus removed his glove and placed his thumb on a small indent in its top. A subtle gleam underneath the pad of his thumb was all that indicated a finger scan and the door unlocked with a soft click. He let her enter first.

It was the last thing she had expected to see.

The bright, artificial white light, almost blinding, filled the entire space around her. The last time she had ever seen something like this was as a child travelling with her parents.

This is impossible…

Hostus nodded. "Yes," he said quietly, "it's what you think it is."

The tunnel stood barely a few inches above their heads but its unearthly look, the dazzling whiteness joining the walls, ceiling and floor into one continuous tube was unmistakable.

A Gateway!

"I thought these were all destroyed in the last War," she said, finally finding her voice.

"All but this one,"explained Hostus. "This is a private gateway; a scaled-down version. One that has been kept secret for centuries, from even some at the highest echelons of power. Sadly, it is but a fraction of of the commercial ones that were destroyed long ago. Not powerful enough to transport more than the occasional one or two travellers."

"Where does this lead to?"

"The planet Skansgarden in the Ellagrin system," he said. "More specifically, the Summer Palace of House Ellagrin. Come, I will show you."

Ellagrin…, reflected Tors uneasily. She had not thought of Ellagrin for a long, long time.

They walked through the brilliant white corridor of light. It was a short walk, no more than ten metres in length and at the end stood a second door, this time made of rosewood and decorated in a marquetry of tortoiseshell and brass. It was slightly smaller than the first, lending Tors to bend her head a little as she stepped through.

Tors blinked in wonder. They were in a sun room but oh what a sun room it was. Constructed mostly out of glass encased in elegant frames and ornamented with lapis lazuli and gold rosettes, daylight streamed in from above and all around, through glass that stretched from marble floor to the glass domed ceiling. It flooded the entire room and reflected off the gilded chairs and gold stucco work. She glanced back at where she had come from. The rosewood door belonged to an antique French armoire in the middle of the room!

But it was what lay outside the glass walls of the sun room that held her speechless. Stretched three hundred and sixty degrees all around them were rolling hills of lush green, and above them a wide open expanse of sky. Tors gazed in amazement at it all. It was not red and hazy but a vivid azure, dazzling and breathtakingly beautiful.

Was Ellagrin always this beautiful?

A woman was sitting on one of the chairs, reading. She glanced up and seeing Hostus, moved elegantly over towards them.

Tors stiffened. She recognised the face; the glittering cobalt eyes. At once her sword was drawn, its tip pointing at Elena's slender neck, keeping her at arms length.

Elena looked just as surprised, although her expression was without any accompanying action.

"What's the meaning of this?" Tors demanded, glaring at Hostus askance.

Hostus placed his hand on her sword and lowered it gently.

"This woman killed Vidar!" protested Tors, her gaze still fixed on Elena's unperturbed expression.

Hostus nodded gravely. "That may be," he said. "You

planned to steal her Eldur after all. But she is the one person that can keep you safe." He looked at her but it was hard to tell what he was thinking, his vizard being only minimally expressive. "This is an old friend and one who will not betray me." Hostus then turned to Lady Elena and bowed. "Your Highness," he said as she came closer.

"How interesting," Lady Elena murmured. Her eyes glittered with sardonic amusement. "Have you brought me a thief or a rebel, Hostus?"

Hostus bowed again, lower this time. "Neither my Lady,"he said. "She does not possess your Eldur, nor is she in alliance with the rebels. I regret we have not been able to trace the Eldur as yet. However I have great need of your assistance."

Lady Elena laughed. "The mighty Hostus needs *my* help?"

"This is Tors," Hostus explained. "She possesses information on the Rebellion which they do not wish known. However skirmishes with the rebels are spreading and fast escalating into a full blown war. I need your help my Lady, to keep her here hidden for the time being."

"Such a lot of effort for one little individual,"she said amusedly. "Surely your men can keep her safe?"

Hostus shook his head, "I'm afraid not, my Lady. Ageronians too it would appear, are after her." He paused and added, "The Emperor I'm afraid seems rather keen on killing our captured rebels before we can extract information from them."

"Ah…," murmured Lady Elena who seemed to take that as sufficient explanation.

"It is for this reason that I look to your wisdom and discretion. I will return for Tors once the fighting has stopped." Hostus stopped and waited as Lady Elena approached Tors.

"My…," she said, looking closely at Tors. Her eyes seemed to emit a glow from within, "how *very* interesting..." Then abruptly, she appeared to have made up her mind. "Very well Hostus," she said, her lips curling slightly. "I shall assist you. In good faith and perhaps one day, I shall call in my favours."

Hostus bowed.

"But Host—" began Tors but Lady Elena stopped her and held her gaze stolidly. Her eyes softened a little. "We may have our differences, you and I," she said quietly, "But I know well enough when political stakes require one to cast pettiness aside. Hostus is a friend and ally, and we have depended much on each other over the years. If he has entrusted your safe-keeping with me, then I shall honour it."

She turned to Hostus and said, "The Summer Palace is almost exclusively mine. Niklas never stays here—he hates it. She can stay with the *servi* on the West Wing where she will be safe from encounters with any of the lesser royals."

Tors regarded her uncomfortably. However, there was something to be said for this as a hiding place, especially for someone potentially wanted by every single inhabitant of the Realms. *At any rate this would certainly be the last place Akseli or anyone for that matter would ever look...*

"Thank you my Lady." Hostus kissed her hand, nodded at Tors and disappeared back into the Gateway before Tors could say anything further.

FITTING IN

SUMMER PALACE, ELLAGRIN

The West Wing of the Summer Palace was, Tors supposed, as good a hiding place as any with the added bonus of not being in the Realm where she could be spotted by Akseli's spies. Set aside for use by staff and servants in order to provide for the smooth running of the palace, the West Wing bustled with cleaners, cooks, handmaids, guards and all manner of staff tasked with serving the steady stream of foreign to outlandish-looking guests Lady Elena seemed to constantly receive. And when it came to people, she certainly liked variety for even those who worked here were as diverse and exotic-looking as the guests they served. All this provided a constant eddy of people and enough cover and anonymity for anyone who wished to remain inconspicuous. Compared with the quiet and more private East Wing which was solely restricted to Lady Elena and some lesser members of the royal court, the West Wing ran as a separate ecosystem of its own with its very own particular set of chores and purposeful activities.

"By Ysgarh, you'd think a pair of pigs lived here!" complained

Agneta as she and Tors heaved the heavy basket of dirty linen out of the room. The two were hard at work cleaning out the guest apartments in the West Wing. During her stay here, Elena had tasked Tors to work as a scullery maid, pairing her up with Agneta who talked incessantly and asked a lot of questions.

Far too many questions, noted Tors cynically. *No doubt to uncover as much information from me as she possibly can.*

Today they had to clean out the rooms recently vacated by Lord Goran, his wife and their entourage—just a few of the steady stream of guests that seemed to frequent the palace and attend the many parties hosted by Lady Elena.

"Leave the linen by the door whilst I empty out the buckets," instructed Agneta as she disappeared into the toilet. Tors deposited the heavy basket of dirty linen by the door with a loud thump and instantly regretted not placing it down gently. She snuffled with revulsion as the resulting whiff of putrid smells wafted straight into her nostrils. Agneta was right and judging from the filth and food stains on the sheets, Lord Goran and his wife did indeed live like pigs.

"Right, let's get out of here," called Agneta, carrying a bucket and a mop in each hand. She looked at Tors and nodded bossily at the linen basket, "Go on, get that..."

Tors shot her a dirty look and reached down to lift the heavy basket. *Why am I not surprised she went for the mop and buckets?*

Agneta shooed her out of the room and closed the door behind them. Tors turned to go, basket in her arms, and then —"Ooof!", bumped into one of the palace guards.

Dressed in standard indigo uniform, he towered over the two women, broad-shouldered, and sporting an unruly tuft of hair at the top that spouted over his close-cropped sides like a blonde firework. "Woahhhh!" he exclaimed as he moved out of her way. He glanced at Tors, then at Agneta with her buckets and mops and grinned. "Agneta! What are you doing with mop and buckets? Have you been punished?"

Agneta stomped on his foot. "Shut up Sigurd," she snapped at him. "This is none of your business." She nodded towards Tors and continued, "We're just cleaning up after Lord Goran and his party."

The big lumbering Sigurd turned back to look at Tors, peering over the large load she held in her basket. She wobbled a bit at its weight. "Whoops!" said Sigurd, reaching out to steady her. "You need a hand?" Tors shook her head firmly but Sigurd reached forward from behind her anyway, both hands caging her on each side, and said rather salaciously, "Here little lady, let me help y—"

Tors elbowed him in the rib before he could finish, dropping the heavy basket on his foot at the same time.

"Oww!" yelled Sigurd. He grabbed at her to stop his fall but unfortunately for him, that move too, was misconstrued by Tors who retaliated instantly. "Ow! Ow! *Oww*!" continued Sigurd as her left leg went under his to hook it.

In a single swift stroke, her other hand reached for his sword and pulled it out as he fell.

"OOOF!" went Sigurd as he laid on his back, eyes centred on the pointed end of his sword in his face. "Okay! Okay!" he said, putting both his hands up. "I was just trying to help, that's all."

Agneta gave a cackle of laughter as Tors lowered the sword and handed it back to him. She extended her hand to help him up.

"You have a firm grip," said Sigurd as he took it, "and you seem pretty good with the sword..."

"Very good in fact," came a cool voice from behind. The

three of them whirled round in surprise, to see Lady Elena standing behind them in the corridor.

Sigurd knelt. "My lady," he said, bowing as Agneta curtseyed beside him.

"You'll have to pardon some of the palace guards here," Elena said, her eyes firmly on Tors who had remained steadfastly upright. "Not all have manners these days," she said. She smiled. "Perhaps being a scullery maid isn't the most suitable job for you here."

She looked Tors up and down, her cobalt blue eyes sharp and piercing. "I need bodyguard," she said brightly, "and on certain occasions, one that is less conspicuous than my tall Varg." Her eyes glittered. "Perhaps you could be my bodyguard instead of cleaning the toilets." Elena turned to Sigurd. "When are the next try outs for new recruits?"

"Two days' time, my lady," answered Sigurd. "We have them weekly, every Fredag."

"Good," said Elena and turned back to Tors. "I want *you* to try out for them."

"I hardly think I'd be suitable for something as important as this…my lady," Tors replied, returning her gaze with a level look. *And why by Dyaeus would I want to anyway? I'd rather clean toilets for the rest of my stay here, than be anywhere near you.*

Elena lifted her hand. "It is not for discussion," she said, smiling sweetly. "Think of it as a step up from menial labour," she continued. Her face appeared amiable enough although her eyes were anything but.

I've seen that look before, observed Tors warily. *When a cat plays with a mouse before eating it…*

"See to it she tries out," Lady Elena instructed Sigurd and walked off.

* * *

THE LAST DAY of the week or Fredag as the Ellagrins call it, arrived and as instructed Sigurd came to collect her for the try-outs.

"We get all sorts come here to apply for the position of palace guard," he explained, sounding more like a tourist guide than a palace guard in charge of the event.

He probably also thinks I'm scared out of my wits, thought Tors amusedly as Sigurd continued with his rather apologetic ramblings.

"Two rounds each—first, recruit against recruit, then the winner against a palace guard," said Sigurd. "Those who try out are mostly civilians and farmers, many from the smaller provinces outside the cities." He eyed Tors and nodded. "There won't be many ex-military if at all, so you'll be on fairly equal footing."

He beckoned her over to the line of potential recruits and handed her one of the wooden truncheons being issued out. "Here," he said with a smile, "you'll be relieved to know you won't be using swords. Just these for the first round. After that it's hand to hand combat."

Tors looked at the truncheon, unconcerned.

"I ah... got to go," said Sigurd leaving her in the waiting line. "I'm supposed to see to things. See you in the arena later!" He gave her a friendly nod and walked off to the other side of the open-air courtyard to get the trials started.

Half an hour later, the trials began. Tors looked on as the first two candidates circled, facing each other before launching into combat, truncheons flying at each other. *I don't need to win,* she told herself, *I just need to fend off most hits and then lose the round.* She really didn't fancy being Lady Elena's bodyguard at all. *The further away from that woman the better.* She didn't trust Elena, no matter what Hostus said. *I'd rather clean out shit all day than be near the snake that killed Vidar...*

The bell rang indicating her turn next.

Tors entered the ring, conscious of the cheering and jeering that seemed to have increased in volume and excitement with each bout. Although strictly disallowed, she was sure bets were being drawn, especially amongst the palace guards watching each combat session.

In the far right corner where the crowd had parted slightly to give her an uninterrupted view of the proceedings, stood Lady Elena with Varg, her giant of a bodyguard, and two of her handmaids.

"Next!" shouted Sigurd waving Tors and her opponent into the centre.

Tors got into position inside the ring, small, slim and dressed in a plain tunic and trousers loaned from one of the younger squires. Facing her was a brutish-looking chap with arms like tree trunks. He was slightly shorter than the others before him but still a good foot taller than her. Tors eyed him casually, oblivious to the scornful jeers and heckles from the crowd at the seemingly unfair pairing of the two of them.

"Begin," Sigurd called out and the bell clanged.

Tors faced up to the man. He grinned at her and encouraged by the resultant laughs from the crowd, beckoned her with a derisive wave of his hand. His other hand, firmly grasping his truncheon, trembled with an eagerness to use it on her.

"C'mon get on with it! Forget the foreplay!" yelled one of the onlookers. A chorus of laughter and jeering followed which seemed to push him into action. With an impatient grunt, he launched himself at her, truncheon raised and teeth bared. His club went wide past her head as she swerved swiftly to the side. She smacked her truncheon squarely on the back of his head as his body moved forward past her.

Don't knock him out, she told herself as she leapt back into a defensive position to face him once more.

"You're letting the little girl beat you up!" jeered someone, which made the back of his neck flush beet-red. Angered, he whirled round and lunged for Tors. She side-stepped and then hit him between the shoulders with her truncheon next. It was too easy. Like most brutes, her opponent relied on his bulk and strength, but little else.

He went back for her, yelling obscenities, truncheon held high ready to swing at her again. That left him wide open in the front so she jabbed him in the solar plexus with hers. Coughing, he staggered backwards, doubled in pain and dropped his truncheon.

Dyaeus, Tors thought to herself, *how the hell am I supposed to actually lose?* She remained facing him and lowered her truncheon.

He looked at her a little uncertainly and then decided to try once more. His dignity was at stake. A few from the crowd were heckling and laughing by now. He launched himself at her but this time Tors didn't strike back. She let him grapple her and grapple her he did, his trunk-like arms wrapped around her squeezing her tight.

By Dyaeus, hurry up and declare him the winner already! She could hardly breathe. But he had other ideas. Eyes blazing mad, he threw her to the ground, lifted his truncheon and aimed for her head.

The damn meathead wants to smash my head in! Tors could hear Sigurd yelling for him to stop and the bell clanging wildly in the background but he was too mad with anger to hear anything. *Bugger!* thought Tors. Faced with the option of having her head bashed in or having to overthrow him, she hooked her leg under his, dislodged him off his feet and flipped him to the ground. Then with a mighty blow, she knocked him out with her truncheon.

The crowd went wild! Some cheered and many cussed, having lost their bets.

Tors looked down at her felled opponent and sighed.

"ROUND TWO!" called out Sigurd, grinning at her.

Tors could tell he was relieved no heads were crushed in the last round, least of all hers. She saw him pause as Elena bent to whisper something in his ear and his face changed.

He seemed uncertain and asked her something back. Elena nodded. "We don't favour recruits with differential treatment, do we now?" she said loudly to him whilst looking at Tors. The last comment, uttered loud enough for her to catch, made Tors a little uneasy.

Reluctantly Sigurd removed his cloak and stepped into the ring. The crowd clapped, eager to watch what would happen next.

"You're up against me, kid," Sigurd said to Tors. "If you do as well as you did before, you'll be fine," he added, giving her an encouraging look.

Someone rang the bell and they circled, facing each other.

The fight ended quicker than she had expected. She allowed Sigurd to get a hold on her, pretending to be too slow in avoiding him. She didn't really punch much so they ended up wrestling hand to hand in the process.

"*C'mon*!" he urged after beating her down the second time. "I know you can fight better than this!"

Tors whacked him on the jaw. He retaliated with a similar blow which she didn't block. It hurt bad. Then she moved to punch him at the side but he caught her wrist and held her as she wriggled to get free.

Aaargh! This was harder than she thought—to fight without properly fighting.

Come on, finish me off dammit! But Sigurd wasn't angry enough to do that.

So she yanked her hand free, then brought her knee up between his legs. "Pussy!" she taunted.

The move obviously worked and Sigurd's face screwed up in an angry grimace. He took one look at her and finally swung his fist at her in full force.

It landed full in her face, bursting her bottom lip before blackness swallowed her.

A PLAN BACKFIRES

Tors awoke to find herself laying on a daybed in one of the drawing rooms of the palace. It was sometime around noon and the sun streamed in strongly through the open windows, assaulting her eyes. She blinked with difficulty, her eyelids heavy, and tried to clear her hazy vision.

The delicate but haughty features of Lady Elena came into focus. Elena was bending over her, her face in full frontal view and her pale golden hair enveloped in a nimbus of light. Wisps of it trailed downwards, hanging over Tors' face and she was dabbing Tors' lip with a ball of cotton wool soaked in some herbal liquid which gave off a vinegarish tang. It smarted terribly and Tors flinched. Gingerly, she touched her mouth to examine it. It was swollen and the bottom lip had definitely split.

"Well, when it comes to combat, I guess you're not as accomplished as I had thought," murmured Elena. " Pity..."She continued to dab gently at Tors' face, her own—flawless and unblemished—seemingly stricken at the sight of the bruises.

"What will Hostus think of me if he sees you like this," she tutted, "and supposedly under my care as well."

"Like what?" mumbled Tors. She had difficulty saying the words. Even the insides of her mouth felt swollen.

Elena smiled and shook her head, then reached for a small antique-looking hand mirror on the side table. She held it in front of Tors so she could see for herself.

Tors struggled to sit up, her ribs hurt like mad. When she finally succeeded in doing so, she glanced at her reflection and winced. The bruises on her mouth and cheek—a solid shade of indigo—were fast turning yellowy-brown at the edges, as was her split lip, which looked dark, angry and crusted. *By Dyaeus, I look like hell.* A quick glance at Lady Elena told her that contrary to the sympathetic tone of her voice, Elena anything but stricken by her injuries.

"It will heal soon," said Elena casually as she put down the mirror and cotton wool. She bade her handmaid take them away and clear the table. "And before you know it, you'll be looking your usual lovely self when Hostus comes back for you," she said. Elena put a cup of warm tea in her hands. "Drink this," she said. "It'll make you feel better."

When Tors made no move to take it, Elena snatched it back and took an impatient sip from it. "There!" she said, before placing the cup back in Tors' hands, "I'm not trying to poison you, alright?"

Tors tried to raise an eyebrow but deciding that was too painful and far too difficult, took a sip of the tea instead. Elena nodded satisfactorily and turned to adjust Tors' blankets about her.

"So, how do you know Hostus anyway?" she asked casually.

Tors said nothing. *Like I'm going to tell you anything,* she thought, watching Elena. *You of all people.* She lifted her hand to touch her swollen face and recoiled instantly. That was a mistake. Touching it was agony and by Dyaeus, it throbbed so bad it made her dizzy. Tors leant back into the daybed with a groan. *Even a hog on a spit looks better than me at the moment.*

"And the rebellion?" continued Elena as if this were merely a convivial tea and chat between two ladies. "Were you always part of them?"

Tors remained stubbornly silent to her probing. She wondered if it was possible to die from incessant interrogation of this sort.

Lady Elena smiled at her. "That man—that night at my apartment—," she said, "the one who escaped…he was the leader of the Rebellion was he not?"

Tors put on her blankest stare in response.

"He was rather good-looking," mused Lady Elena, seemingly oblivious to Tors' lack of contribution to the conversation, "and I thought perhaps he has traces of Ellagrin ancestry." She leant forward and lowered her voice, her eyes gleamed with a touch of mirth, "Tell me, were you two close? Or did he leave you behind?"

Tors returned her look of interest with a level the-hell-I'm-going-to-tell-you-anything gaze, and proceeded to get off the daybed. Her vision swam and the room whirled round her as her feet touched the floor.

"Now, now, not yet," said Lady Elena, edging her back onto the daybed. "You are in no position to get up just yet. You need to rest." She patted Tors gently on the arm. "I shan't annoy you anymore, I promise."

Tors eyed her coldly but said nothing.

Lady Elena paused a moment. "Well, if it's any consolation, it did not look like he wanted to leave you behind," she said, gathering up her skirt to go. "Don't worry yourself about your chores for now," she said as she departed. "Rest as long as you need to until you feel better." She paused before the door and looked back, her eyes centering on Tors like a hawk's. "I will put you to something less strenuous until you've healed" she murmured. "You will work as one of my handmaids as I will need an extra pair of hands soon..."

She nodded to herself and explained why. "You see, my brother the Emperor, is coming to visit."

* * *

True to her word, the following week when Tors felt well enough to resume her duties at the palace, she was instructed to shadow Lady Elena's handmaids and help out in the various duties.

Those closest to Lady Elena helped with her hair, her dressing and other such matters concerned with her upkeep and appearance, whilst others like Tors and those outside the inner circle as it were, would see to things like breakfast, the sewing, drawing Elena's baths and some light cleaning duties.

Being her handmaid is just as bad as being her bodyguard, if not worse, brooded Tors as she knocked on Agneta's door. Tors gave a scornful snort. It seemed that Agneta too had been fortuitous enough to be promoted to handmaid as well although unlike her, Agneta miraculously appeared to be adept at her handmaid duties despite having just started the same time as Tors.

"Ah, you are here," said Agneta imperiously as she opened the door to let Tors in. "We must hurry and get you ready," she said, "His Excellency is here already."

"Who?"

"The Emperor, foolish girl," said Agneta, tugging Tors' tunic off her. She flew to the wardrobe, picked out a green silk gown and proceeded to dress Tors in it.

"I can't wear *that*," protested Tors, eyeing the dress with trepidation as Agneta pulled it over her head. It had a cinched waist, a terribly constricted bodice and a fairly low décolletage.

"It's a dress for goodness sake," retorted Agneta, lacing up the bodice quickly with her nimble fingers. "It's not like you've not seen one before." She tugged and adjusted it swiftly into place. "We can't have you wear a tunic and trousers. By Ysgarh, that will really make you stand out,"she continued, sweeping out any creases in the swathes of fabric that made up the skirt. "There! What a beautiful dress." She stood back to admire her handiwork, panting slightly with the exertion of having to dress Tors in double quick time. Agneta nodded approvingly. "Not bad," she said, "not bad at all." Then, snapping her fingers, she ushered Tors out of the room. "Come! We have to go. Lady Elena is expecting us to attend to her and Emperor Niklas in his private solar. "

* * *

"AH THERE YOU ARE AGNETA," said Lady Elena as they entered the chamber. Lying languidly on the chaise, she beckoned them to come closer. Beside her, reclining in a large, ornate chair, was the Emperor Niklas, legs stretched out before him like a resting lion. He hardly looked up, preferring to nurse his glass of amarinthe instead.

"Agneta, would you please fetch the bloodfruit?" purred Elena. She turned to her brother. "The orchards here have produced an outstanding crop this year," she said, "and I thought you might like to taste some."

But Niklas dismissed the offer with a wave of his hand. "I have no interest in fruit, sister," he growled. He knocked back the rest of his amarinthe in a single gulp and tapped his fingers impatiently on the sides of the glass.

"I think His Excellency is in need of a top up," Elena said, gesturing at Tors to move. Reluctantly, Tors walked across the room to take the decanter from the much more responsive Agneta who had jumped to her feet to retrieve it in the first place. Tors approached Niklas to serve him.

Yes, this is definitely worse than being a bodyguard, she reflected sourly as she walked across towards him to fill his goblet. She eyed him warily from the corner of her eye.

The Emperor was in many ways very much like Elena. Like male and female versions of each other, Niklas was tall, blonde and well-built. His features a masculine version of Elena's—elegant and haughty—but beautiful nonetheless.

As Tors neared him, she felt the icy flicker of his gaze upon her. If Elena's cold, calculative nature gave her the shivers, the Niklas' vibes downright creeped her out. Still, she poured the amarinthe smoothly into his goblet and proceeded to retreat back to her position behind Agneta.

And then his hand shot out to grab her by the wrist. Tors froze. She hadn't anticipated this.

"And who have we here?" Niklas asked. He held her wrist with an iron grip. Tors kept her gaze downwards, pretending not to notice his roving eyes. She wished she hadn't agreed to the dress Agneta had chosen for her.

Elena let out an amused laugh. "Oh, my new handmaid, brother. Lent to me to help out with extra chores, seeing as you're visiting ...." Her lips curled as she continued, "You can borrow her if you like."

Tors bristled. *So that's why you made me your handmaid.*

Niklas looked at Tors, his piercing blue eyes met her fiery green ones with equal potency. But he was not interested, she could tell. With a careless laugh, he released her wrist and turned to Elena, fixing his stolid stare on her instead. A shiver rippled through Tors.

"I have not had the pleasure of your company for quite a while, dear sister," he said slowly, as he reached out to pull and caress Elena's hand. He seemed to enjoy watching her previously playful expression change. "And there are things we have to catch up on. Matters which I have not forgotten..." There was something in his voice that made Tors turn cold.

Niklas' mouth grew tight and hard as he pulled Elena towards him roughly. "Leave us!" he snarled at Tors and Agneta.

Agneta fled without needing to be told twice, whilst Tors followed her to the door, retreating backwards, her eyes not leaving Elena and the Emperor.

Elena's eyes, bright with wicked mirth moments ago, now appeared dead and vacant. She looked across the room at Tors, and for a brief moment those cobalt eyes came alive with a flash of hate.

As Niklas stood up to remove his belt, that look turned, first into desperation, and then as the door shut behind Tors, into despair.

ELENA

It was a quiet night. So quiet the chirr of the weetabugs could not be detected even with the windows of the sun room thrown open to let the night air in.

Elena sat at her gilded writing desk and breathed in the cool air. She welcomed the silence and with Niklas having left the Summer Palace to return to his base at the Royal Palace in Namsos, all seemed that much more peaceful.

She shook off all thoughts of Niklas. *No. Thinking of him will drive me to madness.* She turned back to the accounts and buried her thoughts there as she had done so many times before.

The door of the armoire creaked slightly as it opened and Elena looked up, half expecting to see Hostus. However it was quite a different guest that came through the cabinet. One that she had not seen for quite some time.

"My dear aunt," greeted Lady Elena warmly, after recovering from her surprise and rose to embrace the regal-looking older woman.

"Elena," murmured Queen Alin, walking over with the lethal grace of a lioness.

"How wonderful to see you aunt Alin—you look well," said Elena, looking her up and down with affection. "It has been quite a few years..."

"Decades,"corrected Queen Alin, looking at her keenly. " You could have come to see me," she said in gentle admonishment.

Perhaps... but even then, you wouldn't have been able to help me. Elena smiled. "You know Niklas," she murmured. "There is no love lost between he and anyone from the Ageron household." There was a brief quiver of vulnerability in her voice. *Hold yourself together Elena...*

Queen Alin snorted. "Even his kin?"

Elena patted her aunt's arm affectionately. "You know how he is—from the day you married into House Ageron, he has considered you a traitor to ours. It would be harder for me to explain your presence if he found out. But fortunately, he is not here and as *you* are," she winked at her aunt, "we shall make the most of it, shall we?"

"Indeed we must," replied Queen Alin, placated. "It has been too long. Why have you not come to see me in Ageron?"

"There is much rioting and unrest in the Realms,"replied Elena, pouring her a drink. "Thus for reasons of safety, I had been advised to stay away. Tell me, how is the Emperor Akseli?"

"I am well and he is," said the Queen with a slight grimace, "...most *trying*."

Lady Elena smiled. "Well, he is now Emperor of the Realms," she said, handing Queen Alin her drink, "and heavy is the head that wears the crown as they say."

"Hmmph," came Queen Alin's terse reply. She eyed the faint bruise on Elena's outstretched arm as she accepted the glass of *amarinthe* but said nothing. Instead she asked cheerfully, "And how are things, my dear?"

Elena shrugged and casually arranged herself on the daybed, "Nothing much. The usual. The Winter Carnivale is of course approaching and Niklas insists I refrain from dancing all night." She rolled her eyes, "If I am expected to sit at his table all night, I shall die of unimaginable tedium."

"Well, the Winter Carnivale is the most important festival of the year after all," said Queen Alin, "and a seat next to him is always a good reminder to the Doges as to who has Niklas' ear."

Just like old times, thought Elena. *She has never quite left Ellagrin politics.*

Queen Alin sipped her amarinthe and leant back into her chair. "And the Carnivale aside, anything else of interest these days?"

"Nothing particularly exciting," replied Elena, "Although...,"she said, eyeing her aunt wryly, "a certain someone has me babysitting one of his prisoners. Away from the eyes of *your son...*"

Queen Alin lifted an eyebrow. "Interesting," she said. "Concealed from my Akseli you say? A prisoner?"

Elena nodded, smiling conspiratorially. "A prisoner," she affirmed, "One of the rebels who stole my Eldur in fact."

Queen Alin sat forward suddenly. "*What?*"

"Yes," nodded Elena, looking at her aunt keenly, "but sadly I have been given instructions not to terminate her."

"Her...," repeated Queen Alin. Her eyes gleamed with a far-off look. "And why is that?"

"I'm not entirely sure,"replied Lady Elena, twirling her glass languidly. "However I have agreed to help him. You know me... I prefer to be owed to than the other way around."

"And what does this rebel look like?"

"Female," replied Elena. "Pretty," she added a little reluctantly, "and Ageronian I believe, although she has rather peculiar features for one. She's here—I've left her in the West wing so that we don't have to see each other."

Queen Alin was silent. To Elena, that silence spoke volumes.

"Well?" she urged. "What *is* it, dear aunt?"

The old dowager stood up slowly. Her eyes glittered like artic ice. "By Ysgarh," she whispered with a slight tremble in her voice, "it is by sheer *luck* we've been handed a windfall!" Queen Alin produced a puck-shaped device from her purse. "I came to show you this," she said, placing it in Elena's hand, trembling a little. "But never, of all things, did I ever imagine…" She broke off mid sentence, then not finding the words merely said, "Have a look!"

The puck flickered to life and projected a vid into mid air. It was a recording of one of the old rooms in the ancient quarters of the Red Palace—a small circular room with an object suspended atop a pedestal in the middle, illuminated by a single spotlight. A few minutes later, a figure entered the room. Elena stiffened. Then that figure approached the object and touched it.

Elena gasped. The object unfurled and although the image was blurry, it was clear to Elena what it was. She had been privileged enough to have been shown it before. It was the oldest living being in the galaxy: the Oracle.

"The Oracle has awoken?" she breathed, looking at her aunt.

Queen Alin nodded. "Yes," she said, "but more interesting than that, *listen...*" She tapped the puck gently to increase the volume.

Elena's eyes widened and gleamed as she listened. When it was finished, she took the puck, placed it in the incinerator and destroyed it. The two women sat without speaking for a few moments.

"So she's the Key," said Elena at long last, leaning back.

Queen Alin nodded. "He didn't tell you?"

Elena bit her lip. "No he didn't," she finally admitted.

Her companion said nothing.

"Why?" muttered Elena and looked at her aunt, "*Why*? What is he playing at?"

"I have a theory," said Queen Alin, "but *you* will need to put it to the test to find out."

"What do I have to do?" asked Elena quietly. Her eyes flickered with a cold blue light from within.

TORS

Tors looked on as she scrubbed the stone balustrade of the terrace overlooking the patio below. Around her and below, shouts and jeers erupted at intervals, coming from the off-duty palace guards gathered around to watch the action. The current pair sparring below were hard at it. This was the only part of her 'stay' at the Palace that she found entertaining amidst all this menial work she had been assigned.

After Emperor Niklas' visit, whilst Agneta resumed her original role as handmaid, Lady Elena had sent Tors back to scullery duties, preferring to have nothing to do with her. It was a blessing in Tors' estimation.

She shuddered slightly at the recollection of Niklas that day.

Elena didn't make me handmaid to serve him, she realised. *She was going to serve me up ...* ***to*** *him.* Tors had expected to feel smug after that incident but instead, she found herself feeling sorry for Elena.

She lobbed her brush at the bucket standing in the far end

of the patio. It landed dead centre with a splash. Tors grimaced slightly as she straightened up to relieve the stiffness in her back. Scullery duties were hard work, and sorry or not, Lady Elena had certainly put some thought into ways to make her 'fit in' with the servants here.

I could technically, just leave, she noted to herself, *although Hostus will have a field day if I disappeared again for the next two hundred years.* She entertained that thought as she watched the fight go on.

These sparring sessions were a daily affair organised by the palace guards at the end of their day shifts, where they pitted against each other in hand-to-hand combat. Ever since her failed tryouts, the guards had kind of adopted her as one of their fold and they didn't seem to mind her watching and even joining in their bets. And these bouts were interesting to watch. They kept her mind off him. Mostly.

She had not seen him since the day he left her with Elena. *Is he still fighting the Rebellion? Trying to stop the riots?*

She rubbed her arms to massage the ache out from them. *Do I trust him enough to stay here? With an Ellagrin who seems to gain nothing by harbouring me here and probably wants me dead for stealing her prized Eldur in the first place? What if Emperor Akseli found out about his involvement in all this?*

He had always protected her, even when she was a mere urchin in the slums of Ceos, in ways that were sometimes unorthodox. *And almost always without offering any explanation whatsoever.*

She had felt a similar protectiveness back in the caves at Alandia, but more than that, there was now something else between the two of them. Something that now muddied the straightforward relationship between guardian and protege.

Why do I care if something happens to him? Thinking about someone other than herself was in itself a novel experience for Tors, one she was not used to dealing with. She wasn't sure what to make of it.

She went to retrieve her bucket and then turned her attention to the fight in front in attempt to shut out her confused emotions. As the sun dipped behind the manicured hedges of the palace gardens and the evening sky faded into soft shades of pinks, blues and buttery gold, the current match drew to a close. Tors leant over the balustrade to have a closer look.

Henrik's knees buckled as Magnus, the heavier of the two, had him in a headlock, closing off his oxygen supply. Magnus used his weight to pin Henrik down and as he tightened his grip, Henrik weakened. At the referee's signal, Magnus finally let go, leaving Henrik on his knees, heaving and gasping for air. Shouts and jeers from the others arose as the referee signalled the end of that round.

"By Ysgarh! I believe I've just lost two hundred *ore* to Viljar for that!" groaned Sigurd, pointing at the breathless Henrik. He nudged Tors at the elbow, "How much did you lose?"

"Fifty," came the answer from Tors. *Shame I hadn't counted on Magnus' stamina against Henrik's technique...*

Sigurd's ocean-blue eyes glinted with mirth. "Well," he said, puffing up his chest, "I'm up against Magnus next and you'd better have bet on me!"

Tors gave a chuckle. "I did, but are you sure you can handle him? Even Henrik couldn't today."

Sigurd gave a snort. "Hah! But I'm stronger than Henrik."

Tors' lips curled in amusement. The reliance of Ellagrins on strength far outweighed their use of technique.

"Well, stand back and enjoy the show," Sigurd said jovially. "I'll show you how it's done." He grabbed a drinking horn from Odo the squire's ice bucket. Like others around them, he had been drinking all afternoon and his face was flushed with the effects of the guards' home-made brew.

"Here, this one's on me," he said, shoving the drink at Tors. "Now watch me beat Magnus..."

Tors smiled, set her bucket down and took the drink as Sigurd swaggered into the combat circle. She was about to place her bet when a glimpse of a familiar shape caught her attention; the dark cloak and the unmistakeable vizard. He strode past the pavilions into the distance ahead. Her heart gave a little leap.

Hostus?

She couldn't be sure but the man walked with the same gait.

"Hey, where are you going?" yelled Sigurd as Tors turned abruptly and marched off towards the pavilions.

Sigurd lifted his hands in resignation, then turned back to face Magnus in the ring.

* * *

TORS RAN AFTER THE FIGURE, trying to catch up. Several times she almost lost sight of him as he strode swiftly, deftly avoiding the group of noble ladies strolling along the arched walkway in their evening walk.

He was heading into the Palace building itself now, towards the East Wing.

Tors slowed down to a brisk walking pace. She had to be more careful now as there were less people there and her running would be noticed.

What is he doing here?

Up the stairs he went, light as a panther, swiftly covering its sweeping length in barely a handful of strides. Then into the stone passageway leading towards the Royal residences.

Tors followed cautiously behind, taking care to duck

behind the pillars whenever he slowed down, lest he turned around to look.

This was ridiculous. She didn't know why she was doing this. If it was Hostus, then surely there was no need for this furtiveness. And if it wasn't him, well why was she doing this? But something was telling her to stay the course and remain hidden.

I'm sure it's Hostus and perhaps I'll finally find out what it is between him and this Lady Elena, Tors told herself. *Is he in league with the Ellagrins? Is this another one of Hostus' plans?*

She realised with sheepish surprise, that it wasn't really any of these reasons. More than anything else, she just wanted to see him again.

Ahead, he paused outside one of the doors along the long, stone corridor.

Tors ducked behind the pillar just as he turned to check his surroundings. Holding her breath, she counted to five before sticking out her head to have a look.

Bad timing! He had disappeared, presumably into one of the rooms before she had time to see which one.

Padding noiselessly along the corridor, she stopped outside roughly where he had stood earlier and tried to decide. *It would be one of these doors, judging from where he was standing a moment ago.*

She noticed one of them slightly ajar. A streak of light bled through the crack, like a golden needle across the stark, stone floor.

Tors pushed it open gently and tiptoed in.

The antechamber was illuminated by the soft light of flickering candles with thick, elaborate curtains partitioning it with the one beyond. The sound of a woman's laughter floated across.

Tors stepped quietly forward until she reached the

doorway separating the two rooms, its heavy drapery partially obscuring her view. Tentatively, she lifted the heavy brocade and peered in.

Lady Elena was on the bed, her naked body barely sheathed in a long, chiffon chemise. Standing over her was Hostus, his vizard expressionless, looking impassive as ever. Elena stretched a shapely arm towards him.

"My darling," she said languorously and pulled him close. She draped his arms around her. "You have been away for far too long and I have missed you terribly."

Hostus pulled back from her. "You said it was of utmost urgency," he said. "The rebel woman—has something happened to her? Is she harmed?"

Elena gave him a curious glance, then smiled. "I have been reading the classics," she continued, ignoring his questions. "Did you know the name Hostus comes from the ancient word *hostis*, meaning foe or stranger?"

She laughed again, this time wickedly. "Is that why you chose it? To be known as that? To her? Now that *is* amusing, the games you play..."

Tors' heart started to thrum fast. *What does she mean? What games...?*

"No games, Elena," replied Hostus sternly. "What is it you have to tell me that cannot wait?"

Elena's laugh filled the room. There was a steely edge to it. "A little bird tells me that this Tors is not just a prized rebel. In fact, I've been told she is more than that." Elena's eyes widened as she added, "Oh, much, much more…"

"And what is that?" asked Hostus. It was clear his patience was wearing thin.

Elena's eyes glittered. "I hear she is the *Key*," she whispered, nodding conspiratorially. She moved closer to him. "Is that why you are protecting her? Your little project? Have you found out how to get her to open the Gates?"

"I have found out nothing as yet," replied Hostus gruffly.

Undaunted, Elena pressed closer. She made a soft tutt in reproof. "Tell me," she said, "why did you hide this fact from me? This discovery changes everything. We have used the Nehisi for centuries. Why shouldn't you and I share the spoils of the very last one?" Her lips curled at the thought.

Then leaning back, she drew up her gossamer gown, hitching it up to her knees. Elena laughed. "If the Lagentian Gate is to be reopened," she declared, deviantly spreading her thighs, "then I'd like to propose a new union between our two Houses..."

But Hostus' gaze remained firmly on her face.

Annoyed, Elena wrapped her long legs around him and before he had time to react, pulled him around and down onto the bed in one swift move. There she sat straddling him from the top and with both hands clasping his, pressed them down above his head.

"My dear Lord Draeger," she said dangerously as she bent voluptuously over him, "the strain of all this fighting seems to have taken its toll on you and dampened your reflexes." Her left hand came down to caress the line of his cheek whilst her right, fingers still intertwined with his, slowly moved his hand to the back of his head, just behind his ear. With a deft flick, she pressed his thumb against the vizard and whipped it off.

He lurched forward, but not in time. He snatched at thin air.

"There!" Elena said triumphantly, "That's much better. When I make love to a man, I usually like to see his face!"

He attempted to push her away but too late.

And then he flinched. The periphery of his vision caught

Tors' silhouette at the doorway. He turned sharply to see her standing staring at him.

At *them.*

Tors drew her breath in sharply. Those basilisk eyes. Now she remembered why she called him Lizard Man. Except it seemed he wasn't Hostus either. Elena had called him Draeger. Lord *Draeger*—none other than the Supreme Commander and brother to Emperor Akseli.

Now that is amusing, the games you play... We have used the Nehisi for centuries... Elena's laugh and scornful words rang in her ears.

I have been played for a fool! Tors turned and fled.

"No... wait!" said Draeger hoarsely, pushing Elena away. He started after Tors but Elena clung onto his arm, slowing him down.

"But what's the matter, my love?" she asked laughingly.

Draeger turned to face her, the strain evident in his face. "You planned this, didn't you?" he said as he pushed her away and darted out of the chamber in pursuit.

* * *

Tors had already reached the bottom of the stairs and was making her way through the corridor, her footsteps on the stone tiles echoing wildly.

He spotted her trying to open a portal but for some reason failed to do so. Her gait was uneven. Something was off.

She stumbled ahead, now making her way to the Sun room.

His heart sank as it dawned on him that if she couldn't open a portal herself to escape, she was going to get out via the private gateway.

No, no no, he thought, kicking himself for all this. He had to stop her. The Red Palace was a far riskier place than here on Ellagrin. But she wasn't thinking. He knew that. She just wanted out of here at any cost.

The Sun Room was just ahead.

I have to get to her. Keep her safe. But as he approached, he found his way barred by a team of guards, their weapons pointed directly at him.

Moments later, Elena caught up behind him, surrounded by yet another team of guards.

"You will let me through," growled Draeger.

Elena's eyes met his squarely. "Why?" she challenged.

"You know why," he answered gruffly. "The fate of my people depend on it."

"The fate of your people?" sneered Elena. She laughed. "I'm sure Akseli has *that* under control."

"You don't understand," said Draeger. "Akseli—"

"Akseli will deal with her with what's best for your people in mind," Elena answered, cutting him off. She walked up to him and reached out to stroke his face, smiling beguilingly, but he recoiled from her.

"I have to go after her," he said.

Displeasure flashed in her eyes in an instant. "Wrong answer," she said dangerously. She gave a nod and her guards moved in quickly to disarm and restrain him.

"What are you playing at, Elena?" Draeger asked hoarsely.

Elena laughed as she gestured her men to bring him along. They moved away from the Sun Room towards a different section of the East Wing, where the private offices stood. Elena knocked on a door and opened it.

Standing by the window was the tall commanding figure of Emperor Niklas.

"My dear brother," she said coolly as Emperor Niklas turned to look, "may I present to you the Supreme

Commander Draeger of Ageron." She approached him and placed one hand on his chest, the other over his shoulder, and looked back at Lord Draeger.

Niklas' smile went wide and his eyes glittered, much like his sister's as he looked at Draeger.

"See how I have proven my loyalty to you?" purred Elena.

Niklas gave a loud laugh. "I told you before," he said looking at Draeger, his voice acid, "that if I ever caught you here on Ellagrin soil, the only way you'd ever get back to the Realm would be in a box."

Lady Elena looked at her brother and smiled. "Indeed," she said nodding, "although I thought perhaps we could keep him here for a while before you dispose of him. You can certainly revisit those treaties you've been concerned about, brother."

"Indeed sister," mused Niklas as a self-satisfied smile curled upon his lips.

* * *

MEANWHILE, on the other side of the private portal, light years away, Tors stumbled through into the Red Palace. Her surroundings churned and swirled around her. Her vision blurred.

I have been drugged... But how? When?

In her foggy state, she recalled Sigurd. He had handed her the drink.

*Was this all set up? Was Sigurd in it too? But why? And Hostus... or Draeger...*that was the cruelest, bitterest part of it all.

I'm such a fool! Her cheeks burned at the thought.

Stupid, stupid fool! Was this all orchestrated by him and Elena?

Her heart sank. *If he planned all this, did I then unwittingly put Marcus and his people in danger? Did my naïveté cost Jula her life?*

But she didn't have time to think about all this, for a set of hands picked her up as she toppled over.

Tors looked up only to see the cruel smile of Akseli the Younger loom in front of her, moments before she blacked out.

PART VIII

CITY OF THE DEAD

CITY OF THE DEAD

LAGENTIA, AGERON

It was dark but not because of the night. The solid structure of the Hex which covered the entire city of Lagentia, former capital of Ageron and known to all as the City of the Dead, blocked all light from outside and like an impenetrable tomb it sealed the ancient city from the outside world.

They had come in via the sole entrance point of the structure which would lead them into the city itself. Here, a set of doors barred the way: a thicker outer door and a smaller inner one, with a section in between for the incineration chamber. Tors looked at the doors and shuddered.

This was built to keep whatever's inside from getting out.

The first set of doors were massive, thick, heavy metal hunks which shuddered and groaned when pulled. As the Reds heaved to open them, their rusty hinges screamed with excruciation from centuries of disuse. Walking past, Tors noted the stark absence of any door handle or grips with which to pull them from the inside.

There was never any expectation for the Hex to be opened from the inside. Ever.

Through these doors, they entered what the men referred to as the outer ring: airtight chambers that went round the base of the structure like complex chambers of an ancient beehive. There, they had waited whilst incinerators were activated in the inner ring. A loud klaxon and flashing lights signalled the start of the incineration process and despite the continuous blare of the warning signals, Tors could hear the roar of the flames as they raged inside the airlock. A few minutes later, the warning sounds halted and the unlocking mechanism kicked into action, admitting them into the inner chamber. There a final set of doors greeted them and unlike the metal doors previously, these were smooth and flush against the smooth inner wall of the Hex.

Solislite. Tors recognised the alloy's untarnished silveriness despite her drugged state as the seamless doors parted to let them in.

Akseli strode through without hesitation as the Reds flanking him moved to install lightsticks to illuminate the way. Tors found herself shoved along roughly by her minders as the entire entourage made their way through the eerily empty streets, lighting their path as they progressed.

A city frozen in time. Tors looked at the desolate city that lay beyond as they walked through the main boulevard, their footsteps echoing eerily in the empty streets. The partially-melted remains of a hovertug greeted them at the first turning, followed by a few disintegrated carcasses of citygliders, and here and there scattered amidst the concrete and dust, lay effects belonging to the inhabitants of a city snuffed out of existence in an instant. *No bodies, no bones,* noted Tors. *Not all things survive a nuclear blast...*

The Reds set up the lightsticks as they went along and as

they gradually progressed, their lit path brought an increasingly bright but unnatural glow to the city, like an illuminated trail snaking through it. Eventually after three quarters of an hour, they reached the concourse of Lagentia's Central Station.

The station itself was located on a slight hill in the centre of the city, offering them a vantage point from which to survey the city. Where lit, the ruins of Lagentia lay before them, revealing hints of its former glory.

It was beautiful once…

Big blocks of stone, once belonging to the city's majestic towers and minarets, littered the streets like carelessly tossed giant dice, some glinting with traces of gold in their cracked seams. And interspersed with these were the main commercial buildings of the former capital. Most of them were made from stone and as such, survived the bombardment of nukes dropped over the past century and a half in attempt to wipe out the LON. From her vantage point, Tors could make out the crumbling outline of neighbourhoods and the streets that ran through them. Around the city squares, grim columns of pillared buildings stood like tattered lost children amidst the ruins of what used to be shops, hospitals, museums and galleries.

However, appreciation of the unparalleled views from her position was the furthest thing on Tors' mind at that moment. At Akseli's command, the Reds had trussed her up, arms and legs akimbo, to the power receptacle of the Gate Control room whose location afforded her that uninterrupted view of the city. The rest of that room was mostly gone, leaving only the skeletal remains of two out of four walls, minus all the windows and a partial ceiling, all this giving rise to that unobstructed view. But next to the Control room was the monument they had all come this far for.

The Lagentian Gate, an impressive, overpowering metal arc stood quietly overlooking the platform of the station. Massive but elegant, it was a monument of antiquated beauty standing untarnished even until this day and stretching at slightly under a thousand metres in radius, a testament to the finesse and unquestionable engineering skill of the Tilkoens.

Tors strained against her shackles but their metal clasps held her hands fast and kept them apart. *My hands,* she thought desperately, *I can't cleave an opening into the Ether like this.* She was also still too drugged up to be able to do so even if her hands were free. She was however not too groggy to notice her immediate surroundings.

A control panel stood stolidly in the corner—a grey and impassive chunk of machinery sealed in solislite but inert without any Eldur to power it up and bereft of its destination beacon to link it to its sister Gate on the other side. The Eldur would have been suspended in the power receptacle where Tors now dangled. She could guess what would happen next; she had read enough stories from the past to know. Once they turned this on, she would act in place of the Eldur and beacon, and as the machinery sucked the life out of her, the Gateway would open once again as it had done centuries ago.

But could it work? Would it work? Those stories were so old they bordered on myth. Even if it did work, she wondered how long it would stay open until it depleted her of her life-force. *A Gate this size, probably not very long,* she thought grimly. Tors strained against her shackles once more. It was not the Gate that unsettled her.

There is something else here...

She had sensed it the moment she stepped into this place. Something dark and sickly, that spread like a foul stench. Like a maladour, it filled her very soul with a sense of foreboding and dread. She looked around for it. Ahead, the Reds were clearing the area of the station concourse.

"Here!" alerted one of them, pointing at a patch of dark vegetation covering one side of the steps. The other who was holding what looked like a massive bazooka, pointed it at the creeper and pulled the trigger. A stream of flames emanated from the gun, searing the LON. Tors thought she saw it recoil back moments before it was torched.

"Astounding isn't it?" murmured the Emperor Akseli as he stepped onto the platform and stood alongside her. He was dressed in full military regalia and his golden armour gleamed beneath his dark cloak. He looked up at the arc of the gate. "The fact that this still stands after all these centuries is a testament to Ageronian architecture."

"Tilkoen," corrected Tors. She was having trouble focussing and Akseli's shiny armour seemed to ripple in front of her.

"What did you say?" asked the Emperor contemptuously.

"A testament to the *Tilkoens*," said Tors. "It was the Tilkoens who discovered solislite... and built this Gate with it whilst you Ageronians were still chipping away at your stone buildings like primates."

The Emperor laughed dismissively. "What the Tilkoens excelled in technology, they lacked in vision," he said. "It was Ageronian vision that created all this. My grandfather, Ageron II." He walked over to the control panel and tapped on it. "Do you know how these Gates were first set up?"

His fingers hovered over an empty oblong recess within the control panel. "Each Gate has what we call a beacon: a detachable device containing location information of the gate's counterpart at the other end. So here in this receptacle, there would have been a beacon with the coordinates of the Namsos Gate on the other end, and at Namsos there would be a beacon containing this gate's location. To establish a gateway, each gate needs its beacon and an Eldur to power it."

Tors remained silent and he continued. "We paid the Tilkoens to create the technology to invoke these artificial gateways across the Ether but in order to establish each gate's location, its beacon had to be physically carried through the Ether from one endpoint to the other. The Ether, ever-fluctuating and therefore unchartable meant this was the only way the location coordinates of the two endpoint gates could ever be learned," He looked at Tors. "However, there was no way the Tilkoens, or us, or anyone, could enter the Ether. No one but the Nehisi. It was a simple concept really. Like carrying a silk thread across a river in order to establish a rope bridge." He gave Tors a purposeful smile. "And you Nehisi, were our little spiders. The only ones, by freak of nature, who could create an opening into the Ether. So we had you carry the beacons with you, through the Ether to the other side to attach it to the gate there." Akseli's fingers ran over the cold metal of the control panel and stopped above a smooth red disc, "So when the gates were powered up, a connection could be established between the two gates. A Gateway was formed and the rest, as they say, was history."

"But the beacons were destroyed during the war," said Tors looking at the empty oblong niche.

"Ah," replied Akseli unperturbed, "we may no longer have the beacon here on Lagentia, but the beacon on the other end at Namsos—well, it was never destroyed. And now, it has been reinstated at that end." Akseli gave her a chilling smile. "You see," he said, "all we are missing is the ability to connect to Namsos from here, which is where you come in. With *you,* my little spider to punch through into the Ether, the Lagentian Gateway will come to life once more."

"Why are you doing this?" asked Tors.

"Why?" repeated Akseli mockingly.

"Yes," replied Tors. "Why open the Gateway? We both know it's not to evacuate the citizens of the Realm. Not like this. There isn't enough time to move everyone across."

Akseli's mouth twisted into a terrible mockery of a smile. "No," he replied, agreeing. "You are right. What do I care about the Exodus anyway?" He laughed. "This isn't to let our people across. We aren't opening the Gate to let people out."

His voice grew cold and calculating. "No indeed," he said, his teeth glittering. "We are opening it to let people *in*."

DRAEGER

SUMMER PALACE, ELLAGRIN

Meanwhile in the dregs of the Summer Palace in Ellagrin, Draeger paced up and down the flagstones. He had been thrown in a holding cell and judging by the muffled sounds coming from above, one directly below the ballroom of the Summer Palace. A sonorous blare of trumpets had begun, heralding the arrival of the guests for the annual Winter Carnivale.

Perhaps now would be the opportune time to escape, he considered, *whilst everyone's preoccupied with festivities.* He rasped his fingers agitatedly. He had been careless. He should have seen the signs. But what was Elena playing at, handing him to Niklas? This was an act of aggression and Elena was far too calculating to embark on an all-out war if she could get her way via diplomacy. He played back the events over the last few hours and wondered if Tors had managed to steal away from the Red Palace. A foreboding sense of unease swept over him.

This was planned. She planned all this... for Tors to see us together. And to deliver her into Akseli's clutches. If this had been staged, then Tors' chances were not looking good. Akseli would have certainly been lying in wait for her and Dyaeus only knew what he planned to do with her.

Draeger looked around trying to find a means of escape but before he had time to decide, a guard appeared with Elena and beside her, a massive hulk of a bodyguard. She motioned for the guard to unlock the cell door.

"Come," she said and motioned for her giant bodyguard to move aside for Draeger. "Varg, let him pass."

"Where are we going?" asked Draeger as he was escorted up the steps out of the dungeons and in Elena's wake.

She turned around to face him. "To the ball of course," she answered, her smile acid.

They stopped at the top of the stairs where a handmaiden stood waiting, holding a tray brimming with what looked like piles of bright feathers. On closer inspection, they turned out to be a selection of masks. Elena picked an indigo humming-bird and handed it to Draeger. Then she donned hers—a whimsical interpretation of a bird of prey in bright orange feathers, speckled with glittering blue crystals. She regarded him icily behind her mask; her cobalt blue eyes flickered with a perilous light.

She is angry.

He glanced at her once more and corrected himself. *No. Jealous.*

His heart sank. *Of all reasons, Elena... and what by Dyaeus have you plotted and agreed with Akseli?*

Elena led them up to the ballroom with Varg her huge bodyguard lumbering beside her on her left. Their footsteps rang off the flagstones and echoed all the way up the vaulted ceiling as they joined the throng of guests making their way into the Hall. Down the corridor they walked, beneath its row of brightly lit sconces. Elena was dressed very grandly, in a lavish gown of tangerine, complete with an effervescent train of the lightest silk in vivid carmine. As they progressed she nodded subtly at the guards positioned along the way. They moved in to join her until a natural barrier formed between their little group and the other guests walking alongside.

Perhaps now would be a little tricky to slip away, Draeger decided, looking at their burgeoning entourage and the growing number of guards blocking him off from any means of escape. He decided at any rate, that he needed to find out more about Elena's plans before plotting his getaway.

THE BALLROOM of the Summer Palace was an effusion of light and splendour, its majestic proportions made all the bigger by the profusion of white inside. The fluted columns of the room were twined with white blooms and exotic foliage in every conceivable shade of white and green, and the air was filled with the heady scent of lilies, jasmine and other exotic florals. Opalescent lightglobes of various sizes—some large, others no bigger than the size of a cup—hung above the tables like glowing pearls, casting a soft warm glow on the party below. Ten long tables, each nearly the length of the hall itself were arranged in rows, perpendicular to the royal dais which stood raised a few feet above ground. Each table was covered in snow-white linen and decorated with tall crystal vases filled with iridescent frost-coloured sugarpalms, their sculptural fronds spilling over like sparkling feathers. They made their way to the main table where Elena motioned him to sit beside her.

Niklas, ensconced at the throne and flushed with amarinthe, was deep into festivities. He eyed Draeger suspiciously but at the sight of Varg and the rather hefty assemblage of guards stationed behind him, raised his glass at him with a derisive smile. He was clearly used to his sister's eccentricities.

The Carnivale had begun.

Draeger sat and looked at the colourful riot of preening and posing guests seated at the tables below. Seated at his table overlooking theirs, were Elena, the Emperor Niklas and further along, twenty or so Doges. Every so often, a Doge would approach Niklas to try and engage him in conversation. Draeger observed with wry amusement, each of them tread gingerly past the glut of guards behind him and Elena, as if it were the most normal thing in the world at a banquet table. He pondered his chances against Varg in order to make an exit. *Perhaps when Niklas makes his toast,* he decided as he sipped his amarinthe politely.

Niklas did not overly concern him for if there was one thing Niklas liked more than killing, it was torture and Niklas hadn't had his fun with him yet. No, it would not be the end of him, not until Niklas had had his fun and there was some perverse consolation in that. His own brother Akseli however, now that was another matter. Akseli was unpredictable and at that moment, Draeger wasn't sure what his plans were for Tors. That, more than anything, worried him most.

The celebrations began with the feasting. Food, fresh, lavishly prepared and plentiful, was brought in and served, platter after laden platter, along with copious amounts of amarinthe. Roasted pheasants, smoked scomber, veal escalopes slathered in honey and molasses, accompanied fresh salads and exquisite grains. Elena was talking earnestly to Niklas, her head bent towards him, their conversation too faint to catch but they were clearly engrossed in their discussions. Once or twice Elena threw her head back, laughing at a private joke shared between them.

Draeger observed how remarkably alike the two siblings

looked, Elena almost the twin counterpart to Niklas, both tall, handsome-looking and golden. The lustre of their Ellagrin ancestry shone forth making them seemed almost ethereal. Niklas was rubbing Elena's back as he was talking to her and she seemed to welcome the newfound closeness between them. Brought on no doubt, thought Draeger with reproach, by Elena's offering of him to Niklas.

A faint chime of a gong sounded and the guests hushed to a respectful silence. Emperor Niklas got to his feet as Elena reached over to hand him his drink, her gloved hand lingering over the mouth of his glass as she did so. As the clapping subsided, Niklas raised his glass.

"Welcome, my lords and ladies!" His voice boomed across the Hall. "This is an auspicious day indeed," he said and waved his glass mockingly at Draeger. "In fact so auspicious we have dignitaries from far and wide joining us."

Draeger grimaced slightly at the insinuation.

Niklas raised his glass and added, casting a treacherous smile at Draeger. "Let this day mark also, the beginning of a new chapter in Ellagrin history," he declared. He smiled at the crowd. "The day Ellagrin reclaims its glory and its pride from the Ageronian swine who have kept us down for so long." There was a hint of puzzlement from the guests but Niklas declined to elaborate further. With both arms outstretched, he proclaimed, "Let the Winter Carnivale begin!"

A loud cheer erupted from the guests as they raised their glasses to their emperor.

Niklas lifted his to his lips and downed the amarinthe in one go, wiping his mouth with a sweep of the back of his hand. His smile widened as applause echoed deafeningly around.

With the toast done, Draeger readied himself to make a break for his escape but—

The Emperor's smile froze mid-way.

Draeger stiffened. Something felt very wrong.

Niklas clutched at his throat and spluttered. His face turned a ripe purple. Mottled with pinpricks of red, dark veins began to appear, lacing their way up his neck and face.

"*Niklas?*" Elena had rushed over to his side but by this time, Niklas was thrashing, tearing at his throat and choking fitfully. The whites of his eyes had turned blood-red.

"Help him!" screamed Elena looking round. "HELP him!!" she screamed again as he gasped and choked, bloody spittle frothing over his lips. She clutched at him tightly as the guests recoiled in horror. Then his body spasmed and folded, weighing down upon her. "Niklas! Niklas!" Elena struggled to hold him up as his body slid to the floor.

Someone, presumably a physician, clambered onto the dais to assist but it was too late. Niklas' body lay crumpled on the floor in a heap, heavy and lifeless.

The physician looked at Elena and shook his head.

"No… NOOO!" She shook his body, frantically at first and then she stopped and stood up slowly. Draeger shifted uncomfortably as Elena turned to face him.

No, you wouldn't dare... He stared at her in disbelief as she pointed a trembling finger at him.

"Traitor! *Murderer!*" Her voice rang loud and clear this time. Loud enough to reach even the farthest ends of the Hall.

The guards flew into action, grabbed Draeger and held him down but before they could establish their hold on him, he slammed his entire body backwards, knocking them off him like bowling pins and made for the exit. But Varg was faster, surprisingly fast for someone his size. He loomed before Draeger, cutting off his escape, and before Draeger knew it, he found himself crashing down into solid wood, pinioned to the table by the giant.

Elena walked over and whipped off his mask to reveal his face for all to see. "This!" she shouted. "*This* is the treachery of House Ageron! The Emperor has been poisoned and here sits the Supreme Commander of Ageron in our midst! Assassin!" She looked at him, eyes ablaze, "MURDERER!"

At her signal, Varg released an arm to reach for his sword to deliver retribution. Sensing his chance, Draeger wrenched himself free. Elena recoiled as he relieved Varg of his sword, tearing it from its black scabbard and then swiftly dodging the giant's iron embrace. Slashing left and right, he cleared a way and scrambled for the exit. The guards gave chase but Draeger, for once thankful of his familiarity with the palace grounds garnered through past discreet visits to Elena—*visits that were never anything more than politically motivated,* he reminded himself—swiftly made his way to the Sun room and into the secret portal.

He sprinted through the portal's white passageway and just before reaching the other end, he turned back briefly to look.

Elena was standing at the entrance staring after him.

Her face was closed, cold and expressionless. He had half-expected her to call her men to the portal to give chase but she had taken no action.

What have you done Elena?

And then slowly she closed the door of the armoire on him. It would seem that whatever it was that had occurred, he had served his purpose in it...

THE LOST KEY

RED PALACE, AGERON

Back on Ageron, Akseli's private residences at the Red Palace were searched and found to be empty, the Emperor himself nowhere to be found.

Within the confines of his private solar, Draeger paced up and down agitatedly. "Where is he, Rasmus? Where could he have taken her?"

The Chancellor answered him with concern. "The guards have searched the entire palace, my lord. Nothing. But what makes you think the Emperor has her? She could have come through the private portal and from here, made her escape anywhere. "

Draeger shook his head. "No," he said uneasily. "Akseli has her, I know it. He and Elena planned this."

The Chancellor looked at him. "How did that happen?"

"I hid her," said Draeger, "with Elena..." Words could not possibly describe the regret he felt at that moment. "She's been in Ellagrin, at Elena's Summer Palace all this time."

The Chancellor raised an eyebrow.

Draeger groaned in response. "It was the only place Akseli

wouldn't think of finding her," he explained. "It was the safest place I could think of to hide her. If anyone else found out she was the Key..." He paused, shaking his head. "I thought it was the only place no one from here could reach her. I just never anticipated Elena would..."

The Chancellor patted his shoulder. "I don't think any of us could have guessed that," he said. "But why would Elena side Akseli? And then conspire to murder her own brother?"

"Perhaps he has become too unstable," said Draeger. "He is very like their father Mikael."

"Well, with Niklas dead, she will be looking to seal her position as ruler of House Ellagrin," said Rasmus, "but the Doges would never stand for it."

Draeger nodded agreeing. "She'll need support," he said.

"Yes, but in Ellagrin, the Doges control the army," said the Chancellor.

Draeger looked at him, his eyes darkened considerably. "Which is why she'll need support from elsewhere—"

"Akseli," finished the Chancellor grimly.

Draeger nodded. "But he doesn't have military support—the legions answer to me."

"Unless he seizes control somehow," said the Chancellor slowly. He shifted uncomfortably. "Unless he overthrows our own army. But with what? He can't, surely. At any rate your armies are dispersed all over the planets to quell the rioting—"

They stopped and looked at each other. The Chancellor answered his own question. "...which is *exactly* what he wants." The old man sat down. "Your brother has cunningly kept us occupied with matters of the Carinthia and on the riots," he said. "Away from here—Amorgos. Away from our capital planet."

Draeger sat down as the pin dropped like a big stone. "Niklas mentioned reclaiming Ellagrin's glory just before he died," he said. He shook his head and looked at Rasmus. "Akseli and Elena planned this all along. She got Niklas to give the order for the Ellagrin army to take over Amorgos."

"With our armies dispersed all over the Realm, the Ellagrin army alone will be enough to take over our capital planet," Rasmus continued for him. The old man's voice shook slightly at the audacity of the plan. "If our capital planet falls, all of Ageron will fall..."

Draeger nodded. "He's using the Ellagrin army to take control of Ageron—"

"And in return, with the Ageron army behind her, the Doges will not dare defy her claim for the Ellagrin throne," finished the Chancellor.

Draeger stood up. "Akseli means to open the Lagentian Gateway! That's where he's taken her!"

"But my lord, you don't have enough men. The nearest legion is on Othon. It will be three days to get them here. We have perhaps a hundred strong here loyal to you. Akseli has several times that with him at the moment and you will need at least a thousand if you are to stand a chance against invading Ellagrins," warned Rasmus.

"I have to get her," said Draeger hoarsely as he made for the door.

"Where are you going my lord?" Rasmus asked. Even without being a military man, he knew the odds were not in Draeger's favour.

"To get us some backup," Draeger said.

"Backup? From where?"

Draeger's mouth hardened into a thin line. "From the most unlikely of sources, Rasmus," he said and strode out.

ENEMIES TO ALLIES

Marcus waited to hear Pihla's confirmation on their preflight checks. He was feeling ill at ease and wanted to leave for their new base as soon as they were ready. There was an unsettling feeling in the pit of his stomach that hadn't gone away ever since the day they parted ways with Tors at the Peaks of Minos.

He wondered if he had done the right thing in letting her go with that centurion. *I hope she's not walked into the jaws of a lion.*

He pulled absently at the crate fastenings to check that they were secure. Tors wouldn't have listened to him anyway, especially after Jula's death. He shook his head. *If I hadn't forced her to help us steal the Eldur in the first place, Jula would have been alive still. Perhaps she had a point after all. Was this really the price of freedom and if so, was all this worth it?*

"Engine's purring like a well-fed kitty," Pihla said, hitting the hatch button with a slam of her fist. "We're good to go, boss."

As the hatch of the shuttle closed in, a cloaked figure

bounded up the retreating gangway. He moved quickly and slipped in before the hatch was fully closed.

Marcus grabbed his gun. "YOU!" he exclaimed, aiming it at the intruder.

It was the centurion Tors left with at the Peaks.

"What are you doing on my ship?" Marcus demanded.

The man held out his hands. "I need your help,"he said.

Marcus laughed sardonically. "You have your legion," he said. "Why would you need my help?"

The centurion nodded. "The Emperor has her," he explained.

"What do you mean the Emperor has her?" demanded Marcus. "The Emperor has Tors?"

"Yes," the centurion answered, heavy-heartedly, "Akseli has her. Look, we don't have much time—"

"You *bastard*!" Marcus started forward but Pihla held him back before he could lay one on the man. "You sold her out didn't you?"

"No," said the centurion. "She got captured."

"You were supposed to keep her safe!" Marcus said hoarsely. "And safe from him of all people!" He punched at the wall panel. *I should have taken her with me that day, by force if I had to.*

The centurion ran his fingers through his hair, deeply troubled. "Where I took her, I thought I could keep her safe." He shook his head. "I was wrong."

"Yes," Marcus replied coldly, "dead wrong. And you have some nerve coming here!"

The centurion held out his hands. "I need your help," he pressed, "to get her out. Please...there isn't much time. She's in danger."

Marcus eyed him sardonically. "You want our help to

break her out? And why aren't you doing that yourself? Oh wait, or would that be *treason?*"

"I do not have enough men," explained the centurion, "but I know where he is holding her and I can get us in to extract her. However I cannot do it alone."

"I don't know," said Marcus narrowing his eyes. "How can I know we can trust you? And that this is not a trap to bag yourself the Rebellion in exchange?"

"Because I of all people, given a choice, would *not* be one to make a deal with the Rebellion," said the centurion. He reached behind his ear and pressed the hidden clasp releasing his vizard. The exoskeleton sagged and the vizard dropped hanging loosely around the collarbone.

"Well, I'll be damned," whistled Marcus softly as Lord Draeger's face was revealed to him and Pihla.

"By Dyaeus!" Pihla swore. "The Supreme Commander himself!"

"Y'know," said Marcus, his voice deadly quiet, "we could kill you right now and end all the Rebellion's problems instantly."

Draeger squared up to him, his eyes strange and obsidian. "No you won't," he said evenly. "You can't. But if you did, my brother will have full control over the armies and *that*," Draeger continued, "even *you* would not want." He looked at Marcus. "Please, I am asking you to help me free her, before he kills her."

"Do we know where she is?" asked Marcus, casting his mind back to the various prisons he had frequented in the past. *The Amorgos Central Penitentiary I can do,* he thought, *the Red Palace might be trickier...*

"Yes," answered Draeger, "the City of the Dead."

Pihla, who was taking a swig of her drink, spewed it out in surprise. "What? She's in Lagentia?"

"I had no idea the City of the Dead was even accessible," said Marcus at last. "Why by Dyaeus have they taken her there?"

"He's about to open the Gateway,"replied Draeger, "with her."

"What do you mean 'with her'?" asked Marcus.

Lord Draeger frowned and looked out the window. "She is the Key," he said, "…the last Nehisi."

"By Dyaeus, mother of all shit storms," whispered Pihla.

"Well I'll be damned,"said Marcus and sat down on one of the crates. "I did not see that coming..."

"So that's why she's never bothered wanting a ride out of here," said Pihla softly. "She can go anywhere she wants. Huh." She paused in thought.

"So he's going to use her to force open the Gateway," said Marcus, "but the last time they strapped one of her kind to the Gate..." He trailed off. Unlike most, Marcus knew what actually happened in Lagentia all those years ago. The source that supplied him that information had known the Customs Vilicus himself.

Draeger nodded. "Yes, it will kill her."

Marcus sat thinking. "But why does Akseli want to open the Gateway? Opening it that way won't work for very long. Certainly not long enough to evacuate the entire population of the Realm."

Pihla agreed and pointed out. "There have been no mobilisation or any comms to that effect so he's obviously not doing this as part of the Exodus—"

"Which can only mean one thing…," chimed in Marcus. His eyes widened as the truth dawned on him.

Draeger nodded.

"*Invasion*," said Marcus, finishing his own sentence and leant back.

Pihla looked at them uneasily. "But that doesn't make sense," she said. "The Lagentian Gateway connects us to Ellagrin. Why would our Emperor let the Ellagrins in? Emperor Niklas has been the enemy since the day his father waged war on House Ageron."

Draeger shook his head. "Niklas was tricked into giving the order to invade us by his sister." He paused briefly. "She had other ideas once that order was given."

"I bet," said Marcus. He remembered those cold, blue eyes.

"Niklas is dead," said Draeger.

"Emperor Niklas is dead?" said Pihla, incredulous.

Draeger nodded. "Elena poisoned him, although unfortunately it would appear that I've been made the scapegoat for his murder."

"So Elena and our Emperor Akseli..." Marcus rubbed his chin thoughtfully.

"Yes," said Draeger, "we believe she's getting the Ellagrin army to invade and take over Amorgos. Our capital planet is undefended at the moment—we have but a fraction of the thousands we expect to come through the Gateway from Ellagrin."

"Well, we wouldn't have that many soldiers on Amorgos at any given time anyway," said Marcus. "It's not like we were expecting an invasion from an old enemy light years away and cut off from us for the last two centuries."

"No," agreed Draeger but added ruefully, "but I should have seen the signs."

"Where is the rest of the Ageron army?" asked Pihla.

"All over the Realm putting out riots," Draeger said. "Riots started by Akseli. In the Rebellion's name. "

Pihla snorted. "Well, I never expected *that*," she said.

"There is another complication," Draeger added.

"No kidding..."

"There is a creature that resides in Lagentia," Draeger continued. "The LON. It will make a break for the Ether when the Gateway is re-opened."

"A creature?" asked Pihla, "Inside Lagentia? I don't understand. Wasn't Lagentia sealed in the toxic leak?"

Draeger sighed. "There is no toxic leak," he said. "This creature, this LON—"

"The Light of Nehisi," interrupted Marcus.

Lord Draeger eyed him appraisingly.

"It's some creature evolved from the Light of Nehisi plant the Ellagrins gave them centuries ago," explained Marcus.

"How...?" began Pihla and then waved the rest of her question away in resignation. No surprise there—Marcus often knew things most didn't.

"I thought it had been nuked and more than once," Marcus said. "Wouldn't it be gone by now?"

Draeger shook his head. "Weakened," he said, "but still there. However, it may well turn out to be our solution to the Ellagrin invasion."

"So in addition to invading Ellagrins, we have to watch out for the LON in Lagentia,"said Marcus, thoughtfully.

"My brother knows little about the LON and cares even less," said Draeger. "He has never fought it nor seen it up close. As such, he underestimates it, as do those who have not had the unenviable task of destroying it."

"But you've tried haven't you,"said Pihla, "...to destroy it?"

"Several times over the years, yes," said Draeger. "More recently about fifty years ago. We had nuked it again but when we checked, it was still very much alive. If my guess is correct, the Ellagrins will be no match for the LON. Added to that, the Ellagrins will all be coming through the Gateway, making it a bottleneck and one that can be exploited to great effect."

"So we use the LON to fight the Ellagrins," said Marcus.

"*If* Akseli opens the Gateway before we reach her," said Draeger.

"But if we can get to Tors *before* she activates the Gateway, then we won't even have to deal with the Ellagrins," said Pihla.

Draeger nodded. "I have a small cohort to storm the city but I cannot gather anymore than that at such short notice."

"We can rustle up about a thousand strong," said Marcus, "but that's the best I can do with what little time we have."

Draeger nodded. "That may well be sufficient. Now, we have to move quickly in case Elena manages to get a message across to Akseli that I have escaped. We have fewer men than I'd like so we'll need the element of surprise."

"Invasion...," pondered Marcus. "Who would've thought there was something worse than having to fight you guys." He grinned at the irony.

"Well then," he said, ducking into the cockpit where Pihla was already firing up the engines, "what are we waiting for?"

PART IX

BATTLE

LAGENTIA

They said Tilkoen engineering outlived not only wars but civilisations. In the gloom of the city lit only by the portable lights brought in by Akseli's men, the pale gleam of the Lagentian Gate stretched into the darkness above, filling Tors with the sinking feeling that the saying probably held true.

Akseli had his chief technician inspect her shackles one last time. These were a recent addition, designed to keep both palms closed around the metal rods in its middle. Locked in, they were a snug fit, providing no room to move and no leeway to release her grip on them. No way to break the circuit. Satisfied, the man nodded towards the Emperor indicating all was in order.

"You know," said Akseli airily, "they say Ellagrin's Winter Carnivale is the most lavish of all celebrations, surpassing even those of Ageron's. You would have been able to witness it for yourself if you hadn't run here instead. Sadly, I believe the current celebrations may have just about ended by now." He laughed. "Fortunately for you, we are about to witness an even grander spectacle here, made possible by you. One that has not been seen for centuries."

"You are insane," Tors replied, straining at her wrists but the clasps were so tight her hands barely moved. "What can you possibly hope to achieve by opening the Gateway? It won't remain open for long—I won't survive long enough to keep it going indefinitely. No single Nehisi can power something this large for long."

Akseli looked amused. His smile widened but there was venom in his eyes. "Ah," he said, "but with careful planning, you will last a few days; ample time for what I have planned. But for now, I only need a few hours..."

Tors replied through gritted teeth, "You may not have a few hours. There is something else here." Her eyes fell on the LON still being cleared by Akseli's men and their blowtorches. As the crumbled pillars glimmered in the pulsing glow of their fires, she could have sworn the dark shimmering mass of vines crept back across the cracked stone floors from where they'd been burned off. The dark sickly feeling she felt was growing stronger. She shuddered at the sight of its black tendrils.

Something was brewing. Something insidious and strong.

"What?" Akseli's eyes followed her gaze. "You mean the LON?" He laughed carelessly. "Are you afraid of a *plant*?" He reached out to the wall, its edges sparsely covered with a few LON vines where the blowtorches had missed, and plucked a tendril from its stem. It came off easily and he twirled the dark offshoot in his hand. It was jet black and smooth, giving off a slight sheen as he turned it from side to side. Nestled underneath the leaf itself was a tiny, needle-like barb.

"You superstitious fools," he said. "It's nothing but a weed. Detonations and centuries of being sealed in darkness may not have killed it entirely but without any source of nourishment, it's nothing more than a dying creeper." He laughed out loud and with disdain. "This is not some mythical monster. It is the superstitions and stories of fools that have transformed this weed into a monster. When this is finished, we'll burn the very last of this overgrown vegetation off the face of this planet."

A gust of wind swept past, throwing eddying clouds of fine dust across the floor. As Akseli busied himself with questioning the chief technician, Tors' nostrils detected the waft of centuries-old dust mingled with fresh air from the outside. *A breeze...but the Hex is sealed.*

She felt his presence although it filled her with bittersweet tumult. *He's here. Draeger...*

ZUUUT! A shot fired towards Akseli, just missing his head. He whirled round. Resentment burned in his eyes.

"Get that sniper!" he growled at his men. "And seal the entrance to the City! My brother is here. Keep his soldiers out until the Gateway is opened. There can't be many of them so it shouldn't be too difficult to pick them off if they try to force their way in through the entrance." Then turning back to Tors, he instructed the chief technician to turn the Gate on.

Tors could feel it powering up and as it did so, a slow but steady tingle built up within her. A vibrating hum reverberated through her entire being.

Then pain.

Tors stifled a cry. It was pain like nothing she had experienced before. Pain that resembled her insides, from the tip of her scalp to the ends of her toes, being sucked out slowly. Next to them, the arc of the Lagentian Gate overlooking the platform began to emit a soft white glow and the metal rods in her grasp started to get very hot. Tors' muscles tightened as the agonising sensation coursed through her body, squeezing her capillaries and raising the temperature of the blood in her vessels. In the corner of her eye, she thought she saw the LON flail in response.

The ground shook suddenly as a blast hit the entrance to the City.

They're trying to blast their way in...

Akseli's guards had sealed the heavy doors shut in order to keep Draeger's men out, but the repeated assaults on it was beginning to weaken its jamb. Further ahead on the concourse, several of Akseli's guards continued to incinerate any LON that covered the concourse in front of the Gate.

They're clearing an awful large area of ground, thought Tors as she struggled to remain lucid. *Whatever he means to let through the Gate will require a lot of space.* Then it dawned on her. *An army. He means to let an army in.*

An Ellagrin army!

One massive enough to overthrow the capital and take over the whole of Amorgos. As Draeger told her once: *Amorgos is the centre of power. If Amorgos falls, so will the rest of the Realm.*

"Why would you let the Ellagrins in?" she gasped. "Our enemies!"

Akseli gave a ragged laugh. "Call it the dawn of a new partnership," he said.

"But Draeger and Elena..." Her mind flashed back to the moment she saw them together. "I don't understand...," she faltered. The pain of betrayal seemed to sear through her very being.

"Draeger and Elena?" Akseli threw his head back in laughter. It was filled with hate and bitterness. "No, no," he continued, "you have it all wrong. You are all fools, and my brother the biggest fool of all!" His mouth twisted into a terrible smile, "You see, Elena is not on his side. She is on *mine*."

"You're letting the Ellagrins invade us," said Tors. "Are you mad?"

Akseli regarded her contemptuously. "Once Amorgos falls into my hands, the rest will follow. The Realms will finally answer to me, not my brother."

"It will never work," said Tors. "Draeger still leads the army."

Akseli laughed again. "What army?" he answered. "They are dispersed all over the empire, quelling so-called rebellion riots. Riots I've started for this very purpose. This will all be over by the time I'm finished."

But Tors was no longer listening. By now the pain had become almost unbearable. It throbbed and pulsed, piercing her insides in short, sharp stabs. In the haze of her agony, her head lolled helplessly backwards. There, she stared at the ceiling and in the corners of the room where the blowtorches had not reached were patches of the LON.

I must be hallucinating, she thought, for the patches of LON there were moving, almost imperceptibly, but moving nonetheless with a slow, regular undulation. Forcing her head up, she looked further afield towards the edge of the concourse where the LON grew thick and lush. These too were moving, although ever so subtly that no one else seemed to have noticed. A chill went through Tors: they were moving with the same unnatural rhythm and *in synch* with the LON in the room.

This is no plant.

By now the wave of pain coursing through her surged. Tors screamed. The Gate glowed ever brighter and in tandem, her entire body seemed to glow too, her veins showing up as dark lattices beneath her pale skin. As the ancient contraption whirred on, gorging on and sucking the force inside her, her body glowed semi-translucent like a surreal effigy lit from inside by a white light and as she weakened, so did the bleak, repressive feeling grow and enlarge within her. Tors struggled to keep it at bay as the pain became all encompassing. She felt it more keenly than ever now, except this time, she was too weak to fight it. Now, this dark, insidious feeling began to seep into her mind, soaking in like a sickness.

And then it spoke.

THE LON

Its voice resounded in her head as clearly and as intimately as if they were conversing in a small room. The whirring of machinery and the shouts of the men all disappeared, swallowed up by the total silence that surrounded *that* voice. A voice completely devoid of any human inflections or emotion but complex and tinctured with an indescribably alien quality.

Free me. Free us, it said in a multitude of alien voices, all discordant and singsong. An overlay of tremolos, jarring and hypnotic at the same time.

Tors shook her head in attempt to maintain a mental distance between her and It. *By Dyaeus, if the Gate doesn't kill me, this creature may well finish the job.*

I cannot, she said to it. *I am bound and cannot get free.* She strained helplessly at her shackles. *Why don't you help me get free first,* she said in pain.

Oh the pain. The pain was unbearable. Bright shards of light now danced in her vision, eclipsing her view of the outside world, forcing her to look inward, into her mind's eye, back to It.

Open the Gate and we will help you, the LON replied. *It is time. Time to grow. To spread. You must free us.* ***Join us.*** The last two words were accompanied by a sense of hunger and the shape of intent behind them hit her like a shockwave.

Tors fought to hide her sense of revulsion when, to her horror, she realised she understood what the LON meant. She understood the manner in which they assimilated others, how they survived. It was as if she were the LON itself. She felt their ravenous craving.

Help me! she screamed again, trying to push the LON out from her mind. This was not how it was supposed to happen. She couldn't fight them like this. Not when she felt and thought as they did. Not when she ran the risk of *becoming* like them.

Free us first, they said. *Open the Gate. Open it! Open it and we shall take you with us.*

Tors struggled until she could not hold herself up anymore. She fell back into her bonds, hanging helplessly. *There will be soldiers when the Gate opens...* The thought escaped her mind.

We know. We feel them. We will make them join us.

Tors shuddered at the thought but a final excruciating blast of pain jolted her back to the present. It surged through her body expelling all conscious thought until only agony remained. *Like being burned from the inside out.*

She was beyond pain.

Then a blinding flash of light illuminated the inside of the Gate. Like a conjurer's act, it elongated into a ribbon of light, winding itself round and round and spreading concentrically until a tunnel of pure white formed and extended impossibly inwards towards a point within the tunnel itself, stretching a few hundred yards into another world.

"By Dyaeus, it's working!" Akseli shouted excitedly.

The faint sound of marching resounded from within the tunnel, gradually getting louder and louder, until the first legion of Ellagrin soldiers, five thousand-strong, standing abreast and decked in indigo uniforms appeared at the mouth of the Gate. Behind them were many, many more—a sea of soldiers stretching all the way into the tunnel as far as the eye could see.

Another blast from the city entrance, followed by a resounding crash. Akseli averted his eyes reluctantly away from the visitors. The Hex had been breached and Draeger's men had begun streaming into the city.

"Keep them away from the Gate!" Akseli screamed down from where he stood. "We don't need very long!" His eyes gleamed in eager anticipation. The Ellagrins, once in, would outnumber the paltry company of rebels and Reds ten to one.

He will have them completely slaughtered, thought Tors at the sight of the advancing Ellagrins.

Then an unearthly screech filled the air. Its harsh, alien discordance wrenched Tors from her haze of pain. Before her very eyes, the LON seemed to gather up, detaching itself from the walls, the pavements, the streets.

*It's **moving**. It senses the Ether.*

A darkened mass of tendrils poured in on itself like thick morass from all corners of the city, and converged on the concourse. Tors screamed hysterically.

The weed had become a Hydra.

Flowing thickly, the LON seemed to triple in size, towering high, as high as the Gate itself, and like a massive, hideous viper, it launched its entire mass at the clutch of Akseli's guards and their blowtorches, driving millions of barbs through their very torsos before any of them had a chance to react. And then it turned and hurtled towards the control room where Akseli stood.

The Emperor leapt off the platform before the LON could touch him. The head technician however, was not so lucky.

Tors looked on in horror as the LON enveloped him like a swarm of black locusts.

See? We will help you, the voices sang dissonantly as the immense entity seemed to cover only him with laser precision, leaving Tors, dangling nearby, untouched. *But first, we* ***feed...***

The man's face convulsed trying to speak as he seemed to melt into the dark quivering mass.

Her stomach churned. *He's being eaten alive.*

When his mouth opened to scream, more black tendrils spilled out of his throat.

NOOOOO!! Tors screamed and turned away in revulsion.

The LON diverted its attention back to the Gateway. Screams from the Ellagrins exiting the Gateway soon punctured the air as the LON plunged through and launched itself at them.

Propelling itself forward like a fluid, darkened mass, it continued its murderous ripple whilst on the other side of the platform

Emperor Akseli looked on, paralysed, at the vision of bodies melting on contact with the squirming, crawling, putrid tide of the LON.

Incompatible, the LON projected to the horrified Tors, *but ingestible.* It swept through the Gateway gorging itself on the now fleeing Ellagrins, enveloping them in its deadly embrace and then absorbing them like a fly digesting a liquidised lunch. The more it consumed, the larger it grew. Now every square inch of the inside of the Gateway tunnel was covered with its quivering biomass. The sterile white tunnel of the Gateway now resembled the pulsing insides of an intestine.

Soon it will realise it cannot get through the constructs of the Gateway into the Ether itself, realised Tors. *Then it will come for me...* She struggled to keep hold of her faculties. The pain made it almost impossible to breathe and she could no longer focus on what was going on around her.

In the midst of all this, she felt a tugging at her wrists. Opening an eye, she observed oddly detachedly, Marcus next to her trying to undo her shackles.

"Stay with me," he said as he worked frantically at the metal clasps.

Marcus...

He held a plasma cutter in his hands. They were bleeding as he worked the cutter over her shackles again and again in attempt to cut through.

"No Marcus...," she tried to tell him. *You can't cut me loose... you mustn't. Not whilst the LON is in the tunnel itself. If the Gateway connection is broken whilst the LON remains inside it, it will be dropped in the Ether. It will be free.*

The Gate whirred on, drawing from her relentlessly and Tors felt her life literally draining away as she drifted in and out of consciousness. Everything in sight seemed to be dissolving. Dissolving into a multitude of dazzling white points and emptying out of her in streams of white light.

Rivulets of light...

Like rivulets of water running through the gutters in Ceos.

Why Ceos? she wondered, surprised herself. Ceos with its stinking towns and dirty rundown shanties, and the despairing faces, worn down by hardship and toughened with cheap liquor. Rat-Boy, district gangs and dealers. Stims. Stench. Sickness. So awful it seemed beautiful.

Funny how beautiful things look on the cusp of death. Only then did it occur to Tors that she was about to die.

"No, no, no,… stay with me!"

She could hear Marcus calling out to her as she felt herself succumbing to the devouring brightness. He sounded so very far away.

Marcus...

Marcus who taught her the meaning of trust.

He showed me Jula's location knowing full well I could have taken her away with me anytime after that. And yet, he trusted me not to walk away. He trusted me not to leave the thousands on the Tethys without an Eldur. Beautiful blonde Marcus...

Her mind flicked to the other side of the coin. Where one shone bright as day, the other dark as night.

Draeger...

Draeger who embodied discipline and duty.

He taught me to accept my past and my destiny.

She flinched. *He also taught me the meaning of love... and of pain.*

Pain. The pain of betrayal. The pain of loss. Jula.

Jula...

For a brief moment, Jula's smile shone in her mind with that same bright light.

She took a stand. She chose a side. She sacrificed herself so that others could live...

Tors' eyes filled with tears as she slipped further into bright oblivion.

THE SOUNDS of gunfire reverberated round the station. A full blown skirmish was in play as Draeger's men and rebels now fired upon Akseli's soldiers and any straggling Ellagrins running out of the Gate attempting to evade the LON.

"Keep them away from the Gate!" Akseli screamed uselessly in the midst of gunfire. "We need to give the Ellagrins enough time to enter!" But it was an unrealistic assertion, for the Ellagrins themselves were fighting for survival as the LON continued its horrific onslaught to satiate its hunger.

"Marcus! *Hurry*!" Someone was yelling.

"Stay with me! Stay with me..." Marcus' voice sounded distant and was fading fast. Tors could feel him tugging at the metal surrounding her wrist.

No, Marcus...not whilst it's in the tunnel.

He gave a final wrench and ripped out the first clasp. The Gate flickered as Tors loosened her grip on the first contact rod. It was a split-second pause, but noticeable enough.

"Uh-oh..." Tors heard Marcus utter as they both sensed the LON stop in its tracks.

From the corner of her eye, something large and dark advanced. Like a snake, the LON had gathered itself up from the Gateway tunnel and spun round, rapidly leaving the Gateway clear and white again as it receded like a mudslide and made a beeline for them.

"Shit! Shit! Shit!" Marcus cursed, hurriedly yanking at the shackle. It had come loose but not free and Tors' hand was still clenched around it. But the LON was approaching with lightning speed. Hurtling towards them, it launched itself at Marcus, bouncing him off the platform in the impact. He fell onto the concourse below.

Join us. It spoke into her mind as it slithered up the metal frame towards her loosened hand. *Free us. Open it, open it. Show us how...*

Wrapping its tendrils around it, it now clamped Tors' hand tightly round the rod again, as if willing her to conjure an escape route into the Ether.

Tors kept her mind as empty as she could to avoid it finding out how to escape.

With the circuit now complete once more, the Gate whirred on and as Tors slipped away into unconsciousness, it latched itself around her ankles. Like a snake, it coiled around her legs, climbing insidiously up and up, probing tentatively.

Tors felt it continue its way up; a peculiar sensation, like thousands of hairy spiders brushing against her skin.

All the time, the relentless draining by the Gate was taking its toll. Her heart laboured hard within her chest, exerted to its limits and unable to withstand the pain anymore she fell back into her bonds, hanging from her chains.

Still, the LON continued its insidious climb up her thighs, its tendrils spreading out, seeking. Up and up until it found what it was looking for between them.

No, protested Tors weakly as it slid into her. There was no pain but the violation filled her with fear and revulsion. She understood what was about to happen. She sensed its alienness and its instinct to bind, to integrate. To *transform* its host.

Stop, she screamed, trying to drive it away with her thoughts but the LON continued its path inward, unflinching.

Then a sudden jolt.

It retracted as if it had touched something unpleasant. Like an electric shock. An alien screech filled her head as the LON recoiled and slid out.

Tors felt its pain, like it had touched something extremely hot within her. And then she knew. Even before it said anything to her.

Zygote, it screamed and projected what Tors sensed was its equivalent of a shudder of abhorrence.

Another screech of pain. This time it was external.

She could feel the heat from the plasma shot aimed just

below her ankle. It was Marcus who had fired and burnt off a sizeable chunk of tendrils there.

Rapidly, the LON withdrew the rest of it from her, sliding and slipping off her in slick, receding slaps but the part of it twined around her hand and the contact rod remained steadfastly in place.

Still strung up, Tors was suddenly aware that she was cold and she began to feel that soft, weak sensation of drifting into unconsciousness.

"Hey, hey..." Marcus was shaking her.

When she opened her eyes again, it was Marcus beside her once more and next to him the blurry movements of Draeger, hacking at the LON with his sword.

"Don't go anywhere, okay? Stay with me..."

Tors tried to hang onto Marcus' voice. He struggled to remove the second shackle and nearby, she could hear the rhythmic *chunk*! of Draeger hacking and chopping the LON.

With the LON temporarily out of the Gateway tunnel, the Ellagrin army or what was left of it, surged through. Now they swarmed onto the platform but Draeger's Reds and the rebels were ready for them. Unleashing a barrage of firepower onto the incoming Ellagrins, they cut them down as they poured in from the Gateway.

"NOOOOO!" Akseli's maniacal howl punctured through the clamour of artillery and Tors heard the thin whistle of a blade as it sliced through the air nearby, aiming for Draeger.

In her dimming vision she saw Draeger whirl round to meet Akseli's sword with his, blocking its lethal path. It slid down the length of the emperor's sword with a shrill metallic squeal and pushed him backwards.

"Why are you doing this?" Draeger cried as their swords clashed.

"Because *I* am Emperor!" came Akseli's answer spewed with hate. "I AM! Not you!"

"I have never coveted Father's throne…" Draeger's blade met Akseli's with a cold, sharp ring.

Akseli lunged once more, got blocked and leapt back, laughing bitterly. "No? You run the Realm as if it were yours. You and your toy soldiers. I will not play the puppet anymore. *I* am Emperor of Ageron! *EMPEROR*! Not you!"

"If the Ellagrins invade, there will be no Ageron!"

"You fool! What do you know about politics?" A sharp clang and the metallic shirr of blade upon blade.

"What did you offer Elena?" asked Draeger. His question was met with a ragged laugh, full of contempt and derision.

"I gave her what you couldn't brother, even after all these years of useless foreplay. A trade, brother. A *trade*. A proper deal that adds up. Not like the half-arsed ones you've been knocking up."

"Fool, this is no trade! You have allowed us to be invaded!"

"You don't get it do you? Father's obedient little soldier…" Akseli's eyes blazed with resentment. "With Elena's army, I will take back what is rightfully mine—I will take back Ageron from you! From YOU! And with House Ageron behind her, the Doges loyal to Niklas will not dare go against her. And here's the thing…"—there was utter contempt in his voice now—"here's the thing you never had the courage or foresight to carry out." Akseli's eyes shone with a mad zeal. "Why waste another century trying to reopen the Gateways destroyed in the War? Is that even possible? And so what if it were? There is no more trade to be had between Ageron and the rest of the galaxy. The Realm is dying. When our suns go nova, there will be *no more Ageron*! The Age of Prosperity is gone. *GONE*! Our industries, our commerce—gone! We will have *nothing*, not even the land beneath our feet on to live on."

Akseli advanced. "But with the Key," he continued savagely, "we can move our armies to Ellagrin—our warships, our destroyers, our weapons, our men. With our combined armies, it will be enough to launch an offensive from the Ellagrin system against nearby Tilkoen. From Ellagrin, our combined armies will reach them in five to seven years, and in a few years after that, it will be all over. A short, cheap war and Tilkoen with its land and resources will be ours."

Akseli's eyes gleamed greedily. "In the meantime, the Exodus can continue as best it can—does it matter if a few stragglers don't make it out in time? And by the time our spacecarriers reach Ellagrin, we will have conquered all the land we need to spread out."

"You are executing nothing more than a land grab," said Draeger.

"Too crass for you brother?" said Akseli. "The Tilkoens will never expect it as Ellagrin alone has never had a large enough army to invade anyone. We'll even divide the spoils between our two Houses. Used sparingly, the Key will last us till the invasion is over, with enough time to expatriate members of the ruling classes before we deplete her of her life-force."

He shook his fist furiously. "We are Ageronians by Dyaeus. *Ageronians*! Not pitiful refugees begging around for a place to stay. I *will* have my empire back, even if it means I take one by force!"

"War is not the solution to our problems," Draeger replied hoarsely, " and neither is invasion." He glanced at Tors. "...nor the sacrifice of the last Nehisi for your greed and glory." Something in his voice broke at the last sentence.

Akseli let out a harsh laugh. "Says the Commander who has killed thousands in the last few wars. That is precious coming from you, brother."

"You know what I mean Akseli," growled Draeger. "This is no way to rule an empire."

"And what do you know about ruling an empire?" Akseli charged at Draeger with all his might.

At that same moment, Marcus yanked at the second shackle one last time. He heaved at the metal, putting his entire body weight against it. The final wrench was accompanied by a yell. And then it creaked open. Without wasting a moment, Marcus fired his plasma gun at the remaining LON attached stubbornly around the first shackle and moved to extricate Tors' hand from the contact rods.

Quickly whilst the LON is outside the Gateway... but Tors was too weak to tell him.

As Draeger lifted up his sword to meet Akseli's blow, the Gateway flickered.

The sound of the gate winding down, its tunnel dimming and sputtering seemed to jerk the LON back into action. With a desperate screech, it surged back into the Gateway tunnel and as Marcus lifted Tors away from her shackles, the Gateway powered off.

"NOOOOO!" screamed Akseli, as his blade shattered on impact with Draeger's.

Total darkness engulfed the once blinding Gateway, along with the LON and the Ellagrins in it.

Noooo.... echoed Tors weakly, sensing the sudden absence of the LON.

Akseli staggered backwards and fell to the floor. But before he could get up, Draeger rammed his hilt onto his head and knocked him out cold.

* * *

"You okay?" asked Marcus, looking at Tors. The shooting had ceased and the Reds were rounding up the last few supporters of the Emperor.

"Lord Draeger..." floated the calm voice of Chancellor Rasmus above the sombre bustle of the Reds escorting off their Ellagrin prisoners.

"Chancellor," acknowledged Draeger. "Thank you for coming. We haven't much time." He indicated at Akseli, still unconscious and held up by two Reds. "We have the Emperor detained on the grounds of treason. He is to be put under house arrest with no contact with anyone. No one is to know, not even the Queen Mother. I will deal with him when I return."

The Chancellor gave a brief nod and followed the soldiers as they dragged Akseli away, his flint cloak rippling behind in their wake.

Draeger turned to Tors. He held her by her shoulders. "Ready?" he asked gently.

"Yes," said Tors.

"Can you fight?" he asked, looking at her intently.

Tors nodded.

Marcus interjected. "You cannot be serious! She's in no shape to fight now."

Draeger looked at him gravely. "She has to. And now. Before we lose it in the Ether."

"He's right,"said Tors, stopping Marcus' protest. "I have to finish this."

Draeger nodded. "I'll come with you—there may still be a few Ellagrin soldiers about stranded in the Ether. You will need them out of the way."

"I'm coming too," insisted Marcus not wanting to be left out.

"Us too!" Pihla called out, sprinting up the platform.

Behind her clambered Niko. "And whilst we're at it, would you mind if half your legion came too, Commander?"

Tors smiled and said, "Love your pragmatism Pihla, but opening into the Ether isn't quite as convenient as you think. When I cleave an opening, you have about a minute to step through before it closes on itself. Not long enough for an entire legion to go through I'm afraid."

Pihla shot her a questioning look.

Tors shrugged. "Curtains," she explained. "It's like curtains falling back. It just does that."

"You will have no use for these either,"said Draeger pointing at their guns. "Electronics do not work within the Ether." He handed Tors a sword. She hefted it with practised familiarity and nodded.

"Sans guns is fine by me,"said Pihla, tossing away her gun and pulling her strap, hung cross shouldered, to tighten it. Clamped boldly onto them in front was a fine row of plasma grenades gleaming like a lethal pearl necklace. "I'll use these babies instead."

Niko unsheathed his sword. "Ready when you are," he said, gripping the hilt determinedly.

"Ready?" asked Tors, looking round.

Marcus patted his sword and nodded grimly. "Let's hunt," he said.

With that, Tors took a deep breath and cleaved an opening for them to step through.

SHOWDOWN

Pihla gagged as soon as she tried to breathe. *So this is what it truly feels like to be in the Ether.*

It was cool and viscous, and breathing in it felt a lot like drowning. Her heart began to pound in panic. Then she felt Tors touch her arm.

Tors signalled for her to relax and she nodded in response. She looked round and tried to take her mind off the peculiar discomfort of breathing but the claustrophobic darkness did little to make things better. With no visible horizon, the Ether appeared to have neither ground nor sky and as the gloom wrapped around her like quicksand, she found herself once more sucking desperately, trying to breathe. Unfortunately, the harder she tried to inhale, the more she gagged as her bodily instincts resisted the notion that the substance she was drawing in would not drown her.

Keep calm! Keep calm! she repeated to herself. *Tors said you could breathe in this stuff.* But Pihla could feel the sense of alarm bubbling up even as she fought to keep it down. *This is why the Gateways were built. To artificially wall-off the Ether so people like me wouldn't have to breathe in this goop. By Dyaeus, I feel like I'm drowning in thick tuber porridge!*

In time, logic prevailed and the feeling of panic subsided as her breathing adjusted, much as her eyes did to her surroundings. She could make out the others standing nearby also acclimatising to the Ether. Niko was standing a few paces in front. She shouted out to him but found her words silent, reaching neither of their ears. The Ether it seemed, carried no sound.

Looking down, her gaze traced her arms in the heavy dimness. She noted they were outlined by a faint glow. With no apparent source of light, the Ether itself seemed to emit a faint luminescence of its own, almost impossible to notice at first, but enough along with its leaden viscosity to give it a certain feeling of substance.

Tors had walked ahead some way but how far ahead Pihla could not tell, for devoid of objects, there was no way to gauge distance within the planes of the Ether.

The winds were picking up now, whirling round her and whipping her cloak about. She could feel it buffeting against her the length of her body. *How strange to not hear any of this,* she thought as she felt the frenzied flapping of her cloak against her arms and legs.

Tors signalled for them to follow her.

Marcus moved first, walking a few feet behind her, his sword unsheathed, his demeanour pumped like a soldier advancing into battle.

This place unnerves him, noted Pihla, *I've never seen him this tense...*

By contrast Niko strode behind Marcus, looking around uneasily, disquieted by the unnaturalness of the place. Pihla knew him well enough to sense from his gait that he too was finding the discomfort of breathing in the Ether a struggle.

She followed them both, careful to keep close whilst Draeger walked alongside all of them, his strides long and easy as if strolling in a park.

They continued, but how far and in what direction she hadn't a clue. Tors however seemed to know where they were heading for she kept a firm and confident pace.

By Dyaeus, she'd better be able to get us back home after all this, thought Pihla. To die here would be like being trapped in hell —stranded in the dark with no food, no water and no way out. *I wonder what happened to the Ellagrins in the Gateway tunnel when it disconnected?* Pihla shuddered at the very thought, remembering Pappi and her in the Arnemetiaen Gateway all those years ago. *That could have been us...*

It wasn't long before she found her answer. A darkened pile, barely visible to the eye.

Bones.

A pile of humanoid remains lay amidst a few shreds of clothing. Here, there, Pihla recognised a femur, a partial sternum, a jawbone. Where the flesh had sloughed off, they showed up white against the dimness of their surroundings.

Tors gave a wave urging them to continue and they all moved on, leaving behind the grisly mound. Whatever it was that devoured those people had done so recently.

More bones...

Tors appeared to be following the gruesome trail of remains.

Marcus bent down and picked something from a macabre mound ahead and showed it to them. It was a torn-off cuff of a sleeve, and on it clearly visible, the outline of a sheaf of wheat woven in gold thread: the sigil of House Ellagrin.

Could this have belonged to the same Ellagrins in the Gateway earlier? Pihla gestured at Niko to ask, only to receive his standard I-have-no-idea look in return.

Idiot, she mouthed and was about to take a closer look when a flicker of a movement arrested her attention.

She froze.

The others instinctively swivelled towards the source of her attention.

Tors reacted almost immediately. Pushing Niko out of the way, she reached for her sword.

The LON lashed at empty air where Niko stood moments earlier as Tors drove her sword upwards, slicing into the creature before rolling away out of its grasp. It emerged out of the darkness, surging and towering above them.

Pihla's eyes widened. *There are hundreds of them...*

Hundreds of Ellagrins, as far as she could see, submerged, trapped within its shimmering, writhing mass of black.

Tors stood back and lowered her sword as they all stared aghast at the nightmare before their very eyes.

They're still alive.

Engorged with Ellagrins, the LON now loomed over Pihla, double its size. An arm dangled from it. Pihla blanched. A soldier reached out from the locked embrace of worming tendrils, his eyes wide and unseeing. At first his mouth peeled opened as if to scream, then it froze midway before more vines plunged through his shoulder blades and burst forth from his sternum spreading wide like a flowering bud.

Pihla screamed noiselessly into the Ether.

Like husking a coconut, the LON cracked open his torso into two. Bile rose in her throat, acid and burning. She cowered, then retched and watched with horror as the LON advanced, its vines coiling and uncoiling menacingly.

The creature towered high above her and made ready to engulf her next. Its width spanned across like a massive quivering wall.

There was nowhere to escape.

Pihla glanced at Niko one last time, made her peace with death and closed her eyes. *This is it.*

A moment passed and Pihla opened her eyes to peek.

The LON twisted and snapped, hung limp before her, with Tors crouched down on one knee next to it.

Is it dead? Her gaze followed on from the hacked portion of the LON in hope before sinking once more in despair. *If that was a man, then the part Tors had cut off was only a finger!*

Tors stood her ground and shook her sword, discarding bits of vine, barb, blood and bone from it like droplets off a drenched dog.

Hefting it meditatively, she scrutinised the LON's heaving bulk and weighed up her next move. *It's grown so big I can't see where it begins nor ends...*

The creature slithered to and fro and began to gather itself up. It no longer sought to communicate with her. Instead Tors sensed its bellicosity.

It knows we won't let it live.

She felt its bone-chilling intent. *It knows it will have to kill us to escape.*

She stared at its massive form towering over her. *And it's not afraid...*

Beside her stood Draeger, poised and ready, and on her left, Marcus who was shifting warily, his eyes never leaving the creature.

Then without warning, the LON lashed at them like a thousand bullwhips all at once.

As it lunged forward to attack, Tors let loose the invisible forces she exerted headlong into it. They slammed into the creature, causing shock waves to reverberate around the group knocking them off their feet.

Undeterred, the creature lashed back, its vines thrashing like a thousand angry scorpion tails.

Tors quickly sidestepped but not before one of them pierced through her left pectoral, just missing her heart by centimetres. She stumbled backwards in pain.

Pihla and Niko advanced to attack.

However the LON seemed to anticipate their every move, blocking their blows with its wall of quivering twines and unleashing its barbs like a fluid and deadly mass of striking snakes.

Beside them, Draeger worked swiftly, slashing and slicing, whilst Marcus laboured away, hacking at anything that moved in order to whittle down any amount of the the LON possible.

But the creature was smart and within seconds it had utilised its bulk to separate the group: Niko and Pihla on one side of its hulking mass, Marcus and Draeger on the other, and Tors at its tail end.

On and on the LON attacked. Sharp and relentless.

Marcus went down first. Tors' heart lurched as the vines stabbed viciously at him one after another as he rolled on and on, trying to dodge out of their way.

Draeger reached out to help Marcus back up on his feet, but as he did, the tendrils slapped across his own legs and coiled round his ankle. Finding purchase, the LON picked him up and dangled him a good eight metres in the air whilst another vine, thick as a spear, angled itself at his torso ready to impale him.

Tors let loose a stricken surge of power towards it. This time the vine burst into flame. The LON recoiled but hurled Draeger twenty metres into the emptiness beyond.

On the other side, Pihla, having dodged and hacked at the ever-changing ripple of tendrils and barbs was slowly being separated from Niko by the LON's rippling bulk.

By Dyaeus we're fighting a thousand arms and legs, Tors thought to herself, *except we're tiring much faster than it is.* As the creature's mass shifted and moved some more, Tors glimpsed past its bulk.

Niko!

Fenced in on all sides by the LON, Niko had been forced into a corner. Surrounded by tendrils shifting overhead, they descended down towards him, pushing slick and quivering. Like vipers, they converged.

Before Tors could react, Pihla lurched towards him in desperation and ripped out one of her grenades. She pulled the pin and mustering enough strength to get its trajectory just high enough to miss Niko, hurled it into the descending thicket.

The Ether above Niko's head rippled and blurred as the grenade punched through the LON, its superheated plasma ripping through and burning it. As the jet of flame enveloped the creature, Niko dived for cover. The LON, still ablaze, advanced doggedly towards them like some hellish vision, its vines lashing and aglow like whips driven by phantoms. A straggler hit Niko and wrapped itself around his foot. A brief mist of blood besmeared Pihla's face as its lethal barbs pierced into him and the LON lifted him up.

Pihla screamed mutedly as she threw herself forward to grab him.

Tors could tell he was screaming too, scrabbling at his foot, then at his leg before finally clawing at his thigh as the LON coiled its way up.

She looked at both of them, so far away, and tried frantically to work out how to get past the LON to them. Her strength was ebbing as quickly as the blood she was losing from her punctured wound.

Meanwhile, Pihla was desperately giving her all to save Niko and Niko, in turn, was trying to escape and push her away from danger at the same time.

Draeger was nowhere to be seen and Marcus had long disappeared from view somewhere in the midst of the LON's moving mass.

Tors' heart sank in despair. Was this how it was all going to end?

By Dyaeus, if it is then I'll take you with me!

Jula's last words came to her unbidden. Jula who never did anything for anyone in the past, but who sacrificed herself in the end to save Marie and her two boys.

Tors thought of Pihla and Niko next. They protected each other so fiercely without regard for their own lives.

Then Marcus, who had risked everything so that everyone had an equal chance for survival.

And finally Draeger, driven by duty and bound by belief to save the Realm and its people.

So be it.

This would be no different to the day Rat-Boy raised his machete at her.

All or nothing.

Closing her eyes, Tors looked inward for strength.

The Ether is a substance and like any other substance, it can be manipulated. Draeger's words echoed in her mind and Tors began to gather the Ether around her.

An aurora shimmer of its invisible forces began to build up, expanding like a glowing ball and filling the atmosphere. All around static mounted. In front, Pihla, still struggling to hold onto Niko, paused for a split second to stare at at the hulking mass of the LON about to consume her friend.

Then like a mini nova flaring in the darkness, a blazing arc of light surged, sweeping over the LON and causing it to release Niko.

Seizing her chance, Pihla grabbed him by the front of his tunic and dragged him away from the quivering mass.

They staggered back, shielding their eyes from the blinding light and nearly falling over each other. The air had become superheated and sweat was pouring down Pihla's neck, pooling in the hollow of her collarbone. She clutched Niko in fear. *Will we all die with the creature in this hellfire...?*

From behind the flare of the blast strode Tors, her silhouette glowing so bright it was barely visible against the blinding explosion. The LON retreated, flailing, its vines swinging like scythes but Tors followed it with arms outstretched. Her eyes now shone with a terrible light.

Pihla shuddered. They were incandescent. As were her mouth and ears. In fact, light poured out from her entire body, so hot and white it tinged with blue. The LON, in final desperation and unable to escape, stopped retreating and moved to launch itself at her.

Pihla held her breath and watched.

And then, like an angry nightmarish swarm, it hurtled at Tors with all its might!

Tors stood her ground. The air around the two shimmered luminously white, so bright that Pihla had to raise her hand to shield her eyes. Through the gaps between her fingers, she could make out the two battling one another: the demon—a wild tangle of fiery threads, thrashing and writhing, and the slayer—a sphere of light, borne out of the same elemental fire.

Same but different, thought Pihla as she stared transfixed. *The LON, Tors, the Nehisi... they are all manifestations of the Ether.*

The creature was trying to envelop Tors in its lethal embrace, flailing painfully where her aura touched it but slowly, slowly, Pihla could see its hulking quivering mass close over Tors.

Her heart sank. *It's too massive. It will engulf her. We cannot win by battle...*

But Tors, it seemed, appeared undaunted. Between the

cracks of her fingers, Pihla saw her pause. She noted that Tors' demeanour was no longer bent with the intent of advancement, and her gait no longer emanated the belligerence of attack.

She does not intend to beat it. She's ***never*** *intended to beat it! No! Don't do it...!*

From the corner of her eye, Pihla glimpsed Draeger mouth the same protest and leap desperately towards Tors. But he was too late.

Arms clutched tightly in front of her chest, she lifted her head and as her mouth opened, light poured out.

The LON flailed wildly but she did not falter.

Pihla felt the Ether around her swirl as the force unleashed began sucking in the Ether, engulfing her and the others in, pulling them in towards the adversarial pair like minnows caught in a whirlpool.

As the final brilliance enveloped the LON it twisted and writhed. Its vines began to snap, break and burst into flame.

Pihla reached for Niko but found to her dismay that he had spiralled away from her. Further ahead she spotted Marcus hurtling into the vortex of light. Grappling uselessly at emptiness, her arms flailed wildly as she tried to slow down her hurtling self, but to no avail.

There will be no coming back from this one, not this time...

The world whirled around her as they hurtled towards the blinding ball of brilliance, pulled in by the rippling forces.

And then it stopped.

Behind, a darkness engulfed them as the blazing sphere rapidly diminished, along with the LON, now dead and blackened to a crisp.

* * *

SHE SHOULD HAVE DIED.

Draeger picked her up, cradling her as if she were a child. Her hair smouldered but the rest of her body was cold to the touch. He brushed her face lightly and when her eyelids flickered open, relief washed over him like a tidal wave.

You're not done yet my wild one...

His eyes swept over her and he felt a strange mixture of both fierce protectiveness and tenderness. She was so fragile, so delicate, so broken.

Don't you die just yet. They need you. I need you...

He winced at the sight of her weakened body. As she shivered in his arms, her eyes seemed search his as he gazed into hers. She looked so vulnerable, so frail.

What have I done to you?

He pulled her close as if to take away all the hurt he had caused her.

His heart wrenched when he recalled the look on her face when she saw him with Elena. *She must think I had betrayed her, used her. How will I ever make her believe me?*

He gently brushed a wisp of windswept hair from her face. Even now he knew, as he had the moment he set eyes on her in the Oracle's chamber, that he would never be able to stay away from her.

I love you Tors. I always have. Dyaeus help me, I tried not to...

He carried her all the way, the others trudging wearily behind them, guided only by the subtle movements and nudges from her feeble hands as to which way to go until at long last, she signalled for him to stop.

Then, with great effort she cleaved an exit and they all stepped through.

EPILOGUE

RED PALACE, AGERON

The winds had whipped up a dust storm and from the imposing windows of the Red Palace, Chancellor Rasmus looked on as the razor-sharp crags and ravines of the infamous mountains disappeared gradually into the blanketing dust. Above, the twin suns glowered: Romulus dimly red, muted by the burgeoning sandstorm, and Remus its smaller twin, a hazy vermillion sphere in the distance. Every now and then a transient patch of light from them broke through the haze and illuminated a ridge, making it glow briefly.

There is beauty even in such harshness, thought the Chancellor before turning round to face the others in the room.

It had been almost a month after the group emerged from the Ether. Tors had managed to bring them back to the Realm although in her weakened state, they had in fact emerged on the planet Ceos instead of Amorgos.

He looked at them now—still bruised but thankfully on the mend and relatively unharmed. They had all been injured in various ways, Tors much more so than the others and consequently had been placed in the critical care unit for some time. The physician had called him aside after the examination.

But she made me promise not to tell anyone, in particular Lord Draeger himself. He wondered if the child was the Commander's.

The old man surveyed them all, his eyes keen and grey as steel. Lord Draeger aside, they were an interestingly eclectic group and in the course of their preparations over the last few weeks, he had come to know each of them well.

The woman Pihla, was extremely capable and skilled. *It hadn't taken her very long to understand the workings of the ancient beacon,* mused the Chancellor, recalling the days and nights spent by the gifted half-Tilkoen poring over the technical drawings and finally examining the beacon itself.

Niko, the human, also a capable engineer in his own right, had impressed him with his empathy, farsightedness and knowledge of the challenges faced by the Exodus. *He understands the social complexities of the problem,* observed the Chancellor, *and the moral trade-offs that come with it. Impressive indeed and ironic, considering his kind are shorter-lived than most species.*

The old man's gaze wandered over to Marcus. *We may have agreed a truce with the Rebellion but they will no doubt go on without him and continue to build their own ships to evacuate the people.* He wondered where Marcus' motivations now lay. *With the promise of the Gateways reopening, perhaps he sees now that we are not the enemy. Is this why he's here? To help us find and reopen the Gateways?*

But Rasmus' shrewd eyes perceived a different motivation.

Tors was sitting in one of the high-backed chairs at the table and as Marcus leant protectively over her, it dawned on the Chancellor that Ageron's welfare was perhaps not the sole reason in the young man's thoughts.

Well, chuckled the Chancellor to himself at the revelation, *I do believe Lord Draeger has competition...*

Meanwhile, Queen Alin had not taken news of Akseli's house arrest well. This worried the Chancellor slightly. Nevertheless with Draeger's influence, there were few dissidents willing to openly side her, leaving the Queen Mother with no choice but to resentfully abide by the Supreme Commander's decision.

Outside the palace walls, word of the Emperor's treasonous plot had been received by the people of Ageron with much less interest for there were more immediate worries to contend with. Anavio, Bellun and Trimon—planets closest to the suns—had been hit by all manner of natural disasters, from sudden floods, earthquakes and tsunamis to blistering heatwaves and sandstorms. The Chancellor sighed. These had become more frequent of late, each occurrence more violent and more epic than the last—all the signs of the beginnings of the predicted planetary scatterings due to the failing suns.

"Here it is." The Chancellor approached the table with the ancient records in his arms. Placing the heavy tome on the table he turned its yellowed pages gently.

These records have not left their vacuum seal since I was advisor to a young Ageron III...

"There," said the old man. His finger, delicate and papery thin as the document itself, rested on a page above some inscribed words.

Draeger stood up and walked over to stand beside him whilst the rest gathered round to look.

"See here," pointed the Chancellor again. "Our records confirm that the Arnemetiaen Gateway connects two known natural endpoints in the Ether: our Arnemetiaen Gate in Arnemetiae and the Sansari Gate in the Tilkoen city of Sansari on planet Dharan. With the Lagentian Gateway no longer a viable option, the Arnemetiaen Gateway is our next best hope."

"The Arnemetiaen Gateway...," repeated Pihla. She had a haunted look in her eyes.

Chancellor Rasmus glanced at her. *She would have travelled through that to get here from Tilkoen all those years ago.*

"Yes," he continued. "Gateways as you now know, always take the name of their Ageronian endpoints. So the Arnemetian Gateway would have connected our Arnemetiaen Gate with the Sansari Gate."

"And there were other Gateways?" asked Niko.

Chancellor Rasmus nodded. "Three in total," he said. "Three gateways linking the three Great Houses. The Lagentian Gateway which as you know, linked our Lagentian Gate with the Namsos Gate in Ellagrin, the Arnemetiaen Gateway which linked our Arnemetiaen Gate to the Sansari Gate in Tilkoen, and the Leodis Gateway which linked our Leodis Gate to the Huangshan Gate in Yoon."

"Yoon?" queried Tors.

"They are an old dynasty," Draeger said, "but the Yoons have withdrawn from all of civilisation. They cut all ties sometime during the war, destroying the Yoon Gateway themselves and shunning all contact outside their planetary system."

The Chancellor nodded, looking at the Commander. "Lord Draeger's mother was the thirteenth daughter of House Yoon," he said.

"Anyway, Emperor Mikael as you know, was deeply resentful of our monopoly over the Gateways but as the war progressed, it was clear the Ellagrins could not seize control of the Gateways. Mikael eventually destroyed the beacon at the Lagentian Gate and without both endpoints kept alive, the connection that sustained the Gateway was broken and the

Gateway ceased to be. Lagentia went first, then Leodis—which the Yoons themselves initiated—and finally Arnemetiae. ”

“So without beacons at each Gate, we can’t open up the Gateway, is that right?”asked Niko.

“And don’t forget, you need an Eldur at each end as its power source as well,” added Pihla.

“That is correct,”said Chancellor Rasmus. “The surviving beacon at the Namsos end of the Lagentian Gateway enabled Akseli to use Tors on this end to force the Gateway connection back into existence. However, in the case of the Arnemetiaen Gateway, with the beacon on the Sansari end destroyed, even if Tors decided to strap herself to the Arnemetiaen Gate here, we’d have no way to force the Gateway into existence as it wouldn’t have knowledge of our endpoint at Sansari.”

The Chancellor paused for a moment as the group digested his explanations. Then, he continued with a glint in his eyes. “But if we reinstate the beacon there—”

“But you just said it was destroyed by the Ellagrins,” interjected Niko.

The Chancellor nodded. “It was,” he said, “And it would have held within it the link to Arnemetiae.”

“So how would this work?”asked Pihla, thinking aloud. “The Gate at Arnemetiae needs the beacon from Sansari and similarly the Gate at Sansari needs the beacon from Arnemetiae in order to establish both endpoints.”

“Yes,” affirmed the Chancellor, “but don’t forget, the currents of the Ether are ever changing, so the beacons do not hold fixed coordinates of the opposite endpoints. Rather, they in effect retain the *shape* of the link within the Ether, that is to say, the actual journey through the Ether to the opposite side. This is why we’ve always needed a Nehisi to take the beacon from one end to the other through the Ether itself. The beacons build up the actual journey through the Ether within their memory constructs."

"A virtual spider's thread to link two fluctuating points," said Pihla thoughtfully. "Still, you've just said the beacons were destroyed."

"Not both,"answered Chancellor Rasmus. The old man's beard bristled with excitement. "We have the beacon for the Arnemetiaen Gate kept safe all these years but the beacon for Sansari's side—the Emperor Mikael destroyed that during the War, as he fled from Ageron."

"Which means we still can't open up the Gateway," said Niko.

"Indeed," said the Chancellor, "*unless* we take a new beacon through the Ether from Arnemetiae to Sansari in order for it to 'learn' the route. And then install it at Sansari."

He looked at Pihla and smiled. "The beacon you've been studying in the last few weeks was a real beacon, a spare device left with us by the Tilkoens centuries ago. We just didn't have anyone to take it through the Ether to Sansari...," he glanced at Tors and said, " until now."

Pihla's eyes lit up. "And we only need to do this one way as we still have the Arnemetiaen beacon containing Sansari's co-ords," she finished.

Chancellor Rasmus nodded approvingly. "Exactly," he said. "That's the plan! We will be doing what the Nehisi would have done when the very first Gates were built. They carried the beacons from one end to the other to establish the Gateway connections."

"It may take me some time to find Sansari," said Tors thoughtfully, "because I've never known it and apparently it is the hardest of all endpoints to locate." She gave the Chancellor a wry look and asked, "Out of interest, how long did it take the first Nehisi to find Sansari's natural endpoint?"

"Six years," answered the Chancellor. "We already knew of Arnemetiae as a natural endpoint so they entered the Ether from there and began the search. But with Namsos, it took seven teams twenty years after having established the Lagentian endpoint."

He gave her a kindly look. "However as you know, the Ether is ever-changing so none of this gives us any certainty as to where the endpoint is now or how long it'll take you to find it. You could locate it in a month or you could locate it in a decade."

Tors nodded. "It's certainly possible to mount an expedition to locate it with exits from the Ether along the way to replenish supplies and such when needed."

"Yes," nodded the Chancellor, "and I don't need to tell you to be careful whenever you do so—Dyaeus knows what worlds and civilisations you'll encounter on the way!"

"We'll be careful," Tors said reassuringly. *It will be good to be back in the Ether...*

The comfort and seclusion offered there appealed greatly to her. *I cannot stay here in the Realms,* she thought, conscious of the turmoil in her emotions.

She glanced furtively at Draeger. *I cannot face him. Not yet. Not when I don't know how I feel about him., about us... Is there even an 'us'?*

She looked down at herself. *And what of our child?*

"Well, you won't be alone," grinned Pihla. "And this time, I've made some great outworld gear ready for us!"

Tors smiled in reply. *No,* she thought to herself, *I shan't be alone.* New life quickened within her and she felt it more keenly with each passing day.

Draeger looked at Chancellor Rasmus. "She will be well protected," he said quietly. There was an edge to his voice.

Tors glanced at him. *Does he know?* But when he returned her look, she knew he did not.

How can I tell him if I cannot trust him? She winced at the memory of that day in Elena's Summer Palace. *No, I will raise the child on my own. He will not know. He will never know...*

Draeger continued, his tone heavy with reluctance. "Marcus, Niko and Pihla will join the expedition to locate the Sansari Gate. They will act as her protectors. I have to stay here to govern the Realm."

The Chancellor nodded approvingly. "A wise decision," he said. "With your brother's status as yet undetermined until a trial is agreed, he poses a very real threat to the Empire and of course, the Queen Mother..." He paused. "Who knows?"

The old man's shrewd eyes met Draeger's with approbation and a tinge perhaps, of empathy. Lord Draeger did not always care for the intricacies of politics at the Senate but like his father, he had good instinct and his instincts clearly told him that whilst Akseli's status remained uncertain, he was a threat to Draeger's dominion over the Realm. And beneath all of this, he too sensed that Queen Alin posed a danger to the precarious balance of power that could not be underestimated.

And what of Elena? the old Chancellor wondered. Suffice to say, diplomatic ties between the two Houses were severed and the failed invasion had cost House Ellagrin much: not only had their army faced significant losses fighting the LON, the demise of Emperor Niklas would have undoubtedly destabilised the Ellagrin empire.

Without the backing she's been counting on from House Ageron, she'll be hard pressed to hang onto the throne.

Having said that, the Chancellor was well aware of Lady Elena's prowess when it came to politics...

The Chancellor looked at Draeger and wondered what the

Supreme Commander himself made of her betrayal. But Lord Draeger was not one to be swayed by sentimentality.

He is very much like his mother, reflected the Chancellor recalling the enigmatic Lady Yinha, *And no doubt, his judgement will be as pragmatic and as emotionally-detached as his mother's.*

He wondered too what course of action Lord Draeger would take. *War would be a familiar route but the Exodus and our dependency on Ellagrin for resettlements may well temper that. Difficult times lay ahead, especially with this political mess we find ourselves in.*

"It is settled then,"said Chancellor Rasmus, producing a pill-shaped device, small enough to fit snugly in the palm of his hand, and handed it to Tors. "The beacon for the Sansari Gate," he said. "You all know how to operate this—you've been shown all this these last few weeks—and Pihla understands its inner workings and how to make modifications if necessary."

Tors nodded and placed the beacon safely in a pouch hidden within the folds of her tunic.

"Now, the Eldur?" asked the Chancellor.

Marcus patted the hidden pocket within his vest in response. "It's here," he replied.

"Good," nodded the Chancellor. "You have the beacon and the power source," he said.

The old man stood up a little stiffly, then bowed deeply to the group. For the first time in years, Chancellor Rasmus felt his age. *Who would have thought... the Realms at the cusp of extinction, and hanging by a spider's thread.*

The seriousness of their situation weighed on him with devastating acuteness. *There is so much at stake with so small an expedition...*

"I wish you all the best of luck," said the Chancellor, "and may Dyaeus grant us all a successful outcome and your safe journey home."

Stepping aside, it was Lord Draeger's turn to address each of them.

The Supreme Commander turned to face Tors first but she would not meet his gaze. They had not talked since, not least about the day she fled from him at Summer Palace. "Perhaps you'll let me explain?" Draeger offered, "...that day at the Summer Palace. The Lady Elena and I—"

"No," Tors stopped him short, reddening rapidly. Her cheeks burned. *Not here and in front of the others too...* She added firmly, "That would not be necessary." Her voice was hard and unforgiving.

He drew closer but she levered herself away.

Her eyes held his for a brief moment. They had exchanged words the day before. Heated ones. *'The day you saved me from the slums,' she had shouted at him, 'was that because you knew I was going to be useful to you?'* Many words were exchanged but all the wrong ones it seemed, serving only to drive them apart even further, and the ones that needed to be voiced never surfaced.

So many words left unsaid. And too many needed. But this was not the time to say them. *Besides, can I even trust you anymore?*

Perhaps what he would have said, had she let him, could have set the record straight between them. Words that could have perhaps dismantled the wall that now rose between them. Words that she hoped would tell her he didn't betray her, that he didn't use her, and that perhaps aside from the needs of the Realm, just perhaps, he needed her too.

But no words came out.

And then the moment was past.

Draeger turned to shake Niko's hand next, accompanied with some solemn words, then Pihla's and finally Marcus'.

Tors looked on as both men stood facing each other, each effectively squaring the other up. *Bad enough with one of them coming along,* she thought. *Thank Dyaeus I'm not going on the expedition with* ***both*** *of them.* The contesting nature between these two would make the mission unbearable.

Perhaps Marcus coming along was altogether the preferable option. There was a certain ease with him. With charming and cavalier Marcus she felt free, but confusingly and perhaps absurdly, Draeger, dark and laconic, made her feel safe. But thinking about them both addled her. It stifled her and here, she couldn't breathe.

I just don't want to think anymore, she told herself, making up her mind. *It will be as before, as I have always been—free. No ties, no attachments. I will seek refuge in the Ether...*

"Be careful and come back safe," Draeger was saying to Marcus. Despite their differences, Tors could sense he meant it.

"Don't worry," answered Marcus with a glint in his eye, "I'll take good care of her."

Draeger flashed him a look which suggested he was less than pleased with the reply.

Marcus, unperturbed, hoisted up his rucksack and went to stand beside Tors. Then he looked round at the group. "Ready?" he asked.

They all nodded.

With that Tors cleaved an opening into the Ether.

Marcus stepped through, followed by Pihla and then Niko.

Time to go, thought Tors. Her heart gave a familiar leap of anticipation and as the Ether welcomed them into its cool embrace, she cast one last glance at Draeger and the Chancellor before stepping in.

Home... she thought, still very much a child of the Ether herself, and from within its cool dark walls, new worlds beckoned.

ENJOYED THE BOOK?

If you've enjoyed *The Last Nehisi,* ***please leave me a review***—I'd love to know what you think! And if you've loved reading this as much as I did writing it, spread the word!

The prologue of *Search for Sansari,* the upcoming sequel to *The Last Nehisi,* follows. Please note, the final version of the initial chapter may differ slightly from this version.

Join me online for release news, freebies and other exclusives at warwickeden.com

SEARCH FOR SANSARI

PROLOGUE: 213 YEARS AGO

The convoluted corridors of the ancient quarters were Draeger's favourite haunt, out of all the places the sprawling Red Palace had to offer a boy. A labyrinth of passageways beneath the foundations of the palace, they branched and spread out like a vast network of arteries, past the foundations of the palace, beneath neighbouring villages and far and deep into the bowels of the Red Mountain itself. With low ceilings and dark panelled walls, every corridor looked very much like the next one: lined with endless doors —some nondescript, others ornate—and almost always locked shut. Devoid of windows, these passageways gave no indication as to where he was in relation to the palace grounds above.

Draeger wound the string of wool around his hand as he skipped forward, his footsteps muffled by the richly carpeted floor. In his other hand, he held a toy—a figure of an Ageronian soldier complete with red cloak and sword—a recent gift from Father. The claustrophobic tangle of passageways didn't bother him and his eyes adapted easily to the scant light offered by the wall sconces, enabling him to view his surroundings as if it were bright as day. It was only in the dark that Draeger felt truly at ease, where his strange basilisk eyes served him best and he didn't feel his unusual looks as keenly noticed by others.

Draeger pulled the string taut, winding it faster and faster round his hand. He knew his way out from memory of course, but this was his way of checking, for there would be no way out if he made a mistake. The ancient quarters were so vast and unmapped that even the servants dared not venture this far in lest they got lost themselves. There would be no one to call out to for help if he got lost here.

Finally he emerged from the tunnels and out onto the courtyard, squinting in the golden sunlight. He tore gleefully through the palace gardens, the twin suns warm on his back and the soft breeze cool on his cheeks. From the gardens Draeger ran on, waving his toy soldier this way and that, through the plant-lined walkways shaded by vines and laden with fruit, until at long last he reached the royal quarters. Here, amidst the tall pines and silver palms that towered over its formal planting, he slowed down, remembering being told off for making too much noise the last time and disturbing Father's consorts.

The royal quarters were a series of self-contained apartments arranged along a terrace that ran on all four sides of a rectangular courtyard in the middle with its majestic pergola overrun with climbing jasmine. Covered by an elegant tiled roof and supported by pillars of marble, these residences and the lush, densely planted courtyard were reserved solely for the Emperor's consorts.

Draeger strolled along, enjoying the cool of the stone slabs beneath his bare feet and stopped to listen to the musical warble of birds in the trees. A warm breeze carried the faint scent of jasmine in the air along with the soft voices of women speaking. He presumed the voices to be one of Father's wives and perhaps her handmaid.

"Please, don't..." a woman pleaded.

Draeger turned towards her voice. It came from behind the door of Lady Cassia. It was ajar by no more than a finger's breadth and a baby's cry drifted out.

Lady Cassia's newborn...

Draeger stepped back, ready to retrace his steps. Only last week, he had been rebuked for disturbing the then heavily pregnant Lady Cassia. And now prince Titus, born only a few days ago, had arrived. Draeger knew Father was keen to see him for Lady Cassia was Father's current favourite and Chancellor Rasmus had mentioned to him that Father would cut short his trip to Vasa to return home if the baby came early.

I wonder if Father's here already? wondered Draeger.

He dropped to his knees and crept forward silently, nudging the door open a little more with the top of his head. He peered in cautiously, careful to stay out of sight. Father was not in the room. Lady Cassia however, was lying on her bed, pale and weakened no doubt, by the strains of birth. Another woman stood over her, holding baby Titus. She had her back towards Draeger but from her blonde locks and the curve of her pregnant belly he recognised her as Lady Alin, another of Father's consorts.

"Please, my Lady," begged Lady Cassia weakly. Her baby mewled like a helpless kitten in Lady Alin's arms.

"Don't you see Lady Cassia," said Lady Alin as she walked over to the baby's cot, still cradling the child in her arms, "the predicament your actions put us in?"

She moved a pillow aside and sat at the foot of Lady Cassia's bed. Then she placed the baby on her lap, and tucked its swaddle back into place. The baby stopped crying and began to make soft gurgling noises instead.

"There," cooed Lady Alin softly as the babe looked into her glacial blue eyes. "I'm not so bad after all, am I?" She stroked the child's face lightly with the tips of her fingers.

Lady Cassia looked at her uncertainly. "Please, Lady Alin," she started again, pleadingly. "We are but sisters in the same household."

"Sisters?" snapped Alin icily. "The audacity to think that! I am daughter of Aleksander, Emperor of Ellagrin. A *royal*, unlike the rest of you whores." She picked up the pillow and examined it with a casual air.

Lady Cassia started crying and shaking. "Please, my Lady," she whimpered. "Titus will not stand in line for the throne. I will make sure of that. You have my word. I *promise* it. Please..."

Lady Alin looked up and studied Lady Cassia's face carefully.

"B...besides," ventured Lady Cassia, "it is not my Titus that is heir to the throne. It is the sorceress' child you want, is it not?"

Lady Alin smiled. "Simple minds," she said with disdain. "You have such simple minds, you peasant crud. One must be systematic. Methodical. Ageron's favourite son will get his turn but now is not the time. Now is the time to clear the rest of the path first."

She lifted the pillow and placed it over the baby's face.

Lady Cassia reached out shaking uncontrollably, her watery eyes wide with fear. "Nooo, please no..." she begged weakly, but her cries rapidly diminished into feeble sobs as she cowered under Lady Alin's stare.

"It will be alright, Lady Cassia." Lady Alin pressed the pillow down hard. The baby squirmed and moved but gave barely a struggle. "I will take care of you, as always." The muffled cries of the infant soon stopped, as did all small movements from underneath the pillow.

Draeger dropped his toy soldier with a clatter.

In an instant, Lady Alin whirled around. Her eyes bore down on him, freezing him to the spot.

"Come in Draeger," she snapped.

Draeger got to his feet reluctantly. His legs felt like lead. Lady Alin got up and walked towards the cot to place the limp body of the baby in it, as if nothing was amiss and it was the most natural thing to do. Lady Cassia on the other hand, looked blankly at the bundle. Her eyes were glazed over and her face streaked with tears. She whimpered quietly like a lost child herself.

Draeger suddenly felt very frightened.

"Come here, child," ordered Lady Alin. Reluctantly, Draeger entered. The force of Lady Alin's voice seemed to have stripped him of what little remaining free will he possessed.

Lady Alin sat down at Lady Cassia's dressing table and beckoned him.

"Let me see you, Draeger," she said pleasantly and bade him stand in front of her. Her cold blue eyes looked at him. They were arctic blue, and reminded Draeger of the glaciers of Foss in Ellagrin—alluring but chilling to the bone. He glanced away and looked down at his feet uncertainly.

"Draeger my sweet, did you see anything?" Lady Alin's words tumbled out easily but Draeger could sense she was staring intently at him as she said them.

Draeger shook his head and turned the other way. He avoided looking at the cot. A sickly feeling churned in his stomach.

"You look pale," Lady Alin continued, smiling at him. "Come, let me cut you some fruit."

She picked up the knife beside Lady Cassia's elegant fruit basket and locking him in between her arms, she reached for a bloodfruit and began peeling it. The jewels in the hilt glinted as her blade slit through the fruit easily, letting its crimson juices drip. Caged in by both her arms, Draeger could feel her pregnant belly brush lightly against his back as she continued to make cuts into the fruit, lacerating its flesh and causing even more deep-red juices to trickle down her hands.

Lady Alin leaned over, so her lips were almost brushing his ears. "So, my young lord," she whispered, handing Draeger a piece of bloodfruit, "what do you think we should do next?"

Draeger looked up. He could see Lady Cassia start to shake again, her eyes transfixed on him. They were blank with terror.

Lady Alin put the rest of the fruit down on the table and rested her hand on Draeger's shoulder. Sticky with juice, the sickly sweet fragrance of the fruit wafted up his nostrils. In her other hand, she still held the knife. This she lifted slowly, its bejewelled hilt holding Draeger transfixed like a snake charmer's pipe. Gradually, she brought it closer, all the time at level with his neck.

Nearer and nearer until it disappeared from the periphery of his vision.

Lady Cassia's eyes widened.

"There you are."

At the sound of the voice behind, Draeger whirled round.

Lady Alin lowered her arms as he turned and ran to his mother, the sorceress Yinha.

"My Lady," greeted Lady Alin coldly as she rose from her seat.

The sorceress nodded as she swept into the chamber, her

dark robes flowing around her like molten tar. She stopped at the foot of Lady Cassia's bed and looked at her. Her eyes, pitch-black like Draeger's resembled endless voids as they stared impassively at Lady Cassia and then at the cot.

Lady Alin shifted uneasily.

"Draeger," said the sorceress, without looking at her son. "Vasili has been looking for you. You are late for your lesson. Why don't you go find him now?"

Draeger nodded relieved and bowing to his mother and the other two, left the room.

The sorceress Yinha turned her attention to Lady Cassia again. "My deepest condolences, Lady Cassia," she said quietly, and shifted her gaze towards Lady Alin.

The two women faced each other squarely, one closed and composed, the other, defiant and dangerous.

"What shall we do next indeed," murmured sorceress Yinha.

Her voice was deceptively soft but before Lady Alin could reply, she continued, this time with a steely edge to it. "I will tell you what will happen next my dear Lady Alin."

From within the folds of her robe, she produced a gold bracelet with the engravings of love symbols.

Lady Alin give a little gasp and tried to snatch it from Lady Yinha but as soon as her hand neared, the bracelet swirled into oblivion beneath the sorceress' robe, leaving her hand to grasp at empty air.

"Yes," the sorceress told her with icy curtesy, "...from now on, you will not so much as *touch* my son." Her eyes bore into the fair queen, unearthly and sharp as obsidian. "In fact, you will protect him and you will make it your prime concern to ensure no harm—not even a scratch—comes to him."

She looked at Queen Alin's belly and gave a chilling smile. "For should even a hair on my son's head is harmed, I shall see to it that your little secret is exposed to all. Ageronians, as you know are by far the most traditionalistic of all Houses in the galaxy. I would hazard a guess a revelation such as this would undoubtedly be punishable by death."

Lady Alin's lips trembled and for a brief moment, anger flashed in her eyes. But she remained silent.

A small whimper escaped Lady Cassia.

The woman had retrieved her baby and was clutching the dead infant to her breast, rocking it gently. She had long ceased crying and her eyes, blank and unseeing, had a half-crazed look about them.

Lady Alin shot a furtive look at Lady Yinha, then at the knife, still slick with traces of bloodfruit on it. Slowly, she picked it up and cleaned the blade with her sleeve. Then, she held it out to Lady Cassia.

Sorceress Yinha's gaze bore into Alin at the audacious move. Her eyes were hard and black. Then she looked at Lady Cassia once more and said, "Perhaps this is the only merciful way out."

With that, the sorceress turned to leave the chamber without looking back.

And as the last of her swirling robes drifted out of the room, Lady Cassia took one more look at the lifeless bundle at her breast, reached for the knife and put it to her wrist as Lady Alin sat patiently to watch her.

Printed in Great Britain
by Amazon

82021403R00246